KU-215-162

ADVENTURE STORIES FOR

BOYS

ADVENTURE STORIES FOR

BOYS

Compiled by Tig Thomas

Miles Kelly

First published as *Classic Adventure Stories* in 2008 by Miles Kelly Publishing Ltd,
Harding's Barn, Bardfield End Green, Thaxted, Essex, CM6 3PX, UK

Copyright © Miles Kelly Publishing Ltd 2008

This edition printed 2014

4 6 8 10 9 7 5

Publishing Director Belinda Gallagher
Creative Director Jo Cowan
Senior Designer Simon Lee
Cover Designer Joe Jones
Production Manager Elizabeth Collins
Reprographics Anthony Cambray, Stephan Davis, Jennifer Hunt
Reprint Manager Lorraine King

All rights reserved. No part of this publication may be reproduced, stored in a retrieval system, or transmitted by any means, electronic, mechanical, photocopying, recording or otherwise without the prior permission of the copyright holder.

ISBN 978-1-84810-614-7

Printed in China

British Library Cataloguing-in-Publication Data
A catalogue record for this book is available from the British Library

ACKNOWLEDGEMENTS
The publishers would like to thank the following artists whose work appears in this book:

Sandeep Kaushik, Mike Lacey, Wes Lowe
Enzo Troiano, Roger Wade Walker, Zoografic

Cover artwork: Oliver Frey

Made with paper from a sustainable forest

www.mileskelly.net
info@mileskelly.net

Foreword

Adventure stories have never gone out of fashion. Authors have been writing about the exploits of heroes and villains that have kept readers on the edge of their seats for centuries. This fabulous collection of tales is no different. Each page is filled with dramatic descriptions of hair-raising escapades that take you on a roller-coaster journey. Split into five sections – **Murder Most Foul**, **Heroes of the Hour**, **In Untrodden Lands**, *The Cruel Sea* and **Escape and Rescue** – this book brings together seventeen of the best adventure plots written by some of the greatest authors. Some tales are extracts from novels such as *Treasure Island*, *Journey to the Centre of the Earth* and *The Count of Monte Cristo*. For these, short summaries are provided. Others are complete short stories in their own right, such as *Love of Life* and *The Hand*. All the stories combine with illustrations that capture the very essence of adventure, and encourage children to read on.

Contents

Section One

Murder Most Foul

Contents

Section Two

Heroes of the Hour

Contents

Section Three

In Untrodden Lands

Contents

Section Four

The Cruel Sea

Contents

Section Five

Escape and Rescue

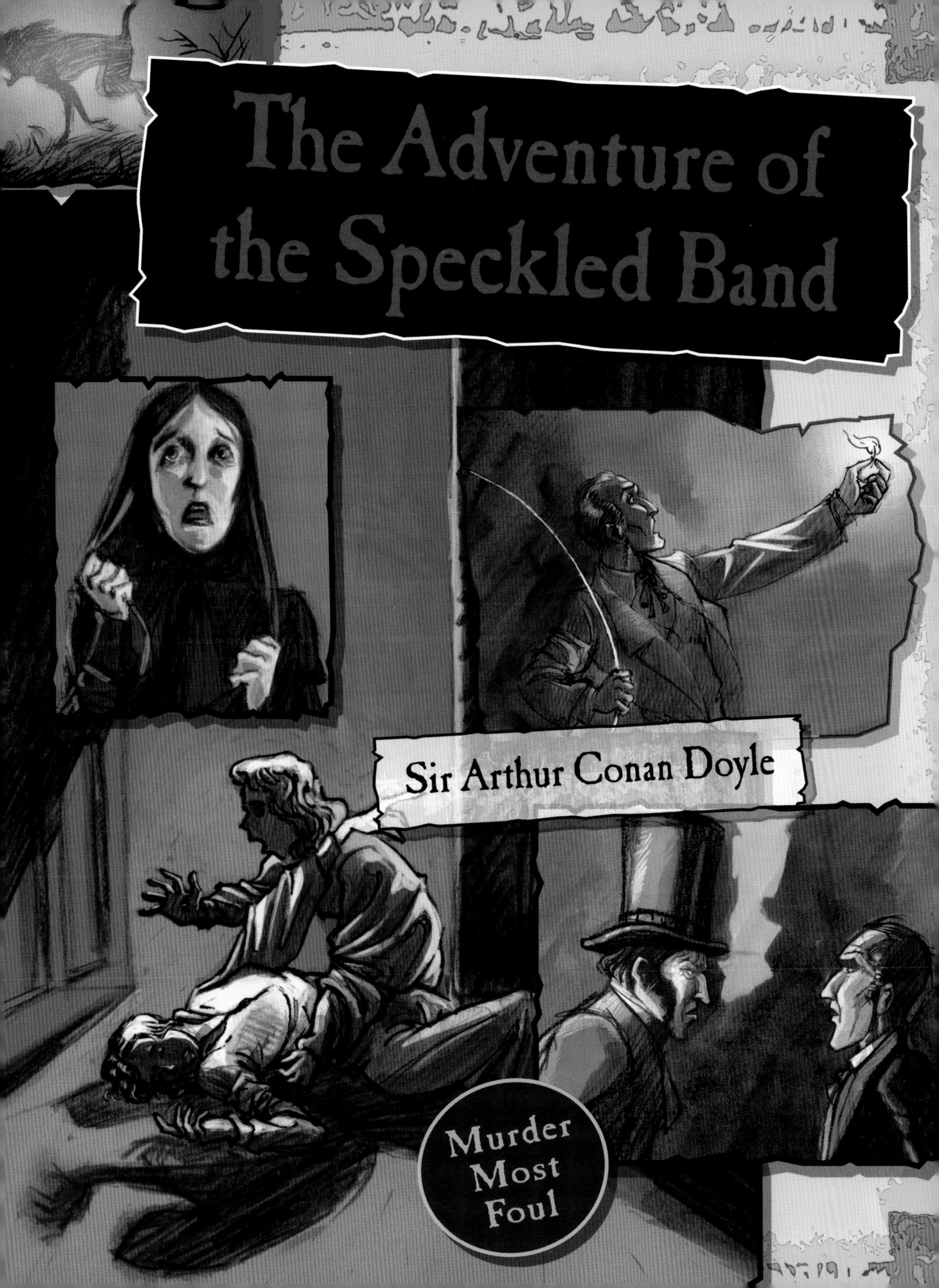
The Adventure of the Speckled Band
Sir Arthur Conan Doyle
Murder Most Foul

The Adventure of the Speckled Band

by

Sir Arthur Conan Doyle

On glancing over my notes of the seventy odd cases in which I have during the last eight years studied the methods of my friend Sherlock Holmes, I find many tragic, some comic, a large number merely strange, but none commonplace; for, working as he did rather for the love of his art than for the acquirement of wealth, he refused to associate himself with any investigation which did not tend towards the unusual, and even the fantastic. Of all these varied cases, however, I cannot recall any which presented more singular features than that which was associated with the well-known Surrey family of the Roylotts of Stoke Moran. The events in question occurred in the early days of my association with Holmes, when we were sharing rooms as bachelors in Baker Street. It is possible that I might have placed them upon record before, but a promise of secrecy was made at the time, from which I have only been freed during the last month by the untimely death of the lady to whom the pledge was given. It is perhaps as well that the facts should now come to light, for I have reasons to know that there are widespread rumours as to the death of Dr. Grimesby Roylott which tend to make the matter even more terrible than the truth.

It was early in April in the year '83 that I woke one morning to find Sherlock Holmes standing, fully dressed, by the side of my bed. He was a late riser, as a rule, and as the clock on the mantelpiece showed me that it was only a quarter-past seven, I blinked up at him in some surprise, and perhaps just a little resentment, for I was myself regular in my habits.

"Very sorry to knock you up, Watson," said he, "but it's the common lot this morning. Mrs. Hudson has been knocked up, she retorted upon me, and I on you."

"What is it, then – a fire?"

"No; a client. It seems that a young lady has arrived in a considerable state of excitement, who insists upon seeing me. She is waiting now in the sitting-room. Now, when young ladies wander about the metropolis at this hour of the morning, and knock sleepy people up out of their beds, I presume that it is something very pressing which they have to communicate. Should it prove to be an interesting case, you would, I am sure, wish to follow it from the outset. I thought, at any rate, that I should call you and give you the chance."

"My dear fellow, I would not miss it for anything."

I had no keener pleasure than in following Holmes in his professional investigations, and in admiring the rapid deductions, as swift as intuitions, and yet always founded on a logical basis with which he unravelled the problems which were submitted to him. I rapidly threw on my clothes and was ready in a few minutes to accompany my friend down to the sitting-room. A lady dressed in black and heavily veiled, who had been sitting in the window, rose as we entered.

"Good-morning, madam," said Holmes cheerily. "My name is Sherlock Holmes. This is my intimate friend and associate, Dr. Watson, before whom you can speak as freely as before myself. Ha! I am glad to see that Mrs. Hudson has had the good sense to light the fire. Pray draw up to it, and I shall order you a cup of hot coffee, for I observe that you are shivering."

"It is not cold which makes me shiver," said the woman in a low voice, changing her seat as requested.

"What, then?"

"It is fear, Mr. Holmes. It is terror." She raised her veil as she spoke, and we could see that she was indeed in a pitiable state of agitation, her face all drawn and grey, with restless frightened eyes,

like those of some hunted animal. Her features and figure were those of a woman of thirty, but her hair was shot with premature grey, and her expression was weary and haggard. Sherlock Holmes ran her over with one of his quick, all-comprehensive glances.

"You must not fear," said he soothingly, bending forward and patting her forearm. "We shall soon set matters right, I have no doubt. You have come in by train this morning, I see."

"You know me, then?"

"No, but I observe the second half of a return ticket in the palm of your left glove. You must have started early, and yet you had a good drive in a dog-cart, along heavy roads, before you reached the station."

The lady gave a violent start and stared in bewilderment at my companion.

"There is no mystery, my dear madam," said he, smiling. "The left arm of your jacket is spattered with mud in no less than seven places. The marks are perfectly fresh. There is no vehicle save a dog-cart which throws up mud in that way, and then only when you sit on the left-hand side of the driver."

"Whatever your reasons may be, you are perfectly correct," said she. "I started from home before six, reached Leatherhead at twenty past, and came in by the first train to Waterloo. Sir, I can stand this strain no longer; I shall go mad if it continues. I have no one to turn to – none, save only one, who cares for me, and he, poor fellow, can be of little aid. I have heard of you, Mr. Holmes; I have heard of you from Mrs. Farintosh, whom you helped in the hour of her sore need. It was from her that I had your address. Oh, sir, do you not think that you could help me, too, and at least throw a little light through the dense darkness which surrounds me? At present it is out of my power to reward you for your services, but in a month or six weeks I shall be married, with the control of my own income, and then at least you shall not find me ungrateful."

Holmes turned to his desk and, unlocking it, drew out a small case-book, which he consulted.

"Farintosh," said he. "Ah yes, I recall the case; it was concerned with an opal tiara. I think it was before your time, Watson. I can only say, madam, that I shall be happy to devote the same care to your case as I did to that of your friend. As to reward, my profession is its own reward; but you are at liberty to defray whatever expenses I may be put to, at the time which suits you best. And now I beg that you will lay before us everything that may help us in forming an opinion upon the matter."

"Alas!" replied our visitor, "the very horror of my situation lies in the fact that my fears are so vague, and my suspicions depend so entirely upon small points, which might seem trivial to another, that even he to whom of all others I have a right to look for help and advice looks upon all that I tell him about it as the fancies of a nervous woman. He does not say so, but I can read it from his soothing answers and averted eyes. But I have heard, Mr. Holmes, that you can see deeply into the manifold wickedness of the human heart. You may advise me how to walk amid the dangers which encompass me."

"I am all attention, madam."

"My name is Helen Stoner, and I am living with my stepfather, who is the last survivor of one of the oldest Saxon families in England, the Roylotts of Stoke Moran, on the western border of Surrey."

Holmes nodded his head. "The name is familiar to me," said he.

"The family was at one time among the richest in England, and the estates extended over the borders into Berkshire in the north, and Hampshire in the west. In the last century, however, four successive heirs were of a dissolute and wasteful disposition, and the family ruin was eventually completed by a gambler in the days of the Regency. Nothing was left save a few acres of ground, and the two-hundred-year-old house, which is itself crushed under a heavy mortgage. The last squire dragged out his existence there, living the horrible life of an aristocratic pauper; but his only son, my stepfather, seeing that he must adapt himself to the new conditions, obtained an advance from a relative, which enabled him to take a medical degree and went out to Calcutta, where, by his professional skill and his force of character, he established a large practice. In a fit of anger, however, caused by some robberies which had been perpetrated in the house, he beat his native butler to death and narrowly escaped a capital sentence. As it was, he suffered a long term of imprisonment and afterwards returned to England a morose and disappointed man.

"When Dr. Roylott was in India he married my mother, Mrs. Stoner, the young widow of Major-General Stoner, of the Bengal Artillery. My sister Julia and I were twins, and we were only two years old at the time of my mother's re-marriage. She had a considerable sum of money – not less than £1000 a year – and this she bequeathed to Dr. Roylott entirely while we resided with him, with a provision that a certain annual sum should be allowed to each of us in the event of our marriage. Shortly after our return to England my mother died – she was killed eight years ago in a railway accident near Crewe. Dr. Roylott then abandoned his attempts to establish himself in practice in London and took us to live with him in the old ancestral house at Stoke Moran. The money which my mother had left was enough for all our wants, and there seemed to be no obstacle to our happiness.

"But a terrible change came over our stepfather about this time. Instead of making friends and exchanging visits with our neighbours, who had at first been overjoyed to see a Roylott of Stoke Moran back in the old family seat, he shut himself up in his house and seldom came out save to indulge in ferocious quarrels with whoever might cross his path. Violence of temper approaching to mania has been hereditary in the men of the family, and in my stepfather's case it had, I believe, been intensified by his long residence in the tropics. A series of disgraceful brawls took place, two of which ended in the police-court, until at last he became the terror of the village, and the folks would fly at his approach, for he is a man of immense strength, and absolutely uncontrollable in his anger.

"Last week he hurled the local blacksmith over a parapet into a stream, and it was only by paying over all the money which I could gather together that I was able to avert another public exposure. He had no friends at all save the wandering gipsies, and he would give these vagabonds leave to encamp upon the few acres of bramble-covered land which represent the family estate, and would accept in return the hospitality of their tents, wandering away with them sometimes for weeks on end. He has a passion also for Indian animals, which are sent over to him by a correspondent, and he has at this moment a cheetah and a baboon, which wander freely over his grounds and are feared by the villagers almost as much as their master.

"You can imagine from what I say that my poor sister Julia and I had no great pleasure in our lives. No servant would stay with us, and for a long time we did all the work of the house. She was but thirty at the time of her death, and yet her hair had already begun to whiten, even as mine has."

"Your sister is dead, then?"

"She died just two years ago, and it is of her death that I wish to speak to you. You can understand that, living the life which I have described, we were little likely to see anyone of our own age and position. We had, however, an aunt, my mother's maiden sister, Miss Honoria Westphail, who lives near Harrow, and we were occasionally allowed to pay short visits at this lady's house. Julia went there at Christmas two years ago, and met there a half-pay major of marines, to whom she became engaged. My stepfather learned of the engagement when my sister returned and offered no objection to the marriage; but within a fortnight of the day which had been fixed for the wedding, the terrible event occurred which has deprived me of my only companion."

Sherlock Holmes had been leaning back in his chair with his eyes closed and his head sunk in a cushion, but he half opened his lids now and glanced across at his visitor.

"Pray be precise as to details," said he.

"It is easy for me to be so, for every event of that dreadful time is seared into my memory. The manor-house is, as I have already said, very old, and only one wing is now inhabited. The bedrooms in this wing are on the ground floor, the sitting-rooms being in the central block of the buildings. Of these bedrooms the first is Dr. Roylott's, the second my sister's, and the third my own. There is no communication between them, but they all open out into the same corridor. Do I make myself plain?"

"Perfectly so."

"The windows of the three rooms open out upon the lawn. That fatal night Dr. Roylott had gone to his room early, though we knew that he had not retired to rest, for my sister was troubled by the smell of the strong Indian cigars which it was his custom to smoke. She left her room, therefore, and came into mine, where she sat for some time, chatting about her approaching wedding. At eleven o'clock she rose to leave me, but she paused at the door and looked back.

my sister was troubled by the smell of the strong Indian cigars

" 'Tell me, Helen,' said she, 'have you ever heard anyone whistle in the dead of the night?'

" 'Never,' said I.

" 'I suppose that you could not possibly whistle, yourself, in your sleep?'

" 'Certainly not. But why?'

" 'Because during the last few nights I have always, about three in the morning, heard a low, clear whistle. I am a light sleeper, and it has awakened me. I cannot tell where it came from – perhaps from the next room, perhaps from the lawn. I thought that I would just ask you whether you had heard it.'

" 'No, I have not. It must be those wretched gipsies in the plantation.'

" 'Very likely. And yet if it were on the lawn, I wonder that you did not hear it also.'

" 'Ah, but I sleep more heavily than you.'

" 'Well, it is of no great consequence, at any rate.' She smiled back at me, closed my door, and a few moments later I heard her key turn in the lock."

"Indeed," said Holmes. "Was it your custom always to lock yourselves in at night?"

"Always."

"And why?"

"I think that I mentioned to you that the doctor kept a cheetah and a baboon. We had no feeling of security unless our doors were locked."

"Quite so. Pray proceed with your statement."

"I could not sleep that night. A vague feeling of impending

misfortune impressed me. My sister and I, you will recollect, were twins, and you know how subtle are the links which bind two souls which are so closely allied. It was a wild night. The wind was howling outside, and the rain was beating and splashing against the windows. Suddenly, amid all the hubbub of the gale, there burst forth the wild scream of a terrified woman. I knew that it was my sister's voice. I sprang from my bed, wrapped a shawl round me, and rushed into the corridor. As I opened my door I seemed to hear a low whistle, such as my sister described, and a few moments later a clanging sound, as if a mass of metal had fallen. As I ran down the passage, my sister's door was unlocked, and revolved slowly upon its hinges. I stared at it horror-stricken, not knowing what was about to issue from it. By the light of the corridor-lamp I saw my sister appear at the opening, her face blanched with terror, her hands groping for help, her whole figure swaying to and fro like that of a drunkard. I ran to her and threw my arms round her, but at that moment her knees seemed to give way and she fell to the ground. She writhed as one who is in terrible pain, and her limbs were dreadfully convulsed. At first I thought that she had not recognised me, but as I bent over her she suddenly shrieked out in a voice which I shall never forget, 'Oh, my God! Helen! It was the band! The speckled band!' There was something else which she would fain have said, and she stabbed with her finger into the air in the direction of the doctor's room, but a fresh convulsion seized her and choked her words. I rushed out, calling loudly for my

stepfather, and I met him hastening from his room in his dressing-gown. When he reached my sister's side she was unconscious, and though he poured brandy down her throat and sent for medical aid from the village, all efforts were in vain, for she slowly sank and died without having recovered her consciousness. Such was the dreadful end of my beloved sister."

"One moment," said Holmes, "are you sure about this whistle and metallic sound? Could you swear to it?"

"That was what the county coroner asked me at the inquiry. It is my strong impression that I heard it, and yet, among the crash of the gale and the creaking of an old house, I may possibly have been deceived."

"Was your sister dressed?"

"No, she was in her night-dress. In her right hand was found the charred stump of a match, and in her left a match-box."

"Showing that she had struck a light and looked about her when the alarm took place. That is important. And what conclusions did the coroner come to?"

"He investigated the case with great care, for Dr. Roylott's conduct had long been notorious in the county, but he was unable to find any satisfactory cause of death. My evidence showed that the door had been fastened upon the inner side, and the windows were blocked by old-fashioned shutters with broad iron bars, which were secured every night. The walls were carefully sounded, and were shown to be quite solid all round, and the flooring was also thoroughly examined, with the same result. The chimney is wide, but is barred up by four large staples. It is certain, therefore, that my sister was quite alone when she met her end. Besides, there were no marks of any violence upon her."

"How about poison?"

"The doctors examined her for it, but without success."

"What do you think that this unfortunate lady died of, then?"

"It is my belief that she died of pure fear and nervous shock, though what it was that frightened her I cannot imagine."

"Were there gipsies in the plantation at the time?"

"Yes, there are nearly always some there."

"Ah, and what did you gather from this allusion to a band – a speckled band?"

"Sometimes I have thought that it was merely the wild talk of delirium, sometimes that it may have referred to some band of people, perhaps to these very gipsies in the plantation. I do not know whether the spotted handkerchiefs which so many of them wear over their heads might have suggested the strange adjective which she used." Holmes shook his head like a man who is far from being satisfied.

"These are very deep waters," said he; "pray go on with your narrative."

"Two years have passed since then, and my life has been until lately lonelier than ever. A month ago, however, a dear friend, whom I have known for many years, has done me the honour to ask my hand in marriage. His name is Armitage – Percy Armitage – the second son of Mr. Armitage, of Crane Water, near Reading. My stepfather has offered no opposition to the match, and we are to be married in the course of the spring. Two days ago some repairs were started in the west wing of the building, and my bedroom wall has been pierced, so that I have had to move into the chamber in which my sister died, and to sleep in the very bed in which she slept. Imagine, then, my thrill of terror when last night, as I lay awake, thinking over her terrible fate, I suddenly heard in the silence of the night the low whistle which had been the herald of her own death. I sprang up and lit the lamp, but nothing was to be seen in the room. I was too shaken to go to bed again, however, so I dressed, and as soon as it was daylight I slipped down, got a dog-cart at the Crown Inn, which is opposite, and drove to Leatherhead, from whence I have come on this morning with the one object of seeing you and asking your advice."

"You have done wisely," said my friend. "But have you told me all?"

"Yes, all."

"Miss Roylott, you have not. You are screening your stepfather."

"Why, what do you mean?"

For answer Holmes pushed back the frill of black lace which fringed the hand that lay upon our visitor's knee. Five little livid spots, the marks of four fingers and a thumb, were printed upon the white wrist.

"You have been cruelly used," said Holmes.

The lady coloured deeply and covered over her injured wrist. "He is a hard man," she said, "and perhaps he hardly knows his own strength."

There was a long silence, during which Holmes leaned his chin upon his hands and stared into the crackling fire.

"This is a very deep business," he said at last. "There are a thousand details which I should desire to know before I decide upon our course of action. Yet we have not a moment to lose. If we were to come to Stoke Moran to-day, would it be possible for us to see over these rooms without the knowledge of your stepfather?"

"As it happens, he spoke of coming into town to-day upon some most important business. It is probable that he will be away all day, and that there would be nothing to disturb you. We have a housekeeper now, but she is old and foolish, and I could easily get her out of the way."

"Excellent. You are not averse to this trip, Watson?"

"By no means."

"Then we shall both come. What are you going to do yourself?"

"I have one or two things which I would wish to do now that I am in town. But I shall return by the twelve o'clock train, so as to be there in time for your coming."

"And you may expect us early in the afternoon. I have myself some small business matters to attend to. Will you not wait and breakfast?"

"No, I must go. My heart is lightened already since I have confided my trouble to you. I shall look forward to seeing you again this afternoon." She dropped her thick black veil over her face and glided from the room.

"And what do you think of it all, Watson?" asked Sherlock Holmes, leaning back in his chair.

"It seems to me to be a most dark and sinister business."

"Dark enough and sinister enough."

"Yet if the lady is correct in saying that the flooring and walls are sound, and that the door, window, and chimney are impassable, then her sister must have been undoubtedly alone when she met her mysterious end."

"What becomes, then, of these nocturnal whistles, and what of the very peculiar words of the dying woman?"

"I cannot think."

"When you combine the ideas of whistles at night, the presence of a band of gipsies who are on intimate terms with this old doctor, the fact that we have every reason to believe that the doctor has an interest in preventing his stepdaughter's marriage, the dying allusion to a band, and, finally, the fact that Miss Helen Stoner heard a metallic clang, which might have been caused by one of those metal bars that secured the shutters falling back into its place, I think that there is good ground to think that the mystery may be cleared along those lines."

"But what, then, did the gipsies do?"

"I cannot imagine."

"I see many objections to any such theory."

"And so do I. It is precisely for that reason that we are going to Stoke Moran this day. I want to see whether the objections are fatal, or if they may be explained away. But what in the name of the devil!"

The ejaculation had been drawn from my companion by the fact that our door had been suddenly dashed open, and that a huge man had framed himself in the aperture. His costume was a peculiar mixture of the professional and of the agricultural, having a black top-hat, a long frock-coat, and a pair of high gaiters, with a hunting-crop swinging in his hand. So tall was he that his hat actually brushed the cross bar of the doorway, and his breadth seemed to span it across from side to side. A large face, seared with a thousand wrinkles, burned yellow with the sun, and marked with every evil passion, was turned from one to the other of us, while his deep-set, bile-shot eyes, and his high, thin, fleshless nose, gave him somewhat the resemblance to a fierce old bird of prey.

"Which of you is Holmes?" asked this apparition.

"My name, sir; but you have the advantage of me," said my companion quietly.

"I am Dr. Grimesby Roylott, of Stoke Moran."

"Indeed, Doctor," said Holmes blandly. "Pray take a seat."

"I will do nothing of the kind. My stepdaughter has been here. I have traced her. What has she been saying to you?"

"It is a little cold for the time of the year," said Holmes.

"What has she been saying to you?" screamed the old man furiously.

"But I have heard that the crocuses promise well," continued my companion imperturbably.

"Ha! You put me off, do you?" said our new visitor, taking a step forward and shaking his hunting-crop. "I know you, you scoundrel! I have heard of you before. You are Holmes, the meddler."

My friend smiled.

"Holmes, the busybody!"

His smile broadened.

"Holmes, the Scotland Yard Jack-in-office!"

Holmes chuckled heartily. "Your conversation is most entertaining," said he. "When you go out close the door, for there is a decided draught."

"I will go when I have said my say. Don't you dare to meddle with my affairs. I know that Miss Stoner has been here. I traced her! I am a dangerous man to fall foul of! See here." He stepped swiftly forward, seized the poker, and bent it into a curve with his huge brown hands.

"See that you keep yourself out of my grip," he snarled, and hurling the twisted poker into the fireplace he strode out of the room.

"He seems a very amiable person," said Holmes, laughing. "I am not quite so bulky, but if he had remained I might have shown him that my grip was not much more feeble than his own." As he spoke he picked up the steel poker and, with a sudden effort, straightened it out again.

"Fancy his having the insolence to confound me with the official detective force! This incident gives zest to our investigation, however, and I only trust that our little friend will not suffer from her imprudence in allowing this brute to trace her. And now, Watson, we shall order breakfast, and afterwards I shall walk down to Doctors' Commons, where I hope to get some data which may help us in this matter."

It was nearly one o'clock when Sherlock Holmes returned from his excursion. He held in his hand a sheet of blue paper, scrawled over with notes and figures.

"I have seen the will of the deceased wife," said he. "To determine its exact meaning I have been obliged to work out the present prices of the investments with which it is concerned. The total income, which at the time of the wife's death was little short of £1100, is now, through the fall in agricultural prices, not more than £750. Each daughter can claim an income of £250, in case of marriage. It is evident, therefore, that if both girls had married, this beauty would have had a mere pittance, while even one of them would cripple him to a very serious extent. My morning's work has not been wasted, since it has proved that he has the very strongest motives for standing in the way of anything of the sort. And now, Watson, this is too serious for dawdling, especially as the old man is aware that we are interesting ourselves in his affairs; so if you are ready, we shall call a cab and drive to Waterloo. I should be very much obliged if you would slip your revolver into your pocket. An Eley's No. 2 is an excellent argument with gentlemen who can twist steel pokers into knots. That and a toothbrush are, I think, all that we need."

At Waterloo we were fortunate in catching a train for Leatherhead, where we hired a trap at the station inn and drove for four or five miles through the lovely Surrey lanes. It was a perfect day, with a bright sun and a few fleecy clouds in the heavens. The trees and wayside hedges were just throwing out their first green shoots, and the air was full of the pleasant smell of the moist earth. To me at least there was a strange contrast between the sweet promise of the spring and this sinister quest upon which we were engaged. My companion sat in the front of the trap, his arms folded, his hat pulled down over his eyes, and his chin sunk upon his breast, buried in the deepest thought. Suddenly, however, he started, tapped me on the shoulder, and pointed over the meadows.

"Look there!" said he.

A heavily timbered park stretched up in a gentle slope, thickening into a grove at the highest point. From amid the branches there jutted out the grey gables and high roof-tree of a very old mansion.

"Stoke Moran?" said he.

"Yes, sir, that be the house of Dr. Grimesby Roylott," remarked the driver.

"There is some building going on there," said Holmes; "that is where we are going."

"There's the village," said the driver, pointing to a cluster of roofs some distance to the left; "but if you want to get to the house, you'll find it shorter to get over this stile, and so by the foot-path over the fields. There it is, where the lady is walking."

"And the lady, I fancy, is Miss Stoner," observed Holmes, shading his eyes. "Yes, I think we had better do as you suggest."

We got off, paid our fare, and the trap rattled back on its way to Leatherhead.

"I thought it as well," said Holmes as we climbed the stile, "that this fellow should think we had come here as architects, or on some definite business. It may stop his gossip. Good-afternoon, Miss Stoner. You see that we have been as good as our word."

Our client of the morning had hurried forward to meet us with a face which spoke her joy. "I have been waiting so eagerly for you," she cried, shaking hands with us warmly. "All has turned out splendidly. Dr. Roylott has gone to town, and it is unlikely that he will be back before evening."

"We have had the pleasure of making the doctor's acquaintance," said Holmes, and in a few words he sketched out what had occurred. Miss Stoner turned white to the lips as she listened.

"Good heavens!" she cried, "he has followed me, then."

"So it appears."

"He is so cunning that I never know when I am safe from him. What will he say when he returns?"

"He must guard himself, for he may find that there is someone more cunning than himself upon his track. You must lock yourself up from him to-night. If he is violent, we shall take you away to your aunt's at Harrow. Now, we must make the best use of our time, so kindly take us at once to the rooms which we are to examine."

The building was of grey, lichen-blotched stone, with a high central portion and two curving wings, like the claws of a crab, thrown out on each side. In one of these wings the windows were broken and blocked with wooden boards, while the roof was partly caved in, a picture of ruin. The central portion was in little better repair, but the right-hand block was comparatively modern, and the blinds in the windows, with the blue smoke curling up from the chimneys, showed that this was where the family resided. Some scaffolding had been erected against the end wall, and the stone-work had been broken into, but there were no signs of any workmen at the moment of our visit. Holmes walked slowly up and down the ill-trimmed lawn and examined with deep attention the outsides of the windows.

"This, I take it, belongs to the room in which you used to sleep, the centre one to your sister's, and the one next to the main building to Dr. Roylott's chamber?"

"Exactly so. But I am now sleeping in the middle one."

"Pending the alterations, as I understand. By the way, there does not seem to be any very pressing need for repairs at that end wall."

"There were none. I believe that it was an excuse to move me from my room."

"Ah! that is suggestive. Now, on the other side of this narrow wing runs the corridor from which these three rooms open. There are windows in it, of course?"

"Yes, but very small ones. Too narrow for anyone to pass through."

"As you both locked your doors at night, your rooms were unapproachable from that side. Now, would you have the kindness to go into your room and bar your shutters?"

Miss Stoner did so, and Holmes, after a careful examination through the open window, endeavoured in every way to force the shutter open, but without success. There was no slit through which a knife could be passed to raise the bar. Then with his lens he tested the hinges, but they were of solid iron, built firmly into the massive masonry. "Hum!" said he, scratching his chin in some perplexity, "my theory certainly presents some difficulties. No one could pass these shutters if they were bolted. Well, we shall see if the inside throws any light upon the matter."

A small side door led into the whitewashed corridor from which the three bedrooms opened. Holmes refused to examine the third chamber, so we passed at once to the second, that in which Miss Stoner was now sleeping, and in which her sister had met with her fate. It was a homely little room, with a low ceiling and a gaping fireplace, after the fashion of old country-houses. A brown chest of drawers stood in one corner, a narrow white-counterpaned bed in another, and a dressing-table on the left-hand side of the window. These articles, with two small wicker-work chairs, made up all the furniture in the room save for a square of Wilton carpet in the centre. The boards round and the panelling of the walls were of brown, worm-eaten oak, so old and discoloured that it may have dated from the original building of the house. Holmes drew one of the chairs into a corner and sat silent, while his eyes travelled round and round and up and down, taking in every detail of the apartment.

"Where does that bell communicate with?" he asked at last pointing to a thick bell-rope which hung down beside the bed, the tassel actually lying upon the pillow.

"It goes to the housekeeper's room."

"It looks newer than the other things?"

"Yes, it was only put there a couple of years ago."

"Your sister asked for it, I suppose?"

"No, I never heard of her using it. We used always to get what we wanted for ourselves."

"Indeed, it seemed unnecessary to put so nice a bell-pull there.

You will excuse me for a few minutes while I satisfy myself as to this floor." He threw himself down upon his face with his lens in his hand and crawled swiftly backward and forward, examining minutely the cracks between the boards. Then he did the same with the wood-work with which the chamber was panelled. Finally he walked over to the bed and spent some time in staring at it and in running his eye up and down the wall. Finally he took the bell-rope in his hand and gave it a brisk tug.

"Why, it's a dummy," said he.

"Won't it ring?"

"No, it is not even attached to a wire. This is very interesting. You can see now that it is fastened to a hook just above where the little opening for the ventilator is."

"How very absurd! I never noticed that before."

"Very strange!" muttered Holmes, pulling at the rope. "There are one or two very singular points about this room. For example, what a fool a builder must be to open a ventilator into another room, when, with the same trouble, he might have communicated with the outside air!"

"That is also quite modern," said the lady.

"Done about the same time as the bell-rope?" remarked Holmes.

"Yes, there were several little changes carried out about that time."

"They seem to have been of a most interesting character – dummy bell-ropes, and ventilators which do not ventilate. With your permission, Miss Stoner, we shall now carry our researches into the inner apartment."

Dr. Grimesby Roylott's chamber was larger than that of his step-daughter, but was as plainly furnished. A camp-bed, a small wooden shelf full of books, mostly of a technical character, an armchair beside the bed, a plain wooden chair against the wall, a round table, and a large iron safe were the principal things which met the eye. Holmes walked slowly round and examined each and all of them with the keenest interest.

"What's in here?" he asked, tapping the safe.

"What's in here?" he asked, tapping the safe.

"My stepfather's business papers."

"Oh! you have seen inside, then?"

"Only once, some years ago. I remember that it was full of papers."

"There isn't a cat in it, for example?"

"No. What a strange idea!"

"Well, look at this!" He took up a small saucer of milk which stood on the top of it.

"No; we don't keep a cat. But there is a cheetah and a baboon."

"Ah, yes, of course! Well, a cheetah is just a big cat, and yet a saucer of milk does not go very far in satisfying its wants, I daresay. There is one point which I should wish to determine." He squatted down in front of the wooden chair and examined the seat of it with the greatest attention.

"Thank you. That is quite settled," said he, rising and putting his lens in his pocket. "Hullo! Here is something interesting!"

The object which had caught his eye was a small dog lash hung on one corner of the bed. The lash, however, was curled upon itself and tied so as to make a loop of whipcord.

"What do you make of that, Watson?"

"It's a common enough lash. But I don't know why it should be tied."

"That is not quite so common, is it? Ah, me! it's a wicked world, and when a clever man turns his brains to crime it is the worst of all. I think that I have seen enough now, Miss Stoner, and with your permission we shall walk out upon the lawn."

I had never seen my friend's face so grim or his brow so dark as it was when we turned from the scene of this investigation. We had walked several times up and down the lawn, neither Miss Stoner nor myself liking to break in upon his thoughts before he roused himself from his reverie.

"It is very essential, Miss Stoner," said he, "that you should absolutely follow my advice in every respect."

"I shall most certainly do so."

"The matter is too serious for any hesitation. Your life may depend upon your compliance."

"I assure you that I am in your hands."

"In the first place, both my friend and I must spend the night in your room."

Both Miss Stoner and I gazed at him in astonishment.

"Yes, it must be so. Let me explain. I believe that that is the village inn over there?"

"Yes, that is the Crown."

"Very good. Your windows would be visible from there?"

"Certainly."

"You must confine yourself to your room, on pretence of a headache, when your stepfather comes back. Then when you hear him retire for the night, you must open the shutters of your window, undo the hasp, put your lamp there as a signal to us, and then withdraw quietly with everything which you are likely to want into the room which you used to occupy. I have no doubt that, in spite of the repairs, you could manage there for one night."

"Oh, yes, easily."

"The rest you will leave in our hands."

"But what will you do?"

"We shall spend the night in your room, and we shall investigate the cause of this noise which has disturbed you."

"I believe, Mr. Holmes, that you have already made up your

mind," said Miss Stoner, laying her hand upon my companion's sleeve.

"Perhaps I have."

"Then, for pity's sake, tell me what was the cause of my sister's death."

"I should prefer to have clearer proofs before I speak."

"You can at least tell me whether my own thought is correct, and if she died from some sudden fright."

"No, I do not think so. I think that there was probably some more tangible cause. And now, Miss Stoner, we must leave you for if Dr. Roylott returned and saw us our journey would be in vain. Good-bye, and be brave, for if you will do what I have told you, you may rest assured that we shall soon drive away the dangers that threaten you."

Sherlock Holmes and I had no difficulty in engaging a bedroom and sitting-room at the Crown Inn. They were on the upper floor, and from our window we could command a view of the avenue gate, and of the inhabited wing of Stoke Moran Manor House. At dusk we saw Dr. Grimesby Roylott drive past, his huge form looming up beside the little figure of the lad who drove him. The boy had some slight difficulty in undoing the heavy iron gates, and we heard the hoarse roar of the doctor's voice and saw the fury with which he shook his clinched fists at him. The trap drove on, and a few minutes later we saw a sudden light spring up among the trees as the lamp was lit in one of the sitting-rooms.

"Do you know, Watson," said Holmes as we sat together in the gathering darkness, "I have really some scruples as to taking you to-night. There is a distinct element of danger."

"Can I be of assistance?"

"Your presence might be invaluable."

"Then I shall certainly come."

"It is very kind of you."

"You speak of danger. You have evidently seen more in these rooms than was visible to me."

"No, but I fancy that I may have deduced a little more. I imagine that you saw all that I did."

"I saw nothing remarkable save the bell-rope, and what purpose that could answer I confess is more than I can imagine."

"You saw the ventilator, too?"

"Yes, but I do not think that it is such a very unusual thing to have a small opening between two rooms. It was so small that a rat could hardly pass through."

"I knew that we should find a ventilator before ever we came to Stoke Moran."

"My dear Holmes!"

"Oh, yes, I did. You remember in her statement she said that her sister could smell Dr. Roylott's cigar. Now, of course that suggested at once that there must be a communication between the two rooms. It could only be a small one, or it would have been remarked upon at the coroner's inquiry. I deduced a ventilator."

"But what harm can there be in that?"

"Well, there is at least a curious coincidence of dates. A ventilator is made, a cord is hung, and a lady who sleeps in the bed dies. Does not that strike you?"

"I cannot as yet see any connection."

"Did you observe anything very peculiar about that bed?"

"No."

"It was clamped to the floor. Did you ever see a bed fastened like that before?"

"I cannot say that I have."

"The lady could not move her bed. It must always be in the same relative position to the ventilator and to the rope – or so we may call it, since it was clearly never meant for a bell-pull."

"Holmes," I cried, "I seem to see dimly what you are hinting at. We are only just in time to prevent some subtle and horrible crime."

"Subtle enough and horrible enough. When a doctor does go wrong he is the first of criminals. He has nerve and he has knowledge. Palmer and Pritchard were among the heads of their profession. This man strikes even deeper, but I think, Watson, that we shall be able to strike deeper still. But we shall have horrors enough before the night is over; for goodness' sake let us have a quiet pipe and turn our minds for a few hours to something more cheerful."

About nine o'clock the light among the trees was extinguished, and all was dark in the direction of the Manor House. Two hours passed slowly away, and then, suddenly, just at the stroke of eleven, a single bright light shone out right in front of us.

"That is our signal," said Holmes, springing to his feet; "it comes from the middle window."

As we passed out he exchanged a few words with the landlord, explaining that we were going on a late visit to an acquaintance, and that it was possible that we might spend the night there. A moment later we were out on the dark road, a chill wind blowing in our faces, and one yellow light twinkling in front of us through the gloom to guide us on our sombre errand.

There was little difficulty in entering the grounds, for unrepaired breaches gaped in the old park wall. Making our way among the trees, we reached the lawn, crossed it, and were about to enter through the window when out from a clump of laurel bushes there darted what seemed to be a hideous and distorted child, who threw itself upon the grass with writhing limbs and then ran swiftly across the lawn into the darkness.

"My God!" I whispered; "did you see it?"

Holmes was for the moment as startled as I.

His hand closed like a vice upon my wrist in his agitation. Then he broke into a low laugh and put his lips to my ear.

"It is a nice household," he murmured. "That is the baboon."

I had forgotten the strange pets which the doctor affected. There was a cheetah, too; perhaps we might find it upon our shoulders at any moment. I confess that I felt easier in my mind when, after following Holmes' example and slipping off my shoes, I found myself inside the bedroom. My companion noiselessly closed the shutters, moved the lamp onto the table, and cast his eyes round the room. All was as we had seen it in the daytime. Then creeping up to me and making a trumpet of his hand, he whispered into my ear again so gently that it was all that I could do to distinguish the words:

"The least sound would be fatal to our plans."

I nodded to show that I had heard.

"We must sit without light. He would see it through the ventilator."

I nodded again.

"Do not go asleep; your very life may depend upon it. Have your pistol ready in case we should need it. I will sit on the side of the bed, and you in that chair."

I took out my revolver and laid it on the corner of the table.

Holmes had brought up a long thin cane, and this he placed upon the bed beside him. By it he laid the box of matches and the stump of a candle. Then he turned down the lamp, and we were left in darkness.

How shall I ever forget that dreadful vigil? I could not hear a sound, not even the drawing of a breath, and yet I knew that my companion sat open-eyed, within a few feet of me, in the same state of nervous tension in which I was myself. The shutters cut off the least ray of light, and we waited in absolute darkness.

From outside came the occasional cry of a night-bird, and once at our very window a long drawn catlike whine, which told us that the cheetah was indeed at liberty. Far away we could hear the deep tones of the parish clock, which boomed out every quarter of an hour. How long they seemed, those quarters! Twelve struck, and one and two and three, and still we sat waiting silently for whatever might befall.

Suddenly there was the momentary gleam of a light up in the direction of the ventilator, which vanished immediately, but was succeeded by a strong smell of burning oil and heated metal. Someone in the next room had lit a dark-lantern. I heard a gentle sound of movement, and then all was silent once more, though the smell grew stronger. For half an hour I sat with straining ears. Then suddenly another sound became audible – a very gentle, soothing sound, like that of a small jet of steam escaping continually from a kettle. The instant that we heard it, Holmes sprang from the bed, struck a match, and lashed furiously with his cane at the bell-pull.

"You see it, Watson?" he yelled. "You see it?"

But I saw nothing. At the moment when Holmes struck the

light I heard a low, clear whistle, but the sudden glare flashing into my weary eyes made it impossible for me to tell what it was at which my friend lashed so savagely. I could, however, see that his face was deadly pale and filled with horror and loathing. He had ceased to strike and was gazing up at the ventilator when suddenly there broke from the silence of the night the most horrible cry to which I have ever listened. It swelled up louder and louder, a hoarse yell of pain and fear and anger all mingled in the one dreadful shriek. They say that away down in the village, and even in the distant parsonage, that cry raised the sleepers from their beds. It struck cold to our hearts, and I stood gazing at Holmes, and he at me, until the last echoes of it had died away into the silence from which it rose.

"What can it mean?" I gasped.

"It means that it is all over," Holmes answered. "And perhaps, after all, it is for the best. Take your pistol, and we will enter Dr. Roylott's room."

With a grave face he lit the lamp and led the way down the corridor. Twice he struck at the chamber door without any reply from within. Then he turned the handle and entered, I at his heels, with the cocked pistol in my hand.

It was a singular sight which met our eyes. On the table stood a dark-lantern with the shutter half open, throwing a brilliant beam of light upon the iron safe, the door of which was ajar. Beside this table, on the wooden chair, sat Dr. Grimesby Roylott clad in a long grey dressing-gown, his bare ankles protruding beneath, and his feet thrust into red heelless Turkish slippers. Across his lap lay the short stock with the long lash which we had noticed during the day. His chin was cocked upward and his eyes were fixed in a dreadful, rigid stare at the corner of the ceiling. Round his brow he had a peculiar yellow band, with brownish speckles, which seemed to be bound tightly round his head. As we entered he made neither sound nor motion.

"The band! the speckled band!" whispered Holmes.

I took a step forward. In an instant his strange headgear began to move, and there reared itself from among his hair the squat diamond-shaped head and puffed neck of a loathsome serpent.

"It is a swamp adder!" cried Holmes; "the deadliest snake in India. He has died within ten seconds of being bitten. Violence does, in truth, recoil upon the violent, and the schemer falls into the pit which he digs for another. Let us thrust this creature back into its den, and we can then remove Miss Stoner to some place of shelter and let the county police know what has happened."

As he spoke he drew the dog-whip swiftly from the dead man's lap, and throwing the noose round the reptile's neck he drew it from its horrid perch and, carrying it at arm's length, threw it into the iron safe, which he closed upon it.

Such are the true facts of the death of Dr. Grimesby Roylott, of Stoke Moran. It is not necessary that I should prolong a narrative which has already run to too great a length by telling how we broke the sad news to the terrified girl, how we conveyed her by the morning train to the care of her good aunt at Harrow, of how the slow process of official inquiry came to the conclusion that the doctor met his fate while indiscreetly playing with a dangerous pet. The little which I had yet to learn of the case was told me by Sherlock Holmes as we travelled back next day.

"I had," said he, "come to an entirely erroneous conclusion which shows, my dear Watson, how dangerous it always is to reason from insufficient data. The presence of the gipsies, and the use of the word 'band,' which was used by the poor girl, no doubt, to explain the appearance which she had caught a hurried glimpse of by the light of her match, were sufficient to put me upon an entirely wrong scent. I can only claim the merit that I instantly reconsidered my position when, however, it became clear to me that whatever danger threatened an occupant of the room could not come either from the window or the door. My attention was speedily drawn, as I have already remarked to you, to this ventilator, and to the bell-rope which hung down to the bed. The discovery that this was a dummy, and that the bed was clamped to the floor, instantly gave rise to the suspicion that the rope was there as a bridge for something passing through the hole and coming to the bed. The idea of a snake instantly occurred to me, and when I coupled it with my knowledge that the doctor was furnished with a supply of creatures from India, I felt that I was probably on the right track. The idea of using a form of poison which could not possibly be discovered by any chemical test was just such a one as would occur to a clever and ruthless man who had had an Eastern training. The rapidity with which such a poison would take effect would also, from his point of view, be an advantage. It would be a sharp-eyed coroner, indeed, who could distinguish the two little dark punctures which would show where the poison fangs had done their work. Then I thought of the whistle. Of course he must recall the snake before the morning light revealed it to the victim. He had trained it, probably by the use of the milk which we saw, to return to him when summoned. He would put it through this ventilator at the hour that he thought best, with the certainty that it would crawl down the rope and land on the bed. It might or might not bite the occupant, perhaps she might escape every night for a week, but sooner or later she must fall a victim.

"I had come to these conclusions before ever I had entered his room. An inspection of his chair showed me that he had been in the habit of standing on it, which of course would be necessary in order that he should reach the ventilator. The sight of the safe, the saucer of milk, and the loop of whipcord were enough to finally dispel any doubts which may have remained. The metallic clang heard by Miss Stoner was obviously caused by her stepfather hastily closing the door of his safe upon its terrible occupant. Having once made up my mind, you know the steps which I took in order to put the matter to the proof. I heard the creature hiss as I have no doubt that you did also, and I instantly lit the light and attacked it."

"With the result of driving it through the ventilator."

"And also with the result of causing it to turn upon its master at the other side. Some of the blows of my cane came home and roused its snakish temper, so that it flew upon the first person it saw. In this way I am no doubt indirectly responsible for Dr. Grimesby Roylott's death, and I cannot say that it is likely to weigh very heavily upon my conscience."

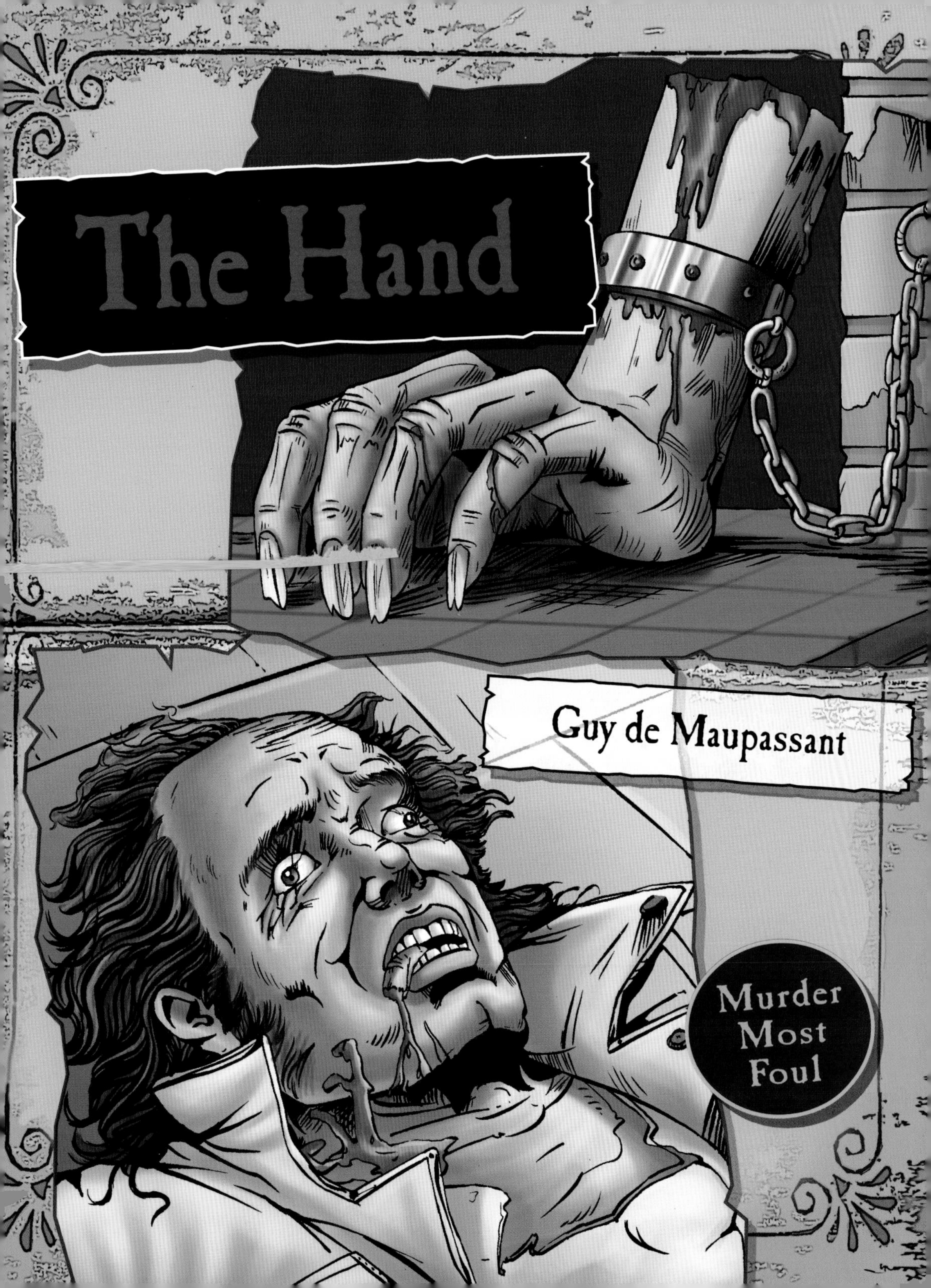
The Hand
Guy de Maupassant
Murder Most Foul

The Hand

by

Guy de Maupassant

All were crowding around M. Bermutier, the judge, who was giving his opinion about the Saint-Cloud mystery. For a month this inexplicable crime had been the talk of Paris. Nobody could make head or tail of it.

M. Bermutier, standing with his back to the fireplace, was talking, citing the evidence, discussing the various theories, but arriving at no conclusion.

Some women had risen, in order to get nearer to him, and were standing with their eyes fastened on the clean-shaven face of the judge, who was saying such weighty things. They were shaking and trembling, moved by fear and curiosity, and by the eager and insatiable desire for the horrible, which haunts the soul of every woman. One of them, paler than the others, said during a pause:

"It's terrible. It verges on the supernatural. The truth will never be known."

The judge turned to her:

"True, madame, it is likely that the actual facts will never be discovered. As for the word 'supernatural' which you have just used, it has nothing to do with the matter. We are in the presence of a very cleverly conceived and executed crime, so well enshrouded in mystery that we cannot disentangle it from the involved circumstances which surround it. But once I had to take charge of an affair in which the uncanny seemed to play a part. In fact, the case became so confused that it had to be given up."

Several women exclaimed at once:

"Oh! Tell us about it!"

M. Bermutier smiled in a dignified manner, as a judge should, and went on:

"Do not think, however, that I, for one minute, ascribed anything in the case to supernatural influences. I believe only in normal causes. But if, instead of using the word 'supernatural' to express what we do not understand, we were simply to make use of the word 'inexplicable,' it would be much better. At any rate, in the affair of which I am about to tell you, it is especially the surrounding, preliminary circumstances which impressed me. Here are the facts:

"I was, at that time, a judge at Ajaccio, a little white city on the edge of a bay which is surrounded by high mountains.

"The majority of the cases which came up before me concerned vendettas. There are some that are superb, dramatic, ferocious, heroic. We find there the most beautiful causes for revenge of which one could dream, enmities hundreds of years old, quieted for a time but never extinguished; abominable stratagems, murders becoming massacres and almost deeds of glory. For two years I heard of nothing but the price of blood, of this terrible Corsican prejudice which compels revenge for insults meted out to the offending person and all his descendants and relatives. I had seen old men, children, cousins murdered; my head was full of these stories.

"One day I learned that an Englishman had just hired a little villa at the end of the bay for several years. He had brought with him a French servant, whom he had engaged on the way at Marseilles.

"Soon this peculiar person, living alone, only going out to hunt and fish, aroused a widespread interest. He never spoke to any one, never went to the town, and every morning he would practice for an hour or so with his revolver and rifle.

"Legends were built up around him. It was said that he was some high personage, fleeing from his fatherland for political reasons; then it was affirmed that he was in hiding after having committed some abominable crime. Some particularly horrible circumstances were even mentioned.

"In my judicial position I thought it necessary to get some information about this man, but it was impossible to learn anything. He called himself Sir John Rowell.

"I therefore had to be satisfied with watching him as closely as I could, but I could see nothing suspicious about his actions.

"However, as rumours about him were growing and becoming more widespread, I decided to try to see this stranger myself, and I began to hunt regularly in the neighbourhood of his grounds.

"For a long time I watched without finding an opportunity. At last it came to me in the shape of a partridge which I shot and killed right in front of the Englishman. My dog fetched it for me, but, taking the bird, I went at once to Sir John Rowell and, begging his pardon, asked him to accept it.

"He was a big man, with red hair and beard, very tall, very broad, a kind of calm and polite Hercules. He had nothing of the so-called British stiffness, and in a broad English accent he thanked me warmly for my attention. At the end of a month we had had five or six conversations.

"One night, at last, as I was passing before his door, I saw him in the garden, seated astride a chair, smoking his pipe. I bowed and he invited me to come in and have a glass of beer. I needed no urging.

"He received me with the most punctilious English courtesy, sang the praises of France and of Corsica, and declared that he was quite in love with this country.

"Then, with great caution and under the guise of a vivid interest, I asked him a few questions about his life and his plans. He answered without embarrassment, telling me that he had travelled a great deal in Africa, in the Indies, in America. He added, laughing:

"'I have had many adventures.'

"Then I turned the conversation on hunting, and he gave me the most curious details on hunting the hippopotamus, the tiger, the elephant and even the gorilla.

"I said:

"'Are all these animals dangerous?'

"He smiled:

"'Oh, no! Man is the worst.'

"And he laughed a good broad laugh, the wholesome laugh of a contented Englishman.

"'I have also frequently been man-hunting.'

"Then he began to talk about weapons, and he invited me to come in and see different makes of guns.

"His parlour was draped in black, black silk embroidered in gold. Big yellow flowers, as brilliant as fire, were worked on the dark material.

"He said:

"'It is a Japanese material.'

"But in the middle of the widest panel a strange thing attracted my attention. A black object stood out against a square of red velvet. I went up to it; it was a hand, a human hand. Not the clean white hand of a skeleton, but a dried black hand, with yellow nails, the muscles exposed and traces of old blood on the bones, which were cut off as clean as though it had been chopped off with an axe, near the middle of the forearm.

"Around the wrist, an enormous iron chain, riveted and soldered to this unclean member, fastened it to the wall by a ring, strong enough to hold an elephant in leash.

"I asked:

"'What is that?'

"The Englishman answered quietly:

"'That is my best enemy. It comes from America, too. The bones were severed by a sword and the skin cut off with a sharp stone and dried in the sun for a week.'

"I touched these human remains, which must have belonged to a giant. The uncommonly long fingers were attached by enormous tendons which still had pieces of skin hanging to them in places. This hand was terrible to see; it made one think of some savage vengeance.

"I said:

"'This man must have been very strong.'

"The Englishman answered quietly:

"'Yes, but I was stronger than he. I put on this chain to hold him.'

"I thought that he was joking. I said:

"'This chain is useless now, the hand won't run away.'

"Sir John Rowell answered seriously:

"'It always wants to go away. This chain is needed.'

"I glanced at him quickly, questioning his face, and I asked myself:

"'Is he an insane man or a practical joker?'

"But his face remained inscrutable, calm and friendly. I turned to other subjects, and admired his rifles.

"However, I noticed that he kept three loaded revolvers in the room, as though constantly in fear of some attack.

"I paid him several calls. Then I did not go any more. People had become used to his presence; everybody had lost interest in him.

"A whole year rolled by. One morning, toward the end of November, my servant awoke me and announced that Sir John Rowell had been murdered during the night.

"Half an hour later I entered the Englishman's house, together with the police commissioner and the captain of the gendarmes. The servant, bewildered and in despair, was crying before the door. At first I suspected this man, but he was innocent.

"The guilty party could never be found.

"On entering Sir John's parlour, I noticed the body, stretched out on its back, in the middle of the room.

"His vest was torn, the sleeve of his jacket had been pulled off, everything pointed to a violent struggle.

"The Englishman had been strangled! His face was black, swollen and frightful, and seemed to express a terrible fear. He held something between his teeth, and his neck, pierced by five or six holes which looked as though they had been made by some iron instrument, was covered with blood.

"A physician joined us. He examined the finger marks on the neck for a long time and then made this strange announcement:

"'It looks as though he had been strangled by a skeleton.'

"A cold chill seemed to run down my back, and I looked over to where I had formerly seen the terrible hand. It was no longer there. The chain was hanging down, broken.

"I bent over the dead man and, in his contracted mouth, I found one of the fingers of this vanished hand, cut – or rather sawed off by the teeth down to the second knuckle.

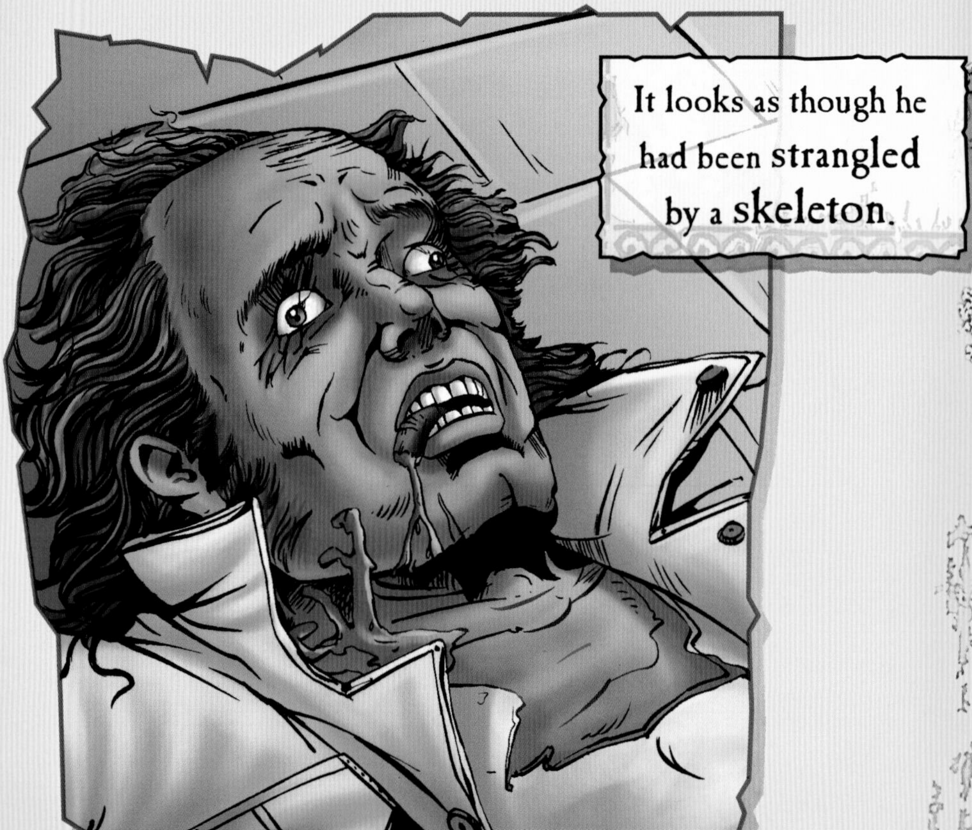

"Then the investigation began. Nothing could be discovered. No door, window or piece of furniture had been forced. The two watch dogs had not been aroused from their sleep.

"Here, in a few words, is the testimony of the servant:

"For a month his master had seemed excited. He had received many letters, which he would immediately burn.

"Often, in a fit of passion which approached madness, he had taken a switch and struck wildly at this dried hand riveted to the wall, and which had disappeared, no one knows how, at the very hour of the crime.

"He would go to bed very late and carefully lock himself in. He always kept weapons within reach. Often at night he would talk loudly, as though he were quarrelling with some one.

"That night, somehow, he had made no noise, and it was only on going to open the windows that the servant had found Sir John murdered. He suspected no one.

"I communicated what I knew of the dead man to the judges and public officials. Throughout the whole island a minute investigation was carried on. Nothing could be found out.

"One night, about three months after the crime, I had a terrible nightmare. I seemed to see the horrible hand running over my curtains and walls like an immense scorpion or spider. Three times I awoke, three times I went to sleep again; three times I saw the hideous object galloping round my room and moving its fingers like legs.

"The following day the hand was brought me, found in the cemetery, on the grave of Sir John Rowell, who had been buried there because we had been unable to find his family. The first finger was missing.

"Ladies, there is my story. I know nothing more."

The women, deeply stirred, were pale and trembling. One of them exclaimed:

"But that is neither a climax nor an explanation! We will be unable to sleep unless you give us your opinion of what had occurred."

The judge smiled severely:

"Oh! Ladies, I shall certainly spoil your terrible dreams. I simply believe that the legitimate owner of the hand was not dead, that he came to get it with his remaining one. But I don't know how. It was a kind of vendetta."

One of the women murmured:

"No, it can't be that."

And the judge, still smiling, said:

"Didn't I tell you that my explanation would not satisfy you?"

Lorna Doone
Blood Upon the Altar
R D Blackmore
Murder Most Foul

The story so far

John Ridd has loved Lorna Doone ever since she was a small girl, but she is a member of a fierce and murderous family, who killed John's father. It is intended that Lorna will marry the head of the family, Carver Doone. After many adventures, John has finally won his lovely Lorna to be his bride. This chapter opens on the day of their wedding, when John is at his happiest.

Blood Upon the Altar
from

Lorna Doone

by

R D Blackmore

However humble I might be, no one knowing anything of our part of the country, would for a moment doubt that now here was a great to do and talk of John Ridd and his wedding. The fierce fight with the Doones so lately, and my leading of the combat (though I fought not more than need be), and the vanishing of Sir Counsellor, and the galloping madness of Carver, and the religious fear of the women that this last was gone to hell – for he himself had declared that his aim, while he cut through the yeomanry – also their remorse, that he should have been made to go thither with all his children left behind – these things, I say (if ever I can again contrive to say anything), had led to the broadest excitement about my wedding of Lorna. We heard that people meant to come from more than thirty miles around, upon excuse of seeing my stature and Lorna's beauty; but in good truth out of sheer curiosity, and the love of meddling.

Our clerk had given notice, that not a man should come inside the door of his church without shilling-fee; and women (as sure to see twice as much) must every one pay two shillings. I thought this wrong; and as church-warden, begged that the money might be paid into mine own hands, when taken. But the clerk said that was against all law; and he had orders from the parson to pay it to him without any delay. So as I always obey the parson, when I care not much about a thing, I let them have it their own way; though feeling inclined to believe, sometimes, that I ought to have some of the money.

Dear mother arranged all the ins and outs of the way in which it was to be done; and Annie and Lizzie, and all the Snowes, and even Ruth Huckaback (who was there, after great persuasion), made such a sweeping of dresses that I scarcely knew where to place my feet, and longed for a staff, to put by their gowns. Then Lorna came out of a pew half-way, in a manner which quite astonished me, and took my left hand in her right, and I prayed God that it were done with.

My darling looked so glorious, that I was afraid of glancing at her, yet took in all her beauty. She was in a fright, no doubt; but nobody should see it; whereas I said (to myself at least), "I will go through it like a grave-digger."

Lorna's dress was of pure white, clouded with faint lavender (for the sake of the old Earl Brandir), and as simple as need be, except for perfect loveliness. I was afraid to look at her, as I said before, except when each of us said, "I will," and then each dwelled upon the other.

It is impossible for any who have not loved as I have to conceive my joy and pride, when after ring and all was done, and the parson had blessed us, Lorna turned to look at me with her glances of subtle fun subdued by this great act.

Her eyes, which none on earth may ever equal, or compare with, told me such a depth of comfort, yet awaiting further commune, that I was almost amazed, thoroughly as I knew them. Darling eyes, the sweetest eyes, the loveliest, the most loving eyes – the sound of a shot rang through the church, and those eyes were filled with death.

Lorna fell across my knees when I was going to kiss her, as the bridegroom is allowed to do, and encouraged, if he needs it; a flood of blood came out upon the yellow wood of the altar steps, and at my feet lay Lorna, trying to tell me some last message out of her faithful eyes. I lifted her up, and petted her, and coaxed her, but it was no good; the only sign of life remaining was a spirt of bright red blood.

Some men know what things befall them in the supreme time

She sighed a long sigh on my
breast, for her last
farewell to life, and then she
grew so cold, and cold, that I
asked the time of year.

of their life – far above the time of death – but to me comes back as a hazy dream, without any knowledge in it, what I did, or felt, or thought, with my wife's arms flagging, flagging, around my neck, as I raised her up, and softly put them there. She sighed a long sigh on my breast, for her last farewell to life, and then she grew so cold, and cold, that I asked the time of year.

It was Whit-Tuesday, and the lilacs all in blossom; and why I thought of the time of year, with the young death in my arms, God or His angels, may decide, having so strangely given us. Enough that so I did, and looked; and our white lilacs were beautiful. Then I laid my wife in my mother's arms, and begging that no one would make a noise, went forth for my revenge.

Of course, I knew who had done it. There was but one man in the world, or at any rate, in our part of it, who could have done such a thing – such a thing. I use no harsher word about it, while I leaped upon our best horse, with bridle but no saddle, and set the head of Kickums towards the course now pointed out to me. Who showed me the course, I cannot tell. I only know that I took it. And the men fell back before me.

Weapon of no sort had I. Unarmed, and wondering at my strange attire (with a bridal vest, wrought by our Annie, and red with the blood of the bride), I went forth just to find out this; whether in this world there be or be not God of justice.

With my vicious horse at a furious speed, I came upon Black Barrow Down, directed by some shout of men, which seemed to me but a whisper. And there, about a furlong before me, rode a man on a great black horse, and I knew that the man was Carver Doone.

"Your life or mine," I said to myself; "as the will of God may be. But we two live not upon this earth, one more hour together."

I knew the strength of this great man; and I knew that he was armed with a gun – if he had time to load again, after shooting my Lorna – or at any rate with pistols, and a horseman's sword as well. Nevertheless, I had no more doubt of killing the man before me than a cook has of spitting a headless fowl.

Sometimes seeing no ground beneath me, and sometimes heeding every leaf, and the crossing of the grass-blades, I followed over the long moor, reckless whether seen or not. But only once the other man turned round and looked back again, and then I was beside a rock, with a reedy swamp behind me.

Although he was so far before me, and riding as hard as ride he might, I saw that he had something on the horse in front of him; something which needed care, and stopped him from looking backward. In the whirling of my wits, I fancied first that this was Lorna; until the scene I had been through fell across hot brain and heart, like the drop at the close of a tragedy. Rushing there through crag and quag, at utmost speed of a maddened horse, I saw, as of another's fate, calmly (as on canvas laid), the brutal deed, the piteous anguish, and the cold despair.

The man turned up the gully leading from the moor to Cloven

Rocks, through which John Fry had tracked Uncle Ben, as of old related. But as Carver entered it, he turned round, and beheld me not a hundred yards behind; and I saw that he was bearing his child, little Ensie, before him. Ensie also descried me, and stretched his hands and cried to me; for the face of his father frightened him.

Carver Doone, with a vile oath, thrust spurs into his flagging horse, and laid one hand on a pistol-stock; whence I knew that his slung carbine had received no bullet since the one that had pierced Lorna. And a cry of triumph rose from the black depths of my heart. What cared I for pistols? I had no spurs, neither was my horse one to need the rowel; I rather held him in than urged him, for he was fresh as ever; and I knew that the black steed in front, if he breasted the steep ascent, where the track divided, must be in our reach at once.

His rider knew this; and, having no room in the rocky channel to turn and fire, drew rein at the crossways sharply, and plunged into the black ravine leading to the Wizard's Slough. "Is it so?" I said to myself with a brain and head cold as iron; "though the foul fiend come from the slough, to save thee; thou shalt carve it, Carver."

I followed my enemy carefully, steadily, even leisurely; for I had him, as in a pitfall, whence no escape might be. He thought that I feared to approach him, for he knew not where he was: and his low disdainful laugh came back. "Laugh he who wins," thought I.

A gnarled and half-starved oak, as stubborn as my own resolve, and smitten by some storm of old, hung from the crag above me. Rising from my horse's back, although I had no stirrups, I caught a limb, and tore it (like a mere wheat-awn) from the socket. Men show the rent even now, with wonder; none with more wonder than myself.

Carver Doone turned the corner suddenly on the black and bottomless bog; with a start of fear he reined back his horse, and I thought he would have turned upon me. But instead of that, he again rode on; hoping to find a way round the side.

Now there is a way between cliff and slough for those who know the ground thoroughly, or have time enough to search it; but for him there was no road, and he lost some time in seeking it. Upon this he made up his mind; and wheeling, fired, and then rode at me.

His bullet struck me somewhere, but I took no heed of that. Fearing only his escape, I laid my horse across the way, and with the limb of the oak struck full on the forehead his charging steed. Ere the slash of the sword came nigh me, man and horse rolled over, and wellnigh bore my own horse down, with the power of their onset.

Carver Doone was somewhat stunned, and could not arise for a moment. Meanwhile I leaped on the ground and awaited, smoothing my hair back, and baring my arms, as though in the ring for wrestling. Then the little boy ran to me, clasped my leg, and looked up at me, and the terror in his eyes made me almost fear myself.

"Ensie, dear," I said quite gently, grieving that he should see his wicked father killed, "run up yonder round the corner and try to find a pretty bunch of bluebells for the lady." The child obeyed me, hanging back, and looking back, and then laughing, while I prepared for business. There and then I might have killed mine enemy, with a single blow, while he lay unconscious; but it would have been foul play.

With a sullen and black scowl, the Carver gathered his mighty limbs, and arose, and looked round for his weapons; but I had put them well away. Then he came to me and gazed; being wont to frighten thus young men.

"I would not harm you, lad," he said, with a lofty style of sneering: "I have punished you enough, for most of your impertinence. For the rest I forgive you; because you have been good and gracious to my little son. Go, and be contented."

For answer, I smote him on the cheek, lightly, and not to hurt him: but to make his blood leap up. I would not sully my tongue by speaking to a man like this.

There was a level space of sward between us and the slough. With the courtesy derived from London, and the processions I had seen, to this place I led him. And that he might breathe himself, and have every fibre cool, and every muscle ready, my hold upon his coat I loosed, and left him to begin with me, whenever he thought proper.

I think that he felt that his time was come. I think he knew from my knitted muscles, and the firm arch of my breast, and the way in which I stood; but most of all from my stern blue eyes; that he had found his master. At any rate a paleness came, an ashy paleness on his cheeks, and the vast calves of his legs bowed in, as if he were out of training.

Seeing this, villain as he was, I offered him first chance. I stretched forth my left hand, as I do to a weaker antagonist, and I let him have the hug of me. But in this I was too generous; having forgotten my pistol-wound, and the cracking of one of my short lower ribs. Carver Doone caught me round the waist, with such a grip as never yet had been laid upon me.

I heard my rib go; I grasped his arm, and tore the muscle out of it (as the string comes out of an orange); then I took him by the throat, which is not allowed in wrestling; but he had snatched at mine; and now was no time of dalliance. In vain he tugged, and strained, and writhed, dashed his bleeding fist into my face, and flung himself on me with gnashing jaws. Beneath the iron of my strength – for God that day was with me – I had him helpless in two minutes, and his fiery eyes lolled out.

"I will not harm thee any more," I cried, so far as I could for panting, the work being very furious: "Carver Doone, thou art beaten: own it, and thank God for it; and go thy way, and repent thyself."

It was all too late. Even if he had yielded in his ravening frenzy – for his beard was like a mad dog's jowl – even if he would have

I will not harm thee any more ... Carver Doone, thou art beaten: own it, and thank God for it; and go thy way, and repent thyself.

owned that, for the first time in his life, he had found his master; it was all too late.

The black bog had him by the feet; the sucking of the ground drew on him, like the thirsty lips of death. In our fury, we had heeded neither wet nor dry; nor thought of earth beneath us. I myself might scarcely leap, with the last spring of o'er-laboured legs, from the engulfing grave of slime. He fell back, with his swarthy breast (from which my gripe had rent all clothing), like a hummock of bog-oak, standing out the quagmire; and then he tossed his arms to heaven, and they were black to the elbow, and the glare of his eyes was ghastly. I could only gaze and pant; for my strength was no more than an infant's, from the fury and the horror. Scarcely could I turn away, while, joint by joint, he sank from sight.

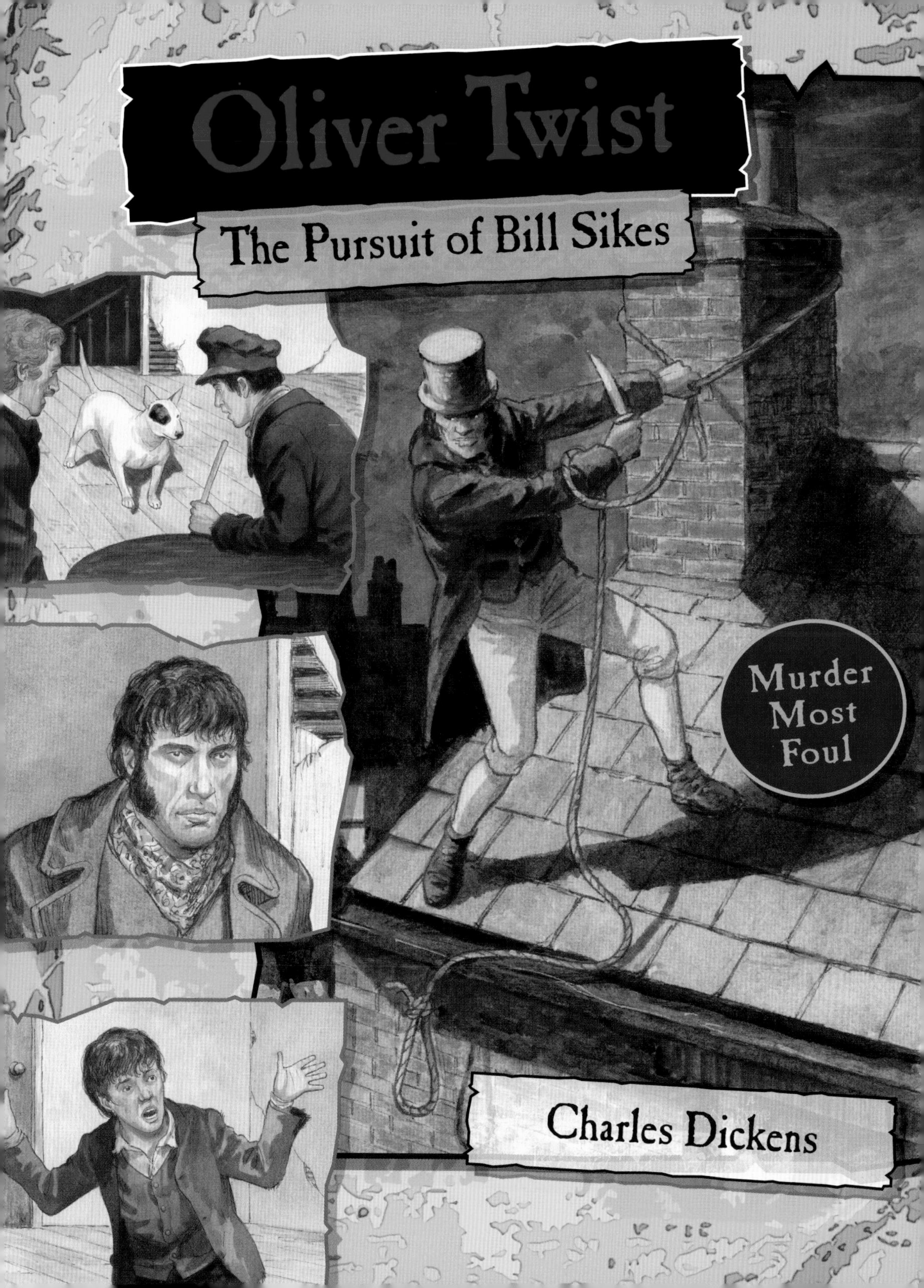
Oliver Twist
The Pursuit of Bill Sikes
Murder Most Foul
Charles Dickens

The story so far

Oliver Twist is the story of a young orphan boy in Victorian London who falls in with a gang of pickpockets and thieves led by an old man called Fagin. Bill Sikes, a dangerous thief, discovers that his girlfriend Nancy has, as he suspected, betrayed him to the police while she was planning to rescue Oliver from the gang. In his fury, Sikes beats her to death. He is now on the run, with all of England on the hunt for him, while his former associates alternate between horror at the murder and fear that Sikes may bring the police upon them.

The Pursuit of Bill Sikes

from

Oliver Twist

by

Charles Dickens

In Jacob's Island, the warehouses are roofless and empty; the walls are crumbling down; the windows are windows no more; the doors are falling into the streets; the chimneys are blackened, but they yield no smoke. Thirty or forty years ago, before losses and chancery suits came upon it, it was a thriving place; but now it is a desolate island indeed. The houses have no owners; they are broken open, and entered upon by those who have the courage; and there they live, and there they die. They must have powerful motives for a secret residence, or be reduced to a destitute condition indeed, who seek a refuge in Jacob's Island.

In an upper room of one of these houses – a detached house of fair size, ruinous in other respects, but strongly defended at door and window: of which house the back commanded the ditch in manner already described – there were assembled three men, who, regarding each other every now and then with looks expressive of perplexity and expectation, sat for some time in profound and gloomy silence. One of these was Toby Crackit, another Mr. Chitling, and the third a robber of fifty years, whose nose had been almost beaten in, in some old scuffle, and whose face bore a frightful scar which might probably be traced to the same occasion. This man was a returned transport, and his name was Kags.

"I wish," said Toby turning to Mr. Chitling, "that you had picked out some other crib when the two old ones got too warm, and had not come here, my fine feller."

"Why didn't you, blunder-head!" said Kags.

"Well, I thought you'd have been a little more glad to see me than this," replied Mr. Chitling, with a melancholy air.

"Why, look'e, young gentleman," said Toby, "when a man keeps himself so very ex-clusive as I have done, and by that means has a snug house over his head with nobody a prying and smelling about it, it's rather a startling thing to have the honour of a wisit from a young gentleman (however respectable and pleasant a person he may be to play cards with at conweniency) circumstanced as you are."

"Especially, when the exclusive young man has got a friend

stopping with him, that's arrived sooner than was expected from foreign parts, and is too modest to want to be presented to the Judges on his return," added Mr. Kags.

There was a short silence, after which Toby Crackit, seeming to abandon as hopeless any further effort to maintain his usual devil-may-care swagger, turned to Chitling and said,

"When was Fagin took then?"

"Just at dinner-time – two o'clock this afternoon. Charley and I made our lucky up the wash-us chimney, and Bolter got into the empty water-butt, head downwards; but his legs were so precious long that they stuck out at the top, and so they took him too."

"And Bet?"

"Poor Bet! She went to see the Body, to speak to who it was," replied Chitling, his countenance falling more and more, "and went off mad, screaming and raving, and beating her head against the boards; so they put a strait-weskut on her and took her to the hospital – and there she is."

"Wot's come of young Bates?" demanded Kags.

"He hung about, not to come over here afore dark, but he'll be here soon," replied Chitling. "There's nowhere else to go to now, for the people at the Cripples are all in custody, and the bar of the ken – I went up there and see it with my own eyes – is filled with traps."

"This is a smash,' observed Toby, biting his lips. "There's more than one will go with this."

"The sessions are on," said Kags: "if they get the inquest over, and Bolter turns King's evidence: as of course he will, from what he's said already: they can prove Fagin an accessory before the fact, and get the trial on on Friday, and he'll swing in six days from this, by G – !"

"You should have heard the people groan," said Chitling; "the officers fought like devils, or they'd have torn him away. He was down once, but they made a ring round him, and fought their way along. You should have seen how he looked about him, all muddy and bleeding, and clung to them as if they were his dearest friends. I can see 'em now, not able to stand upright with the pressing of the mob, and draggin him along amongst 'em; I can see the people jumping up, one behind another, and snarling with their teeth and making at him; I can see the blood upon his hair and beard, and hear the cries with which the women worked themselves into the centre of the crowd at the street corner, and swore they'd tear his heart out!"

The horror-stricken witness of this scene pressed his hands upon his ears, and with his eyes closed got up and paced violently to and fro, like one distracted.

While he was thus engaged, and the two men sat by in silence with their eyes fixed upon the floor, a pattering noise was heard upon the stairs, and Sikes's dog bounded into the room. They ran to the window, downstairs, and into the street. The dog had jumped in at an open window; he made no attempt to follow them, nor was his master to be seen.

"What's the meaning of this?" said Toby when they had returned. "He can't be coming here. I – I – hope not."

"If he was coming here, he'd have come with the dog," said Kags, stooping down to examine the animal, who lay panting on the floor. "Here! Give us some water for him;

he has run himself faint."

"He's drunk it all up, every drop," said Chitling after watching the dog some time in silence. "Covered with mud – lame – half blind – he must have come a long way."

"Where can he have come from!" exclaimed Toby. "He's been to the other kens of course, and finding them filled with strangers come on here, where he's been many a time and often. But where can he have come from first, and how comes he here alone without the other!"

'He' – (none of them called the murderer by his old name) – "He can't have made away with himself. What do you think?" said Chitling.

Toby shook his head.

"If he had," said Kags, "the dog 'ud want to lead us away to where he did it. No. I think he's got out of the country, and left the dog behind. He must have given him the slip somehow, or he wouldn't be so easy."

This solution, appearing the most probable one, was adopted as the right; the dog, creeping under a chair, coiled himself up to sleep, without more notice from anybody.

It being now dark, the shutter was closed, and a candle lighted and placed upon the table. The terrible events of the last two days had made a deep impression on all three, increased by the danger and uncertainty of their own position. They drew their chairs closer together, starting at every sound. They spoke little, and that in whispers, and were as silent and awe-stricken as if the remains of the murdered woman lay in the next room.

They had sat thus, some time, when suddenly was heard a hurried knocking at the door below.

"Young Bates," said Kags, looking angrily round, to check the fear he felt himself.

The knocking came again. No, it wasn't he. He never knocked like that.

Crackit went to the window, and shaking all over, drew in his head. There was no need to tell them who it was; his pale face was enough. The dog too was on the alert in an instant, and ran whining to the door.

"We must let him in," he said, taking up the candle.

"Isn't there any help for it?" asked the other man in a hoarse voice.

"None. He must come in."

"Don't leave us in the dark," said Kags, taking down a candle from the chimney-piece, and lighting it, with such a trembling hand that the knocking was twice repeated before he had finished.

Crackit went down to the door, and returned followed by a man with the lower part of his face buried in a handkerchief, and another tied over his head under his hat. He drew them slowly off. Blanched face, sunken eyes, hollow cheeks, beard of three days' growth, wasted flesh, short thick breath; it was the very ghost of Sikes.

He laid his hand upon a chair which stood in the middle of the room, but shuddering as he was about to drop into it, and seeming to glance over his shoulder, dragged it back close to the wall – as close as it would go – and ground it against it – and sat down.

Not a word had been exchanged. He looked from one to another in silence. If an eye were furtively raised and met his, it was instantly averted. When his hollow voice broke silence, they all three started. They seemed never to have heard its tones before.

"How came that dog here?" he asked.

"Alone. Three hours ago."

"Tonight's paper says that Fagin's took. Is it true, or a lie?"

"True."

They were silent again.

"Damn you all!" said Sikes, passing his hand across his forehead.

"Have you nothing to say to me?"

There was an uneasy movement among them, but nobody spoke.

"You that keep this house," said Sikes, turning his face to Crackit, "do you mean to sell me, or to let me lie here till this hunt is over?"

"You may stop here, if you think it safe," returned the person addressed, after some hesitation.

Sikes carried his eyes slowly up the wall behind him: rather trying to turn his head than actually doing it: and said, "Is – it – the body – is it buried?"

They shook their heads.

"Why isn't it!" he retorted with the same glance behind him. "Wot do they keep such ugly things above the ground for? – Who's that knocking?"

Crackit intimated, by a motion of his hand as he left the room, that there was nothing to fear; and directly came back with Charley Bates behind him. Sikes sat opposite the door, so that the moment the boy entered the room he encountered his figure.

"Toby," said the boy falling back, as Sikes turned his eyes

towards him, "why didn't you tell me this, downstairs?"

There had been something so tremendous in the shrinking off of the three, that the wretched man was willing to propitiate even this lad. Accordingly he nodded, and made as though he would shake hands with him.

"Let me go into some other room," said the boy, retreating still farther.

"Charley!" said Sikes, stepping forward. "Don't you – don't you know me?"

"Don't come nearer me," answered the boy, still retreating, and looking, with horror in his eyes, upon the murderer's face. "You monster!"

The man stopped half-way, and they looked at each other; but Sikes's eyes sunk gradually to the ground.

"Witness you three," cried the boy shaking his clenched fist, and becoming more and more excited as he spoke. "Witness you three – I'm not afraid of him – if they come here after him, I'll give him up; I will. I tell you out at once. He may kill me for it if he likes, or if he dares, but if I am here I'll give him up. I'd give him up if he was to be boiled alive. Murder! Help! If there's the pluck of a man among you three, you'll help me. Murder! Help! Down with him!"

Pouring out these cries, and accompanying them with violent gesticulation, the boy actually threw himself, single-handed, upon the strong man, and in the intensity of his energy and the suddenness of his surprise, brought him heavily to the ground.

The three spectators seemed quite stupefied. They offered no interference, and the boy and man rolled on the ground together; the former, heedless of the blows that showered upon him, wrenching his hands tighter and tighter in the garments about the murderer's breast, and never ceasing to call for help with all his might.

The contest, however, was too unequal to last long. Sikes had him down, and his knee was on his throat, when Crackit pulled him back with a look of alarm, and pointed to the window. There were lights gleaming below, voices in loud and earnest conversation, the tramp of hurried footsteps – endless they seemed in number – crossing the nearest wooden bridge. One man on horseback seemed to be among the crowd; for there was the noise of hoofs rattling on the uneven pavement. The gleam of lights increased; the footsteps came more thickly and noisily on. Then, came a loud knocking at the door, and then a hoarse murmur from such a multitude of angry voices as would have made the boldest quail.

"Help!" shrieked the boy in a voice that rent the air.

"He's here! Break down the door!"

"In the King's name," cried the voices without; and the hoarse cry arose again, but louder.

"Break down the door!" screamed the boy. "I tell you they'll never open it. Run straight to the room where the light is. Break down the door!"

Strokes, thick and heavy, rattled upon the door and lower window-shutters as he ceased to speak, and a loud huzzah burst from the crowd; giving the listener, for the first time, some adequate idea of its immense extent.

"Open the door of some place where I can lock this screeching Hell-babe," cried Sikes fiercely; running to and fro, and dragging the boy, now, as easily as if he were an empty sack. "That door. Quick!" He flung him in, bolted it, and turned the key. "Is the downstairs door fast?"

"Double-locked and chained," replied Crackit, who, with the other two men, still remained quite helpless and bewildered.

"The panels – are they strong?"

"Lined with sheet-iron."

"And the windows too?"

"Yes, and the windows."

"Damn you!" cried the desperate ruffian, throwing up the sash and menacing the crowd. "Do your worst! I'll cheat you yet!"

Of all the terrific yells that ever fell on mortal ears, none could exceed the cry of the infuriated throng. Some shouted to those who were nearest to set the house on fire; others roared to the officers to shoot him dead. Among them all, none showed such fury as the man on horseback, who, throwing himself out of the saddle, and bursting through the crowd as if he were parting water, cried, beneath the window, in a voice that rose above all others, "Twenty guineas to the man who brings a ladder!"

The nearest voices took up the cry, and hundreds echoed it. Some called for ladders, some for sledge-hammers; some ran with torches to and fro as if to seek them, and still came back and roared again; some spent their breath in impotent curses and execrations; some pressed forward with the ecstasy of madmen, and thus impeded the progress of those below; some among the boldest attempted to climb up by the water-spout and crevices in the wall; and all waved to and fro, in the darkness beneath, like a field of corn moved by an angry wind: and joined from time to time in one loud furious roar.

"The tide," cried the murderer, as he staggered back into the room, and shut the faces out, "the tide was in as I came up. Give me a rope, a long rope. They're all in front. I may drop into the Folly Ditch, and clear off that way. Give me a rope, or I shall do three more murders and kill myself."

The panic-stricken men pointed to where such articles were kept; the murderer, hastily selecting the longest and strongest cord, hurried up to the house-top.

All the window in the rear of the house had been long ago bricked up, except one small trap in the room where the boy was locked, and that was too small even for the passage of his body. But, from this aperture, he had never ceased to call on those without, to guard the back; and thus, when the murderer emerged at last on the house-top by the door in the roof, a loud shout proclaimed the fact to those in front, who immediately began to pour round, pressing upon each other in an unbroken stream.

He planted a board, which he had carried up with him for the purpose, so firmly against the door that it must be matter of great difficulty to open it from the inside; and creeping over the tiles, looked over the low parapet.

The water was out, and the ditch a bed of mud.

The crowd had been hushed during these few moments, watching his motions and doubtful of his purpose, but the instant they perceived it and knew it was defeated, they raised a cry of triumphant execration to which all their previous shouting had been whispers. Again and again it rose. Those who were at too great a distance to know its meaning, took up the sound; it echoed and re-echoed; it seemed as though the whole city had poured its population out to curse him.

On pressed the people from the front – on, on, on, in a strong struggling current of angry faces, with here and there a glaring torch to lighten them up, and show them out in all their wrath and passion. The houses on the opposite side of the ditch had been entered by the mob; sashes were thrown up, or torn bodily out; there were tiers and tiers of faces in every window; cluster upon cluster of people clinging to every house-top. Each little bridge (and there were three in sight) bent beneath the weight of the crowd upon it. Still the current poured on to find some nook or hole from which to vent their shouts, and only for an instant see the wretch.

"They have him now," cried a man on the nearest bridge. "Hurrah!"

The crowd grew light with uncovered heads; and again the shout uprose.

"I will give fifty pounds," cried an old gentleman from the same quarter, "to the man who takes him alive. I will remain here, till he come to ask me for it."

There was another roar. At this moment the word was passed among the crowd that the door was forced at last, and that he who had first called for the ladder had mounted into the room. The stream abruptly turned, as this intelligence ran from mouth to mouth; and the people at the windows, seeing those upon the bridges pouring back, quitted their stations, and running into the street, joined the concourse that now thronged pell-mell to the spot they had left: each man crushing and striving with his neighbour, and all panting with impatience to get near the door, and look upon the criminal as the officers brought him out. The cries and shrieks of those who were pressed almost to suffocation, or trampled down and trodden under foot in the confusion, were dreadful; the narrow ways were completely blocked up; and at this time, between the rush of some to regain the space in front of the house, and the unavailing struggles of others to extricate themselves from the mass, the immediate attention was distracted from the murderer, although the universal eagerness for his capture was, if possible, increased.

The man had shrunk down, thoroughly quelled by the ferocity of the crowd, and the impossibility of escape; but seeing this sudden change with no less rapidity than it had occurred, he sprang upon his feet, determined to make one last effort for his life by dropping into the ditch, and, at the risk of being stifled, endeavouring to creep away in the darkness and confusion.

Roused into new strength and energy, and stimulated by the noise within the house which announced that an entrance had really been effected, he set his foot against the stack of chimneys, fastened one end of the rope tightly and firmly round it, and with the other made a strong running noose by the aid of his hands and

teeth almost in a second. He could let himself down by the cord to within a less distance of the ground than his own height, and had his knife ready in his hand to cut it then and drop.

At the very instant when he brought the loop over his head previous to slipping it beneath his armpits, and when the old gentleman before-mentioned (who had clung so tight to the railing of the bridge as to resist the force of the crowd, and retain his position) earnestly warned those about him that the man was about to lower himself down – at that very instant the murderer, looking behind him on the roof, threw his arms above his head, and uttered a yell of terror.

"The eyes again!" he cried in an unearthly screech.

Staggering as if struck by lightning, he lost his balance and tumbled over the parapet. The noose was on his neck. It ran up with his weight, tight as a bow-string, and swift as the arrow it speeds. He fell for five-and-thirty feet. There was a sudden jerk, a terrific convulsion of the limbs; and there he hung, with the open knife clenched in his stiffening hand.

The old chimney quivered with the shock, but stood it bravely. The murderer swung lifeless against the wall; and the boy, thrusting aside the dangling body which obscured his view, called to the people to come and take him out, for God's sake.

A dog, which had lain concealed till now, ran backwards and forwards on the parapet with a dismal howl, and collecting himself for a spring, jumped for the dead man's shoulders. Missing his aim, he fell into the ditch, turning completely over as he went; and striking his head against a stone, dashed out his brains.

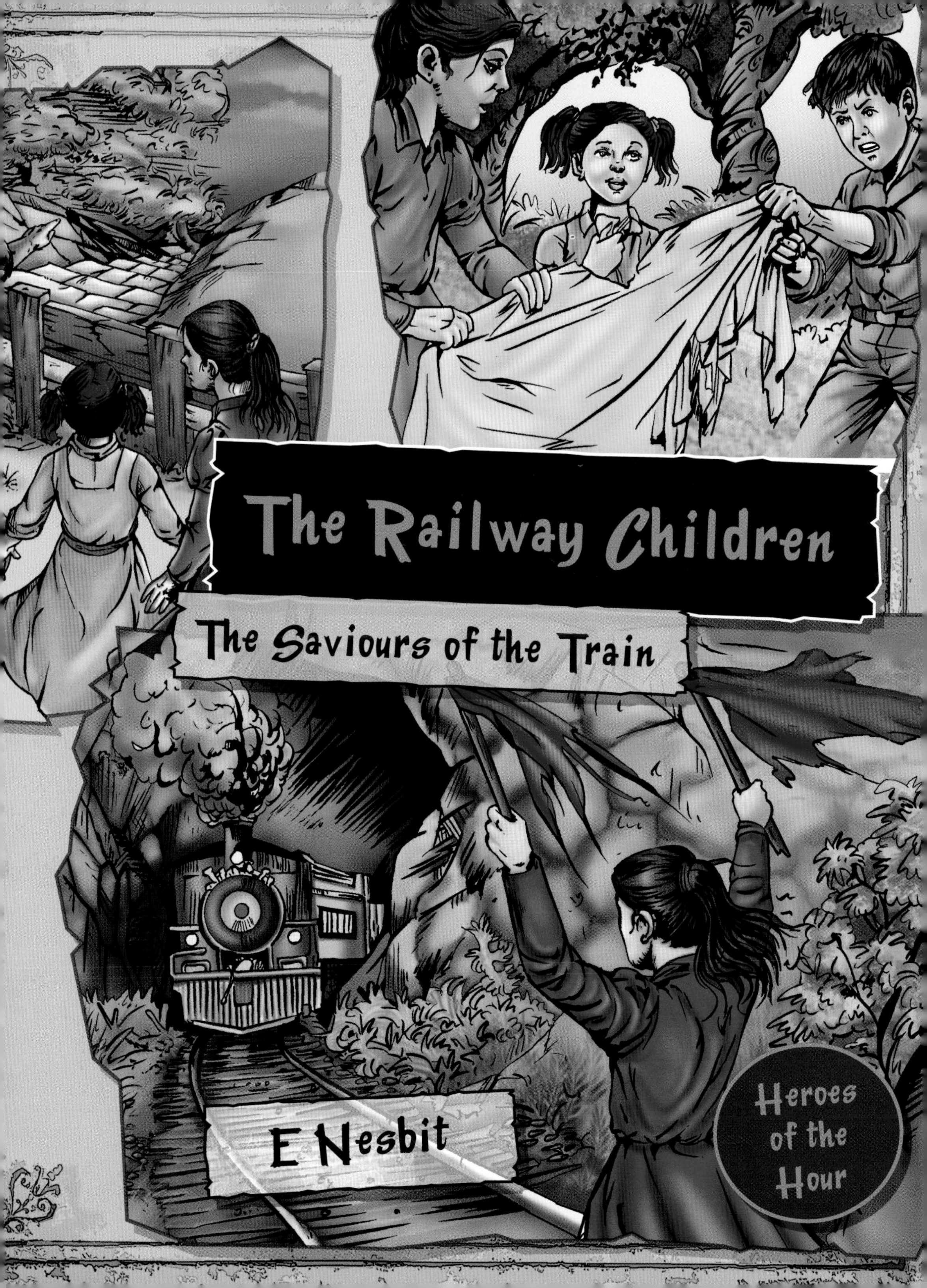
The Railway Children
The Saviours of the Train
E Nesbit
Heroes of the Hour

The story so far

Roberta, Phyllis and Peter have moved to the country with their mother while their father is in prison. They are much poorer than they used to be, but find great pleasure in exploring the nearby railway. Recently, they have taken an ill Russian gentleman into their home, whom their mother is helping to nurse, and the children are determined to find small treats to help him in his recovery.

The Saviours of the Train
from

The Railway Children

by

E Nesbit

The Russian gentleman was so delighted with the strawberries that the three racked their brains to find some other surprise for him. But all the racking did not bring out any idea more novel than wild cherries. And this idea occurred to them next morning. They had seen the blossom on the trees in the spring, and they knew where to look for wild cherries now that cherry time was here. The trees grew all up and along the rocky face of the cliff out of which the mouth of the tunnel opened. There were all sorts of trees there, birches and beeches and baby oaks and hazels, and among them the cherry blossom had shone like snow and silver.

The mouth of the tunnel was some way from Three Chimneys,

so Mother let them take their lunch with them in a basket. And the basket would do to bring the cherries back in if they found any. She also lent them her silver watch so that they should not be late for tea. Peter's Waterbury had taken it into its head not to go since the day when Peter dropped it into the water-butt. And they started. When they got to the top of the cutting, they leaned over the fence and looked down to where the railway lines lay at the bottom of what, as Phyllis said, was exactly like a mountain gorge.

"If it wasn't for the railway at the bottom, it would be as though the foot of man had never been there, wouldn't it?"

The sides of the cutting were of grey stone, very roughly hewn. Indeed, the top part of the cutting had been a little natural glen that had been cut deeper to bring it down to the level of the tunnel's mouth. Among the rocks, grass and flowers grew, and seeds dropped by birds in the crannies of the stone had taken root and grown into bushes and trees that overhung the cutting. Near the tunnel was a flight of steps leading down to the line – just wooden bars roughly fixed into the earth – a very steep and narrow way, more like a ladder than a stair.

"We'd better get down," said Peter; "I'm sure the cherries would be quite easy to get at from the side of the steps. You remember it was there we picked the cherry blossoms that we put on the rabbit's grave."

So they went along the fence towards the little swing gate that is at the top of these steps. And they were almost at the gate when

Bobbie said: –

"Hush. Stop! What's that?"

"That" was a very odd noise indeed – a soft noise, but quite plainly to be heard through the sound of the wind in tree branches, and the hum and whir of the telegraph wires. It was a sort of rustling, whispering sound. As they listened it stopped, and then it began again.

And this time it did not stop, but it grew louder and more rustling and rumbling.

"Look," – cried Peter, suddenly – "the tree over there!"

The tree he pointed at was one of those that have rough grey leaves and white flowers. The berries, when they come, are bright scarlet, but if you pick them, they disappoint you by turning black before you get them home. And, as Peter pointed, the tree was moving – not just the way trees ought to move when the wind blows through them, but all in one piece, as though it were a live creature and were walking down the side of the cutting.

"It's moving!" cried Bobbie. "Oh, look! and so are the others. It's like the woods in Macbeth."

"It's magic," said Phyllis, breathlessly. "I always knew this railway was enchanted."

It really did seem a little like magic. For all the trees for about twenty yards of the opposite bank seemed to be slowly walking down towards the railway line, the tree with the grey leaves bringing up the rear like some old shepherd driving a flock of green sheep.

"What is it? Oh, what is it?" said Phyllis; "it's much too magic for me. I don't like it. Let's go home."

But Bobbie and Peter clung fast to the rail and watched breathlessly. And Phyllis made no movement towards going home by herself.

The trees moved on and on. Some stones and loose earth fell down and rattled on the railway metals far below.

"It's ALL coming down," Peter tried to say, but he found there was hardly any voice to say it with. And, indeed, just as he spoke, the great rock, on the top of which the walking trees were, leaned slowly forward. The trees, ceasing to walk, stood still and shivered. Leaning with the rock, they seemed to hesitate a moment, and then rock and trees and grass and bushes, with a rushing sound, slipped right away from the face of the cutting and fell on the line with a blundering crash that could have been heard half a mile off. A cloud of dust rose up.

"Oh," said Peter, in awestruck tones, "isn't it exactly like when coals come in? – if there wasn't any roof to the cellar and you could see down."

"Look what a great mound it's made!" said Bobbie.

"Yes," said Peter, slowly. He was still leaning on the fence. "Yes," he said again, still more slowly.

Then he stood upright.

"The 11.29 down hasn't gone by yet. We must let them know at the station, or there'll be a most frightful accident."

"Let's run," said Bobbie, and began.

But Peter cried, "Come back!" and looked at Mother's watch. He was very prompt and businesslike, and his face looked whiter than they had ever seen it.

"No time," he said; "it's two miles away, and it's past eleven."

"Couldn't we," suggested Phyllis, breathlessly, "couldn't we climb up a telegraph post and do something to the wires?"

"We don't know how," said Peter.

"They do it in war," said Phyllis; "I know I've heard of it."

"They only CUT them, silly," said Peter, "and that doesn't do any good. And we couldn't cut them even if we got up, and we couldn't get up. If we had anything red, we could get down on the line and wave it."

"But the train wouldn't see us till it got round the corner, and then it could see the mound just as well as us," said Phyllis; "better, because it's much bigger than us."

"If we only had something red," Peter repeated, "we could go round the corner and wave to the train."

"We might wave, anyway."

"They'd only think it was just US, as usual. We've waved so often before. Anyway, let's get down."

They got down the steep stairs. Bobbie was pale and shivering. Peter's face looked thinner than usual. Phyllis was red-faced and damp with anxiety.

"Oh, how hot I am!" she said; "and I thought it was going to be cold; I wish we hadn't put on our – " she stopped short, and then ended in quite a different tone – "our flannel petticoats."

Bobbie turned at the bottom of the stairs.

"Oh, yes," she cried; "THEY'RE red! Let's take them off."

They did, and with the petticoats rolled up under their arms, ran along the railway, skirting the newly fallen mound of stones and rock and earth, and bent, crushed, twisted trees. They ran at their best pace. Peter led, but the girls were not far behind. They reached the corner that hid the mound from the straight line of railway that ran half a mile without curve or corner.

"Now," said Peter, taking hold of the largest flannel petticoat.

"You're not" – Phyllis faltered – "you're not going to TEAR them?"

"Shut up," said Peter, with brief sternness.

"Oh, yes," said Bobbie, "tear them into little bits if you like. Don't you see, Phil, if we can't stop the train, there'll be a real live

accident, with people KILLED. Oh, horrible! Here, Peter, you'll never tear it through the band!"

She took the red flannel petticoat from him and tore it off an inch from the band. Then she tore the other in the same way.

"There!" said Peter, tearing in his turn. He divided each petticoat into three pieces. "Now, we've got six flags." He looked at the watch again. "And we've got seven minutes. We must have flagstaffs."

The knives given to boys are, for some odd reason, seldom of the kind of steel that keeps sharp. The young saplings had to be broken off. Two came up by the roots. The leaves were stripped from them.

"We must cut holes in the flags, and run the sticks through the holes," said Peter. And the holes were cut. The knife was sharp enough to cut flannel with. Two of the flags were set up in heaps of loose stones between the sleepers of the down line. Then Phyllis and Roberta took each a flag, and stood ready to wave it as soon as the train came in sight.

"I shall have the other two myself," said Peter, "because it was my idea to wave something red."

"They're our petticoats, though," Phyllis was beginning, but Bobbie interrupted –

"Oh, what does it matter who waves what, if we can only save the train?"

Perhaps Peter had not rightly calculated the number of minutes it would take the 11.29 to get from the station to the place where they were, or perhaps the train was late. Anyway, it seemed a very long time that they waited.

Phyllis grew impatient. "I expect the watch is wrong, and the train's gone by," said she.

Peter relaxed the heroic attitude he had chosen to show off his two flags. And Bobbie began to feel sick with suspense.

It seemed to her that they had been standing there for hours and hours, holding those silly little red flannel flags that no one would ever notice. The train wouldn't care. It would go rushing by them and tear round the corner and go crashing into that awful mound. And everyone would be killed. Her hands grew very cold and trembled so that she could hardly hold the flag. And then came the distant rumble and hum of the metals, and a puff of white steam showed far away along the stretch of line.

"Stand firm," said Peter, "and wave like mad! When it gets to that big furze bush step back, but go on waving! Don't stand ON the line, Bobbie!"

The train came rattling along very, very fast.

"They don't see us! They won't see us! It's all no good!" cried Bobbie.

The two little flags on the line swayed as the nearing train shook and loosened the heaps of loose stones that held them up. One of them slowly leaned over and fell on the line. Bobbie jumped forward and caught it up, and waved it; her hands did not tremble now.

It seemed that the train came on as fast as ever. It was very near now.

"Keep off the line, you silly cuckoo!" said Peter, fiercely.

"It's no good," Bobbie said again.

"Stand back!" cried Peter, suddenly, and he dragged Phyllis back by the arm.

But Bobbie cried, "Not yet, not yet!" and waved her two flags right over the line. The front of the engine looked black and enormous. Its voice was loud and harsh.

"Oh, stop, stop, stop!" cried Bobbie. No one heard her. At least Peter and Phyllis didn't, for the oncoming rush of the train covered the sound of her voice with a mountain of sound. But afterwards she used to wonder whether the engine itself had not heard her. It seemed almost as though it had – for it slackened swiftly, slackened and stopped, not twenty yards from the place where Bobbie's two flags waved over the line. She saw the great black engine stop dead, but somehow she could not stop waving the flags. And when the driver and the fireman had got off the engine and Peter and Phyllis had gone to meet them and pour out their excited tale of the awful mound just round the corner, Bobbie still waved the flags but more and more feebly and jerkily.

When the others turned towards her she was lying across the line with her hands flung forward and still gripping the sticks of the little red flannel flags.

The engine-driver picked her up, carried her to the train, and laid her on the cushions of a first-class carriage.

"Gone right off in a faint," he said, "poor little woman. And no wonder. I'll just 'ave a look at this 'ere mound of yours, and then we'll run you back to the station and get her seen to."

It was horrible to see Bobbie lying so white and quiet, with her lips blue, and parted.

"I believe that's what people look like when they're dead," whispered Phyllis.

"DON'T!" said Peter, sharply.

They sat by Bobbie on the blue cushions, and the train ran back. Before it reached their station Bobbie had sighed and opened her eyes, and rolled herself over and begun to cry. This cheered the others wonderfully. They had seen her cry before, but they had never seen her faint, nor anyone else, for the matter of that. They had not known what to do when she was fainting, but now she was only crying they could thump her on the back and tell her not to, just as they always did. And presently, when she stopped crying, they were able to laugh at her for being such a coward as to faint.

When the station was reached, the three were the heroes of an agitated meeting on the platform.

The praises they got for their "prompt action," their "common sense," their "ingenuity," were enough to have turned anybody's head. Phyllis enjoyed herself thoroughly. She had never been a real heroine before, and the feeling was delicious. Peter's ears got very red. Yet he, too, enjoyed himself. Only Bobbie wished they all wouldn't. She wanted to get away.

"You'll hear from the Company about this, I expect," said the Station Master.

Bobbie wished she might never hear of it again. She pulled at Peter's jacket.

"Oh, come away, come away! I want to go home," she said.

So they went. And as they went Station Master and Porter and guards and driver and fireman and passengers sent up a cheer.

"Oh, listen," cried Phyllis; "that's for US!"

"Yes," said Peter. "I say, I am glad I thought about something red, and waving it."

"How lucky we DID put on our red flannel petticoats!" said Phyllis.

Bobbie said nothing. She was thinking of the horrible mound, and the trustful train rushing towards it.

"And it was US that saved them," said Peter.

"How dreadful if they had all been killed!" said Phyllis; "wouldn't it, Bobbie?"

"We never got any cherries, after all," said Bobbie.

The others thought her rather heartless.

The Prisoner of Zenda
A Merry Evening with a Distant Relative
Anthony Hope
Heroes of the Hour

The story so far

Rudolf Rassendyll, brother of Lord Burlesdon, has travelled to the European country of Ruritania to see the coronation of the new King, who is also called Rudolf, a member of the royal house of the Elphbergs. Rassendyll is believed to be a distant relative of the king. He certainly has the flaming red hair and long nose for which the King is famous. He has broken his journey at Zenda, the home territory of the King's half-brother, a royal duke called Black Michael. It is common knowledge that Black Michael would like to be King and would seize any excuse to prevent the coronation. Rassendyll is planning to travel on to the capital, Strelsau, to see the coronation.

A Merry Evening with a Distant Relative
from

The Prisoner of Zenda

by

Anthony Hope

I took an early luncheon, and, having bidden my kind entertainers farewell, promising to return to them on my way home, I set out to climb the hill that led to the Castle, and thence to the forest of Zenda. Half an hour's leisurely walking brought me to the Castle. It had been a fortress in old days, and the ancient keep was still in good preservation and very imposing. Behind it stood another portion of the original castle, and behind that again, and separated from it by a deep and broad moat, which ran all round the old buildings, was a handsome modern chateau, erected by the last king, and now forming the country residence of the Duke of Strelsau. The old and the new portions were connected by a drawbridge, and this indirect mode of access formed the only passage between the old building and the outer world; but leading to the modern chateau there was a broad and handsome avenue. It was an ideal residence: when 'Black Michael' desired company, he could dwell in his chateau; if a fit of misanthropy seized him, he had merely to cross the bridge and draw it up after him (it ran on rollers), and nothing short of a regiment and a train of artillery could fetch him out. I went on my way, glad that poor Black Michael, though he could not have the throne or the princess, had, at least, as fine a residence as any prince in Europe.

Soon I entered the forest, and walked on for an hour or more in its cool sombre shade. The great trees enlaced with one another over my head, and the sunshine stole through in patches as bright as diamonds, and hardly bigger. I was enchanted with the place, and, finding a felled tree-trunk, propped my back against it, and stretching my legs out gave myself up to undisturbed contemplation of the solemn beauty of the woods and to the comfort of a good cigar. And when the cigar was finished and I had (I suppose) inhaled as much beauty as I could, I went off into the most delightful sleep, regardless of my train to Strelsau and of the fast-waning afternoon. To remember a train in such a spot would have been rank sacrilege. Instead of that, I fell to dreaming that I was married to the Princess Flavia and dwelt in the Castle of Zenda, and beguiled whole days with my love in the glades of the forest – which made a very pleasant dream. In fact, I was just impressing a fervent kiss on the charming lips of the princess, when I heard (and the voice seemed at first a part of the dream) someone exclaim, in rough strident tones.

"Why, the devil's in it! Shave him, and he'd be the King!"

The idea seemed whimsical enough for a dream: by the sacrifice of my heavy moustache and carefully pointed imperial, I was to be transformed into a monarch! I was about to kiss the princess again, when I arrived (very reluctantly) at the conclusion that I was awake.

I opened my eyes, and found two men regarding me with much curiosity. Both wore shooting costumes and carried guns. One was rather short and very stoutly built, with a big bullet-shaped head, a bristly grey moustache, and small pale-blue eyes, a trifle bloodshot. The other was a slender young fellow, of middle height, dark in complexion, and bearing himself with grace and distinction. I set the one down as an old soldier: the other for a gentleman accustomed to move in good society, but not unused to military life either. It turned out afterwards that my guess was a good one.

The elder man approached me, beckoning the younger to follow. He did so, courteously raising his hat. I rose slowly to my feet.

"He's the height, too!" I heard the elder murmur, as he surveyed my six feet two inches of stature. Then, with a cavalier touch of the cap, he addressed me:

"May I ask your name?"

"As you have taken the first step in the acquaintance, gentlemen," said I, with a smile, "suppose you give me a lead in the matter of names."

The young man stepped forward with a pleasant smile.

"This," said he, "is Colonel Sapt, and I am called Fritz von Tarlenheim: we are both in the service of the King of Ruritania."

I bowed and, baring my head, answered:

"I am Rudolf Rassendyll. I am a traveller from England; and once for a year or two I held a commission from her Majesty the Queen."

"Then we are all brethren of the sword," answered Tarlenheim, holding out his hand, which I took readily.

"Rassendyll, Rassendyll!" muttered Colonel Sapt; then a gleam of intelligence flitted across his face.

"By Heaven!" he cried, "you're of the Burlesdons?"

"My brother is now Lord Burlesdon," said I.

"Thy head betrayeth thee," he chuckled, pointing to my uncovered poll. "Why, Fritz, you know the story?"

The young man glanced apologetically at me. He felt a delicacy which my sister-in-law would have admired. To put him at his ease, I remarked with a smile:

"Ah! the story is known here as well as among us, it seems."

"Known!" cried Sapt. "If you stay here, the deuce a man in all Ruritania will doubt of it – or a woman either."

I began to feel uncomfortable. Had I realized what a very

plainly written pedigree I carried about with me, I should have thought long before I visited Ruritania. However, I was in for it now.

At this moment a ringing voice sounded from the wood behind us:

"Fritz, Fritz! where are you, man?"

Tarlenheim started, and said hastily:

"It's the King!"

Old Sapt chuckled again.

Then a young man jumped out from behind the trunk of a tree and stood beside us. As I looked at him, I uttered an astonished cry; and he, seeing me, drew back in sudden wonder. Saving the hair on my face and a manner of conscious dignity which

his position gave him, saving also that he lacked perhaps half an inch – nay, less than that, but still something – of my height, the King of Ruritania might have been Rudolf Rassendyll, and I, Rudolf, the King.

For an instant we stood motionless, looking at one another. Then I bared my head again and bowed respectfully. The King found his voice, and asked in bewilderment:

"Colonel – Fritz – who is this gentleman?"

I was about to answer, when Colonel Sapt stepped between the King and me, and began to talk to his Majesty in a low growl. The King towered over Sapt, and, as he listened, his eyes now and again sought mine. I looked at him long and carefully. The likeness was certainly astonishing, though I saw the points of difference also. The King's face was slightly more fleshy than mine, the oval of its contour the least trifle more pronounced, and, as I fancied, his mouth lacking something of the firmness (or obstinacy) which was to be gathered from my close-shutting lips. But, for all that, and above all minor distinctions, the likeness rose striking, salient, wonderful.

Sapt ceased speaking, and the King still frowned. Then, gradually, the corners of his mouth began to twitch, his nose came down (as mine does when I laugh), his eyes twinkled, and, behold! he burst into the merriest fit of irrepressible laughter, which rang through the woods and proclaimed him a jovial soul.

"Well met, cousin!" he cried, stepping up to me, clapping me on the back, and laughing still. "You must forgive me if I was taken aback. A man doesn't expect to see double at this time of day, eh, Fritz?"

"I must pray pardon, sire, for my presumption," said I. "I trust it will not forfeit your Majesty's favour."

"By Heaven! you'll always enjoy the King's countenance," he laughed, "whether I like it or not; and, sir, I shall very gladly add to it what services I can. Where are you travelling to?"

"To Strelsau, sire – to the coronation."

The King looked at his friends: he still smiled, though his expression hinted some uneasiness. But the humorous side of the matter caught him again.

"Fritz, Fritz!" he cried, "a thousand crowns for a sight of brother Michael's face when he sees a pair of us!" and the merry laugh rang out again.

"Seriously," observed Fritz von Tarlenheim, "I question Mr. Rassendyll's wisdom in visiting Strelsau just now."

The King lit a cigarette.

"Well, Sapt?" said he, questioningly.

"He mustn't go," growled the old fellow.

"Come, colonel, you mean that I should be in Mr. Rassendyll's debt, if – "

"Oh, ay! wrap it up in the right way," said Sapt, hauling a great pipe out of his pocket.

"Enough, sire," said I. "I'll leave Ruritania today."

"No, by thunder, you shan't – and that's sans phrase, as Sapt likes it. For you shall dine with me tonight, happen what will afterwards. Come, man, you don't meet a new relation every day!"

"We dine sparingly tonight," said Fritz von Tarlenheim.

"Not we – with our new cousin for a guest!" cried the King; and, as Fritz shrugged his shoulders, he added: "Oh! I'll remember our early start, Fritz."

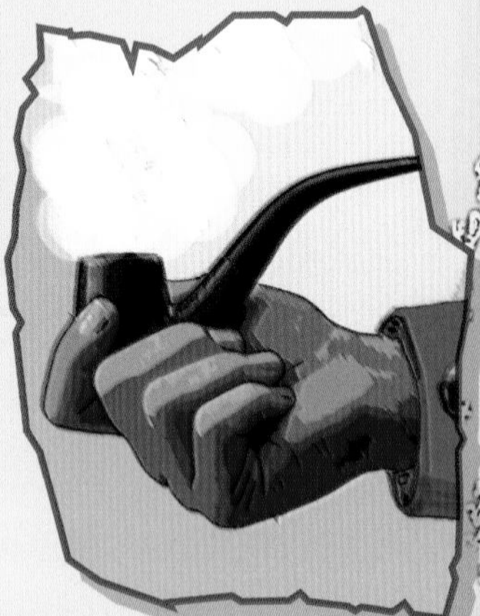

"So will I – tomorrow morning," said old Sapt, pulling at his pipe.

"O wise old Sapt!" cried the King. "Come, Mr. Rassendyll – by the way, what name did they give you?"

"Your Majesty's," I answered, bowing.

"Well, that shows they weren't ashamed of us," he laughed. "Come, then, cousin Rudolf; I've got no house of my own here, but my dear brother Michael lends us a place of his, and we'll make shift to entertain you there;" and he put his arm through mine and, signing to the others to accompany us, walked me off, westerly, through the forest.

We walked for more than half an hour, and the King smoked cigarettes and chattered incessantly. He was full of interest in my family, laughed heartily when I told him of the portraits with Elphberg hair in our galleries, and yet more heartily when he heard that my expedition to Ruritania was a secret one.

"You have to visit your disreputable cousin on the sly, have you?" said he.

Suddenly emerging from the wood, we came on a small and rude hunting-lodge. It was a one-storey building, a sort of bungalow, built entirely of wood. As we approached it, a little man in a plain livery came out to meet us. The only other person I saw about the place was a fat elderly woman, whom I afterwards discovered to be the mother of Johann, the duke's keeper.

"Well, is dinner ready, Josef?" asked the King.

The little servant informed us that it was, and we soon sat down to a plentiful meal. The fare was plain enough: the King ate heartily, Fritz von Tarlenheim delicately, old Sapt voraciously. I played a good knife and fork, as my custom is; the King noticed my performance with approval.

"We're all good trenchermen, we Elphbergs," said he. "But what? – we're eating dry! Wine, Josef! wine, man! Are we beasts, to eat without drinking? Are we cattle, Josef?"

At this reproof Josef hastened to load the table with bottles.

"Remember tomorrow!" said Fritz.

"Ay – tomorrow!" said old Sapt.

The King drained a bumper to his "Cousin Rudolf," as he was gracious – or merry – enough to call me; and I drank its fellow to the "Elphberg Red," whereat he laughed loudly.

Now, be the meat what it might, the wine we drank was beyond all price or praise, and we did it justice. Fritz ventured once to stay the King's hand.

"What?" cried the King. "Remember you start before I do, Master Fritz – you must be more sparing by two hours than I."

Fritz saw that I did not understand.

"The colonel and I," he explained, "leave here at six: we ride down to Zenda and return with the guard of honour to fetch the King at eight, and then we all ride together to the station."

"Hang that same guard!" growled Sapt.

"Oh! it's very civil of my brother to ask the honour for his regiment," said the King. "Come, cousin, you need not start early. Another bottle, man!"

I had another bottle – or, rather, a part of one, for the larger half travelled quickly down his Majesty's throat. Fritz gave up his attempts at persuasion: from persuading, he fell to being persuaded, and soon we were all of us as full of wine as we had any right to be. The King began talking of what he would do in the future, old Sapt of what he had done in the past, Fritz of some beautiful girl or other, and I of the wonderful merits of the Elphberg dynasty. We all talked at once, and followed to the letter Sapt's exhortation to let the morrow take care of itself.

At last the King set down his glass and leant back in his chair.

"I have drunk enough," said he.

"Far be it from me to contradict the King," said I.

Indeed, his remark was most absolutely true – so far as it went.

While I yet spoke, Josef came and set before the King a

marvellous old wicker-covered flagon. It had lain so long in some darkened cellar that it seemed to blink in the candlelight.

"His Highness the Duke of Strelsau bade me set this wine before the King, when the King was weary of all other wines, and pray the King to drink, for the love that he bears his brother."

"Well done, Black Michael!" said the King. "Out with the cork, Josef. Hang him! Did he think I'd flinch from his bottle?"

The bottle was opened, and Josef filled the King's glass. The King tasted it. Then, with a solemnity born of the hour and his own condition, he looked round on us:

"Gentlemen, my friends – Rudolf, my cousin ('tis a scandalous story, Rudolf, on my honour!), everything is yours to the half of Ruritania. But ask me not for a single drop of this divine bottle, which I will drink to the health of that – that sly knave, my brother, Black Michael."

And the King seized the bottle and turned it over his mouth, and drained it and flung it from him, and laid his head on his arms on the table.

And we drank pleasant dreams to his Majesty – and that is all I remember of the evening. Perhaps it is enough.

Whether I had slept a minute or a year I knew not. I awoke with a start and a shiver; my face, hair and clothes dripped water, and opposite me stood old Sapt, a sneering smile on his face and an empty bucket in his hand. On the table by him sat Fritz von Tarlenheim, pale as a ghost and black as a crow under the eyes.

I leapt to my feet in anger.

"Your joke goes too far, sir!" I cried.

"Tut, man, we've no time for quarrelling. Nothing else would rouse you. It's five o'clock."

"I'll thank you, Colonel Sapt – " I began again, hot in spirit, though I was uncommonly cold in body.

"Rassendyll," interrupted Fritz, getting down from the table and taking my arm, "look here."

The King lay full length on the floor. His face was red as his hair, and he breathed heavily. Sapt, the disrespectful old dog, kicked him sharply. He did not stir, nor was there any break in his breathing. I saw that his face and head were wet with water, as were mine.

"We've spent half an hour on him," said Fritz.

"He drank three times what either of you did," growled Sapt.

I knelt down and felt his pulse. It was alarmingly languid and slow. We three looked at one another.

"Was it drugged – that last bottle?" I asked in a whisper.

"I don't know," said Sapt.

"We must get a doctor."

"There's none within ten miles, and a thousand doctors wouldn't take him to Strelsau today. I know the look of it. He'll not move for six or seven hours yet."

"But the coronation!" I cried in horror.

Fritz shrugged his shoulders, as I began to see was his habit on most occasions.

"We must send word that he's ill," he said.

"I suppose so," said I.

Old Sapt, who seemed as fresh as a daisy, had lit his pipe and was puffing hard at it.

"If he's not crowned today," said he, "I'll lay a crown he's never crowned."

"But heavens, why?"

"The whole nation's there to meet him; half the army – ay, and

Black Michael at the head. Shall we send word that the King's drunk?"

"That he's ill," said I, in correction.

"Ill!" echoed Sapt, with a scornful laugh. "They know his illnesses too well. He's been 'ill' before!"

"Well, we must chance what they think," said Fritz helplessly. "I'll carry the news and make the best of it."

Sapt raised his hand.

"Tell me," said he. "Do you think the King was drugged?"

"I do," said I.

"And who drugged him?"

"That damned hound, Black Michael," said Fritz between his teeth.

"Ay," said Sapt, "that he might not come to be crowned. Rassendyll here doesn't know our pretty Michael. What think you, Fritz, has Michael no king ready? Has half Strelsau no other candidate? As God's alive, man the throne's lost if the King show himself not in Strelsau today. I know Black Michael."

"We could carry him there," said I.

"And a very pretty picture he makes," sneered Sapt.

Fritz von Tarlenheim buried his face in his hands. The King breathed loudly and heavily. Sapt stirred him again with his foot.

"The drunken dog!" he said; "but he's an Elphberg and the son of his father, and may I rot in hell before Black Michael sits in his place!"

For a moment or two we were all silent; then Sapt, knitting his bushy grey brows, took his pipe from his mouth and said to me:

"As a man grows old he believes in Fate. Fate sent you here. Fate sends you now to Strelsau."

I staggered back, murmuring "Good God!"

Fritz looked up with an eager, bewildered gaze.

"Impossible!" I muttered. "I should be known."

"It's a risk – against a certainty," said Sapt. "If you shave, I'll wager you'll not be known. Are you afraid?"

"Sir!"

"Come, lad, there, there; but it's your life, you know, if you're known – and mine – and Fritz's here. But, if you don't go, I swear to you Black Michael will sit tonight on the throne, and the King lie in prison or his grave."

"The King would never forgive it," I stammered.

"Are we women? Who cares for his forgiveness?"

The clock ticked fifty times, and sixty and seventy times, as I stood in thought. Then I suppose a look came over my face, for old Sapt caught me by the hand, crying:

"You'll go?"

"Yes, I'll go," said I, and I turned my eyes on the prostrate figure of the King on the floor.

"Tonight," Sapt went on in a hasty whisper, "we are to lodge in the Palace. The moment they leave us you and I will mount our horses – Fritz must stay there and guard the King's room – and ride here at a gallop. The King will be ready – Josef will tell him – and he must ride back with me to Strelsau, and you ride as if the devil were behind you to the frontier."

I took it all in in a second, and nodded my head.

"There's a chance," said Fritz, with his first sign of hopefulness.

"If I escape detection," said I.

"If we're detected," said Sapt. "I'll send Black Michael down below before I go myself, so help me heaven! Sit in that chair, man."

I obeyed him.

He darted from the room, calling "Josef! Josef!" In three minutes he was back, and Josef with him. The latter carried a jug of hot water, soap and razors. He was trembling as Sapt told him how the land lay, and bade him shave me.

Suddenly Fritz smote on his thigh:

"But the guard! They'll know! they'll know!"

"Pooh! We shan't wait for the guard. We'll ride to Hofbau and catch a train there. When they come, the bird'll be flown."

"But the King?"

"The King will be in the wine-cellar. I'm going to carry him there now."

"If they find him?"

"They won't. How should they? Josef will put them off."

"But – "

Sapt stamped his foot.

"We're not playing," he roared. "My God! don't I know the

risk? If they do find him, he's no worse off than if he isn't crowned today in Strelsau."

So speaking, he flung the door open and, stooping, put forth a strength I did not dream he had, and lifted the King in his hands. And as he did so, the old woman, Johann the keeper's mother, stood in the doorway. For a moment she stood, then she turned on her heel, without a sign of surprise, and clattered down the passage.

"Has she heard?" cried Fritz.

"I'll shut her mouth!" said Sapt grimly, and he bore off the King in his arms.

For me, I sat down in an armchair, and as I sat there, half-dazed, Josef clipped and scraped me till my moustache and imperial were things of the past and my face was as bare as the King's. And when Fritz saw me thus he drew a long breath and exclaimed: –

"By Jove, we shall do it!"

It was six o'clock now, and we had no time to lose. Sapt hurried me into the King's room, and I dressed myself in the uniform of a colonel of the Guard, finding time as I slipped on the King's boots to ask Sapt what he had done with the old woman.

"She swore she'd heard nothing," said he; "but to make sure I tied her legs together and put a handkerchief in her mouth and bound her hands, and locked her up in the coal-cellar, next door to the King. Josef will look after them both later on."

Then I burst out laughing, and even old Sapt grimly smiled.

"I fancy," said he, "that when Josef tells them the King is gone they'll think it is because we smelt a rat. For you may swear Black Michael doesn't expect to see him in Strelsau today."

I put the King's helmet on my head. Old Sapt handed me the King's sword, looking at me long and carefully.

"Thank God, he shaved his beard!" he exclaimed.

"Why did he?" I asked.

"Because Princess Flavia said he grazed her cheek when he was graciously pleased to give her a cousinly kiss. Come though, we must ride."

"Is all safe here?"

"Nothing's safe anywhere," said Sapt, "but we can make it no safer."

Fritz now rejoined us in the uniform of a captain in the same regiment as that to which my dress belonged. In four minutes Sapt had arrayed himself in his uniform. Josef called that the horses were ready. We jumped on their backs and started at a rapid trot. The game had begun. What would the issue of it be?

The cool morning air cleared my head, and I was able to take in all Sapt said to me. He was wonderful. Fritz hardly spoke, riding like a man asleep, but Sapt, without another word for the King, began at once to instruct me most minutely in the history of my past life, of my family, of my tastes, pursuits, weaknesses, friends, companions, and servants. He told me the etiquette of the Ruritanian Court, promising to be constantly at my elbow to point out everybody whom I ought to know, and give me hints with what degree of favour to greet them.

"By the way," he said, "you're a Catholic, I suppose?"

"Not I," I answered.

"Lord, he's a heretic!" groaned Sapt, and forthwith he fell to a rudimentary lesson in the practices and observances of the Romish faith.

"Luckily," said he, "you won't be expected to know much, for the King's notoriously lax and careless about such matters. But you must be as civil as butter to the Cardinal. We hope to win him over, because he and Michael have a standing quarrel about their precedence."

We were by now at the station. Fritz had recovered nerve enough to explain to the astonished station master that the King had changed his plans. The train steamed up. We got into a first-class carriage, and Sapt, leaning back on the cushions, went on with his lesson. I looked at my watch – the King's watch it was, of course. It was just eight.

"I wonder if they've gone to look for us," I said.

"I hope they won't find the King," said Fritz nervously, and this time it was Sapt who shrugged his shoulders.

The train travelled well, and at half-past nine, looking out of the window, I saw the towers and spires of a great city.

"Your capital, my liege," grinned old Sapt, with a wave of his hand, and, leaning forward, he laid his finger on my pulse. "A little too quick," said he, in his grumbling tone.

"I'm not made of stone!" I exclaimed.

"You'll do," said he, with a nod. "We must say Fritz here has caught the ague. Drain your flask, Fritz, for heaven's sake, boy!"

Fritz did as he was bid.

"We're an hour early," said Sapt. "We'll send word forward for your Majesty's arrival, for there'll be no one here to meet us yet. And meanwhile – "

"Meanwhile," said I, "the King'll be hanged if he doesn't have some breakfast."

Old Sapt chuckled, and held out his hand.

"You're an Elphberg, every inch of you," said he. Then he paused, and looking at us, said quietly, "God send we may be alive tonight!"

"Amen!" said Fritz von Tarlenheim.

The train stopped. Fritz and Sapt leapt out, uncovered, and held the door for me. I choked down a lump that rose in my throat, settled my helmet firmly on my head, and (I'm not ashamed to say it) breathed a short prayer to God. Then I stepped on the platform of the station at Strelsau.

A moment later, all was bustle and confusion: men hurrying up, hats in hand, and hurrying off again; men conducting me to the buffet; men mounting and riding in hot haste to the quarters of the troops, to the Cathedral, to the residence of Duke Michael. Even as I swallowed the last drop of my cup of coffee, the bells throughout all the city broke out into a joyful peal, and the sound of a military band and of men cheering smote upon my ear.

King Rudolf the Fifth was in his good city of Strelsau! And they shouted outside –

"God save the King!"

Old Sapt's mouth wrinkled into a smile.

"God save 'em both!" he whispered. "Courage, lad!" and I felt his hand press my knee.

With Fritz von Tarlenheim and Colonel Sapt close behind me, I stepped out of the buffet on to the platform. The last thing I did was to feel if my revolver were handy and my sword loose in the scabbard. A gay group of officers and high dignitaries stood awaiting me, at their head a tall old man, covered with medals, and of military bearing. He wore the yellow and red ribbon of the Red Rose of Ruritania – which, by the way, decorated my unworthy breast also.

"Marshal Strakencz," whispered Sapt, and I knew that I was in the presence of the most famous veteran of the Ruritanian army.

Just behind the Marshal stood a short spare man, in flowing robes of black and crimson.

"The Chancellor of the Kingdom," whispered Sapt.

The Marshal greeted me in a few loyal words, and proceeded to deliver an apology from the Duke of Strelsau. The duke, it seemed, had been afflicted with a sudden indisposition which made it impossible for him to come to the station, but he craved leave to await his Majesty at the Cathedral. I expressed my concern, accepted the Marshal's excuses very suavely, and received the compliments of a large number of distinguished personages. No one betrayed the least suspicion, and I felt my nerve returning and the agitated beating of my heart subsiding. But Fritz was still pale, and his hand shook like a leaf as he extended it to the Marshal.

Presently we formed procession and took our way to the door of the station. Here I mounted my horse, the Marshal holding my stirrup. The civil dignitaries went off to their carriages, and I started to ride through the streets with the Marshal on my right and Sapt (who, as my chief aide-de-camp, was entitled to the place) on my left. The city of Strelsau is partly old and partly new. Spacious modern boulevards and residential quarters surround and embrace the narrow, tortuous, and picturesque streets of the original town. In the outer circles the upper classes live; in the inner the shops are situated; and, behind their prosperous fronts, lie hidden populous but wretched lanes and alleys, filled with a poverty-stricken, turbulent, and (in large measure) criminal class. These social and local divisions corresponded, as I knew from Sapt's information, to another division more important to me. The New Town was for the King; but to the Old Town Michael of Strelsau was a hope, a hero, and a darling.

The scene was very brilliant as we passed along the Grand Boulevard and on to the great square where the Royal Palace stood. Here I was in the midst of my devoted adherents. Every house was hung with red and bedecked with flags and mottoes. The streets were lined with raised seats on each side, and I passed along, bowing this way and that, under a shower of cheers, blessings, and waving handkerchiefs. The balconies were full of gaily dressed ladies, who clapped their hands and curtsied and threw their brightest glances at me. A torrent of red roses fell on me; one bloom lodged in my horse's mane, and I took it and stuck it in my coat. The Marshal smiled grimly. I had stolen some glances at his face, but he was too impassive to show me whether his sympathies were with me or not.

"The red rose for the Elphbergs, Marshal," said I gaily, and he nodded.

I have written "gaily," and a strange word it must seem. But the truth is, that I was drunk with excitement. At that moment I believed – I almost believed – that I was in very truth the King; and, with a look of laughing triumph, I raised my eyes to the beauty-laden balconies again . . . and then I started. For, looking down on me, with her handsome face and proud smile, was the lady who had been my fellow traveller – Antoinette de Mauban; and I saw her also start, and her lips moved, and she leant forward and gazed at me. And I, collecting myself, met her eyes full and square, while again I felt my revolver. Suppose she had cried aloud,

Looking down on me, with her handsome face and proud smile, was the lady who had been my fellow traveller — Antoinette de Mauban.

"That's not the King!"

Well, we went by; and then the Marshal, turning round in his saddle, waved his hand, and the Cuirassiers closed round us, so that the crowd could not come near me. We were leaving my quarter and entering Duke Michael's, and this action of the Marshal's showed me more clearly than words what the state of feeling in the town must be. But if Fate made me a King, the least I could do was to play the part handsomely.

"Why this change in our order, Marshal?" said I.

The Marshal bit his white moustache.

"It is more prudent, sire," he murmured.

I drew rein.

"Let those in front ride on," said I, "till they are fifty yards ahead. But do you, Marshal, and Colonel Sapt and my friends, wait here till I have ridden fifty yards. And see that no one is nearer to me. I will have my people see that their King trusts them."

Sapt laid his hand on my arm. I shook him off. The Marshal hesitated.

"Am I not understood?" said I; and, biting his moustache again, he gave the orders. I saw old Sapt smiling into his beard, but he shook his head at me. If I had been killed in open day in the streets of Strelsau, Sapt's position would have been a difficult one.

Perhaps I ought to say that I was dressed all in white, except my boots. I wore a silver helmet with gilt ornaments, and the broad ribbon of the Rose looked well across my chest. I should be paying a poor compliment to the King if I did not set modesty aside and admit that I made a very fine figure. So the people thought; for when I, riding alone, entered the dingy, sparsely decorated, sombre streets of the Old Town, there was first a murmur, then a cheer, and a woman, from a window above a cookshop, cried the old local saying:

"If he's red, he's right!" whereat I laughed and took off my helmet that she might see that I was of the right colour and they cheered me again at that.

It was more interesting riding thus alone, for I heard the comments of the crowd.

"He looks paler than his wont," said one.

"You'd look pale if you lived as he does," was the highly disrespectful retort.

"He's a bigger man than I thought," said another.

"So he had a good jaw under that beard after all," commented a third.

"The pictures of him aren't handsome enough," declared a pretty girl, taking great care that I should hear. No doubt it was mere flattery.

But, in spite of these signs of approval and interest, the mass of the people received me in silence and with sullen looks, and my dear brother's portrait ornamented most of the windows – which was an ironical sort of greeting to the King. I was quite glad that he had been spared the unpleasant sight. He was a man of quick temper, and perhaps he would not have taken it so placidly as I did.

At last we were at the Cathedral. Its great grey front, embellished with hundreds of statues and boasting a pair of the finest oak doors in Europe, rose for the first time before me, and the sudden sense of my audacity almost overcame me. Everything was in a mist as I dismounted. I saw the Marshal and Sapt dimly, and dimly the throng of gorgeously robed priests who awaited me. And my eyes were still dim as I walked up the great nave, with the pealing of the organ in my ears. I saw nothing of the brilliant throng that filled it, I hardly distinguished the stately figure of the Cardinal as he rose from the archiepiscopal throne to greet me. Two faces only stood out side by side clearly before my eyes – the face of a girl, pale and lovely, surmounted by a crown of the glorious Elphberg hair (for in a woman it is glorious), and the face of a man, whose full-blooded red cheeks, black hair, and dark deep eyes told me that at last I was in presence of my brother, Black Michael. And when he saw me his red cheeks went pale all in a moment, and his helmet fell with a clatter on the floor. Till that moment I believe that he had not realized that the King was in very truth come to Strelsau.

Of what followed next I remember nothing. I knelt before the altar and the Cardinal anointed my head. Then I rose to my feet, and stretched out my hand and took from him the crown of Ruritania and set it on my head, and I swore the old oath of the King; and (if it were a sin, may it be forgiven me) I received the

Holy Sacrament there before them all. Then the great organ pealed out again, the Marshal bade the heralds proclaim me, and Rudolf the Fifth was crowned King; of which imposing ceremony an excellent picture hangs now in my dining-room. The portrait of the King is very good.

Then the lady with the pale face and the glorious hair, her train held by two pages, stepped from her place and came to where I stood. And a herald cried:

"Her Royal Highness the Princess Flavia!"

She curtsied low, and put her hand under mine and raised my hand and kissed it. And for an instant I thought what I had best do. Then I drew her to me and kissed her twice on the cheek, and she blushed red, and – then his Eminence the Cardinal Archbishop slipped in front of Black Michael, and kissed my hand and presented me with a letter from the Pope – the first and last which I have received from that exalted quarter!

And then came the Duke of Strelsau. His step trembled, I swear, and he looked to the right and to the left, as a man looks who thinks on flight; and his face was patched with red and white, and his hand shook so that it jumped under mine, and I felt his lips dry and parched. And I glanced at Sapt, who was smiling again into his beard, and, resolutely doing my duty in that station of life to which I had been marvellously called, I took my dear Michael by both hands and kissed him on the cheek. I think we were both glad when that was over!

But neither in the face of the princess nor in that of any other did I see the least doubt or questioning. Yet, had I and the King stood side by side, she could have told us in an instant, or, at least, on a little consideration. But neither she nor anyone else dreamed or imagined that I could be other than the King. So the likeness served, and for an hour I stood there, feeling as weary and blase as though I had been a king all my life; and everybody kissed my hand, and the ambassadors paid me their respects, among them old Lord Topham, at whose house in Grosvenor Square I had danced a score of times. Thank heaven, the old man was as blind as a bat, and did not claim my acquaintance.

Then back we went through the streets to the Palace, and I heard them cheering Black Michael; but he, Fritz told me, sat biting his nails like a man in a reverie, and even his own friends said that he should have made a braver show. I was in a carriage now, side by side with the Princess Flavia, and a rough fellow cried out:

"And when's the wedding?" and as he spoke another struck him in the face, crying "Long live Duke Michael!" and the princess coloured – it was an admirable tint – and looked straight in front of her.

Now I felt in a difficulty, because I had forgotten to ask Sapt the state of my affections, or how far matters had gone between the princess and myself. Frankly, had I been the King, the further they had gone the better should I have been pleased. For I am not a slow-blooded man, and I had not kissed Princess Flavia's cheek for nothing. These thoughts passed through my head, but, not being sure of my ground, I said nothing; and in a moment or two the princess, recovering her equanimity, turned to me.

"Do you know, Rudolf," said she, "you look somehow different today?"

The fact was not surprising, but the remark was disquieting.

"You look," she went on, "more sober, more sedate; you're almost careworn, and I declare you're thinner. Surely it's not possible that you've begun to take anything seriously?"

The princess seemed to hold of the King much the same opinion that Lady Burlesdon held of me.

I braced myself up to the conversation.

"Would that please you?" I asked softly.

"Oh, you know my views," said she, turning her eyes away.

"Whatever pleases you I try to do," I said; and, as I saw her smile and blush, I thought that I was playing the King's hand very well for him. So I continued and what I said was perfectly true:

"I assure you, my dear cousin, that nothing in my life has affected me more than the reception I've been greeted with today."

She smiled brightly, but in an instant grew grave again, and whispered:

"Did you notice Michael?"

"Yes," said I, adding, "he wasn't enjoying himself."

"Do be careful!" she went on. "You don't – indeed you don't – keep enough watch on him. You know – "

"I know," said I, "that he wants what I've got."

"Yes. Hush!"

Then – and I can't justify it, for I committed the King far beyond what I had a right to do – I suppose she carried me off my feet – I went on:

"And perhaps also something which I haven't got yet, but hope to win some day."

This was my answer. Had I been the King, I should have thought it encouraging:

"Haven't you enough responsibilities on you for one day, cousin?"

Bang, bang! Blare, blare! We were at the Palace. Guns were firing and trumpets blowing. Rows of lackeys stood waiting, and, handing the princess up the broad marble staircase, I took formal possession, as a crowned King, of the House of my ancestors, and sat down at my own table, with my cousin on my right hand, on her other side Black Michael, and on my left his Eminence the Cardinal. Behind my chair stood Sapt; and at the end of the table, I saw Fritz von Tarlenheim drain to the bottom his glass of champagne rather sooner than he decently should.

I wondered what the King of Ruritania was doing. We were in the King's dressing-room – Fritz von Tarlenheim, Sapt, and I. I flung myself exhausted into an armchair. Sapt lit his pipe. He uttered no congratulations on the marvellous success of our wild risk, but his whole bearing was eloquent of satisfaction. The triumph, aided perhaps by good wine, had made a new man of Fritz.

"What a day for you to remember!" he cried. "Gad, I'd like to be King for twelve hours myself! But, Rassendyll, you mustn't throw your heart too much into the part. I don't wonder Black Michael looked blacker than ever – you and the princess had so much to say to one another."

"How beautiful she is!" I exclaimed.

"Never mind the woman," growled Sapt. "Are you ready to start?"

"Yes," said I, with a sigh.

It was five o'clock, and at twelve I should be no more than Rudolf Rassendyll. I remarked on it in a joking tone.

"You'll be lucky," observed Sapt grimly, "if you're not the late Rudolf Rassendyll. By Heaven! I feel my head wobbling on my shoulders every minute you're in the city. Do you know, friend, that Michael has had news from Zenda? He went into a room alone to read it – and he came out looking like a man dazed."

"I'm ready," said I, this news making me none the more eager to linger.

Sapt sat down.

"I must write us an order to leave the city. Michael's Governor, you know, and we must be prepared for hindrances. You must sign the order."

"My dear colonel, I've not been bred a forger!"

Out of his pocket Sapt produced a piece of paper.

"There's the King's signature," he said, "and here," he went on, after another search in his pocket, "is some tracing paper. If you can't manage a 'Rudolf' in ten minutes, why – I can."

"Your education has been more comprehensive than mine," said I. "You write it."

And a very tolerable forgery did this versatile hero produce.

"Now, Fritz," said he, "the King goes to bed. He is upset. No one is to see him till nine o'clock tomorrow. You understand – no one?"

"I understand," answered Fritz.

"Michael may come, and claim immediate audience. You'll answer that only princes of the blood are entitled to it."

"That'll annoy Michael," laughed Fritz.

"You quite understand?" asked Sapt again. "If the door of this room is opened while we're away, you're not to be alive to tell us about it."

"I need no schooling, colonel," said Fritz, a trifle haughtily.

"Here, wrap yourself in this big cloak," Sapt continued to me, "and put on this flat cap. My orderly rides with me to the hunting-lodge tonight."

"There's an obstacle," I observed. "The horse doesn't live that can carry me forty miles."

"Oh, yes, he does – two of him: one here – one at the lodge. Now, are you ready?"

"I'm ready," said I.

Fritz held out his hand.

"In case," said he; and we shook hands heartily.

"Damn your sentiment!" growled Sapt. "Come along."

He went, not to the door, but to a panel in the wall.

"In the old King's time," said he, "I knew this way well."

I followed him, and we walked, as I should estimate, near two hundred yards along a narrow passage. Then we came to a stout oak door. Sapt unlocked it. We passed through, and found ourselves in a quiet street that ran along the back of the Palace gardens. A man was waiting for us with two horses. One was a magnificent bay, up to any weight; the other a sturdy brown. Sapt signed to me to mount the bay. Without a word to the man, we mounted and rode away. The town was full of noise and merriment, but we took secluded ways. My cloak was wrapped over half my face; the capacious flat cap hid every lock of my tell-tale hair. By Sapt's directions, I crouched on my saddle, and rode with such a round back as I hope never to exhibit on a horse again. Down a long narrow lane we went, meeting some wanderers and some roisterers; and, as we rode, we heard the Cathedral bells still clanging out their welcome to the King. It was half-past six, and still light. At last we came to the city wall and to a gate.

"Have your weapon ready," whispered Sapt. "We must stop his mouth, if he talks."

I put my hand on my revolver. Sapt hailed the doorkeeper. The stars fought for us! A little girl of fourteen tripped out.

"Please, sir, father's gone to see the King."

"He'd better have stayed here," said Sapt to me, grinning.

"But he said I wasn't to open the gate, sir."

"Did he, my dear?" said Sapt, dismounting. "Then give me the key."

The key was in the child's hand. Sapt gave her a crown.

"Here's an order from the King. Show it to your father. Orderly, open the gate!"

I leapt down. Between us we rolled back the great gate, led our horses out, and closed it again.

"I shall be sorry for the doorkeeper if Michael finds out that he wasn't there. Now then, lad, for a canter. We mustn't go too fast while we're near the town."

Once, however, outside the city, we ran little danger, for everybody else was inside, merry-making; and as the evening fell we quickened our pace, my splendid horse bounding along under me as though I had been a feather. It was a fine night, and presently the moon appeared. We talked little on the way, and chiefly about the progress we were making.

"I wonder what the duke's despatches told him," said I, once.

"Ay, I wonder!" responded Sapt.

We stopped for a draught of wine and to bait our horses, losing half an hour thus. I dared not go into the inn, and stayed with the horses in the stable. Then we went ahead again, and had covered some five-and-twenty miles, when Sapt abruptly stopped.

"Hark!" he cried.

I listened. Away, far behind us, in the still of the evening – it was just half-past nine – we heard the beat of horses' hoofs. The wind blowing strong behind us, carried the sound. I glanced at Sapt.

"Come on!" he cried, and spurred his horse into a gallop. When we next paused to listen, the hoof-beats were not audible, and we relaxed our pace. Then we heard them again. Sapt jumped down and laid his ear to the ground.

"There are two," he said. "They're only a mile behind. Thank God the road curves in and out, and the wind's our way."

We galloped on. We seemed to be holding our own. We had entered the outskirts of the forest of Zenda, and the trees, closing in behind us as the track zigged and zagged, prevented us seeing our pursuers, and them from seeing us.

Another half-hour brought us to a divide of the road. Sapt drew rein.

"To the right is our road," he said. "To the left, to the Castle. Each about eight miles. Get down."

"But they'll be on us!" I cried.

"Get down!" he repeated brusquely; and I obeyed. The wood

was dense up to the very edge of the road. We led our horses into the covert, bound handkerchiefs over their eyes, and stood beside them.

"You want to see who they are?" I whispered.

"Ay, and where they're going," he answered.

I saw that his revolver was in his hand.

Nearer and nearer came the hoofs. The moon shone out now clear and full, so that the road was white with it. The ground was hard, and we had left no traces.

"Here they come!" whispered Sapt.

"It's the duke!"

"I thought so," he answered.

It was the duke; and with him a burly fellow whom I knew well, and who had cause to know me afterwards – Max Holf, brother to Johann the keeper, and body-servant to his Highness. They were up to us: the duke reined up. I saw Sapt's finger curl lovingly towards the trigger. I believe he would have given ten years of his life for a shot; and he could have picked off Black Michael as easily as I could a barn-door fowl in a farmyard. I laid my hand on his arm. He nodded reassuringly: he was always ready to sacrifice inclination to duty.

"Which way?" asked Black Michael.

"To the Castle, your Highness," urged his companion. "There we shall learn the truth."

For an instant the duke hesitated.

"I thought I heard hoofs," said he.

"I think not, your Highness."

"Why shouldn't we go to the lodge?"

"I fear a trap. If all is well, why go to the lodge? If not, it's a snare to trap us."

Suddenly the duke's horse neighed. In an instant we folded our cloaks close round our horses' heads, and, holding them thus, covered the duke and his attendant with our revolvers. If they had found us, they had been dead men, or our prisoners.

Michael waited a moment longer. Then he cried:

"To Zenda, then!" and setting spurs to his horse, galloped on.

Sapt raised his weapon after him, and there was such an expression of wistful regret on his face that I had much ado not to burst out laughing.

For ten minutes we stayed where we were.

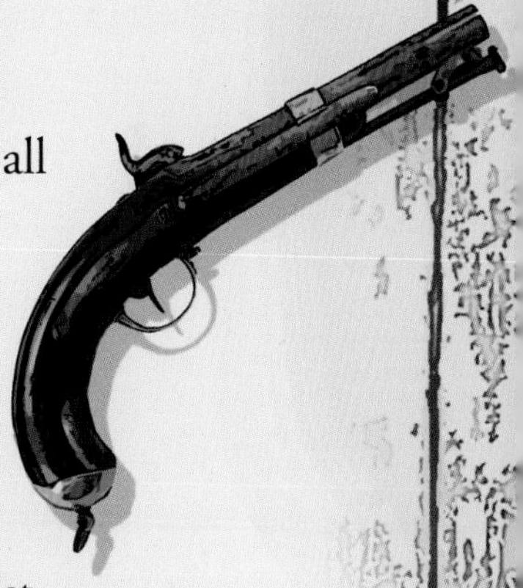

"You see," said Sapt, "they've sent him news that all is well."

"What does that mean?" I asked.

"God knows," said Sapt, frowning heavily. "But it's brought him from Strelsau in a rare puzzle."

Then we mounted, and rode as fast as our weary horses could lay their feet to the ground. For those last eight miles we spoke no more. Our minds were full of apprehension. "All is well." What did it mean? Was all well with the King?

At last the lodge came in sight. Spurring our horses to a last gallop, we rode up to the gate. All was still and quiet. Not a soul came to meet us. We dismounted in haste. Suddenly Sapt caught me by the arm.

"Look there!" he said, pointing to the ground.

I looked down. At my feet lay five or six silk handkerchiefs, torn and slashed and rent. I turned to him questioningly.

"They're what I tied the old woman up with," said he. "Fasten the horses, and come along."

The handle of the door turned without resistance. We passed into the room which had been the scene of last night's bout. It was still strewn with the remnants of our meal and with empty bottles.

"Come on," cried Sapt, whose marvellous composure had at last almost given way.

We rushed down the passage towards the cellars. The door of the coal-cellar stood wide open.

"They found the old woman," said I.

"You might have known that from the handkerchiefs," he said.

Then we came opposite the door of the wine-cellar. It was shut. It looked in all respects as it had looked when we left it that morning.

"Come, it's all right," said I.

A loud oath from Sapt rang out. His face turned pale, and he pointed again at the floor. From under the door a red stain had spread over the floor of the passage and dried there. Sapt sank against the opposite wall. I tried the door. It was locked.

"Where's Josef?" muttered Sapt.

"Where's the King?" I responded.

Sapt took out a flask and put it to his lips. I ran back to the dining-room, and seized a heavy poker from the fireplace. In my terror and excitement I rained blows on the lock of the door, and I fired a cartridge into it. It gave way, and the door swung open.

"Give me a light," said I; but Sapt still leant against the wall.

He was, of course, more moved than I, for he loved his master. Afraid for himself he was not – no man ever saw him that; but to think what might lie in that dark cellar was enough to turn any man's face pale. I went myself, and took a silver candlestick from the dining-table and struck a light, and, as I returned, I felt the hot wax drip on my naked hand as the candle swayed to and fro; so that I cannot afford to despise Colonel Sapt for his agitation.

I came to the door of the cellar. The red stain turning more and more to a dull brown, stretched inside. I walked two yards into the cellar, and held the candle high above my head. I saw the full bins of wine; I saw spiders crawling on the walls; I saw, too, a couple of empty bottles lying on the floor; and then, away in the corner, I saw the body of a man, lying flat on his back, with his arms stretched wide, and a crimson gash across his throat. I walked to him and knelt down beside him, and commended to God the soul

of a faithful man. For it was the body of Josef, the little servant, slain in guarding the King.

I felt a hand on my shoulders, and, turning, saw Sapt, eyes glaring and terror-struck, beside me.

"The King? My God! the King?" he whispered hoarsely.

I threw the candle's gleam over every inch of the cellar.

"The King is not here," said I.

The Lost World
Escape from the Ape Men
Sir Arthur Conan Doyle
Heroes of the Hour

The story so far

Professor Challenger, an eccentric Victorian scientist, is searching for a land on a high plateau in South America where he believes dinosaurs and other extinct creatures may still exist. With him are Lord John Royston, a hunter and English aristocrat, Summerlee, another scientist, and Ned Malone, a journalist who is narrating the story. When they arrive at the plateau, they lose their means of getting back, and discover not only dinosaurs, but also a primitive ape-like species of humans. Malone manages to make his way back to the camp after falling into a trap pit, and finds, to his horror, that his companions have disappeared amid signs of a struggle – and there are blood stains all over the camp.

Escape from the Ape Men
from
The Lost World
by
Sir Arthur Conan Doyle

It was an awesome thing to sleep in that ill-fated camp; and yet it was even more unnerving to do so in the jungle. One or the other it must be. Prudence, on the one hand, warned me that I should remain on guard, but exhausted Nature, on the other, declared that I should do nothing of the kind. I climbed up on to a limb of the great gingko tree, but there was no secure perch on its rounded surface, and I should certainly have fallen off and broken my neck the moment I began to doze. I got down, therefore, and pondered over what I should do. Finally, I closed the door of the zareba, lit three separate fires in a triangle, and having eaten a hearty supper dropped off into a profound sleep, from which I had a strange and most welcome awakening. In the early morning, just as day was breaking, a hand was laid upon my arm, and starting up, with all my nerves in a tingle and my hand feeling for a rifle, I gave a cry of joy as in the cold gray light I saw Lord John Roxton kneeling beside me.

It was he – and yet it was not he. I had left him calm in his bearing, correct in his person, prim in his dress. Now he was pale and wild-eyed, gasping as he breathed like one who has run far and fast. His gaunt face was scratched and bloody, his clothes were hanging in rags, and his hat was gone. I stared in amazement, but he gave me no chance for questions. He was grabbing at our stores all the time he spoke.

"Quick, young fellah! Quick!" he cried. "Every moment counts. Get the rifles, both of them. I have the other two. Now, all the cartridges you can gather. Fill up your pockets. Now, some food. Half a dozen tins will do. That's all right! Don't wait to talk or think. Get a move on, or we are done!"

Still half-awake, and unable to imagine what it all might mean, I found myself hurrying madly after him through the wood, a rifle under each arm and a pile of various stores in my hands. He dodged in and out through the thickest of the scrub until he came to a dense clump of brushwood. Into this he rushed, regardless of thorns, and threw himself into the heart of it, pulling me down by his side.

"There!" he panted. "I think we are safe here. They'll make for the camp as sure as fate. It will be their first idea. But this should puzzle 'em."

"What is it all?" I asked, when I had got my breath. "Where are the professors? And who is it that is after us?"

"The ape-men," he cried. "My God, what brutes! Don't raise your voice, for they have long ears – sharp eyes, too, but no power of scent, so far as I could judge, so I don't think they can sniff us out. Where have you been, young fellah? You were well out of it."

In a few sentences I whispered what I had done.

"Pretty bad," said he, when he had heard of the dinosaur and the pit. "It isn't quite the place for a rest cure. What? But I had no idea what its possibilities were until those devils got hold of us. The man-eatin' Papuans had me once, but they are Chesterfields compared to this crowd."

"How did it happen?" I asked.

"It was in the early mornin'. Our learned friends were just stirrin'. Hadn't even begun to argue yet. Suddenly it rained apes. They came down as thick as apples out of a tree. They had been assemblin' in the dark, I suppose, until that great tree over our heads was heavy with them. I shot one of them through the belly, but before we knew where we were they had us spread-eagled on our backs. I call them apes, but they carried sticks and stones in their hands and jabbered talk to each other, and ended up by tyin' our hands with creepers, so they are ahead of any beast that I have seen in my wanderin's. Ape-men – that's what they are – Missin' Links, and I wish they had stayed missin'. They carried off their wounded comrade – he was bleedin' like a pig – and then they sat around us, and if ever I saw frozen murder it was in their faces. They were big fellows, as big as a man and a deal stronger. Curious glassy gray eyes they have, under red tufts, and they just sat and gloated and gloated. Challenger is no chicken, but even he was cowed. He managed to struggle to his feet, and yelled out at them to have done with it and get it over. I think he had gone a bit off his head at the suddenness of it, for he raged and cursed at them like a lunatic. If they had been a row of his favourite Pressmen he could not have slanged them worse."

"Well, what did they do?" I was enthralled by the strange story which my companion was whispering into my ear, while all the time his keen eyes were shooting in every direction and his hand grasping his cocked rifle.

"I thought it was the end of us, but instead of that it started them on a new line. They all jabbered and chattered together. Then one of them stood out beside Challenger. You'll smile, young fellah, but 'pon my word they might have been kinsmen. I couldn't have believed it if I hadn't seen it with my own eyes. This old ape-man – he was their chief – was a sort of red Challenger, with every one of our friend's beauty points, only just a trifle more so. He had the short body, the big shoulders, the round chest, no neck, a great ruddy frill of a beard, the tufted eyebrows, the 'What do you want, damn you!' look about the eyes, and the whole catalogue. When the ape-man stood by Challenger and put his paw on his shoulder, the thing was complete. Summerlee was a bit hysterical, and he laughed till he cried. The ape-men laughed too – or at least they put up the devil of a cacklin' – and they set to work to drag us off

through the forest. They wouldn't touch the guns and things – thought them dangerous, I expect – but they carried away all our loose food. Summerlee and I got some rough handlin' on the way – there's my skin and my clothes to prove it – for they took us a bee-line through the brambles, and their own hides are like leather. But Challenger was all right. Four of them carried him shoulder high, and he went like a Roman emperor. What's that?"

It was a strange clicking noise in the distance not unlike castanets.

"There they go!" said my companion, slipping cartridges into the second double barrelled "Express." "Load them all up, young fellah my lad, for we're not going to be taken alive, and don't you think it! That's the row they make when they are excited. By George! they'll have something to excite them if they put us up. The 'Last Stand of the Grays' won't be in it. 'With their rifles grasped in their stiffened hands, mid a ring of the dead and dyin',' as some fathead sings. Can you hear them now?"

"Very far away."

"That little lot will do no good, but I expect their search parties are all over the wood. Well, I was telling you my tale of woe. They got us soon to this town of theirs – about a thousand huts of branches and leaves in a great grove of trees near the edge of the cliff. It's three or four miles from here. The filthy beasts fingered me all over, and I feel as if I should never be clean again. They tied us up – the fellow who handled me could tie like a bosun – and there we lay with our toes up, beneath a tree, while a great brute stood guard over us with a club in his hand. When I say 'we' I mean Summerlee and myself. Old Challenger was up a tree, eatin' pines and havin' the time of his life. I'm bound to say that he managed to get some fruit to us, and with his own hands he loosened our bonds. If you'd seen him sitting up in that tree hob-nobbin' with his twin brother – and singin' in that rollin' bass of his, 'Ring out, wild bells,' cause music of any kind seemed to put 'em in a good humour, you'd have smiled; but we weren't in much mood for laughin', as you can guess. They were inclined, within limits, to let him do what he liked, but they drew the line pretty sharply at us. It was a mighty consolation to us all to know that you were runnin' loose and had the archives in your keepin'.

"Well, now, young fellah, I'll tell you what will surprise you. You say you saw signs of men, and fires, traps, and the like. Well, we have seen the natives themselves. Poor devils they were, down-faced little chaps, and had enough to make them so. It seems that the humans hold one side of this plateau – over yonder, where you saw the caves – and the ape-men hold this side, and there is bloody war between them all the time. That's the situation, so far as I could follow it. Well, yesterday the ape-men got hold of a dozen of the humans and brought them in as prisoners. You never heard such a jabberin' and shriekin' in your life. The men were little red fellows, and had been bitten and clawed so that they could hardly walk. The ape-men put two of them to death there and then – fairly pulled the arm off one of them – it was perfectly beastly. Plucky little chaps they are, and hardly gave a squeak. But it turned us absolutely sick. Summerlee fainted, and even Challenger had as much as he could stand. I think they have cleared, don't you?"

We listened intently, but nothing save the calling of the birds broke the deep peace of the forest. Lord Roxton went on with his story.

"I think you have had the escape of your life, young fellah my lad. It was catchin' those Indians that put you clean out of their heads, else they would have been back to the camp for you as sure as fate and gathered you in. Of course, as you said, they have been watchin' us from the beginnin' out of that tree, and they knew perfectly well that we were one short. However, they could think only of this new haul; so it was I, and not a bunch of apes, that dropped in on you in the morning. Well, we had a horrid business afterwards. My God! what a nightmare the whole thing is! You remember the great bristle of sharp canes down below where we found the skeleton of the American? Well, that is just under ape-town, and that's the jumpin'-off place of their prisoners. I expect there's heaps of skeletons there, if we looked for 'em. They have a sort of clear parade-ground on the top, and they make a proper ceremony about it. One by one the poor devils have to jump, and the game is to see whether they are merely dashed to pieces or whether they get skewered on the canes. They took us out to see it, and the whole tribe lined up on the edge. Four of the Indians jumped, and the canes went through 'em like knittin' needles through a pat of butter. No wonder we found that poor Yankee's skeleton with the canes growin' between his ribs. It was horrible – but it was doocedly interestin' too. We were all fascinated to see them take the dive, even when we thought it would be our turn next on the spring-board.

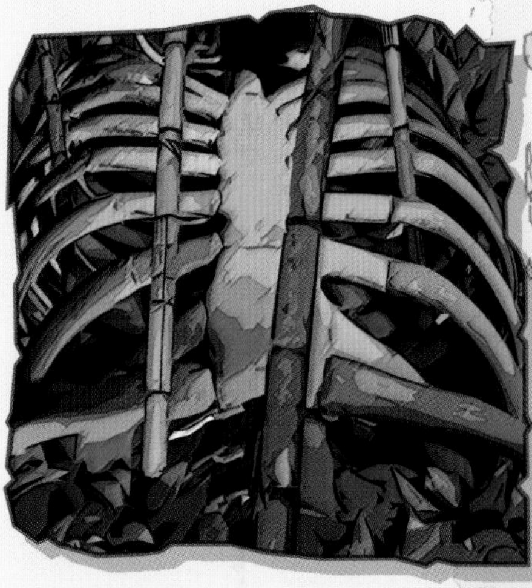

"Well, it wasn't. They kept six of the Indians up for to-day – that's how I understood it – but I fancy we were to be the star performers in the show. Challenger might get off, but Summerlee and I were in the bill. Their language is more than half signs, and it was not hard to follow them. So I thought it was time we made a break for it. I had been plottin' it out a bit, and had one or two things clear in my mind. It was all on me, for Summerlee was useless and Challenger not much better. The only time they got together they got slangin' because they couldn't agree upon the scientific classification of these red-headed devils that had got hold of us. One said it was the dryopithecus of Java, the other said it was pithecanthropus. Madness, I call it – Loonies, both. But, as I say, I had thought out one or two points that were helpful. One was that these brutes could not run as fast as a man in the open. They have short, bandy legs, you see, and heavy bodies. Even Challenger could give a few yards in a hundred to the best of them, and you or I would be a perfect Shrubb. Another point was that they knew nothin' about guns. I don't believe they ever understood how the fellow I shot came by his hurt. If we could get at our guns there was no sayin' what we could do.

"So I broke away early this mornin', gave my guard a kick in the tummy that laid him out, and sprinted for the camp. There I got you and the guns, and here we are."

"But the professors!" I cried, in consternation.

"Well, we must just go back and fetch 'em. I couldn't bring 'em with me. Challenger was up the tree, and Summerlee was not fit for the effort. The only chance was to get the guns and try a rescue. Of course they may scupper them at once in revenge. I don't think they would touch Challenger, but I wouldn't answer for Summerlee. But they would have had him in any case. Of that I am certain. So I haven't made matters any worse by boltin'. But we are honour bound to go back and have them out or see it through with them. So you can make up your soul, young fellah my lad, for it will be one way or the other before evenin'."

I have tried to imitate here Lord Roxton's jerky talk, his short, strong sentences, the half-humorous, half-reckless tone that ran through it all. But he was a born leader. As danger thickened his jaunty manner would increase, his speech become more racy, his cold eyes glitter into ardent life, and his Don Quixote moustache bristle with joyous excitement. His love of danger, his intense appreciation of the drama of an adventure – all the more intense for being held tightly in – his consistent view that every peril in life is a form of sport, a fierce game betwixt you and Fate, with Death as a forfeit, made him a wonderful companion at such hours. If it were not for our fears as to the fate of our companions, it would have been a positive joy to throw myself with such a man into such an affair. We were rising from our brushwood hiding-place when suddenly I felt his grip upon my arm.

"By George!" he whispered, "here they come!"

From where we lay we could look down a brown aisle, arched with green, formed by the trunks and branches. Along this a party of the ape-men were passing. They went in single file, with bent legs and rounded backs, their hands occasionally touching the ground, their heads turning to left and right as they trotted along. Their crouching gait took away from their height, but I should put them at five feet or so, with long arms and enormous chests. Many of them carried sticks, and at the distance they looked like a line of very hairy and deformed human beings. For a moment I caught this clear glimpse of them. Then they were lost among the bushes.

"Not this time," said Lord John, who had caught up his rifle. "Our best chance is to lie quiet until they have given up the search. Then we shall see whether we can't get back to their town and hit 'em where it hurts most. Give 'em an hour and we'll march."

We filled in the time by opening one of our food tins and

making sure of our breakfast. Lord Roxton had had nothing but some fruit since the morning before and ate like a starving man. Then, at last, our pockets bulging with cartridges and a rifle in each hand, we started off upon our mission of rescue. Before leaving it we carefully marked our little hiding-place among the brush-wood and its bearing to Fort Challenger, that we might find it again if we needed it. We slunk through the bushes in silence until we came to the very edge of the cliff, close to the old camp. There we halted, and Lord John gave me some idea of his plans.

"So long as we are among the thick trees these swine are our masters," said he. "They can see us and we cannot see them. But in the open it is different. There we can move faster than they. So we must stick to the open all we can. The edge of the plateau has fewer large trees than further inland. So that's our line of advance. Go slowly, keep your eyes open and your rifle ready. Above all, never let them get you prisoner while there is a cartridge left – that's my last word to you, young fellah."

When we reached the edge of the cliff I looked over and saw our good old black Zambo sitting smoking on a rock below us. I would have given a great deal to have hailed him and told him how we were placed, but it was too dangerous, lest we should be heard. The woods seemed to be full of the ape-men; again and again we heard their curious clicking chatter. At such times we plunged into the nearest clump of bushes and lay still until the sound had passed away. Our advance, therefore, was very slow, and two hours at least must have passed before I saw by Lord John's cautious movements that we must be close to our destination. He motioned to me to lie still, and he crawled forward himself. In a minute he was back again, his face quivering with eagerness.

"Come!" said he. "Come quick! I hope to the Lord we are not too late already!"

I found myself shaking with nervous excitement as I scrambled forward and lay down beside him, looking out through the bushes at a clearing which stretched before us.

It was a sight which I shall never forget until my dying day – so weird, so impossible, that I do not know how I am to make you realize it, or how in a few years I shall bring myself to believe in it if I live to sit once more on a lounge in the Savage Club and look out on the drab solidity of the Embankment. I know that it will seem then to be some wild nightmare, some delirium of fever. Yet I will set it down now, while it is still fresh in my memory, and one at least, the man who lay in the damp grasses by my side, will know if I have lied.

A wide, open space lay before us – some hundreds of yards across – all green turf and low bracken growing to the very edge of the cliff. Round this clearing there was a semi-circle of trees with curious huts built of foliage piled one above the other among the branches. A rookery, with every nest a little house, would best convey the idea. The openings of these huts and the branches of the trees were thronged with a dense mob of ape-people, whom from their size I took to be the females and infants of the tribe. They formed the background of the picture, and were all looking out with eager interest at the same scene which fascinated and bewildered us.

In the open, and near the edge of the cliff, there had assembled a crowd of some hundred of these shaggy, red-haired creatures, many of them of immense size, and all of them horrible to look upon. There was a certain discipline among them, for none of them attempted to break the line which had been formed. In front there stood a small group of Indians – little, clean-limbed, red fellows, whose skins glowed like polished bronze in the strong sunlight. A tall, thin white man was standing beside them, his head bowed, his arms folded, his whole attitude expressive of his horror and dejection. There was no mistaking the angular form of Professor Summerlee.

In front of and around this dejected group of prisoners were several ape-men, who watched them closely and made all escape impossible. Then, right out from all the others and close to the edge of the cliff, were two figures, so strange, and under other circumstances so ludicrous, that they absorbed my attention. The one was our comrade, Professor Challenger. The remains of his coat still hung in strips from his shoulders, but his shirt had been all torn out, and his great beard merged itself in the black tangle which covered his mighty chest. He had lost his hat, and his hair, which had grown long in our wanderings, was flying in wild disorder. A single day seemed to have changed him from the highest product of modern civilization to the most desperate savage in South America. Beside him stood his master, the king of the ape-men. In all things he was, as Lord John had said, the very image of our Professor, save that his colouring was red instead of black. The same short, broad figure, the same heavy shoulders, the same forward hang of the arms, the same bristling beard merging itself in the hairy chest. Only above the eyebrows, where the sloping forehead and low, curved skull of the ape-man were in sharp contrast to the broad brow and magnificent cranium of the European, could one see any marked difference. At every other point the king was an absurd parody of the Professor.

All this, which takes me so long to describe, impressed itself upon me in a few seconds. Then we had very different things to think of, for an active drama was in progress. Two of the ape-men had seized one of the Indians out of the group and dragged him forward to the edge of the cliff. The king raised his hand as a signal. They caught the man by his leg and arm, and swung him three times backwards and forwards with tremendous violence. Then, with a frightful heave they shot the poor wretch over the precipice. With such force did they throw him that he curved high in the air before beginning to drop. As he vanished from sight, the whole assembly, except the guards, rushed forward to the edge of the precipice, and there was a long pause of absolute silence, broken by a mad yell of delight. They sprang about, tossing their long, hairy arms in the air and howling with exultation. Then they fell back from the edge, formed themselves again into line, and waited for the next victim.

This time it was Summerlee. Two of his guards caught him by the wrists and pulled him brutally to the front. His thin figure and long limbs struggled and fluttered like a chicken being dragged from a coop. Challenger had turned to the king and waved his hands frantically before him. He was begging, pleading, imploring for his comrade's life. The ape-man pushed him roughly aside and shook his head. It was the last conscious movement he was to make upon earth. Lord John's rifle cracked, and the king sank down, a tangled red sprawling thing, upon the ground.

"Shoot into the thick of them! Shoot! sonny, shoot!" cried my companion.

There are strange red depths in the soul of the most commonplace man. I am tenderhearted by nature, and have found my eyes moist many a time over the scream of a wounded hare. Yet the blood lust was on me now. I found myself on my feet emptying one magazine, then the other, clicking open the breech to re-load, snapping it to again, while cheering and yelling with pure ferocity and joy of slaughter as I did so. With our four guns the two of us made a horrible havoc. Both the guards who held Summerlee were down, and he was staggering about like a drunken man in his amazement, unable to realize that he was a free man. The dense mob of ape-men ran about in bewilderment, marvelling whence this storm of death was coming or what it might mean. They waved, gesticulated, screamed, and tripped up over those who had fallen. Then, with a sudden impulse, they all rushed in a howling crowd to the trees for shelter, leaving the ground behind them spotted with their stricken comrades. The prisoners were left for the moment standing alone in the middle of the clearing.

Challenger's quick brain had grasped the situation. He seized the bewildered Summerlee by the arm, and they both ran towards us. Two of their guards bounded after them and fell to two bullets from

Lord John. We ran forward into the open to meet our friends, and pressed a loaded rifle into the hands of each. But Summerlee was at the end of his strength. He could hardly totter. Already the ape-men were recovering from their panic. They were coming through the brushwood and threatening to cut us off. Challenger and I ran Summerlee along, one at each of his elbows, while Lord John covered our retreat, firing again and again as savage heads snarled at us out of the bushes. For a mile or more the chattering brutes were at our very heels. Then the pursuit slackened, for they learned our power and would no longer face that unerring rifle. When we had at last reached the camp, we looked back and found ourselves alone.

So it seemed to us; and yet we were mistaken. We had hardly closed the thornbush door of our zareba, clasped each other's hands, and thrown ourselves panting upon the ground beside our spring, when we heard a patter of feet and then a gentle, plaintive crying from outside our entrance. Lord Roxton rushed forward, rifle in hand, and threw it open. There, prostrate upon their faces, lay the little red figures of the four surviving Indians, trembling with fear of us and yet imploring our protection. With an expressive sweep of his hands one of them pointed to the woods around them, and indicated that they were full of danger. Then, darting forward, he threw his arms round Lord John's legs, and rested his face upon them.

"By George!" cried our peer, pulling at his moustache in great perplexity, "I say – what the deuce are we to do with these people? Get up, little chappie, and take your face off my boots."

Summerlee was sitting up and stuffing some tobacco into his old briar.

"We've got to see them safe," said he. "You've pulled us all out of the jaws of death. My word! it was a good bit of work!"

"Admirable!" cried Challenger. "Admirable! Not only we as individuals, but European science collectively, owe you a deep debt of gratitude for what you have done. I do not hesitate to say that the disappearance of Professor Summerlee and myself would have left an appreciable gap in modern zoological history. Our young friend here and you have done most excellently well."

He beamed at us with the old paternal smile, but European science would have been somewhat amazed could they have seen their chosen child, the hope of the future, with his tangled, unkempt head, his bare chest, and his tattered clothes. He had one of the meat-tins between his knees, and sat with a large piece of cold Australian mutton between his fingers. The Indian looked up at him, and then, with a little yelp, cringed to the ground and clung to Lord John's leg.

"Don't you be scared, my bonnie boy," said Lord John, patting the matted head in front of him. "He can't stick your appearance, Challenger; and, by George! I don't wonder. All right, little chap, he's only a human, just the same as the rest of us."

"Really, sir!" cried the Professor.

"Well, it's lucky for you, Challenger, that you ARE a little out of the ordinary. If you hadn't been so like the king – "

"Upon my word, Lord John, you allow yourself great latitude."

"Well, it's a fact."

"I beg, sir, that you will change the subject. Your remarks are irrelevant and unintelligible. The question before us is what are we to do with these Indians? The obvious thing is to escort them home, if we knew where their home was."

"There is no difficulty about that," said I. "They live in the caves on the other side of the central lake."

"Our young friend here knows where they live. I gather that it is some distance."

"A good twenty miles," said I.

Summerlee gave a groan.

"I, for one, could never get there. Surely I hear those brutes still howling upon our track."

As he spoke, from the dark recesses of the woods we heard far away the jabbering cry of the ape-men. The Indians once more set up a feeble wail of fear.

"We must move, and move quick!" said Lord John. "You help Summerlee, young fellah. These Indians will carry stores. Now, then, come along before they can see us."

In less than half-an-hour we had reached our brushwood retreat and concealed ourselves. All day we heard the excited calling of the ape-men in the direction of our old camp, but none of them came our way, and the tired fugitives, red and white, had a long, deep sleep. I was dozing myself in the evening when someone plucked my sleeve, and I found Challenger kneeling beside me.

"You keep a diary of these events, and you expect eventually to publish it, Mr. Malone," said he, with solemnity.

"I am only here as a Press reporter," I answered.

"Exactly. You may have heard some rather fatuous remarks of Lord John Roxton's which seemed to imply that there was some – some resemblance."

"Yes, I heard them."

"I need not say that any publicity given to such an idea – any levity in your narrative of what occurred – would be exceedingly offensive to me."

"I will keep well within the truth."

"Lord John's observations are frequently exceedingly fanciful, and he is capable of attributing the most absurd reasons to the respect which is always shown by the most undeveloped races to dignity and character. You follow my meaning?"

"Entirely."

"I leave the matter to your discretion." Then, after a long pause, he added: "The king of the ape-men was really a creature of great distinction – a most remarkably handsome and intelligent personality. Did it not strike you?"

"A most remarkable creature," said I.

And the Professor, much eased in his mind, settled down to his slumber once more.

Journey to the Centre of the Earth

The Search for Water

Jules Verne

In Untrodden Lands

The story so far

Professor Lidenbrock, a German scientist, has discovered an ancient coded manuscript that tells of a route to the centre of the earth, and he is determined to make the journey. He has hired a guide, Hans, and taken his young nephew, Axel, who narrates the story, with him. The entrance into the subterranean world is through the crater of an extinct volcano in Iceland. The three travellers are now making their way ever downwards through narrow passages.

The Search for Water
from

Journey to the Centre of the Earth

by

Jules Verne

As I had expected from the first, our supply of water gave completely out on our first day's march. Our provision of liquids was reduced to our supply of Schiedam; but this horrible – nay, I will say it – this infernal liquor burnt the throat, and I could not even bear the sight of it. I found the temperature to be stifling. I was paralyzed with fatigue. More than once I was about to fall insensible to the ground. The whole party then halted, and the worthy Icelander and my excellent uncle did their best to console and comfort me. I could, however, plainly see that my uncle was contending painfully against the extreme fatigues of our journey, and the awful torture generated by the absence of water.

At length a time came when I ceased to recollect anything – when all was one awful hideous, fantastic dream!

At last, on Tuesday, the seventh of the month of July, after crawling on our hands and knees for many hours, more dead than alive, we reached the point of junction between the galleries. I lay like a log, an inert mass of human flesh on the arid lava soil. It was then ten in the morning.

Hans and my uncle, leaning against the wall, tried to nibble away at some pieces of biscuit, while deep groans and sighs escaped from my scorched and swollen lips. Then I fell off into a kind of deep lethargy.

Presently I felt my uncle approach, and lift me up tenderly in his arms.

"Poor boy," I heard him say in a tone of deep commiseration.

I was profoundly touched by these words, being by no means accustomed to signs of womanly weakness in the Professor. I caught his trembling hands in mine and gave them a gentle pressure. He allowed me to do so without resistance, looking at me kindly all the time. His eyes were wet with tears.

I then saw him take the gourd which he wore at his side. To my surprise, or rather to my stupefaction, he placed it to my lips.

"Drink, my boy," he said.

Was it possible my ears had not deceived me? Was my uncle

mad? I looked at him, with, I am sure, quite an idiotic expression. I could not believe him. I too much feared the counteraction of disappointment.

"Drink," he said again.

Had I heard aright? Before, however, I could ask myself the question a second time, a mouthful of water cooled my parched lips and throat – one mouthful, but I do believe it brought me back to life.

I thanked my uncle by clasping my hands. My heart was too full to speak.

"Yes," said he, "one mouthful of water, the very last – do you hear, my boy – the very last! I have taken care of it at the bottom of my bottle as the apple of my eye. Twenty times, a hundred times, I have resisted the fearful desire to drink it. But – no – no, Harry, I saved it for you."

"My dear uncle," I exclaimed, and the big tears rolled down my hot and feverish cheeks.

"Yes, my poor boy, I knew that when you reached this place, this crossroad in the earth, you would fall down half dead, and I saved my last drop of water in order to restore you."

"Thanks," I cried; "thanks from my heart."

As little as my thirst was really quenched, I had nevertheless partially recovered my strength. The contracted muscles of my throat relaxed – and the inflammation of my lips in some measure subsided. At all events, I was able to speak.

"Well," I said, "there can be no doubt now as to what we have to do. Water has utterly failed us; our journey is therefore at an end. Let us return."

While I spoke thus, my uncle evidently avoided my face: he held down his head; his eyes were turned in every possible direction but the right one.

"Yes," I continued, getting excited by my own words, "we must go back to Sneffels. May heaven give us strength to enable us once more to revisit the light of day. Would that we now stood on the summit of the crater."

"Go back," said my uncle, speaking to himself, "and must it be so?"

"Go back – yes, and without losing a single moment," I vehemently cried.

For some moments there was silence under that dark and gloomy vault.

"So, my dear Harry," said the Professor in a very singular tone of voice, "those few drops of water have not sufficed to restore your energy and courage."

"Courage!" I cried.

"I see that you are quite as downcast as before – and still give way to discouragement and despair."

What, then, was the man made of, and what other projects were entering his fertile and audacious brain!

"You are not discouraged, sir?"

"What! Give up just as we are on the verge of success?" he cried. "Never, never shall it be said that Professor Hardwigg retreated."

"Then we must make up our minds to perish," I cried with a helpless sigh.

"No, Harry, my boy, certainly not. Go, leave me, I am very far from desiring your death. Take Hans with you. I will go on alone."

"You ask us to leave you?"

"Leave me, I say. I have undertaken this dangerous and perilous adventure. I will carry it to the end – or I will never return to the surface of Mother Earth. Go, Harry – once more I say to you – go!"

My uncle as he spoke was terribly excited. His voice, which before had been tender, almost womanly, became harsh and menacing. He appeared to be struggling with desperate energy against the impossible. I did not wish to abandon him at the bottom of that abyss, while, on the other hand, the instinct of preservation told me to fly.

Meanwhile, our guide was looking on with profound calmness

and indifference. He appeared to be an unconcerned party, and yet he perfectly well knew what was going on between us. Our gestures sufficiently indicated the different roads each wished to follow – and which each tried to influence the other to undertake. But Hans appeared not to take the slightest interest in what was really a question of life and death for us all, but waited quite ready to obey the signal which should say go aloft, or to resume his desperate journey into the interior of the earth.

How then I wished with all my heart and soul that I could make him understand my words. My representations, my sighs and groans, the earnest accents in which I should have spoken would have convinced that cold, hard nature. Those fearful dangers and perils of which the stolid guide had no idea, I would have pointed them out to him – I would have, as it were, made him see and feel. Between us, we might have convinced the obstinate Professor. If the worst had come to the worst, we could have compelled him to return to the summit of Sneffels.

I quietly approached Hans. I caught his hand in mine. He never moved a muscle. I indicated to him the road to the top of the crater. He remained motionless. My panting form, my haggard countenance, must have indicated the extent of my sufferings. The Icelander gently shook his head and pointed to my uncle.

"Master," he said.

The word is Icelandic as well as English.

"The master!" I cried, beside myself with fury – "madman! no –

I tell you he is not the master of our lives; we must fly! we must drag him with us! do you hear me? Do you understand me, I say?"

I have already explained that I held Hans by the arm. I tried to make him rise from his seat. I struggled with him and tried to force him away. My uncle now interposed.

"My good Henry, be calm," he said. "You will obtain nothing from my devoted follower; therefore, listen to what I have to say."

I folded my arms, as well as I could, and looked my uncle full in the face.

"This wretched want of water," he said, "is the sole obstacle to the success of my project. In the entire gallery, made of lava, schist, and coal, it is true we found not one liquid molecule. It is quite possible that we may be more fortunate in the western tunnel."

My sole reply was to shake my head with an air of deep incredulity.

"Listen to me to the end," said the Professor in his well-known lecturing voice. "While you lay yonder without life or motion, I undertook a reconnoitering journey into the conformation of this other gallery. I have discovered that it goes directly downwards into the bowels of the earth, and in a few hours will take us to the old granitic formation. In this we shall undoubtedly find innumerable springs. The nature of the rock makes this a mathematical certainty, and instinct agrees with logic to say that it is so. Now, this is the serious proposition which I have to make to you. When Christopher Columbus asked of his men three days to discover the land of promise, his men ill, terrified, and hopeless, yet gave him three days – and the New World was discovered. Now I, the Christopher Columbus of this subterranean region, only ask of you one more day. If, when that time is expired, I have not found the water of which we are in search, I swear to you, I will give up my mighty enterprise and return to the earth's surface."

Despite my irritation and despair, I knew how much it cost my uncle to make this proposition, and to hold such conciliatory language. Under the circumstances, what could I do but yield?

"Well," I cried, "let it be as you wish, and may heaven reward your superhuman energy. But as, unless we discover water, our hours are numbered, let us lose no time, but go ahead."

Our descent was now resumed by means of the second gallery. Hans took up his post in front as usual. We had not gone more than a hundred yards when the Professor carefully examined the walls.

"This is the primitive formation – we are on the right road – onwards is our hope!"

When the whole earth got cool in the first hours of the world's morning, the diminution of the volume of the earth produced a state of dislocation in its upper crust, followed by ruptures, crevasses and fissures. The passage was a fissure of this kind, through which, ages ago, had flowed the eruptive granite. The thousand windings and turnings formed an inextricable

labyrinth through the ancient soil.

As we descended, successions of layers composing the primitive soil appeared with the utmost fidelity of detail. Geological science considers this primitive soil as the base of the mineral crust, and it has recognized that it is composed of three different strata or layers, all resting on the immovable rock known as granite.

No mineralogists had even found themselves placed in such a marvellous position to study nature in all her real and naked beauty. The sounding rod, a mere machine, could not bring to the surface of the earth the objects of value for the study of its internal structure, which we were about to see with our own eyes, to touch with our own hands.

Remember that I am writing this after the journey.

Across the streak of the rocks, coloured by beautiful green tints, wound metallic threads of copper, of manganese, with traces of platinum and gold. I could not help gazing at these riches buried in the entrails of Mother Earth, and of which no man would have the enjoyment to the end of time! These treasures – mighty and inexhaustible, were buried in the morning of the earth's history, at such awful depths, that no crowbar or pickax will ever drag them from their tomb!

The light of our Ruhmkorff's coil, increased tenfold by the myriad of prismatic masses of rock, sent its jets of fire in every direction, and I could fancy myself travelling through a huge hollow diamond, the rays of which produced myriads of extraordinary effects.

Towards six o'clock, this festival of light began sensibly and visibly to decrease, and soon almost ceased. The sides of the gallery assumed a crystallized tint, with a sombre hue; white mica began to commingle more freely with feldspar and quartz, to form what may be called the true rock – the stone which is hard above all, that supports, without being crushed, the four stories of the earth's soil.

We were walled by an immense prison of granite!

It was now eight o'clock, and still there was no sign of water. The sufferings I endured were horrible. My uncle now kept at the head of our little column. Nothing could induce him to stop. I, meanwhile, had but one real thought. My ear was keenly on the watch to catch the sound of a spring. But no pleasant sound of falling water fell upon my listening ear.

The light of our Ruhmkorff's coil, increased tenfold by the myriad of prismatic masses of rock, sent its jets of fire in every direction

But at last the time came when my limbs refused to carry me longer. I contended heroically against the terrible tortures I endured, because I did not wish to compel my uncle to halt. To him I knew this would be the last fatal stroke.

Suddenly I felt a deadly faintness come over me. My eyes could no longer see; my knees shook. I gave one despairing cry – and fell!

"Help, help, I am dying!"

My uncle turned and slowly retraced his steps. He looked at me with folded arms, and then allowed one sentence to escape, in hollow accents, from his lips:

"All is over."

The last thing I saw was a face fearfully distorted with pain and sorrow; and then my eyes closed.

When I again opened them, I saw my companions lying near me, motionless, wrapped in their huge travelling rugs. Were they asleep or dead? For myself, sleep was wholly out of the question. My fainting fit over, I was wakeful as the lark. I suffered too much for sleep to visit my eyelids – the more, that I thought myself sick unto death – dying. The last words spoken by my uncle seemed to be buzzing in my ears – all is over! And it was probable that he was right. In the state of prostration to which I was reduced, it was madness to think of ever again seeing the light of day.

Above were miles upon miles of the earth's crust. As I thought of it, I could fancy the whole weight resting on my shoulders. I was crushed, annihilated! and exhausted myself in vain attempts to turn in my granite bed.

Hours upon hours passed away. A profound and terrible silence reigned around us – a silence of the tomb. Nothing could make itself heard through these gigantic walls of granite. The very thought was stupendous.

Presently, despite my apathy, despite the kind of deadly calm into which I was cast, something aroused me. It was a slight but peculiar noise. While I was watching intently, I observed that the tunnel was becoming dark. Then gazing through the dim light that remained, I thought I saw the Icelander taking his departure, lamp in hand.

Why had he acted thus? Did Hans the guide mean to abandon us? My uncle lay fast asleep – or dead. I tried to cry out, and arouse him. My voice, feebly issuing from my parched and fevered lips, found no echo in that fearful place. My throat was dry, my tongue stuck to the roof of my mouth. The obscurity had by this time become intense, and at last even the faint sound of the guide's

footsteps was lost in the blank distance. My soul seemed filled with anguish, and death appeared welcome, only let it come quickly.

"Hans is leaving us," I cried. "Hans – Hans, if you are a man, come back."

These words were spoken to myself. They could not be heard aloud. Nevertheless, after the first few moments of terror were over, I was ashamed of my suspicions against a man who hitherto had behaved so admirably. Nothing in his conduct or character justified suspicion. Moreover, a moment's reflection reassured me. His departure could not be a flight. Instead of ascending the gallery, he was going deeper down into the gulf. Had he had any bad design, his way would have been upwards.

This reasoning calmed me a little and I began to hope!

The good, and peaceful, and imperturbable Hans would certainly not have arisen from his sleep without some serious and grave motive. Was he bent on a voyage of discovery? During the deep, still silence of the night had he at last heard that sweet murmur about which we were all so anxious?

During a long, long, weary hour, there crossed my wildly delirious brain all sorts of reasons as to what could have aroused our quiet and faithful guide. The most absurd and ridiculous ideas passed through my head, each more impossible than the other.

I believe I was either half or wholly mad.

Suddenly, however, there arose, as it were from the depths of the earth, a voice of comfort. It was the sound of footsteps! Hans was returning.

Presently the uncertain light began to shine upon the walls of the passage, and then it came in view far down the sloping tunnel. At length Hans himself appeared.

He approached my uncle, placed his hand upon his shoulder, and gently awakened him. My uncle, as soon as he saw who it was, instantly arose.

"Well!" exclaimed the Professor.

"Vatten," said the hunter.

I did not know a single word of the Danish language, and yet by a sort of mysterious instinct I understood what the guide had said.

"Water, water!" I cried, in a wild and frantic tone, clapping my hands, and gesticulating like a madman.

"Water!" murmured my uncle, in a voice of deep emotion and gratitude. "Hvar?" ("Where?")

"Nedat." ("Below.")

"Where? below!" I understood every word. I had caught the hunter by the hands, and I shook them heartily, while he looked on with perfect calmness.

The preparations for our departure did not take long, and we were soon making a rapid descent into the tunnel.

An hour later we had advanced a thousand yards, and descended two thousand feet.

At this moment I heard an accustomed and well-known sound running along the floors of the granite rock – a kind of dull and sullen roar, like that of a distant waterfall.

During the first half hour of our advance, not finding the discovered spring, my feelings of intense suffering appeared to return. Once more I began to lose all hope. My uncle, however, observing how downhearted I was again becoming, took up the conversation.

"Hans was right," he exclaimed enthusiastically; "that is the dull roaring of a torrent."

"A torrent," I cried, delighted at even hearing the welcome words.

"There's not the slightest doubt about it," he replied, "a subterranean river is flowing beside us."

I made no reply, but hastened on, once more animated by hope. I began not even to feel the deep fatigue which hitherto had overpowered me. The very sound of this glorious murmuring water already refreshed me. We could hear it increasing in volume every moment. The torrent, which for a long time could be heard flowing over our heads, now ran distinctly along the left wall, roaring, rushing, spluttering, and still falling.

Several times I passed my hand across the rock hoping to find some trace of humidity – of the slightest percolation. Alas! in vain.

Again a half hour passed in the same weary toil. Again we advanced.

It now became evident that the hunter, during his absence, had not been able to carry his researches any farther. Guided by an instinct peculiar to the dwellers in mountain regions and water finders, he 'smelt' the living spring through the rock. Still he had not seen the precious liquid. He had neither quenched his own thirst, nor brought us one drop in his gourd.

Moreover, we soon made the disastrous discovery that, if our progress continued, we should soon be moving away from the torrent, the sound of which gradually diminished. We turned back. Hans halted at the precise spot where the sound of the torrent appeared nearest.

I could bear the suspense and suffering no longer, and seated myself against the wall, behind which I could hear the water seething and effervescing not two feet away. But a solid wall of granite still separated us from it!

Hans looked keenly at me, and, strange enough, for once I thought I saw a smile on his imperturbable face.

He rose from a stone on which he had been seated, and took up the lamp. I could not help rising and following. He moved slowly along the firm and solid granite wall. I watched him with mingled curiosity and eagerness. Presently he halted and placed his ear against the dry stone, moving slowly along and listening with the most extreme care and attention. I understood at once that he was searching for the exact spot where the torrent's roar was most plainly heard. This point he soon found in the lateral wall on the left side, about three feet above the level of the tunnel floor.

I was in a state of intense excitement. I scarcely dared believe what the eider-duck hunter was about to do. It was, however, impossible in a moment more not to both understand and applaud, and even to smother him in my embraces, when I saw him raise the heavy crowbar and commence an attack upon the rock itself.

"Saved!" I cried.

"Yes," cried my uncle, even more excited and delighted than myself; "Hans is quite right. Oh, the worthy, excellent man! We should never have thought of such an idea."

And nobody else, I think, would have done so. Such a process, simple as it seemed, would most certainly not have entered our heads. Nothing could be more dangerous than to begin to work with pickaxes in that particular part of the globe. Supposing while he was at work a break-up were to take place, and supposing the torrent once having gained an inch were to take an ell, and come pouring bodily through the broken rock!

Not one of these dangers was chimerical. They were only too real. But at that moment no fear of falling in of the roof, or even of inundation was capable of stopping us. Our thirst was so intense that to quench it we would have dug below the bed of old Ocean itself.

Hans went quietly to work – a work which neither my uncle nor I would have undertaken at any price. Our impatience was so great that if we had once begun with pickax and crowbar, the rock would soon have split into a hundred fragments. The guide, on the contrary, calm, ready, moderate, wore away the hard rock by little steady blows of his instrument, making no attempt at a larger hole than about six inches. As I stood, I heard, or I thought I heard, the roar of the torrent momentarily increasing in loudness, and at times I almost felt the pleasant sensation of water upon my parched lips.

At the end of what appeared an age, Hans had made a hole which enabled his crowbar to enter two feet into the solid rock. He had been at work exactly an hour. It appeared a dozen. I was getting wild with impatience. My uncle began to think of using more violent measures. I had the greatest difficulty in checking him. He had indeed just got hold of his crowbar when a loud and welcome hiss was heard. Then a stream, or rather jet, of water burst through the wall and came out with such force as to hit the opposite side!

Hans, the guide, who was half upset by the shock, was scarcely able to keep down a cry of pain and grief. I understood his meaning when, plunging my hands into the sparkling jet, I myself gave a wild and frantic cry. The water was scalding hot!

"Boiling," I cried, in bitter disappointment.

"Well, never mind," said my uncle, "it will soon get cool."

The tunnel began to be filled by clouds of vapour, while a small

stream ran away into the interior of the earth. In a short time we had some sufficiently cool to drink. We swallowed it in huge mouthfuls.

Oh! what exalted delight – what rich and incomparable luxury! What was this water, whence did it come? To us what was that? The simple fact was – it was water; and, though still with a tingle of warmth about it, it brought back to the heart, that life which, but for it, must surely have faded away. I drank greedily, almost without tasting it.

When, however, I had almost quenched my ravenous thirst, I made a discovery.

"Why, it is chalybeate water!"

"A most excellent stomachic," replied my uncle, "and highly mineralized. Here is a journey worth twenty to Spa."

"It's very good," I replied.

"I should think so. Water found six miles underground. There is a peculiarly inky flavor about it, which is by no means disagreeable. Hans may congratulate himself on having made a rare discovery. What do you say, nephew, according to the usual custom of travellers, to name the stream after him?"

"Good," said I. And the name of 'Hansbach' ('Hans Brook') was at once agreed upon.

Hans was not a bit more proud after hearing our determination than he was before. After having taken a very small modicum of the welcome refreshment, he had seated himself in a corner with his usual imperturbable gravity.

"Now," said I, "it is not worth while letting this water run to waste."

"What is the use," replied my uncle, "the source from which this river rises is inexhaustible."

"Never mind," I continued, "let us fill our goatskin and gourds, and then try to stop the opening up."

My advice, after some hesitation, was followed or attempted to be followed. Hans picked up all the broken pieces of granite he had knocked out, and using some tow he happened to have about him, tried to shut up the fissure he had made in the wall. All he did was to scald his hands. The pressure was too great, and all our attempts were utter failures.

"It is evident," I remarked, "that the upper surface of these springs is situated at a very great height above – as we may fairly infer from the great pressure of the jet."

"That is by no means doubtful," replied my uncle, "if this column of water is about thirty-two thousand feet high, the atmospheric pressure must be something enormous. But a new idea has just struck me."

"And what is that?"

"Why be at so much trouble to close this aperture?"

"Because – "

I hesitated and stammered, having no real reason.

"When our water bottles are empty, we are not at all sure that we shall be able to fill them," observed my uncle.

"I think that is very probable."

"Well, then, let this water run. It will, of course, naturally follow in our track, and will serve to guide and refresh us."

"I think the idea a good one," I cried in reply, "and with this rivulet as a companion, there is no further reason why we should not succeed in our marvelous project."

"Ah, my boy," said the Professor, laughing, "after all, you are coming round."

"More than that, I am now confident of ultimate success."

"One moment, nephew mine. Let us begin by taking some hours of repose."

I had utterly forgotten that it was night. The chronometer, however, informed me of the fact. Soon we were sufficiently restored and refreshed, and had all fallen into a profound sleep.

By the next day we had nearly forgotten our past sufferings. The first sensation I experienced was surprise at not being thirsty, and I actually asked myself the reason. The running stream, which flowed in rippling wavelets at my feet, was the satisfactory reply.

We breakfasted with a good appetite, and then drank our fill of the excellent water. I felt myself quite a new man, ready to go anywhere my uncle chose to lead. I began to think. Why should not a man as seriously convinced as my uncle, succeed, with so excellent a guide as worthy Hans, and so devoted a nephew as myself? These were the brilliant ideas which now invaded my brain. Had the proposition now been made to go back to the summit of Mount Sneffels, I should have declined the offer in a most indignant manner.

But fortunately there was no question of going up. We were about to descend farther into the interior of the earth.

"Let us be moving," I cried, awakening the echoes of the old world.

We resumed our march on Thursday at eight o'clock in the morning. The great granite tunnel, as it went round by sinuous and winding ways, presented every now and then sharp turns, and in fact all the appearance of a labyrinth. Its direction, however, was in general towards the southwest. My uncle made several pauses in order to consult his compass.

The gallery now began to trend downwards in a horizontal

direction, with about two inches of fall in every furlong. The murmuring stream flowed quietly at our feet. I could not but compare it to some familiar spirit, guiding us through the earth, and I dabbled my fingers in its tepid water, which sang like a naiad as we progressed. My good humour began to assume a mythological character.

As for my uncle he began to complain of the horizontal character of the road. His route, he found, began to be indefinitely prolonged, instead of "sliding down the celestial ray," according to his expression.

But we had no choice; and as long as our road led towards the centre – however little progress we made, there was no reason to complain.

Moreover, from time to time the slopes were much greater, the naiad sang more loudly, and we began to dip downwards in earnest.

As yet, however, I felt no painful sensation. I had not got over the excitement of the discovery of water.

That day and the next we did a considerable amount of horizontal, and relatively very little vertical, travelling.

On Friday evening, the tenth of July, according to our estimation, we ought to have been thirty leagues to the southeast of Reykjavik, and about two leagues and a half deep. We now received a rather startling surprise.

Under our feet there opened a horrible well. My uncle was so delighted that he actually clapped his hands – as he saw how steep and sharp was the descent.

"Ah, ah!" he cried, in rapturous delight; "this takes us a long way. Look at the projections of the rock. Hah!" he exclaimed, "it's a fearful staircase!"

Hans, however, who in all our troubles had never given up the ropes, took care so to dispose of them as to prevent any accidents. Our descent then began. I dare not call it a perilous descent, for I was already too familiar with that sort of work to look upon it as anything but a very ordinary affair.

This well was a kind of narrow opening in the massive granite of the kind known as a fissure. The contraction of the terrestrial scaffolding, when it suddenly cooled, had been evidently the cause. If it had ever served in former times as a kind of funnel through which passed the eruptive masses vomited by Sneffels, I was at a loss to explain how it had left no mark. We were, in fact, descending a spiral, something like those winding staircases in use in modern houses.

We were compelled every quarter of an hour or thereabouts to sit down in order to rest our legs. Our calves ached. We then seated ourselves on some projecting rock with our legs hanging over, and gossiped while we ate a mouthful – drinking still from the pleasantly warm running stream which had not deserted us.

It is scarcely necessary to say that in this curiously shaped fissure the Hansbach had become a cascade to the detriment of its

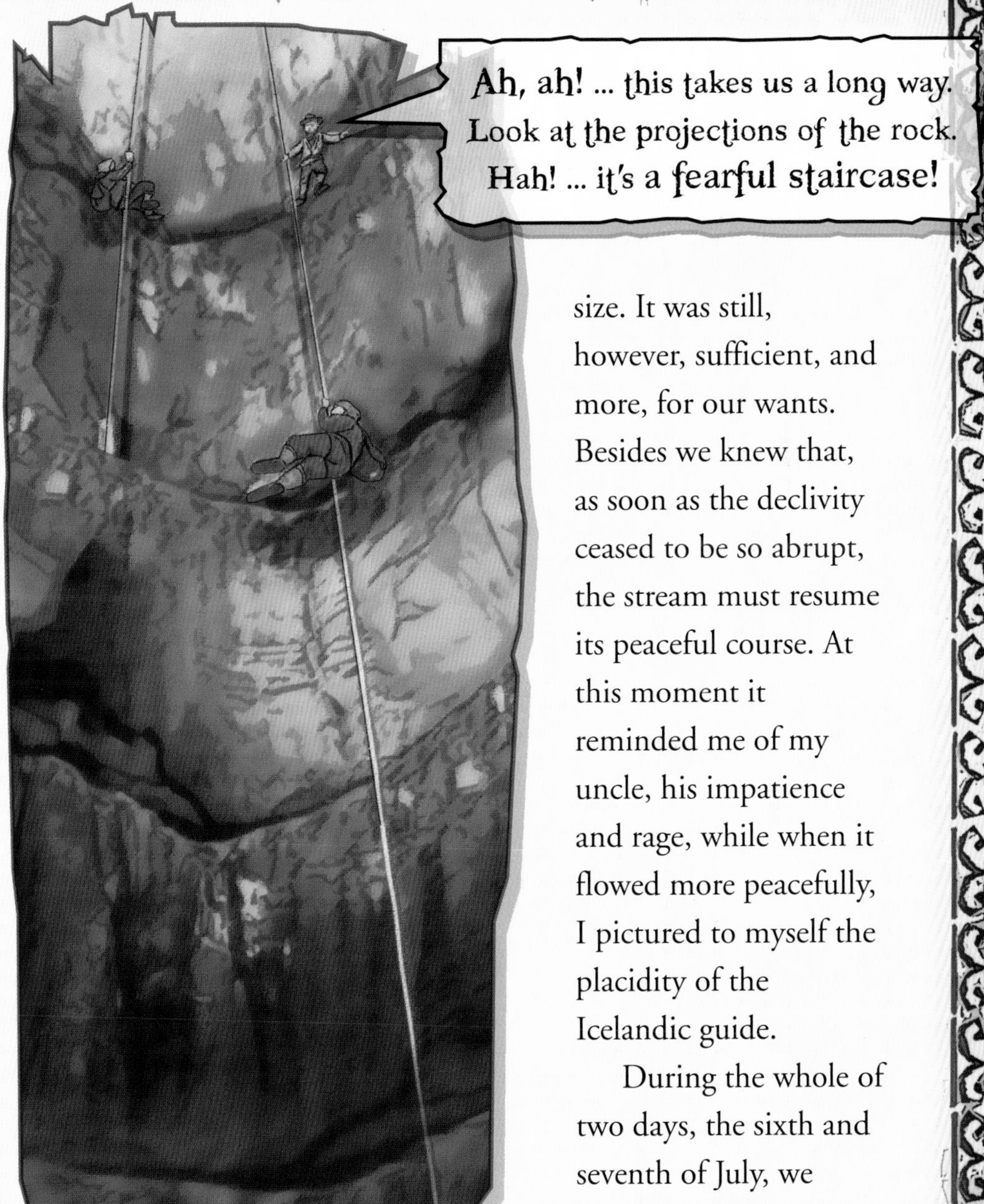

size. It was still, however, sufficient, and more, for our wants. Besides we knew that, as soon as the declivity ceased to be so abrupt, the stream must resume its peaceful course. At this moment it reminded me of my uncle, his impatience and rage, while when it flowed more peacefully, I pictured to myself the placidity of the Icelandic guide.

During the whole of two days, the sixth and seventh of July, we followed the extraordinary spiral staircase of the fissure, penetrating two leagues farther into the crust of the earth, which put us five leagues below the level of the sea. On the eighth, however, at twelve o'clock in the day, the fissure suddenly assumed a much more gentle slope still trending in a southeast direction.

The road now became comparatively easy, and at the same time dreadfully monotonous. It would have been difficult for matters to have turned out otherwise. Our peculiar journey had no chance of being diversified by landscape and scenery. At all events, such was my idea.

At length, on Wednesday the fifteenth, we were actually seven leagues (twenty-one miles) below the surface of the earth, and fifty leagues distant from the mountain of Sneffels. Though, if the truth be told, we were very tired, our health had resisted all suffering, and was in a most satisfactory state. Our traveler's box of medicaments had not even been opened.

My uncle was careful to note every hour the indications of the compass, of the manometer, and of the thermometer, all which he afterwards published in his elaborate philosophical and scientific account of our remarkable voyage. He was therefore able to give an exact relation of the situation. When, therefore, he informed me that we were fifty leagues in a horizontal direction distant from our starting point, I could not suppress a loud exclamation.

"What is the matter now?" cried my uncle.

"Nothing very important, only an idea has entered my head,"

was my reply.

"Well, out with it, My boy."

"It is my opinion that if your calculations are correct we are no longer under Iceland."

"Do you think so?"

"We can very easily find out," I replied, pulling out a map and compasses.

"You see," I said, after careful measurement, "that I am not mistaken. We are far beyond Cape Portland; and those fifty leagues to the southeast will take us into the open sea."

"Under the open sea," cried my uncle, rubbing his hands with a delighted air.

"Yes," I cried, "no doubt old Ocean flows over our heads!"

"Well, my dear boy, what can be more natural! Do you not know that in the neighbourhood of Newcastle there are coal mines which have been worked far out under the sea?"

Now my worthy uncle, the Professor, no doubt regarded this discovery as a very simple fact, but to me the idea was by no means a pleasant one. And yet when one came to think the matter over seriously, what mattered it whether the plains and mountains of Iceland were suspended over our devoted heads, or the mighty billows of the Atlantic Ocean? The whole question rested on the solidity of the granite roof above us. However, I soon got used to the ideal for the passage now level, now running down, and still always to the southeast, kept going deeper and deeper into the profound abysses of Mother Earth.

Three days later, on the eighteenth day of July, on a Saturday, we reached a kind of vast grotto. My uncle here paid Hans his usual rix-dollars, and it was decided that the next day should be a day of rest.

It must in all truth be confessed, things as yet had gone on well, and I should have acted in bad taste to have complained. If the true medium of our difficulties did not increase, it was within the range of possibility that we might ultimately reach the end of our journey. Then what glory would be ours! I began in the newly aroused ardour of my soul to speak enthusiastically to the Professor. Well, was I serious? The whole state in which we existed was a mystery – and it was impossible to know whether or not I was in earnest.

For several days after our memorable halt, the slopes became more rapid – some were even of a most frightful character – almost vertical, so that we were forever going down into the solid interior mass. During some days, we actually descended a league and a half, even two leagues towards the centre of the earth. The descents were sufficiently perilous, and while we were engaged in them we learned fully to appreciate the marvelous coolness of our guide, Hans.

Without him we should have been wholly lost. The grave and impassible Icelander devoted himself to us with the most incomprehensible sang-froid and ease; and, thanks to him, many a dangerous pass was got over, where, but for him, we should inevitably have stuck fast.

His silence increased every day. I think that we began to be influenced by this peculiar trait in his character. It is certain that the inanimate objects by which you are surrounded have a direct action on the brain. It must be that a man who shuts himself up between four walls must lose the faculty of associating ideas and words. How many persons condemned to the horrors of solitary confinement have gone mad – simply because the thinking faculties have lain dormant!

During the two weeks that followed our last interesting conversation, there occurred nothing worthy of being especially recorded.

I have, while writing these memoirs, taxed my memory in vain for one incident of travel during this particular period.

But the next event to be related is terrible indeed. Its very memory, even now, makes my soul shudder, and my blood run cold.

It was on the seventh of August. Our constant and successive descents had taken us quite thirty leagues into the interior of the earth, that is to say that there were above us thirty leagues, nearly a hundred miles, of rocks, and oceans, and continents, and towns, to say nothing of living inhabitants. We were in a southeasterly direction, about two hundred leagues from Iceland.

On that memorable day the tunnel had begun to assume an almost horizontal course.

I was on this occasion walking on in front. My uncle had charge of one of the Ruhmkorff coils, I had possession of the other. By means of its light I was busy examining the different layers of granite. I was completely absorbed in my work.

Suddenly halting and turning round, I found that I was alone!

"Well," thought I to myself, "I have certainly been walking too fast – or else Hans and my uncle have stopped to rest. The best thing I can do is to go back and find them. Luckily, there is very little ascent to tire me."

I accordingly retraced my steps and, while doing so, walked for at least a quarter of an hour. Rather uneasy, I paused and looked eagerly around. Not a living soul. I called aloud. No reply. My voice was lost amid the myriad cavernous echoes it aroused!

I began for the first time to feel seriously uneasy. A cold shiver shook my whole body, and perspiration, chill and terrible, burst upon my skin.

"I must be calm," I said, speaking aloud, as boys whistle to drive away fear. "There can be no doubt that I shall find my companions. There cannot be two roads. It is certain that I was considerably ahead; all I have to do is to go back."

Having come to this determination I ascended the tunnel for at least half an hour, unable to decide if I had ever seen certain landmarks before. Every now and then I paused to discover if any loud appeal was made to me, well knowing that in that dense and intensified atmosphere I should hear it a long way off. But no. The most extraordinary silence reigned in this immense gallery. Only the echoes of my own footsteps could be heard.

At last I stopped. I could scarcely realize the fact of my isolation. I was quite willing to think that I had made a mistake, but not that I was lost. If I had made a mistake, I might find my way; if lost – I shuddered to think of it.

"Come, come," said I to myself, "since there is only one road, and they must come by it, we shall at last meet. All I have to do is still to go upwards. Perhaps, however, not seeing me, and forgetting I was ahead, they may have gone back in search of me. Still, even in this case, if I make haste, I shall get up to them. There can be no doubt about the matter."

But as I spoke these last words aloud, it would have been quite clear to any listener – had there been one – that I was by no means convinced of the fact. Moreover in order to associate together these simple ideas and to reunite them under the form of reasoning, required some time. I could not all at once bring my brain to think.

Then another dread doubt fell upon my soul. After all, was I ahead? Of course I was. Hans was no doubt following behind preceded by my uncle. I perfectly recollected his having stopped for a moment to strap his baggage on his shoulder. I now remembered this trifling detail. It was, I believe, just at that very moment that I had determined to continue my route.

"Again," thought I, reasoning as calmly as was possible, "there is another sure means of not losing my way, a thread to guide me through the labyrinthine subterraneous retreat – one which I had forgotten – my faithful river."

This course of reasoning roused my drooping spirits, and I resolved to resume my journey without further delay. No time was to be lost.

It was at this moment that I had reason to bless the thoughtfulness of my uncle, when he refused to allow the eider hunter to close the orifices of the hot spring – that small fissure in the great mass of granite. This beneficent spring after having saved us from thirst during so many days would now enable me to regain the right road.

Having come to this mental decision, I made up my mind, before I started upwards, that ablution would certainly do me a great deal of good.

I stopped to plunge my hands and forehead in the pleasant water of the Hansbach stream, blessing its presence as a certain consolation.

Conceive my horror and stupefaction! I was treading a hard, dusty, shingly road of granite. The stream on which I reckoned had wholly disappeared!

No words in any human language can depict my utter despair. I was literally buried alive; with no other expectation before me but

to die in all the slow horrible torture of hunger and thirst.

Mechanically I crawled about, feeling the dry and arid rock. Never to my fancy had I ever felt anything so dry.

But, I frantically asked myself, how had I lost the course of the flowing stream? There could be no doubt it had ceased to flow in the gallery in which I now was. Now I began to understand the cause of the strange silence which prevailed when last I tried if any appeal from my companions might perchance reach my ear.

Conceive my horror and stupefaction! The stream on which I reckoned had wholly disappeared!

It so happened that when I first took an imprudent step in the wrong direction, I did not perceive the absence of the all-important stream.

It was now quite evident that when we halted, another tunnel must have received the waters of the little torrent, and that I had unconsciously entered a different gallery. To what unknown depths had my companions gone? Where was I?

How to get back! Clue or landmark there was absolutely none! My feet left no signs on the granite and shingle. My brain throbbed with agony as I tried to discover the solution of this terrible problem. My situation, after all sophistry and reflection, had finally to be summed up in three awful words –

Lost! Lost!! LOST!!!

Lost at a depth which, to my finite understanding, appeared to be immeasurable.

These thirty leagues of the crust of the earth weighed upon my shoulders like the globe on the shoulders of Atlas. I felt myself crushed by the awful weight. It was indeed a position to drive the sanest man to madness!

I tried to bring my thoughts back to the things of the world so long forgotten. It was with the greatest difficulty that I succeeded in doing so. Hamburg, the house on the Konigstrasse, my dear cousin Gretchen – all that world which had before vanished like a shadow floated before my now vivid imagination.

There they were before me, but how unreal. Under the influence of a terrible hallucination I saw all the incidents of our journey pass before me like the scenes of a panorama. The ship and its inmates, Iceland, M. Fridriksson, and the great summit of Mount Sneffels! I said to myself that, if in my position I retained the most faint and shadowy outline of a hope, it would be a sure sign of approaching delirium. It were better to give way wholly to despair!

In fact, did I but reason with calmness and philosophy, what human power was there in existence able to take me back to the surface of the earth, and ready, too, to split asunder, to rend in twain those huge and mighty vaults which stand above my head? Who could enable me to find my road – and regain my companions?

Insensate folly and madness to entertain even a shadow of hope!

"Oh, Uncle!" was my despairing cry.

This was the only word of reproach which came to my lips; for I thoroughly understood how deeply and sorrowfully the worthy Professor would regret my loss, and how in his turn he would patiently seek for me.

When I at last began to resign myself to the fact that no further aid was to be expected from man, and knowing that I was utterly powerless to do anything for my own salvation, I kneeled with earnest fervor and asked assistance from Heaven. The remembrance of my innocent childhood, the memory of my mother, known only in my infancy, came welling forth from my heart. I had recourse to prayer. And little as I had a right to be remembered by Him whom I had forgotten in the hour of prosperity, and whom I so tardily invoked, I prayed earnestly and sincerely.

This renewal of my youthful faith brought about a much greater amount of calm, and I was enabled to concentrate all my strength and intelligence on the terrible realities of my unprecedented situation.

I had about me that which I had at first wholly forgotten – three days' provisions. Moreover, my water bottle was quite full.

Nevertheless, the one thing which it was impossible to do was to remain alone. Try to find my companions I must, at any price. But which course should I take? Should I go upwards, or again descend? Doubtless it was right to retrace my steps in an upward direction.

By doing this with care and coolness, I must reach the point where I had turned away from the rippling stream. I must find the fatal bifurcation or fork. Once at this spot, once the river at my feet, I could, at all events, regain the awful crater of Mount Sneffels. Why had I not thought of this before? This, at last, was a reasonable hope of safety. The most important thing, then, to be done was to discover the bed of the Hansbach.

After a slight meal and a draught of water, I rose like a giant refreshed. Leaning heavily on my pole, I began the ascent of the gallery. The slope was very rapid and rather difficult. But I advanced hopefully and carefully, like a man who at last is making his way out of a forest, and knows there is only one road to follow.

During one whole hour nothing happened to check my progress. As I advanced, I tried to recollect the shape of the tunnel – to recall to my memory certain projections of rocks – to persuade myself that I had followed certain winding routes before. But no one particular sign could I bring to mind, and I was soon forced to allow that this gallery would never take me back to the point at which I had separated myself from my companions. It was absolutely without issue – a mere blind alley in the earth.

The moment at length came when, facing the solid rock, I knew my fate, and fell inanimate on the arid floor!

To describe the horrible state of despair and fear into which I then fell would now be vain and impossible. My last hope, the courage which had sustained me, drooped before the sight of this pitiless granite rock!

Lost in a vast labyrinth, the sinuosities of which spread in every direction, without guide, clue or compass, I knew it was a vain and useless task to attempt flight. All that remained to me was to lie down and die. To lie down and die the most cruel and horrible of deaths!

In my state of mind, the idea came into my head that one day perhaps, when my fossil bones were found, their discovery so far below the level of the earth might give rise to solemn and interesting scientific discussions.

I tried to cry aloud, but hoarse, hollow, and inarticulate sounds alone could make themselves heard through my parched lips. I literally panted for breath.

In the midst of all these horrible sources of anguish and despair, a new horror took possession of my soul. My lamp, by falling down, had got out of order. I had no means of repairing it. Its light was already becoming paler and paler, and soon would expire.

With a strange sense of resignation and despair, I watched the luminous current in the coil getting less and less. A procession of shadows moved flashing along the granite wall. I scarcely dared to lower my eyelids, fearing to lose the last spark of this fugitive light. Every instant it seemed to me that it was about to vanish and to leave me forever – in utter darkness!

At last, one final trembling flame remained in the lamp; I followed it with all my power of vision; I gasped for breath; I concentrated upon it all the power of my soul, as upon the last scintillation of light I was ever destined to see: and then I was to be lost forever in Cimmerian and tenebrous shades.

A wild and plaintive cry escaped my lips. On earth during the most profound and comparatively complete darkness, light never allows a complete destruction and extinction of its power. Light is so diffuse, so subtle, that it permeates everywhere, and whatever little may remain, the retina of the eye will succeed in finding it.

In this place nothing – the absolute obscurity made me blind in every sense.

My head was now wholly lost. I raised my arms, trying the effects of the feeling in getting against the cold stone wall. It was painful in the extreme. Madness must have taken possession of me. I knew not what I did. I began to run, to fly, rushing at haphazard in this inextricable labyrinth, always going downwards, running wildly underneath the terrestrial crust, like an inhabitant of the subterranean furnaces, screaming, roaring, howling, until bruised by the pointed rocks, falling and picking myself up all covered with blood, seeking madly to drink the blood which dripped from my torn features, mad because this blood only trickled over my face, and watching always for this horrid wall which ever presented to me the fearful obstacle against which I could not dash my head.

Where was I going? It was impossible to say. I was perfectly ignorant of the matter.

Several hours passed in this way. After a long time, having utterly exhausted my strength, I fell a heavy inert mass along the side of the tunnel, and lost consciousness.

When at last I came back to a sense of life and being, my face was wet, but wet, as I soon knew, with tears. How long this state of insensibility lasted, it is quite impossible for me now to say. I had no means left to me of taking any account of time. Never since the creation of the world had such a solitude as mine existed. I was completely abandoned.

After my fall I lost much blood. I felt myself flooded with the life-giving liquid. My first sensation was perhaps a natural one. Why was I not dead? Because I was alive, there was something left to do. I tried to make up my mind to think no longer. As far as I was able, I drove away all ideas, and utterly overcome by pain and grief, I crouched against the granite wall.

I just commenced to feel the fainting coming on again, and the sensation that this was the last struggle before complete annihilation – when, on a sudden, a violent uproar reached my ears. It had some resemblance to the prolonged rumbling voice of thunder, and I clearly distinguished sonorous voices, lost one after the other, in the distant depths of the gulf.

Whence came this noise? Naturally, it was to be supposed from new phenomena which were taking place in the bosom of the solid mass of Mother Earth! The explosion of some gaseous vapours, or the fall of some solid, of the granitic or other rock.

Again I listened with deep attention. I was extremely anxious to hear if this strange and inexplicable sound was likely to be renewed! A whole quarter of an hour elapsed in painful expectation. Deep and solemn silence reigned in the tunnel. So still that I could hear the beatings of my own heart! I waited, waited with a strange kind of hopefulness.

Suddenly my ear, which leaned accidentally against the wall, appeared to catch, as it were, the faintest echo of a sound. I thought that I heard vague, incoherent and distant voices. I quivered all over with excitement and hope!

"It must be hallucination," I cried. "It cannot be! it is not true!"

But no! By listening more attentively, I really did convince myself that what I heard was truly the sound of human voices. To make any meaning out of the sound, however, was beyond my power. I was too weak even to hear distinctly. Still it was a positive fact that someone was speaking. Of that I was quite certain.

There was a moment of fear. A dread fell upon my soul that it might be my own words brought back to me by a distant echo. Perhaps without knowing it, I might have been crying aloud. I resolutely closed my lips, and once more placed my ear to the huge granite wall.

Yes, for certain. It was in truth the sound of human voices.

I now by the exercise of great determination dragged myself along the sides of the cavern, until I reached a point where I could hear more distinctly. But though I could detect the sound, I could only make out uncertain, strange, and incomprehensible words. They reached my ear as if they had been spoken in a low tone – murmured, as it were, afar off.

At last, I made out the word forlorad repeated several times in a tone betokening great mental anguish and sorrow.

What could this word mean, and who was speaking it? It must be either my uncle or the guide Hans! If, therefore, I could hear them, they must surely be able to hear me.

"Help," I cried at the top of my voice; "help, I am dying!"

I then listened with scarcely a breath; I panted for the slightest sound in the darkness – a cry, a sigh, a question! But silence reigned supreme. No answer came! In this way some minutes passed. A whole flood of ideas flashed through my mind. I began to fear that my voice, weakened by sickness and suffering, could not reach my companions who were in search of me.

"It must be they," I cried; "who else could by any possibility be buried a hundred miles below the level of the earth?" The mere supposition was preposterous.

I began, therefore, to listen again with the most breathless attention. As I moved my ears along the side of the place I was in, I found a mathematical point as it were, where the voices appeared to attain their maximum of intensity. The word forlorad again distinctly reached my ear. Then came again that rolling noise like thunder which had awakened me out of torpor.

"I begin to understand," I said to myself after some little time devoted to reflection; "it is not through the solid mass that the sound reaches my ears. The walls of my cavernous retreat are of solid granite, and the most fearful explosion would not make uproar enough to penetrate them. The sound must come along the gallery itself. The place I was in must possess some peculiar acoustic properties of its own."

Again I listened; and this time – yes, this time – I heard my name distinctly pronounced: cast as it were into space.

It was my uncle, the Professor, who was speaking. He was in

conversation with the guide, and the word which had so often reached my ears, forlorad, was a Danish expression.

Then I understood it all. In order to make myself heard, I too must speak as it were along the side of the gallery, which would carry the sound of my voice just as the wire carries the electric fluid from point to point.

But there was no time to lose. If my companions were only to remove a few feet from where they stood, the acoustic effect would be over, my Whispering Gallery would be destroyed. I again therefore crawled towards the wall, and said as clearly and distinctly as I could:

"Uncle Hardwigg."

I then awaited a reply.

Sound does not possess the property of traveling with such extreme rapidity. Besides the density of the air at that depth from light and motion was very far from adding to the rapidity of circulation. Several seconds elapsed, which to my excited imagination, appeared ages; and these words reached my eager ears, and moved my wildly beating heart:

"Harry, my boy, is that you?"

A short delay between question and answer.

"Yes – yes."

"Where are you?"

"Lost!"

"And your lamp?"

"Out."

"But the guiding stream?"

"Is lost!"

"Keep your courage, Harry. We will do our best."

"One moment, my uncle," I cried; "I have no longer strength to answer your questions. But – for heaven's sake – do you – continue – to speak – to me!" Absolute silence, I felt, would be annihilation.

"Keep up your courage," said my uncle. "As you are so weak, do not speak. We have been searching for you in all directions, both by going upwards and downwards in the gallery. My dear boy, I had begun to give over all hope – and you can never know what bitter tears of sorrow and regret I have shed. At last, supposing you to be still on the road beside the Hansbach, we again descended, firing off guns as signals. Now, however, that we have found you, and that our voices reach each other, it may be a long time before we actually meet. We are conversing by means of some extraordinary acoustic arrangement of the labyrinth. But do not despair, my dear boy. It is something gained even to hear each other."

While he was speaking, my brain was at work reflecting. A certain undefined hope, vague and shapeless as yet, made my heart beat wildly. In the first place, it was absolutely necessary for me to know one thing. I once more, therefore, leaned my head against the wall, which I almost touched with my lips, and again spoke.

"Uncle."

"My boy?" was his answer after a few moments.

"It is of the utmost consequence that we should know how far we are asunder."

"That is not difficult."

"You have your chronometer at hand?" I asked.

"Certainly."

"Well, take it into your hand. Pronounce my name, noting exactly the second at which you speak. I will reply as soon as I hear your words – and you will then note exactly the moment at which my reply reaches you."

"Very good; and the mean time between my question and your answer will be the time occupied by my voice in reaching you."

"That is exactly what I mean, Uncle," was my eager reply.

"Are you ready?"

"Yes."

"Well, make ready, I am about to pronounce your name," said the Professor.

I applied my ear close to the sides of the cavernous gallery, and as soon as the word "Harry" reached my ear, I turned round and, placing my lips to the wall, repeated the sound.

"Forty seconds," said my uncle. "There has elapsed forty seconds between the two words. The sound, therefore, takes twenty seconds to ascend. Now, allowing a thousand and twenty feet for every second – we have twenty thousand four hundred feet – a league and a half and one-eighth."

These words fell on my soul like a kind of death knell.

"A league and a half," I muttered in a low and despairing voice.

"It shall be got over, my boy," cried my uncle in a cheery tone; "depend on us."

"But do you know whether to ascend or descend?" I asked faintly enough.

"We have to descend, and I will tell you why. You have reached a vast open space, a kind of bare crossroad, from which galleries diverge in every direction. That in which you are now lying must necessarily bring you to this point, for it appears that all these mighty fissures, these fractures of the globe's interior, radiate from the vast cavern which we at this moment occupy. Rouse yourself, then, have courage and continue your route. Walk if you can, if not drag yourself along – slide, if nothing else is possible. The slope must be rather rapid – and you will find strong arms to receive you at the end of your journey. Make a start, like a good fellow."

These words served to rouse some kind of courage in my sinking frame.

"Farewell for the present, good uncle, I am about to take my departure. As soon as I start, our voices will cease to commingle. Farewell, then, until we meet again."

"Adieu, Harry – until we say Welcome." Such were the last

words which reached my anxious ears before I commenced my weary and almost hopeless journey.

This wonderful and surprising conversation which took place through the vast mass of the earth's labyrinth, these words exchanged, the speakers being about five miles apart – ended with hopeful and pleasant expressions. I breathed one more prayer to Heaven, I sent up words of thanksgiving – believing in my inmost heart that He had led me to the only place where the voices of my friends could reach my ears.

This apparently astounding acoustic mystery is easily explainable by simple natural laws; it arose from the conductibility of the rock. There are many instances of this singular propagation of sound which are not perceptible in its less mediate positions. In the interior gallery of St. Paul's, and amid the curious caverns in Sicily, these phenomena are observable. The most marvelous of them all is known as the Ear of Dionysius.

These memories of the past, of my early reading and studies, came fresh to my thoughts. Moreover, I began to reason that if my uncle and I could communicate at so great a distance, no serious obstacle could exist between us. All I had to do was to follow the direction whence the sound had reached me; and logically putting it, I must reach him if my strength did not fail.

I accordingly rose to my feet. I soon found, however, that I could not walk; that I must drag myself along. The slope as I expected was very rapid; but I allowed myself to slip down.

Soon the rapidity of the descent began to assume frightful proportions; and menaced a fearful fall. I clutched at the sides; I grasped at projections of rocks; I threw myself backwards. All in vain. My weakness was so great I could do nothing to save myself.

Suddenly earth failed me.

I was first launched into a dark and gloomy void. I then struck against the projecting asperities of a vertical gallery, a perfect well. My head bounded against a pointed rock, and I lost all knowledge of existence. As far as I was concerned, death had claimed me for his own.

When I returned to the consciousness of existence, I found myself surrounded by a kind of semiobscurity, lying on some thick and soft coverlets. My uncle was watching – his eyes fixed intently on my countenance, a grave expression on his face, a tear in his eye. At the first sigh which struggled from my bosom, he took hold of my hand. When he saw my eyes open and fix themselves upon his, he uttered a loud cry of loud cry of joy. "He lives! he lives!"

"Yes, my good uncle," I whispered.

"My dear boy," continued the grim Professor, clasping me to his heart, "you are saved!"

King Solomon's Mines

A Visit to King Solomon's Mines

H Rider Haggard

The story so far

Allan Quatermain, the narrator of the story, is travelling in a remote part of Africa with two companions, Good, a soldier, and Sir Henry Curtis. Sir Henry has invited the other two on a mission to find his brother, who disappeared when he went on the trail of the great treasure hidden in King Solomon's Mines. Quatermain knows of two other attempts to find the treasure, one by a Portuguese explorer who travelled there three hundred years ago, and another by a man who searched for it in more recent times. During their quest, the three explorers rid the country of Kukuanaland of its cruel king, Twala, and put a new king on the throne – a man who is travelling with them as their servant, but is in fact the rightful heir. The new king then helps the men to travel to the mines, accompanied by his trusted counsellor Infadoos, the evil witch doctor Gagool, and a young servant girl Foulata who has fallen deeply in love with Good.

A Visit to King Solomon's Mines
from
King Solomon's Mines
by
H Rider Haggard

It was already dark on the third day after the scene described in the previous chapter when we camped in some huts at the foot of the 'Three Witches', as the triangle of mountains is called to which Solomon's Great Road runs. Our party consisted of our three selves and Foulata, who waited on us – especially on Good – Infadoos, Gagool, who was borne along in a litter, inside which she could be heard muttering and cursing all day long, and a party of guards and attendants. The mountains, or rather the three peaks of the mountain, for the mass was evidently the result of a solitary upheaval, were, as I have said, in the form of a triangle, of which the base was towards us, one peak being on our right, one on our left, and one straight in front of us. Never shall I forget the sight afforded by those three towering peaks in the early sunlight of the following morning. High, high above us, up into the blue air, soared their twisted snow-wreaths. Beneath the snow-line the peaks were purple with heaths, and so were the wild moors that ran up the slopes towards them. Straight before us the white ribbon of Solomon's Great Road stretched away uphill to the foot of the centre peak, about five miles from us, and there stopped. It was its terminus.

I had better leave the feelings of intense excitement with which

we set out on our march that morning to the imagination of those who read this history. At last we were drawing near to the wonderful mines that had been the cause of the miserable death of the old Portuguese Dom three centuries ago, of my poor friend, his ill-starred descendant, and also, as we feared, of George Curtis, Sir Henry's brother. Were we destined, after all that we had gone through, to fare any better? Evil befell them, as that old fiend Gagool said; would it also befall us? Somehow, as we were marching up that last stretch of beautiful road, I could not help feeling a little superstitious about the matter, and so I think did Good and Sir Henry.

For an hour and a half or more we tramped on up the heather-fringed way, going so fast in our excitement that the bearers of Gagool's hammock could scarcely keep pace with us, and its occupant piped out to us to stop.

"Walk more slowly, white men," she said, projecting her hideous shrivelled countenance between the grass curtains, and fixing her gleaming eyes upon us; "why will ye run to meet the evil that shall befall you, ye seekers after treasure?" and she laughed that horrible laugh which always sent a cold shiver down my back, and for a while quite took the enthusiasm out of us.

However, on we went, till we saw before us, and between ourselves and the peak, a vast circular hole with sloping sides, three hundred feet or more in depth, and quite half a mile round.

"Can't you guess what this is?" I said to Sir Henry and Good, who were staring in astonishment at the awful pit before us.

They shook their heads.

"Then it is clear that you have never seen the diamond diggings at Kimberley. You may depend on it that this is Solomon's Diamond Mine. Look there," I said, pointing to the strata of stiff blue clay which were yet to be seen among the grass and bushes that clothed the sides of the pit, "the formation is the same. I'll be bound that if we went down there we should find 'pipes' of soapy brecciated rock. Look, too," and I pointed to a series of worn flat slabs of stone that were placed on a gentle slope below the level of a watercourse which in some past age had been cut out of the solid rock; "if those are not tables once used to wash the 'stuff,' I'm a Dutchman."

At the edge of this vast hole, which was none other than the pit marked on the old Dom's map, the Great Road branched into two and circumvented it. In many places, by the way, this surrounding road was built entirely out of blocks of stone, apparently with the object of supporting the edges of the pit and preventing falls of reef. Along this path we pressed, driven by curiosity to see what were the three towering objects which we could discern from the hither side of the great gulf. As we drew near we perceived that they were Colossi of some sort or another, and rightly conjectured that before us sat the three "Silent Ones" that are held in such awe by the Kukuana people. But it was not until we were quite close to them that we recognised the full majesty of these 'Silent Ones'.

There, upon huge pedestals of dark rock, sculptured with rude emblems of the Phallic worship, separated from each other by a distance of forty paces, and looking down the road which crossed some sixty miles of plain to Loo, were three colossal seated forms – two male and one female – each measuring about thirty feet from the crown of its head to the pedestal.

The female form, which was nude, was of great though severe beauty, but unfortunately the features had been injured by centuries of exposure to the weather. Rising from either side of her head were the points of a crescent. The two male Colossi, on the contrary, were draped, and presented a terrifying cast of features, especially the one to our right, which had the face of a devil. That to our left was serene in countenance, but the calm upon it seemed dreadful. It was the calm of that inhuman cruelty, Sir Henry remarked, which the ancients attributed to beings potent for good, who could yet watch the sufferings of humanity, if not without rejoicing, at least without sorrow. These three statues form a most awe-inspiring trinity, as they sit there in their solitude, and gaze out across the plain for ever.

Contemplating these 'Silent Ones', as the Kukuanas call them, an intense curiosity again seized us to know whose were the hands which had shaped them, who it was that had dug the pit and made the road. Whilst I was gazing and wondering, suddenly it occurred to me – being familiar with the Old Testament – that Solomon went astray after strange gods, the names of three of whom I remembered – 'Ashtoreth, the goddess of the Zidonians, Chemosh, the god of the Moabites, and Milcom, the god of the children of Ammon' – and I suggested to my companions that the figures before us might represent these false and exploded divinities.

"Hum," said Sir Henry, who is a scholar, having taken a high degree in classics at college, "there may be something in that; Ashtoreth of the Hebrews was the Astarte of the Phoenicians, who were the great traders of Solomon's time. Astarte, who afterwards became the Aphrodite of the Greeks, was represented with horns like the half-moon, and there on the brow of the female figure are distinct horns. Perhaps these Colossi were designed by some Phœnician official who managed the mines. Who can say?" Before we had finished examining these extraordinary relics of remoteantiquity, Infadoos came up, and having saluted the 'Silent Ones' by lifting his spear, asked us if we intended entering the "Place of Death" at once, or if we would wait till after we had taken food at mid-day. If we were ready to go at once, Gagool had announced her willingness to guide us. As it was not later than eleven o'clock – driven to it by a burning curiosity – we announced our intention of proceeding instantly, and I suggested that, in case we should be detained in the cave, we should take some food with us. Accordingly Gagool's litter was brought up, and that lady herself assisted out of it. Meanwhile Foulata, at my request, stored some 'biltong', or dried game-flesh, together with a couple of gourds of water, in a reed basket with a hinged cover. Straight in front of us, at a distance of some fifty paces from the backs of the Colossi, rose a sheer wall of rock, eighty feet or more in height, that gradually sloped upwards till it formed the base of the lofty snow-wreathed peak, which soared into the air three thousand feet above us. As soon as she was clear of her hammock, Gagool cast one evil grin upon us, and then, leaning on a stick, hobbled off towards the face of this wall. We followed her till we came to a narrow portal solidly arched that looked like the opening of a gallery of a mine.

Here Gagool was waiting for us, still with that evil grin upon her horrid face.

"Now, white men from the Stars," she piped; "great warriors, Incubu, Bougwan, and Macumazahn the wise, are ye ready? Behold, I am here to do the bidding of my lord the king, and to show you the store of bright stones. Ha! ha! ha!"

"We are ready," I said.

"Good, good! Make strong your hearts to bear what ye shall see. Comest thou too, Infadoos, thou who didst betray thy master?"

Infadoos frowned as he answered –

"Nay, I come not; it is not for me to enter there. But thou, Gagool, curb thy tongue, and beware how thou dealest with my lords. At thy hands will I require them, and if a hair of them be hurt, Gagool, be'st thou fifty times a witch, thou shalt die. Hearest thou?"

"I hear Infadoos; I know thee, thou didst ever love big words; when thou wast a babe I remember thou didst threaten thine own mother. That was but the other day. But, fear not, fear not, I live only to do the bidding of the king. I have done the bidding of many kings, Infadoos, till in the end they did mine. Ha! ha! I go to look upon their faces once more, and Twala's also! Come on, come on, here is the lamp," and she drew a large gourd full of oil, and fitted with a rush wick, from under her fur cloak.

"Art thou coming, Foulata?" asked Good in his villainous Kitchen Kukuana, in which he had been improving himself under that young lady's tuition.

"I fear, my lord," the girl answered timidly.

"Then give me the basket."

"Nay, my lord, whither thou goest there I go also."

"The deuce you will!" thought I to myself; "that may be rather awkward if we ever get out of this."

Without further ado Gagool plunged into the passage, which was wide enough to admit of two walking abreast, and quite dark. We followed the sound of her voice as she piped to us to come on, in some fear and trembling, which was not allayed by the flutter of a sudden rush of wings.

"Hullo! what's that?" halloed Good; "somebody hit me in the face."

"Bats," said I; "on you go."

When, so far as we could judge, we had gone some fifty paces, we perceived that the passage was growing faintly light. Another minute, and we were in perhaps the most wonderful place that the eyes of living man have beheld.

Let the reader picture to himself the hall of the vastest cathedral he ever stood in, windowless indeed, but dimly lighted from above, presumably by shafts connected with the outer air and driven in the roof, which arched away a hundred feet above our heads, and he will get some idea of the size of the enormous cave in which we found ourselves, with the difference that this cathedral designed

... this cathedral designed by nature was loftier and wider than any built by man.

by nature was loftier and wider than any built by man. But its stupendous size was the least of the wonders of the place, for running in rows adown its length were gigantic pillars of what looked like ice, but were, in reality, huge stalactites. It is impossible for me to convey any idea of the overpowering beauty and grandeur of these pillars of white spar, some of which were not less than twenty feet in diameter at the base, and sprang up in lofty and yet delicate beauty sheer to the distant roof. Others again were in process of formation. On the rock floor there was in these cases what looked, Sir Henry said, exactly like a broken column in an old Grecian temple, whilst high above, depending from the roof, the point of a huge icicle could be dimly seen.

Even as we gazed we could hear the process going on, for presently with a tiny splash a drop of water would fall from the far-off icicle on to the column below. On some columns the drops only fell once in two or three minutes, and in these cases it would be an interesting calculation to discover how long, at that rate of dripping, it would take to form a pillar, say eighty feet by ten in diameter. That the process, in at least one instance, was incalculably slow, the following example will suffice to show. Cut on one of these pillars we discovered the crude likeness of a mummy, by the head of which sat what appeared to be the figure of an Egyptian god, doubtless the handiwork of some old-world labourer in the mine. This work of art was executed at the natural height at which an idle fellow, be he Phœnician workman or

British cad, is in the habit of trying to immortalise himself at the expense of nature's masterpieces, namely, about five feet from the ground. Yet at the time that we saw it, which must have been nearly three thousand years after the date of the execution of the carving, the column was only eight feet high, and was still in process of formation, which gives a rate of growth of a foot to a thousand years, or an inch and a fraction to a century. This we knew because, as we were standing by it, we heard a drop of water fall.

Sometimes the stalagmites took strange forms, presumably where the dropping of the water had not always been on the same spot. Thus, one huge mass, which must have weighed a hundred tons or so, was in the shape of a pulpit, beautifully fretted over outside with a design that looked like lace. Others resembled strange beasts, and on the sides of the cave were fanlike ivory tracings, such as the frost leaves upon a pane.

Out of the vast main aisle there opened here and there smaller caves, exactly, Sir Henry said, as chapels open out of great cathedrals. Some were large, but one or two – and this is a wonderful instance of how nature carries out her handiwork by the same unvarying laws, utterly irrespective of size – were tiny. One little nook, for instance, was no larger than an unusually big doll's house, and yet it might have been a model for the whole place, for the water dropped, tiny icicles hung, and spar columns were forming in just the same way.

We had not, however, enough time to examine this beautiful cavern so thoroughly as we should have liked to do, since unfortunately, Gagool seemed to be indifferent as to stalactites, and only anxious to get her business over. This annoyed me the more, as I was particularly anxious to discover, if possible, by what system the light was admitted into the cave, and whether it was by the hand of man or by that of nature that this was done; also if the place had been used in any way in ancient times, as seemed probable. However, we consoled ourselves with the idea that we would investigate it thoroughly on our way back, and followed on at the heels of our uncanny guide.

On she led us, straight to the top of the vast and silent cave, where we found another doorway, not arched as the first was, but square at the top, something like the doorways of Egyptian temples.

"Are ye prepared to enter the Place of Death, white men?" asked Gagool, evidently with a view to making us feel uncomfortable.

"Lead on, Macduff," said Good solemnly, trying to look as though he was not at all alarmed, as indeed we all did except Foulata, who caught Good by the arm for protection.

"This is getting rather ghastly," said Sir Henry, peeping into the dark passageway. "Come on, Quatermain – seniores priores. We mustn't keep the old lady waiting!" and he politely made way for me to lead the van, for which inwardly I did not bless him.

Tap, tap, went old Gagool's stick down the passage, as she

trotted along, chuckling hideously; and still overcome by some unaccountable presentiment of evil, I hung back.

"Come, get on, old fellow," said Good, "or we shall lose our fair guide."

Thus adjured, I started down the passage, and after about twenty paces found myself in a gloomy apartment some forty feet long, by thirty broad, and thirty high, which in some past age evidently had been hollowed, by hand-labour, out of the mountain. This apartment was not nearly so well lighted as the vast stalactite ante-cave, and at the first glance all I could discern was a massive stone table running down its length, with a colossal white figure at its head, and life- sized white figures all round it. Next I discovered a brown thing, seated on the table in the centre, and in another moment my eyes grew accustomed to the light, and I saw what all these things were, and was tailing out of the place as hard as my legs could carry me.

I am not a nervous man in a general way, and very little troubled with superstitions, of which I have lived to see the folly; but I am free to own that this sight quite upset me, and had it not been that Sir Henry caught me by the collar and held me, I do honestly believe that in another five minutes I should have been outside the stalactite cave, and that a promise of all the diamonds in Kimberley would not have induced me to enter it again. But he held me tight, so I stopped because I could not help myself. Next second, however, his eyes became accustomed to the light, and he let go of me, and began to mop the perspiration off his forehead. As for Good, he swore feebly, while Foulata threw her arms round his neck and shrieked.

Only Gagool chuckled loud and long.

It was a ghastly sight. There at the end of the long stone table, holding in his skeleton fingers a great white spear, sat Death himself, shaped in the form of a colossal human skeleton, fifteen feet or more in height. High above his head he held the spear, as though in the act to strike; one bony hand rested on the stone table before him, in the position a man assumes on rising from his seat, whilst his frame was bent forward so that the vertebræ of the neck and the grinning, gleaming skull projected towards us, and fixed its hollow eye-places upon us, the jaws a little open, as though it were about to speak.

"Great heavens!" said I faintly, at last, "what can it be?"

"And what are those things?" asked Good, pointing to the white company round the table.

"And what on earth is that thing?" said Sir Henry, pointing to the brown creature seated on the table.

"Hee! hee! hee!" laughed Gagool. "To those who enter the Hall of the Dead, evil comes. Hee! hee! hee! ha! ha!"

"Come, Incubu, brave in battle, come and see him thou slewest;" and the old creature caught Curtis' coat in her skinny fingers, and led him away towards the table. We followed.

Presently she stopped and pointed at the brown object seated on the table. Sir Henry looked, and started back with an exclamation; and no wonder, for there, quite naked, the head which Curtis' battle-axe had shorn from the body resting on its knees, was the gaunt corpse of Twala, the last king of the Kukuanas. Yes, there, the head perched upon the knees, it sat in all its ugliness, the vertebræ projecting a full inch above the level of the shrunken flesh of the neck, for all the world like a black double of Hamilton Tighe. Over the surface of the corpse there was gathered a thin glassy film, that made its appearance yet more appalling, for which we were, at the moment, quite unable to account, till presently we observed that from the roof of the chamber the water fell steadily, drip! drop! drip! on to the neck of the corpse, whence it ran down over the entire surface, and finally escaped into the rock through a tiny hole in the table. Then I guessed what the film was – Twala's body was being transformed into a stalactite.

A look at the white forms seated on the stone bench which ran round that ghastly board confirmed this view. They were human bodies indeed, or rather they had been human; now they were stalactites. This was the way in which the Kukuana people had from time immemorial preserved their royal dead. They petrified them. What the exact system might be, if there was any, beyond the placing of them for a long period of years under the drip, I never discovered, but there they sat, iced over and preserved for ever by the siliceous fluid.

Anything more awe-inspiring than the spectacle of this long line of departed royalties (there were twenty-seven of them, the last being Ignosi's father), wrapped, each of them, in a shroud of ice-like spar, through which the features could be dimly discovered, and seated round that inhospitable board, with Death himself for a host, it is impossible to imagine. That the practice of thus preserving their kings must have been an ancient one is evident from the number, which, allowing for an average reign of fifteen years, supposing that every king who reigned was placed here – an improbable thing, as some are sure to have perished in battle far from home – would fix the date of its commencement at four and a quarter centuries back.

But the colossal Death, who sits at the head of the board, is far older than that, and, unless I am much mistaken, owes his origin to the same artist who designed the three Colossi. He is hewn out of a single stalactite, and, looked at as a work of art, is most admirably conceived and executed. Good, who understands such things, declared that, so far as he could see, the anatomical design of the skeleton is perfect down to the smallest bones.

My own idea is, that this terrific object was a freak of fancy on the part of some old-world sculptor, and that its presence had suggested to the Kukuanas the idea of placing their royal dead under its awful presidency. Or perhaps it was set there to frighten away any marauders who might have designs upon the treasure chamber beyond. I cannot say. All I can do is to describe it as it is, and the reader must form his own conclusion.

Such, at any rate, was the White Death and such were the White Dead!

While we were engaged in recovering from our fright, and in examining the grisly wonders of the Place of Death, Gagool had been differently occupied. Somehow or other – for she was marvellously active when she chose – she had scrambled on to the great table, and made her way to where our departed friend Twala was placed, under the drip, to see, suggested Good, how he was 'pickling', or for some dark purpose of her own. Then, after bending down to kiss his icy lips as though in affectionate greeting, she hobbled back, stopping now and again to address the remark, the tenor of which I could not catch, to one or other of the shrouded forms, just as you or I might welcome an old acquaintance. Having gone through this mysterious and horrible ceremony, she squatted herself down on the table immediately under the White Death, and began, so far as I could make out, to offer up prayers. The spectacle of this wicked creature pouring out supplications, evil ones no doubt, to the arch enemy of mankind, was so uncanny that it caused us to hasten our inspection.

"Now, Gagool," said I, in a low voice – somehow one did not dare to speak above a whisper in that place – "lead us to the chamber."

The old witch promptly scrambled down from the table.

"My lords are not afraid?" she said, leering up into my face.

"Lead on."

"Good, my lords;" and she hobbled round to the back of the great Death. "Here is the chamber; let my lords light the lamp, and enter," and she placed the gourd full of oil upon the floor, and leaned herself against the side of the cave. I took out a match, of which we had still a few in a box, and lit a rush wick, and then looked for the doorway, but there was nothing before us except the solid rock. Gagool grinned. "The way is there, my lords. Ha! ha! ha!"

"Do not jest with us," I said sternly.

"I jest not, my lords. See!" and she pointed at the rock.

As she did so, on holding up the lamp we perceived that a mass of stone was rising slowly from the floor and vanishing into the rock above, where doubtless there is a cavity prepared to receive it.

The mass was of the width of a good-sized door, about ten feet high and not less than five feet thick. It must have weighed at least twenty or thirty tons, and was clearly moved upon some simple balance principle of counter-weights, probably the same as that by which the opening and shutting of an ordinary modern window is arranged. How the principle was set in motion, of course none of us saw; Gagool was careful to avoid this; but I have little doubt that there was some very simple lever, which was moved ever so little by pressure at a secret spot, thereby throwing additional weight on to the hidden counter-balances, and causing the

monolith to be lifted from the ground.

Very slowly and gently the great stone raised itself, till at last it had vanished altogether, and a dark hole presented itself to us in the place which the door had filled.

Our excitement was so intense, as we saw the way to Solomon's treasure chamber thrown open at last, that I for one began to tremble and shake. Would it prove a hoax after all, I wondered, or was old Da Silvestra right? Were there vast hoards of wealth hidden in that dark place, hoards which would make us the richest men in the whole world? We should know in a minute or two.

"Enter, white men from the Stars," said Gagool, advancing into the doorway; "but first hear your servant, Gagool the old. The bright stones that ye will see were dug out of the pit over which the Silent Ones are set, and stored here, I know not by whom, for that was done longer ago than even I remember. But once has this place been entered since the time that those who hid the stones departed in haste, leaving them behind. The report of the treasure went down indeed among the people who lived in the country from age to age, but none knew where the chamber was, nor the secret of the door. But it happened that a white man reached this country from over the mountains – perchance he too came 'from the Stars' – and was well received by the king of that day. He it is who sits yonder," and she pointed to the fifth king at the table of the Dead. "And it came to pass that he and a woman of the country who was with him journeyed to this place, and that by chance the woman learnt the secret of the door – a thousand years might ye search, but ye should never find that secret. Then the white man entered with the woman, and found the stones, and filled with stones the skin of a small goat, which the woman had with her to hold food. And as he was going from the chamber he took up one more stone, a large one, and held it in his hand."

Here she paused.

"Well," I asked, breathless with interest as we all were, "what happened to Da Silvestra?"

The old hag started at the mention of the name.

"How knowest thou the dead man's name?" she asked sharply; and then, without waiting for an answer, went on –

"None can tell what happened; but it came about that the white man was frightened, for he flung down the goat-skin, with the stones, and fled out with only the one stone in his hand, and that the king took, and it is the stone which thou, Macumazahn, didst take from Twala's brow."

"Have none entered here since?" I asked, peering again down the dark passage.

"None, my lords. Only the secret of the door has been kept, and every king has opened it, though he has not entered. There is a saying, that those who enter there will die within a moon, even as the white man died in the cave upon the mountain, where ye found him, Macumazahn, and therefore the kings do not enter. Ha! ha! mine are true words."

Our eyes met as she said it, and I turned sick and cold. How did the old hag know all these things?

"Enter, my lords. If I speak truth, the goat-skin with the stones will lie upon the floor; and if there is truth as to whether it is death to enter here, that ye will learn afterwards. Ha! ha! ha!" and she hobbled through the doorway, bearing the light with her; but I confess that once more I hesitated about following.

"Oh, confound it all!" said Good; "here goes. I am not going to be frightened by that old devil;" and followed by Foulata, who, however, evidently did not at all like the business, for she was shivering with fear, he plunged into the passage after Gagool – an example which we quickly followed.

A few yards down the passage, in the narrow way hewn out of the living rock, Gagool had paused, and was waiting for us.

"See, my lords," she said, holding the light before her, "those who stored the treasure here fled in haste, and bethought them to guard against any who should find the secret of the door, but had not the time," and she pointed to large square blocks of stone, which, to the height of two courses (about two feet three), had been placed across the passage with a view to walling it up. Along the side of the passage were similar blocks ready for use, and, most curious of all, a heap of mortar and a couple of trowels, which tools, so far as we had time to examine them, appeared to be of a similar shape and make to those used by workmen to this day.

Here Foulata, who had been in a state of great fear and

agitation throughout, said that she felt faint and could go no farther, but would wait there. Accordingly we set her down on the unfinished wall, placing the basket of provisions by her side, and left her to recover.

Following the passage for about fifteen paces farther, we came suddenly to an elaborately painted wooden door. It was standing wide open. Whoever was last there had either not found the time to shut it, or had forgotten to do so.

Across the threshold of this door lay a skin bag, formed of a goat-skin, that appeared to be full of pebbles.

"Hee! hee! white men," sniggered Gagool, as the light from the lamp fell upon it. "What did I tell you, that the white man who came here fled in haste, and dropped the woman's bag – behold it! Look within also and ye will find a water-gourd amongst the stones."

Good stooped down and lifted it. It was heavy and jingled.

"By Jove! I believe it's full of diamonds," he said, in an awed whisper; and, indeed, the idea of a small goat-skin full of diamonds is enough to awe anybody.

"Go on," said Sir Henry impatiently. "Here, old lady, give me the lamp," and taking it from Gagool's hand, he stepped through the doorway and held it high above his head.

We pressed in after him, forgetful for the moment of the bag of diamonds, and found ourselves in King Solomon's treasure chamber.

At first, all that the somewhat faint light given by the lamp revealed was a room hewn out of the living rock, and apparently not more than ten feet square. Next there came into sight, stored one on the other to the arch of the roof, a splendid collection of elephant-tusks. How many of them there were we did not know, for of course we could not see to what depth they went back, but there could not have been less than the ends of four or five hundred tusks of the first quality visible to our eyes. There, alone, was enough ivory to make a man wealthy for life. Perhaps, I thought, it was from this very store that Solomon drew the raw material for his 'great throne of ivory', of which "there was not the like made in any kingdom."

On the opposite side of the chamber were about a score of wooden boxes, something like Martini-Henry ammunition boxes, only rather larger, and painted red.

"There are the diamonds," cried I; "bring the light."

Sir Henry did so, holding it close to the top box, of which the lid, rendered rotten by time even in that dry place, appeared to have been smashed in, probably by Da Silvestra himself. Pushing my hand through the hole in the lid I drew it out full, not of diamonds, but of gold pieces, of a shape that none of us had seen before, and with what looked like Hebrew characters stamped upon them.

"Ah!" I said, replacing the coin, "we shan't go back empty-handed, anyhow. There must be a couple of thousand pieces in

each box, and there are eighteen boxes. I suppose this was the money to pay the workmen and merchants."

"Well," put in Good, "I think that is the lot; I don't see any diamonds, unless the old Portuguese put them all into his bag."

"Let my lords look yonder where it is darkest, if they would find the stones," said Gagool, interpreting our looks. "There my lords will find a nook, and three stone chests in the nook, two sealed and one open."

Before translating this to Sir Henry, who carried the light, I could not resist asking how she knew these things, if no one had entered the place since the white man, generations ago.

"Ah, Macumazahn, the watcher by night," was the mocking answer, "ye who dwell in the stars, do ye not know that some live long, and that some have eyes which can see through rock? Ha! ha! ha!"

"Look in that corner, Curtis," I said, indicating the spot Gagool had pointed out.

"Hullo, you fellows," he cried, "here's a recess. Great heavens! see here."

We hurried up to where he was standing in a nook, shaped something like a small bow window. Against the wall of this recess were placed three stone chests, each about two feet square. Two were fitted with stone lids, the lid of the third rested against the side of the chest, which was open.

"See!" he repeated hoarsely, holding the lamp over the open chest. We looked, and for a moment could make nothing out, on account of a silvery sheen which dazzled us. When our eyes grew used to it we saw that the chest was three-parts full of uncut diamonds, most of them of considerable size. Stooping, I picked some up. Yes, there was no doubt of it, there was the unmistakable soapy feel about them.

I fairly gasped as I dropped them.

"We are the richest men in the whole world," I said. "Monte Christo was a fool to us."

"We shall flood the market with diamonds," said Good.

"Got to get them there first," suggested Sir Henry.

We stood still with pale faces and stared at each other, the lantern in the middle and the glimmering gems below, as though we were conspirators about to commit a crime, instead of being, as we thought, the most fortunate men on earth.

"Hee! hee! hee!" cackled old Gagool behind us, as she flitted about like a vampire bat. "There are the bright stones ye love, white men, as many as ye will; take them, run them through your fingers, eat of them, hee! hee! drink of them, ha! ha!"

At that moment there was something so ridiculous to my mind at the idea of eating and drinking diamonds, that I began to laugh outrageously, an example which the others followed, without knowing why. There we stood and shrieked with laughter over the gems that were ours, which had been found for us thousands of years ago by the patient delvers in the great hole yonder, and stored for us by Solomon's long-dead overseer, whose name, perchance, was written in the characters stamped on the faded wax that yet adhered to the lids of the chest. Solomon never got them, nor David, or Da Silvestra, nor anybody else. We had got them: there before us were millions of pounds' worth of diamonds, and thousands of pounds' worth of gold and ivory only waiting to be taken away.

Suddenly the fit passed off, and we stopped laughing.

"Open the other chests, white men," croaked Gagool, "there are surely more therein. Take your fill, white lords! Ha! ha! take your fill."

Thus adjured, we set to work to pull up the stone lids on the other two, first – not without a feeling of sacrilege – breaking the seals that fastened them.

Hoorah! they were full too, full to the brim; at least, the second one was; no wretched burglarious Da Silvestra had been filling goat-skins out of that. As for the third chest, it was only about a fourth full, but the stones were all picked ones; none less than twenty carats, and some of them as large as pigeon-eggs. A good many of these bigger ones, however, we could see by holding them up to the light, were a little yellow, "off coloured," as they call it at Kimberley.

What we did not see, however, was the look of fearful malevolence that old Gagool favoured us with as she crept, crept like a snake, out of the treasure chamber and down the passage towards the door of solid rock.

Hark! Cry upon cry comes ringing up the vaulted path. It is Foulata's voice!

"Oh, Bougwan! help! help! the stone falls!"

"Leave go, girl! Then – "

"Help! help! she has stabbed me!"

By now we are running down the passage, and this is what the light from the lamp shows us. The door of the rock is closing down slowly; it is not three feet from the floor. Near it struggle Foulata and Gagool. The red blood of the former runs to her knee, but still the brave girl holds the old witch, who fights like a wild cat. Ah! she is free! Foulata falls, and Gagool throws herself on the ground, to twist like a snake through the crack of the closing stone. She is under – ah! god! too late! too late! The stone nips her, and she yells in agony. Down, down it comes, all the thirty tons of it, slowly pressing her old body against the rock below. Shriek upon shriek, such as we have never heard, then a long sickening crunch, and the door was shut just as, rushing down the passage, we hurled ourselves against it.

It was all done in four seconds.

Then we turned to Foulata. The poor girl was stabbed in the body, and I saw that she could not live long.

"Ah! Bougwan, I die!" gasped the beautiful creature. "She crept out – Gagool; I did not see her, I was faint – and the door began to fall; then she came back, and was looking up the path – I saw her come in through the slowly falling door, and caught her and held her, and she stabbed me, and I die, Bougwan!"

"Poor girl! poor girl!" Good cried in his distress; and then, as he could do nothing else, he fell to kissing her.

"Bougwan," she said, after a pause, "is Macumazahn there?

It grows so dark, I cannot see."

"Here I am, Foulata."

"Macumazahn, be my tongue for a moment, I pray thee, for Bougwan cannot understand me, and before I go into the darkness I would speak to him a word."

"Say on, Foulata, I will render it."

"Say to my lord, Bougwan, that – I love him, and that I am glad to die because I know that he cannot cumber his life with such as I am, for the sun may not mate with the darkness, nor the white with the black.

"Say that, since I saw him, at times I have felt as though there were a bird in my bosom, which would one day fly hence and sing elsewhere. Even now, though I cannot lift my hand, and my brain grows cold, I do not feel as though my heart were dying; it is so full of love that it could live ten thousand years, and yet be young. Say that if I live again, mayhap I shall see him in the Stars, and that – I will search them all, though perchance there I should still be black and he would – still be white. Say – nay, Macumazahn, say no more, save that I love – Oh, hold me closer, Bougwan, I cannot feel thine arms – oh! oh! "

"She is dead – she is dead!" muttered Good, rising in grief, the tears running down his honest face.

"You need not let that trouble you, old fellow," said Sir Henry.

"Eh!" exclaimed Good; "what do you mean?"

"I mean that you will soon be in a position to join her. Man, don't you see that we are buried alive?"

Until Sir Henry uttered these words I do not think that the full horror of what had happened had come home to us, preoccupied as we were with the sight of poor Foulata's end. But now we understood. The ponderous mass of rock had closed, probably for ever, for the only brain which knew its secret was crushed to powder beneath its weight. This was a door that none could hope to force with anything short of dynamite in large quantities. And we were on the wrong side!

For a few minutes we stood horrified, there over the corpse of Foulata. All the manhood seemed to have gone out of us. The first shock of this idea of the slow and miserable end that awaited us was overpowering. We saw it all now; that fiend Gagool had planned this snare for us from the first.

It would have been just the jest that her evil mind would have rejoiced in, the idea of the three white men, whom, for some reason of her own, she had always hated, slowly perishing of thirst and hunger in the company of the treasure they had coveted. Now I saw the point of that sneer of hers about eating and drinking the diamonds. Probably somebody had tried to serve the poor old Dom in the same way, when he abandoned the skin full of jewels.

"This will never do," said Sir Henry hoarsely; "the lamp will soon go out. Let us see if we can't find the spring that works the rock."

We sprang forward with desperate energy, and, standing in a

bloody ooze, began to feel up and down the door and the sides of the passage. But no knob or spring could we discover.

"Depend on it," I said, "it does not work from the inside; if it did Gagool would not have risked trying to crawl underneath the stone. It was the knowledge of this that made her try to escape at all hazards, curse her."

"At all events," said Sir Henry, with a hard little laugh, "retribution was swift; hers was almost as awful an end as ours is likely to be. We can do nothing with the door; let us go back to the treasure room."

We turned and went, and as we passed it I perceived by the unfinished wall across the passage the basket of food which poor Foulata had carried. I took it up, and brought it with me to the accursed treasure chamber that was to be our grave. Then we returned and reverently bore in Foulata's corpse, laying it on the floor by the boxes of coin.

Next we seated ourselves, leaning our backs against the three stone chests which contained the priceless treasure.

"Let us divide the food," said Sir Henry, "so as to make it last as long as possible." Accordingly we did so. It would, we reckoned, make four infinitesimally small meals for each of us, enough, say, to support life for a couple of days. Besides the 'biltong', or dried game-flesh, there were two gourds of water, each of which held not more than a quart.

"Now," said Sir Henry grimly, "let us eat and drink, for

to-morrow we die."

We each ate a small portion of the 'biltong', and drank a sip of water. Needless to say, we had but little appetite, though we were sadly in need of food, and felt better after swallowing it. Then we got up and made a systematic examination of the walls of our prison-house, in the faint hope of finding some means of exit, sounding them and the floor carefully.

There was none. It was not probable that there would be any to a treasure chamber.

The lamp began to burn dim. The fat was nearly exhausted.

"Quatermain," said Sir Henry, "what is the time – your watch goes?"

I drew it out, and looked at it. It was six o'clock; we had entered the cave at eleven.

"Infadoos will miss us," I suggested. "If we do not return to-night he will search for us in the morning, Curtis."

"He may search in vain. He does not know the secret of the door, nor even where it is. No living person knew it yesterday, except Gagool. To-day no one knows it. Even if he found the door he could not break it down. All the Kukuana army could not break through five feet of living rock. My friends, I see nothing for it but to bow ourselves to the will of the Almighty. The search for treasure has brought many to a bad end; we shall go to swell their number."

The lamp grew dimmer yet.

Presently it flared up and showed the whole scene in strong relief, the great mass of white tusks, the boxes of gold, the corpse of the poor Foulata stretched before them, the goat-skin full of treasure, the dim glimmer of the diamonds, and the wild, wan faces of us three white men seated there awaiting death by starvation.

Then the flame sank and expired.

I can give no adequate description of the horrors of the night which followed. Mercifully they were to some extent mitigated by sleep, for even in such a position as ours wearied nature will sometimes assert itself. But I, at any rate, found it impossible to sleep much. Putting aside the terrifying thought of our impending doom – for the bravest man on earth might well quail from such a fate as awaited us, and I never made any pretensions to be brave – the silence itself was too great to allow of it. Reader, you may have lain awake at night and thought the quiet oppressive, but I say with confidence that you can have no idea what a vivid, tangible thing is perfect stillness. On the surface of the earth there is always some sound or motion, and though it may in itself be imperceptible, yet it deadens the sharp edge of absolute silence. But here there was none. We were buried in the bowels of a huge snow-clad peak. Thousands of feet above us the fresh air rushed over the white snow, but no sound of it reached us. We were separated by a long tunnel and five feet of rock even from the awful Chamber of the Dead; and the dead make no noise. Did we not know it who lay by poor Foulata's side? The crashing of all the artillery of earth and heaven could not have come to our ears in our living tomb. We were cut off from every echo of the world – we were as men already in the grave.

Then the irony of the situation forced itself upon me. There around us lay treasures enough to pay off a moderate national debt, or to build a fleet of ironclads, and yet we would have bartered them all gladly for the faintest chance of escape. Soon, doubtless, we should be rejoiced to exchange them for a bit of food or a cup of water, and, after that, even for the privilege of a speedy close to our sufferings. Truly wealth, which men spend their lives in acquiring, is a valueless thing at the last.

And so the night wore on.

"Good," said Sir Henry's voice at last, and it sounded awful in the intense stillness, "how many matches have you in the box?"

"Eight, Curtis."

"Strike one and let us see the time."

He did so, and in contrast to the dense darkness the flame nearly blinded us. It was five o'clock by my watch. The beautiful dawn was now blushing on the snow-wreaths far over our heads, and the breeze would be stirring the night mists in the hollows.

"We had better eat something and keep up our strength," I suggested.

"What is the good of eating?" answered Good; "the sooner we die and get it over the better."

"While there is life there is hope," said Sir Henry.

Accordingly we ate and sipped some water, and another period of time elapsed. Then Sir Henry suggested that it might be well to get as near the door as possible and halloa, on the faint chance of somebody catching a sound outside. Accordingly Good, who, from long practice at sea, has a fine piercing note, groped his way down the passage and set to work. I must say that he made a most diabolical noise. I never heard such yells; but it might have been a mosquito buzzing for all the effect they produced.

After a while he gave it up and came back very thirsty, and had to drink. Then we stopped yelling, as it encroached on the supply of water.

So we sat down once more against the chests of useless diamonds in that dreadful inaction which was one of the hardest circumstances of our fate; and I am bound to say that, for my part, I gave way in despair. Laying my head against Sir Henry's broad shoulder I burst into tears; and I think that I heard Good gulping away on the other side, and swearing hoarsely at himself for doing so.

Ah, how good and brave that great man was! Had we been two frightened children, and he our nurse, he could not have treated us more tenderly. Forgetting his own share of miseries, he did all he could to soothe our broken nerves, telling stories of men who had been in somewhat similar circumstances, and miraculously escaped; and when these failed to cheer us, pointing out how, after all, it was only anticipating an end which must come to us all, that it would soon be over, and that death from exhaustion was a merciful one (which is not true). Then, in a diffident sort of way, as once before I had heard him do, he suggested that we should throw ourselves on the mercy of a higher Power, which for my part I did with great vigour.

His is a beautiful character, very quiet, but very strong.

And so somehow the day went as the night had gone, if, indeed, one can use these terms where all was densest night, and when I lit a match to see the time it was seven o'clock.

Once more we ate and drank, and as we did so an idea occurred to me.

"How is it," said I, "that the air in this place keeps fresh? It is thick and heavy, but it is perfectly fresh."

"Great heavens!" said Good, starting up, "I never thought of that. It can't come through the stone door, for it's air-tight, if ever a door was. It must come from somewhere. It there were no current of air in the place we should have been stifled or poisoned when we first came in. Let us have a look."

It was wonderful what a change this mere spark of hope wrought in us. In a moment we were all three groping about on our hands and knees, feeling for the slightest indication of a draught. Presently my ardour received a check. I put my hand on something cold. It was dead Foulata's face.

For an hour or more we went on feeling about, till at last Sir Henry and I gave it up in despair, having been considerably hurt by constantly knocking our heads against tusks, chests, and the sides of the chamber. But Good still persevered, saying, with an approach to cheerfulness, that it was better than doing nothing.

"I say, you fellows," he said presently, in a constrained sort of voice, "come here."

Needless to say we scrambled towards him quickly enough.

"Quatermain, put your hand here where mine is. Now, do you feel anything?"

"I think I feel air coming up."

"Now listen." He rose and stamped upon the place, and a flame of hope shot up in our hearts. It rang hollow. With trembling hands I lit a match. I had only three left, and we saw that we were in the angle of the far corner of the chamber, a fact that accounted for our not having noticed the hollow sound of the place during our former exhaustive examination. As the match burnt we scrutinised the spot. There was a join in the solid rock floor, and, great heavens! there, let in level with the rock, was a stone ring. We said no word, we were too excited, and our hearts beat too wildly with hope to allow us to speak. Good had a knife, at the back of which was one of those hooks that are made to extract stones from horses' hoofs. He opened it, and scratched round the ring with it. Finally he worked it under, and levered away gently for fear of breaking the hook. The ring began to move. Being of stone it had not rusted fast in all the centuries it had lain there, as would have been the case had it been of iron. Presently it was upright. Then he thrust his hands into it and tugged with all his force, but nothing budged.

"Let me try," I said impatiently, for the situation of the stone, right in the angle of the corner, was such that it was impossible for two to pull at once. I took hold and strained away, but no results.

Then Sir Henry tried and failed.

Taking the hook again, Good scratched all round the crack where we felt the air coming up.

"Now, Curtis," he said, "tackle on, and put your back into it;

There was a join in the solid rock floor, and, great heavens! there, let in level with the rock, was a stone ring.

you are as strong as two. Stop," and he took off a stout black silk handkerchief, which, true to his habits of neatness, he still wore, and ran it through the ring. "Quatermain, get Curtis round the middle and pull for dear life when I give the word. Now."

Sir Henry put out all his enormous strength, and Good and I did the same, with such power as nature had given us.

"Heave! heave! it's giving," gasped Sir Henry; and I heard the muscles of his great back cracking. Suddenly there was a grating sound, then a rush of air, and we were all on our backs on the floor with a heavy flag-stone upon the top of us. Sir Henry's strength had done it, and never did muscular power stand a man in better stead.

"Light a match, Quatermain," he said, so soon as we had picked ourselves up and got our breath; "carefully, now."

I did so, and there before us, Heaven be praised! was the first step of a stone stair.

"Now what is to be done?" asked Good.

"Follow the stair, of course, and trust to Providence."

"Stop!" said Sir Henry; "Quatermain, get the bit of biltong and the water that are left; we may want them."

I went, creeping back to our place by the chests for that purpose, and as I was coming away an idea struck me. We had not thought much of the diamonds for the last twenty-four hours or so; indeed, the very idea of diamonds was nauseous, seeing what they had entailed upon us; but, reflected I, I may as well pocket some in case we ever should get out of this ghastly hole. So I just put my fist into the first chest and filled all the available pockets of my old shooting-coat and trousers, topping up – this was a happy thought – with a few handfuls of big ones from the third chest. Also, by an afterthought, I stuffed Foulata's basket, which, except for one water-gourd and a little biltong, was empty now, with great quantities of the stones.

"I say, you fellows," I sang out, "won't you take some diamonds with you? I've filled my pockets and the basket."

"Oh, come on, Quatermain! and hang the diamonds!" said Sir Henry. "I hope that I may never see another."

As for Good, he made no answer. He was, I think, taking his last farewell of all that was left of the poor girl who had loved him so well. And curious as it may seem to you, my reader, sitting at home at ease and reflecting on the vast, indeed the immeasurable, wealth which we were thus abandoning, I can assure you that if you had passed some twenty-eight hours with next to nothing to eat and drink in that place, you would not have cared to cumber yourself with diamonds whilst plunging down into the unknown bowels of the earth, in the wild hope of escape from an agonising death. If from the habits of a lifetime, it had not become a sort of second nature with me never to leave anything worth having behind if there was the slightest chance of my being able to carry it away, I am sure that I should not have bothered to fill my pockets and that basket.

"Come on, Quatermain," repeated Sir Henry, who was already standing on the first step of the stone stair. "Steady, I will go first."

"Mind where you put your feet, there may be some awful hole underneath," I answered.

"Much more likely to be another room," said Sir Henry, while he descended slowly, counting the steps as he went.

When he got to "fifteen" he stopped. "Here's the bottom," he said. "Thank goodness! I think it's a passage. Follow me down."

Good went next, and I came last, carrying the basket, and on reaching the bottom lit one of the two remaining matches. By its light we could just see that we were standing in a narrow tunnel, which ran right and left at right angles to the staircase we had descended. Before we could make out any more, the match burnt my fingers and went out. Then arose the delicate question of which way to go. Of course, it was impossible to know what the tunnel was, or where it led to, and yet to turn one way might lead us to safety, and the other to destruction. We were utterly perplexed, till suddenly it struck Good that when I had lit the match the draught of the passage blew the flame to the left.

"Let us go against the draught," he said; "air draws inwards, not outwards."

We took this suggestion, and feeling along the wall with our hands, whilst trying the ground before us at every step, we departed from that accursed treasure chamber on our terrible quest for life. If ever it should be entered again by living man, which I do not think probable, he will find tokens of our visit in the open chests of jewels, the empty lamp, and the white bones of poor Foulata.

When we had groped our way for about a quarter of an hour along the passage, suddenly it took a sharp turn, or else was bisected by another, which we followed, only in course of time to be led into a third. And so it went on for some hours. We seemed to be in a stone labyrinth that led nowhere. What all these passages are, of course I cannot say, but we thought that they must be the ancient workings of a mine, of which the various shafts and adits travelled hither and thither as the ore led them. This is the only way in which we could account for such a multitude of galleries.

At length we halted, thoroughly worn out with fatigue and with that hope deferred which maketh the heart sick, and ate up our poor remaining piece of biltong and drank our last sup of water, for our throats were like lime-kilns. It seemed to us that we had escaped Death in the darkness of the treasure chamber only to meet him in the darkness of the tunnels.

As we stood, once more utterly depressed, I thought that I caught a sound, to which I called the attention of the others. It was very faint and very far off, but it was a sound, a faint, murmuring sound, for the others heard it too, and no words can describe the blessedness of it after all those hours of utter, awful stillness.

"By heaven! it's running water," said Good. "Come on."

Off we started again in the direction from which the faint murmur seemed to come, groping our way as before along the rocky walls. I remember that I laid down the basket full of diamonds, wishing to be rid of its weight, but on second thoughts took it up again. One might as well die rich as poor, I reflected. As we went the sound became more and more audible, till at last it seemed quite loud in the quiet. On, yet on; now we could distinctly make out the unmistakable swirl of rushing water. And yet how could there be running water in the bowels of the earth? Now we were quite near it, and Good, who was leading, swore that he could smell it.

"Go gently, Good," said Sir Henry, "we must be close." Splash! and a cry from Good.

He had fallen in.

"Good! Good! where are you?" we shouted, in terrified distress. To our intense relief an answer came back in a choky voice.

"All right; I've got hold of a rock. Strike a light to show me where you are."

Hastily I lit the last remaining match. Its faint gleam discovered to us a dark mass of water running at our feet. How wide it was we could not see, but there, some way out, was the dark form of our companion hanging on to a projecting rock.

"Stand clear to catch me," sung out Good. "I must swim for it."

Then we heard a splash, and a great struggle. Another minute and he had grabbed at and caught Sir Henry's outstretched hand, and we had pulled him up high and dry into the tunnel.

"My word!" he said, between his gasps, "that was touch and go. If I hadn't managed to catch that rock, and known how to swim, I should have been done. It runs like a mill-race, and I could feel no bottom."

We dared not follow the banks of the subterranean river for fear lest we should fall into it again in the darkness. So after Good had rested a while, and we had drunk our fill of the water, which was sweet and fresh, and washed our faces, that needed it sadly, as well as we could, we started from the banks of this African Styx, and began to retrace our steps along the tunnel, Good dripping unpleasantly in front of us. At length we came to another gallery leading to our right.

"We may as well take it," said Sir Henry wearily; "all roads are alike here; we can only go on till we drop."

Slowly, for a long, long while, we stumbled, utterly exhausted, along this new tunnel, Sir Henry now leading the way. Again I thought of abandoning that basket, but did not.

Suddenly he stopped, and we bumped up against him.

"Look!" he whispered, "is my brain going, or is that light?"

We stared with all our eyes, and there, yes, there, far ahead of us, was a faint, glimmering spot, no larger than a cottage window pane. It was so faint that I doubt if any eyes, except those which, like ours, had for days seen nothing but blackness, could have perceived it at all.

With a gasp of hope we pushed on. In five minutes there was no longer any doubt; it was a patch of faint light. A minute more and a breath of real live air was fanning us. On we struggled. All at once the tunnel narrowed. Sir Henry went on his knees. Smaller yet it grew, till it was only the size of a large fox's earth – it was earth now, mind you; the rock had ceased.

A squeeze, a struggle, and Sir Henry was out, and so was Good, and so was I, dragging Foulata's basket after me; and there above us were the blessed stars, and in our nostrils was the sweet air. Then suddenly something gave, and we were all rolling over and over and over through grass and bushes and soft, wet soil.

The basket caught in something and I stopped. Sitting up I halloed lustily. An answering shout came from below, where Sir Henry's wild career had been checked by some level ground. I scrambled to him, and found him unhurt, though breathless. Then we looked for Good. A little way off we discovered him also, hammed in a forked root. He was a good deal knocked about, but soon came to himself.

We sat down together, there on the grass, and the revulsion of feeling was so great that really I think we cried with joy. We had escaped from that awful dungeon, which was so near to becoming our grave. Surely some merciful Power guided our footsteps to the jackal hole, for that is what it must have been, at the termination

of the tunnel. And see, yonder on the mountains the dawn we had never thought to look upon again was blushing rosy red.

Presently the grey light stole down the slopes, and we saw that we were at the bottom, or rather, nearly at the bottom, of the vast pit in front of the entrance to the cave. Now we could make out the dim forms of the three Colossi who sat upon its verge. Doubtless those awful passages, along which we had wandered the livelong night, had been originally in some way connected with the great diamond mine. As for the subterranean river in the bowels of the mountain, Heaven only knows what it is, or whence it flows, or whither it goes. I, for one, have no anxiety to trace its course.

Lighter it grew, and lighter yet. We could see each other now, and such a spectacle as we presented I have never set eyes on before or since. Gaunt-cheeked, hollow-eyed wretches, smeared all over with dust and mud, bruised, bleeding, the long fear of imminent death yet written on our countenances, we were, indeed, a sight to frighten the daylight. And yet it is a solemn fact that Good's eye-glass was still fixed in Good's eye. I doubt whether he had ever taken it out at all. Neither the darkness, nor the plunge in the subterranean river, nor the roll down the slope, had been able to separate Good and his eye-glass.

Presently we rose, fearing that our limbs would stiffen if we stopped there longer, and commenced with slow and painful steps to struggle up the sloping sides of the great pit. For an hour or more we toiled steadfastly up the blue clay, dragging ourselves on by the help of the roots and grasses with which it was clothed. But now I had no more thought of leaving the basket; indeed, nothing but death should have parted us.

At last it was done, and we stood by the great road, on that side of the pit which is opposite to the Colossi.

At the side of the road, a hundred yards off, a fire was burning in front of some huts, and round the fire were figures. We staggered towards them, supporting one another, and halting every few paces. Presently one of the figures rose, saw us and fell on to the ground, crying out for fear.

"Infadoos, Infadoos! it is we, thy friends."

He rose; he ran to us, staring wildly, and still shaking with fear.

"Oh, my lords, my lords, it is indeed you come back from the dead! – come back from the dead!"

And the old warrior flung himself down before us, and clasping Sir Henry's knees, he wept aloud for joy.

Love of Life
In Untrodden Lands
Jack London

Love of Life

by

Jack London

"This out of all will remain –
They have lived and have tossed:
So much of the game will be gain,
Though the gold of the dice has been lost."

They limped painfully down the bank, and once the foremost of the two men staggered among the rough-strewn rocks. They were tired and weak, and their faces had the drawn expression of patience which comes of hardship long endured. They were heavily burdened with blanket packs which were strapped to their shoulders. Head-straps, passing across the forehead, helped support these packs. Each man carried a rifle. They walked in a stooped posture, the shoulders well forward, the head still farther forward, the eyes bent upon the ground.

"I wish we had just about two of them cartridges that's layin' in that cache of ourn," said the second man.

His voice was utterly and drearily expressionless. He spoke without enthusiasm; and the first man, limping into the milky stream that foamed over the rocks, vouchsafed no reply.

The other man followed at his heels. They did not remove their foot-gear, though the water was icy cold – so cold that their ankles ached and their feet went numb. In places the water dashed against their knees, and both men staggered for footing.

The man who followed slipped on a smooth boulder, nearly fell, but recovered himself with a violent effort, at the same time uttering a sharp exclamation of pain. He seemed faint and dizzy and put out his free hand while he reeled, as though seeking support against the air. When he had steadied himself he stepped forward, but reeled again and nearly fell. Then he stood still and looked at the other man, who had never turned his head.

The man stood still for fully a minute, as though debating with himself. Then he called out:

"I say, Bill, I've sprained my ankle."

Bill staggered on through the milky water. He did not look around. The man watched him go, and though his face was expressionless as ever, his eyes were like the eyes of a wounded deer.

The other man limped up the farther bank and continued straight on without looking back. The man in the stream watched him. His lips trembled a little, so that the rough thatch of brown hair which covered them was visibly agitated. His tongue even strayed out to moisten them.

"Bill!" he cried out.

It was the pleading cry of a strong man in distress, but Bill's head did not turn. The man watched him go, limping grotesquely and lurching forward with a stammering gait up the slow slope toward the soft sky-line of the low-lying hill. He watched him go till he passed over the crest and disappeared. Then he turned his gaze and slowly took in the circle of the world that remained to him now that Bill was gone.

Near the horizon the sun was smouldering dimly, almost obscured by formless mists and vapors, which gave an impression of mass and density without outline or tangibility. The man pulled out his watch, the while resting his weight on one leg. It was four o'clock, and as the season was near the last of July or first of August, – he did not know the precise date within a week or two, – he knew that the sun roughly marked the northwest. He looked to the south and knew that somewhere beyond those bleak hills lay the Great Bear Lake; also, he knew that in that direction the Arctic Circle cut its forbidding way across the Canadian Barrens. This stream in which he stood was a feeder to the Coppermine River, which in turn flowed north and emptied into Coronation Gulf and the Arctic Ocean. He had never been there, but he had seen it, once, on a Hudson Bay Company chart.

Again his gaze completed the circle of the world about him. It was not a heartening spectacle. Everywhere was soft sky-line. The hills were all low-lying. There were no trees, no shrubs, no grasses – naught but a tremendous and terrible desolation that sent fear swiftly dawning into his eyes.

"Bill!" he whispered, once and twice; "Bill!"

He cowered in the midst of the milky water, as though the vastness were pressing in upon him with overwhelming force, brutally crushing him with its complacent awfulness. He began to shake as with an ague-fit, till the gun fell from his hand with a splash. This served to rouse him. He fought with his fear and pulled himself together, groping in the water and recovering the weapon. He hitched his pack farther over on his left shoulder, so as to take a portion of its weight from off the injured ankle. Then he proceeded, slowly and carefully, wincing with pain, to the bank.

He did not stop. With a desperation that was madness, unmindful of the pain, he hurried up the slope to the crest of the hill over which his comrade had disappeared – more grotesque and comical by far than that limping, jerking comrade.

But at the crest he saw a shallow valley, empty of life. He fought with his fear again, overcame it, hitched the pack still farther over on his left shoulder, and lurched on down the slope.

The bottom of the valley was soggy with water, which the thick moss held, spongelike, close to the surface. This water squirted out from under his feet at every step, and each time he lifted a foot the action culminated in a sucking sound as the wet moss reluctantly released its grip. He picked his way from muskeg to muskeg, and followed the other man's footsteps along and across the rocky ledges which thrust like islets through the sea of moss.

Though alone, he was not lost. Farther on he knew he would come to where dead spruce and fir, very small and weazened, bordered the shore of a little lake, the TITCHIN-NICHILIE, in the tongue of the country, the "land of little sticks." And into that lake flowed a small stream, the water of which was not milky. There was rush-grass on that stream – this he remembered well – but no timber, and he would follow it till its first trickle ceased at a divide. He would cross this divide to the first trickle of another stream, flowing to the west, which he would follow until it emptied into the river Dease, and here he would find a cache under an upturned canoe and piled over with many rocks. And in this cache would be ammunition for his empty gun, fish-hooks and lines, a small net – all the utilities for the killing and snaring of food. Also, he would find flour, – not much, – a piece of bacon, and some beans.

Bill would be waiting for him there, and they would paddle away south down the Dease to the Great Bear Lake. And south across the lake they would go, ever south, till they gained the Mackenzie. And south, still south, they would go, while the winter raced vainly after them, and the ice formed in the eddies, and the days grew chill and crisp, south to some warm Hudson Bay Company post, where timber grew tall and generous and there was grub without end.

These were the thoughts of the man as he strove onward. But hard as he strove with his body, he strove equally hard with his mind, trying to think that Bill had not deserted him, that Bill would surely wait for him at the cache. He was compelled to think this thought, or else there would not be any use to strive, and he would have lain down and died. And as the dim ball of the sun sank slowly into the northwest he covered every inch – and many times – of his and Bill's flight south before the downcoming winter. And he conned the grub of the cache and the grub of the Hudson Bay Company post over and over again. He had not eaten for two days; for a far longer time he had not had all he wanted to eat. Often he stooped and picked pale muskeg berries, put them into his mouth, and chewed and swallowed them. A muskeg berry is a bit of seed enclosed in a bit of water. In the mouth the water melts away and the seed chews sharp and bitter. The man knew there was no nourishment in the berries, but he chewed them patiently with a hope greater than knowledge and defying experience.

At nine o'clock he stubbed his toe on a rocky ledge, and from sheer weariness and weakness staggered and fell. He lay for some time, without movement, on his side. Then he slipped out of the pack-straps and clumsily dragged himself into a sitting posture. It was not yet dark, and in the lingering twilight he groped about among the rocks for shreds of dry moss. When he had gathered a heap he built a fire, – a smouldering, smudgy fire, – and put a tin pot of water on to boil.

He unwrapped his pack and the first thing he did was to count his matches. There were sixty-seven. He counted them three times to make sure. He divided them into several portions, wrapping them in oil paper, disposing of one bunch in his empty tobacco pouch, of another bunch in the inside band of his battered hat, of a third bunch under his shirt on the chest. This accomplished, a panic came upon him, and

he unwrapped them all and counted them again. There were still sixty-seven.

He dried his wet foot-gear by the fire. The moccasins were in soggy shreds. The blanket socks were worn through in places, and his feet were raw and bleeding. His ankle was throbbing, and he gave it an examination. It had swollen to the size of his knee. He tore a long strip from one of his two blankets and bound the ankle tightly. He tore other strips and bound them about his feet to serve for both moccasins and socks. Then he drank the pot of water, steaming hot, wound his watch, and crawled between his blankets.

He slept like a dead man. The brief darkness around midnight came and went. The sun arose in the northeast – at least the day dawned in that quarter, for the sun was hidden by gray clouds.

At six o'clock he awoke, quietly lying on his back. He gazed straight up into the gray sky and knew that he was hungry. As he rolled over on his elbow he was startled by a loud snort, and saw a bull caribou regarding him with alert curiosity. The animal was not mere than fifty feet away, and instantly into the man's mind leaped the vision and the savor of a caribou steak sizzling and frying over a fire. Mechanically he reached for the empty gun, drew a bead, and pulled the trigger. The bull snorted and leaped away, his hoofs rattling and clattering as he fled across the ledges.

The man cursed and flung the empty gun from him. He groaned aloud as he started to drag himself to his feet. It was a slow and arduous task.

His joints were like rusty hinges. They worked harshly in their sockets, with much friction, and each bending or unbending was accomplished only through a sheer exertion of will. When he finally gained his feet, another minute or so was consumed in straightening up, so that he could stand erect as a man should stand.

He crawled up a small knoll and surveyed the prospect. There were no trees, no bushes, nothing but a gray sea of moss scarcely diversified by gray rocks, gray lakelets, and gray streamlets. The sky was gray. There was no sun nor hint of sun. He had no idea of north, and he had forgotten the way he had come to this spot the night before. But he was not lost. He knew that. Soon he would come to the land of the little sticks. He felt that it lay off to the left somewhere, not far – possibly just over the next low hill.

He went back to put his pack into shape for travelling. He assured himself of the existence of his three separate parcels of matches, though he did not stop to count them. But he did linger, debating, over a squat moose-hide sack. It was not large. He could hide it under his two hands. He knew that it weighed fifteen pounds, – as much as all the rest of the pack, – and it worried him. He finally set it to one side and proceeded to roll the pack. He paused to gaze at the squat moose-hide sack. He picked it up hastily with a defiant glance about him, as though the desolation were trying to rob him of it; and when he rose to his feet to stagger on into the day, it was included in the pack on his back.

He bore away to the left, stopping now and again to eat

muskeg berries. His ankle had stiffened, his limp was more pronounced, but the pain of it was as nothing compared with the pain of his stomach. The hunger pangs were sharp. They gnawed and gnawed until he could not keep his mind steady on the course he must pursue to gain the land of little sticks. The muskeg berries did not allay this gnawing, while they made his tongue and the roof of his mouth sore with their irritating bite.

He came upon a valley where rock ptarmigan rose on whirring wings from the ledges and muskegs. Ker – ker – ker was the cry they made. He threw stones at them, but could not hit them. He placed his pack on the ground and stalked them as a cat stalks a sparrow. The sharp rocks cut through his pants' legs till his knees left a trail of blood; but the hurt was lost in the hurt of his hunger. He squirmed over the wet moss, saturating his clothes and chilling his body; but he was not aware of it, so great was his fever for food. And always the ptarmigan rose, whirring, before him, till their ker – ker – ker became a mock to him, and he cursed them and cried aloud at them with their own cry.

Once he crawled upon one that must have been asleep. He did not see it till it shot up in his face from its rocky nook. He made a clutch as startled as was the rise of the ptarmigan, and there remained in his hand three tail-feathers. As he watched its flight he hated it, as though it had done him some terrible wrong. Then he returned and shouldered his pack.

As the day wore along he came into valleys or swales where

game was more plentiful. A band of caribou passed by, twenty and odd animals, tantalizingly within rifle range. He felt a wild desire to run after them, a certitude that he could run them down. A black fox came toward him, carrying a ptarmigan in his mouth. The man shouted. It was a fearful cry, but the fox, leaping away in fright, did not drop the ptarmigan.

Late in the afternoon he followed a stream, milky with lime, which ran through sparse patches of rush-grass. Grasping these rushes firmly near the root, he pulled up what resembled a young onion-sprout no larger than a shingle-nail. It was tender, and his teeth sank into it with a crunch that promised deliciously of food. But its fibers were tough. It was composed of stringy filaments saturated with water, like the berries, and devoid of nourishment. He threw off his pack and went into the rush-grass on hands and knees, crunching and munching, like some bovine creature.

He was very weary and often wished to rest – to lie down and sleep; but he was continually driven on – not so much by his desire to gain the land of little sticks as by his hunger. He searched little ponds for frogs and dug up the earth with his nails for worms, though he knew in spite that neither frogs nor worms existed so far north.

He looked into every pool of water vainly, until, as the long twilight came on, he discovered a solitary fish, the size of a minnow, in such a pool. He plunged his arm in up to the shoulder, but it eluded him. He reached for it with both hands and stirred up the milky mud at the bottom. In his excitement he fell in, wetting himself to the waist. Then the water was too muddy to admit of his seeing the fish, and he was compelled to wait until the sediment had settled.

The pursuit was renewed, till the water was again muddied. But he could not wait. He unstrapped the tin bucket and began to bale the pool. He baled wildly at first, splashing himself and flinging the water so short a distance that it ran back into the pool. He worked

more carefully, striving to be cool, though his heart was pounding against his chest and his hands were trembling. At the end of half an hour the pool was nearly dry. Not a cupful of water remained. And there was no fish. He found a hidden crevice among the stones through which it had escaped to the adjoining and larger pool – a pool which he could not empty in a night and a day. Had he known of the crevice, he could have closed it with a rock at the beginning and the fish would have been his.

Thus he thought, and crumpled up and sank down upon the wet earth. At first he cried softly to himself, then he cried loudly to the pitiless desolation that ringed him around; and for a long time after he was shaken by great dry sobs.

He built a fire and warmed himself by drinking quarts of hot water, and made camp on a rocky ledge in the same fashion he had the night before. The last thing he did was to see that his matches were dry and to wind his watch. The blankets were wet and clammy. His ankle pulsed with pain. But he knew only that he was hungry, and through his restless sleep he dreamed of feasts and banquets and of food served and spread in all imaginable ways.

He awoke chilled and sick. There was no sun. The gray of earth and sky had become deeper, more profound. A raw wind was blowing, and the first flurries of snow were whitening the hilltops. The air about him thickened and grew white while he made a fire and boiled more water. It was wet snow, half rain, and the flakes were large and soggy. At first they melted as soon as they came in contact with the earth, but ever more fell, covering the ground, putting out the fire, spoiling his supply of moss-fuel.

This was a signal for him to strap on his pack and stumble onward, he knew not where. He was not concerned with the land of little sticks, nor with Bill and the cache under the upturned canoe by the river Dease. He was mastered by the verb "to eat." He was hunger-mad. He took no heed of the course he pursued, so long as that course led him through the swale bottoms. He felt his way through the wet snow to the watery muskeg berries, and went by feel as he pulled up the rush-grass by the roots. But it was tasteless stuff and did not satisfy. He found a weed that tasted sour and he ate all he could find of it, which was not much, for it was a creeping growth, easily hidden under the several inches of snow.

He had no fire that night, nor hot water, and crawled under his blanket to sleep the broken hunger-sleep. The snow turned into a cold rain. He awakened many times to feel it falling on his upturned face. Day came – a gray day and no sun. It had ceased raining. The keenness of his hunger had departed. Sensibility, as far as concerned the yearning for food, had been exhausted. There was a dull, heavy ache in his stomach, but it did not bother him so much. He was more rational, and once more he was chiefly interested in the land of little sticks and the cache by the river Dease.

He ripped the remnant of one of his blankets into strips and bound his bleeding feet. Also, he recinched the injured ankle and prepared himself for a day of travel. When he came to his pack, he paused long over the squat moose-hide sack, but in the end it went with him.

The snow had melted under the rain, and only the hilltops showed white. The sun came out, and he succeeded in locating the points of the compass, though he knew now that he was lost. Perhaps, in his previous days' wanderings, he had edged away too far to the left. He now bore off to the right to counteract the possible deviation from his true course.

Though the hunger pangs were no longer so exquisite, he realized that he was weak. He was compelled to pause for frequent rests, when he attacked the muskeg berries and rush-grass patches. His tongue felt dry and large, as though covered with a fine hairy growth, and it tasted bitter in his mouth. His heart gave him a great deal of trouble. When he had travelled a few minutes it would begin a remorseless thump, thump, thump, and then leap up and away in a painful flutter of beats that choked him and made him go faint and dizzy.

In the middle of the day he found two minnows in a large pool. It was impossible to bale it, but he was calmer now and managed to catch them in his tin bucket. They were no longer than his little finger, but he was not particularly hungry. The dull ache in his stomach had been growing duller and fainter. It seemed almost that his stomach was dozing. He ate the fish raw, masticating with painstaking care, for the eating was an act of pure reason. While he had no desire to eat, he knew that he must eat to live.

In the evening he caught three more minnows, eating two and saving the third for breakfast. The sun had dried stray shreds of moss, and he was able to warm himself with hot water. He had not covered more than ten miles that day; and the next day, travelling whenever his heart permitted him, he covered no more than five miles. But his stomach did not give him the slightest uneasiness. It had gone to sleep. He was in a strange country, too, and the caribou were growing more plentiful, also the wolves. Often their yelps drifted across the desolation, and once he saw three of them slinking away before his path.

Another night; and in the morning, being more rational, he untied the leather string that fastened the squat moose-hide sack. From its open mouth poured a yellow stream of coarse gold-dust and nuggets. He roughly divided the gold in halves, caching one half on a prominent ledge, wrapped in a piece of blanket, and returning the other half to the sack. He also began to use strips of the one remaining blanket for his feet. He still clung to his gun, for there were cartridges in that cache by the river Dease.

This was a day of fog, and this day hunger awoke in him again. He was very weak and was afflicted with a giddiness which at times blinded him. It was no uncommon thing now for him to stumble and fall; and stumbling once, he fell squarely into a ptarmigan nest. There were four newly hatched chicks, a day old – little specks of pulsating life no more than a mouthful; and he ate them ravenously, thrusting them alive into his mouth and

crunching them like egg-shells between his teeth. The mother ptarmigan beat about him with great outcry. He used his gun as a club with which to knock her over, but she dodged out of reach. He threw stones at her and with one chance shot broke a wing. Then she fluttered away, running, trailing the broken wing, with him in pursuit.

The little chicks had no more than whetted his appetite. He hopped and bobbed clumsily along on his injured ankle, throwing stones and screaming hoarsely at times; at other times hopping and bobbing silently along, picking himself up grimly and patiently when he fell, or rubbing his eyes with his hand when the giddiness threatened to overpower him.

The chase led him across swampy ground in the bottom of the valley, and he came upon footprints in the soggy moss. They were not his own – he could see that. They must be Bill's. But he could not stop, for the mother ptarmigan was running on. He would catch her first, then he would return and investigate.

He exhausted the mother ptarmigan; but he exhausted himself. She lay panting on her side. He lay panting on his side, a dozen feet away, unable to crawl to her. And as he recovered she recovered, fluttering out of reach as his hungry hand went out to her. The chase was resumed. Night settled down and she escaped. He stumbled from weakness and pitched head foremost on his face, cutting his cheek, his pack upon his back. He did not move for a long while; then he rolled over on his side, wound his watch, and lay there until morning.

Another day of fog. Half of his last blanket had gone into foot-wrappings. He failed to pick up Bill's trail. It did not matter. His hunger was driving him too compellingly – only – only he wondered if Bill, too, were lost. By midday the irk of his pack became too oppressive. Again he divided the gold, this time merely spilling half of it on the ground. In the afternoon he threw the rest of it away, there remaining to him only the half-blanket, the tin bucket, and the rifle.

An hallucination began to trouble him. He felt confident that one cartridge remained to him. It was in the chamber of the rifle and he had overlooked it. On the other hand, he knew all the time that the chamber was empty. But the hallucination persisted. He fought it off for hours, then threw his rifle open and was confronted with emptiness. The disappointment was as bitter as though he had really expected to find the cartridge.

He plodded on for half an hour, when the hallucination arose again. Again he fought it, and still it persisted, till for very relief he opened his rifle to unconvince himself. At times his mind wandered farther afield, and he plodded on, a mere automaton, strange conceits and whimsicalities gnawing at his brain like worms. But these excursions out of the real were of brief duration, for ever the pangs of the hunger-bite called him back. He was jerked back abruptly once from such an excursion by a sight that caused him nearly to faint. He reeled and swayed, doddering like a drunken man to keep from falling. Before him stood a horse. A horse! He could not believe his eyes. A thick mist was in them, intershot with sparkling points of light. He rubbed his eyes savagely to clear his vision, and beheld, not a horse, but a great brown bear. The animal was studying him with bellicose curiosity.

The man had brought his gun halfway to his shoulder before he realized. He lowered it and drew his hunting-knife from its beaded sheath at his hip. Before him was meat and life. He ran his thumb along the edge of his knife. It was sharp. The point was sharp. He would fling himself upon the bear and kill it. But his heart began its warning thump, thump, thump. Then followed the wild upward leap and tattoo of flutters, the pressing as of an iron band about his forehead, the creeping of the dizziness into his brain.

His desperate courage was evicted by a great surge of fear. In his weakness, what if the animal attacked him? He drew himself up to his most imposing stature, gripping the knife and staring hard at the bear. The bear advanced clumsily a couple of steps, reared up, and gave vent to a tentative growl. If the man ran, he would run after him; but the man did not run. He was animated now with the courage of fear. He, too, growled, savagely, terribly, voicing the fear that is to life germane and that lies twisted about life's deepest roots.

The bear edged away to one side, growling menacingly, himself appalled by this mysterious creature that appeared upright and unafraid. But the man did not move. He stood like a statue till the danger was past, when he yielded to a fit of trembling and sank down into the wet moss. He pulled himself together and went on, afraid now in a new way. It was not the fear that he should die passively from lack of food, but that he should be destroyed violently before starvation had exhausted the last particle of the endeavor in him that made toward surviving. There were the wolves. Back and forth across the desolation drifted their howls, weaving the very air into a fabric of menace that was so tangible that he found himself, arms in the air, pressing it back from him as it might be the walls of a wind-blown tent.

Now and again the wolves, in packs of two and three, crossed his path. But they sheered clear of him. They were not in sufficient numbers, and besides they were hunting the caribou, which did not battle, while this strange creature that walked erect might scratch and bite.

In the late afternoon he came upon scattered bones where the wolves had made a kill. The debris had been a caribou calf an hour before, squawking and running and very much alive. He contemplated the bones, clean-picked and polished, pink with the cell-life in them which had not yet died. Could it possibly be that he might be that ere the day was done! Such was life, eh? A vain and fleeting thing. It was only life that pained. There was no hurt in death. To die was to sleep. It meant cessation, rest. Then why was he not content to die?

But he did not moralize long. He was squatting in the moss, a bone in his mouth, sucking at the shreds of life that still dyed it faintly pink. The sweet meaty taste, thin and elusive almost as a memory, maddened him. He closed his jaws on the bones and crunched. Sometimes it was the bone that broke, sometimes his teeth. Then he crushed the bones between rocks, pounded them to a pulp, and swallowed them. He pounded his fingers, too, in his haste, and yet found a moment in which to feel surprise at the fact that his fingers did not hurt much when caught under the descending rock.

Came frightful days of snow and rain. He did not know when

he made camp, when he broke camp. He travelled in the night as much as in the day. He rested wherever he fell, crawled on whenever the dying life in him flickered up and burned less dimly. He, as a man, no longer strove. It was the life in him, unwilling to die, that drove him on. He did not suffer. His nerves had become blunted, numb, while his mind was filled with weird visions and delicious dreams.

But ever he sucked and chewed on the crushed bones of the caribou calf, the least remnants of which he had gathered up and carried with him. He crossed no more hills or divides, but automatically followed a large stream which flowed through a wide and shallow valley. He did not see this stream nor this valley. He saw nothing save visions. Soul and body walked or crawled side by side, yet apart, so slender was the thread that bound them.

He awoke in his right mind, lying on his back on a rocky ledge. The sun was shining bright and warm. Afar off he heard the squawking of caribou calves. He was aware of vague memories of rain and wind and snow, but whether he had been beaten by the storm for two days or two weeks he did not know.

For some time he lay without movement, the genial sunshine pouring upon him and saturating his miserable body with its warmth. A fine day, he thought. Perhaps he could manage to locate himself. By a painful effort he rolled over on his side. Below him flowed a wide and sluggish river. Its unfamiliarity puzzled him. Slowly he followed it with his eyes, winding in wide sweeps among the bleak, bare hills, bleaker and barer and lower-lying than any hills he had yet encountered. Slowly, deliberately, without excitement or more than the most casual interest, he followed the course of the strange stream toward the sky-line and saw it emptying into a bright and shining sea. He was still unexcited. Most unusual, he thought, a vision or a mirage – more likely a vision, a trick of his disordered mind. He was confirmed in this by sight of a ship lying at anchor in the midst of the shining sea. He closed his eyes for a while, then opened them. Strange how the vision persisted! Yet not strange. He knew there were no seas or ships in the heart of the barren lands, just as he had known there was no cartridge in the empty rifle.

He heard a snuffle behind him – a half-choking gasp or cough. Very slowly, because of his exceeding weakness and stiffness, he rolled over on his other side. He could see nothing near at hand, but he waited patiently. Again came the snuffle and cough, and outlined between two jagged rocks not a score of feet away he made out the gray head of a wolf. The sharp ears were not pricked so sharply as he had seen them on other wolves; the eyes were bleared and bloodshot, the head seemed to droop limply and forlornly. The animal blinked continually in the sunshine. It seemed sick. As he looked it snuffled and coughed again.

This, at least, was real, he thought, and turned on the other side so that he might see the reality of the world which had been veiled from him before by the vision. But the sea still shone in the distance and the ship was plainly discernible. Was it reality, after all? He closed his eyes for a long while and thought, and then it came to him. He had been making north by east, away from the Dease Divide and into the Coppermine Valley. This wide and sluggish river was the Coppermine. That shining sea was the Arctic Ocean. That ship was a whaler, strayed east, far east, from the mouth of the Mackenzie, and it was lying at anchor in Coronation Gulf. He remembered the Hudson Bay Company chart he had seen long ago, and it was all clear and reasonable to him.

He sat up and turned his attention to immediate affairs. He had worn through the blanket-wrappings, and his feet were shapeless lumps of raw meat. His last blanket was gone. Rifle and knife were both missing. He had

outlined between two jagged rocks not a score of feet away he made out the gray head of a wolf...

lost his hat somewhere, with the bunch of matches in the band, but the matches against his chest were safe and dry inside the tobacco pouch and oil paper. He looked at his watch. It marked eleven o'clock and was still running. Evidently he had kept it wound.

He was calm and collected. Though extremely weak, he had no sensation of pain. He was not hungry. The thought of food was not even pleasant to him, and whatever he did was done by his reason alone. He ripped off his pants' legs to the knees and bound them about his feet. Somehow he had succeeded in retaining the tin bucket. He would have some hot water before he began what he foresaw was to be a terrible journey to the ship.

His movements were slow. He shook as with a palsy. When he started to collect dry moss, he found he could not rise to his feet. He tried again and again, then contented himself with crawling about on hands and knees. Once he crawled near to the sick wolf. The animal dragged itself reluctantly out of his way, licking its chops with a tongue which seemed hardly to have the strength to curl. The man noticed that the tongue was not the customary healthy red. It was a yellowish brown and seemed coated with a rough and half-dry mucus.

After he had drunk a quart of hot water the man found he was able to stand, and even to walk as well as a dying man might be supposed to walk. Every minute or so he was compelled to rest. His steps were feeble and uncertain, just as the wolf's that trailed him were feeble and uncertain; and that night, when the shining sea was blotted out by blackness, he knew he was nearer to it by no more than four miles.

Throughout the night he heard the cough of the sick wolf, and now and then the squawking of the caribou calves. There was life all around him, but it was strong life, very much alive and well, and he knew the sick wolf clung to the sick man's trail in the hope that the man would die first. In the morning, on opening his eyes, he beheld it regarding him with a wistful and hungry stare. It stood crouched, with tail between its legs, like a miserable and woe-begone dog. It shivered in the chill morning wind, and grinned dispiritedly when the man spoke to it in a voice that achieved no more than a hoarse whisper.

The sun rose brightly, and all morning the man tottered and fell toward the ship on the shining sea. The weather was perfect. It was the brief Indian Summer of the high latitudes. It might last a week. To-morrow or next day it might he gone.

In the afternoon the man came upon a trail. It was of another man, who did not walk, but who dragged himself on all fours. The man thought it might be Bill, but he thought in a dull, uninterested way. He had no curiosity. In fact, sensation and emotion had left him. He was no longer susceptible to pain. Stomach and nerves had gone to sleep. Yet the life that was in him drove him on. He was very weary, but it refused to die. It was because it refused to die that he still ate muskeg berries and minnows, drank his hot water, and kept a wary eye on the sick wolf.

He followed the trail of the other man who dragged himself along, and soon came to the end of it – a few fresh-picked bones where the soggy moss was marked by the foot-pads of many wolves. He saw a squat moose-hide sack, mate to his own, which had been torn by sharp teeth. He picked it up, though its weight was almost too much for his feeble fingers. Bill had carried it to the last. Ha! ha! He would have the laugh on Bill. He would survive and carry it to the ship in the shining sea. His mirth was hoarse and ghastly, like a raven's croak, and the sick wolf joined him, howling lugubriously. The man ceased suddenly. How could he have the laugh on Bill if that were Bill; if those bones, so pinky-white and clean, were Bill?

He turned away. Well, Bill had deserted him; but he would not take the gold, nor would he suck Bill's bones. Bill would have, though, had it been the other way around, he mused as he staggered on.

He came to a pool of water. Stooping over in quest of minnows, he jerked his head back as though he had been stung. He had caught sight of his reflected face. So horrible was it that sensibility awoke long enough to be shocked. There were three minnows in the pool, which was too large to drain; and after several ineffectual attempts to catch them in the tin bucket he forbore. He was afraid, because of his great weakness, that he might fall in and drown. It was for this reason that he did not trust himself to the river astride one of the many drift-logs which lined its sand-spits.

That day he decreased the distance between him and the ship by three miles; the next day by two – for he was crawling now as Bill had crawled; and the end of the fifth day found the ship still seven miles away and him unable to make even a mile a day. Still the Indian Summer held on, and he continued to crawl and faint, turn and turn about; and ever the sick wolf coughed and wheezed at his heels. His knees had become raw meat like his feet, and though he padded them with the shirt from his back it was a red track he left behind him on the moss and stones. Once, glancing back, he saw the wolf licking hungrily his bleeding trail, and he saw sharply what his own end might be – unless – unless he could get the wolf. Then began as grim a tragedy of existence as was ever played – a sick man that crawled, a sick wolf that limped, two creatures dragging their dying carcasses across the desolation and hunting each other's lives.

Had it been a well wolf, it would not have mattered so much to the man; but the thought of going to feed the maw of that loathsome and all but dead thing was repugnant to him. He was finicky. His mind had begun to wander again, and to be perplexed by hallucinations, while his lucid intervals grew rarer and shorter.

He was awakened once from a faint by a wheeze close in his ear. The wolf leaped lamely back, losing its footing and falling in its weakness. It was ludicrous, but he was not amused. Nor was he even afraid. He was too far gone for that. But his mind was for the moment clear, and he lay and considered. The ship was no more than four miles away. He could see it quite distinctly when he rubbed the mists out of his eyes, and he could see the white sail of a small boat cutting the water of the shining sea. But he could never crawl those four miles. He knew that, and was very calm in the knowledge. He knew that he could not crawl half a mile. And yet he wanted to live. It was unreasonable that he should die after all he had undergone. Fate asked too much of him. And, dying, he declined to die. It was stark madness, perhaps, but in the very grip of Death he defied Death and refused to die.

He closed his eyes and composed himself with infinite precaution. He steeled himself to keep above the suffocating languor that lapped like a rising tide through all the wells of his being. It was very like a sea, this deadly languor, that rose and rose and drowned his consciousness bit by bit. Sometimes he was all but submerged, swimming through oblivion with a faltering stroke; and again, by some strange alchemy of soul, he would find another shred of will and strike out more strongly.

Without movement he lay on his back, and he could hear, slowly drawing near and nearer, the wheezing intake and output of the sick wolf's breath. It drew closer, ever closer, through an infinitude of time, and he did not move. It was at his ear. The harsh dry tongue grated like sandpaper against his cheek. His hands shot out – or at least he willed them to shoot out.

He could see the **white sail** of a small boat cutting the water of the shining sea.

The fingers were curved like talons, but they closed on empty air. Swiftness and certitude require strength, and the man had not this strength.

The patience of the wolf was terrible. The man's patience was no less terrible. For half a day he lay motionless, fighting off unconsciousness and waiting for the thing that was to feed upon him and upon which he wished to feed. Sometimes the languid sea rose over him and he dreamed long dreams; but ever through it all, waking and dreaming, he waited for the wheezing breath and the harsh caress of the tongue.

He did not hear the breath, and he slipped slowly from some dream to the feel of the tongue along his hand. He waited. The fangs pressed softly; the pressure increased; the wolf was exerting its last strength in an effort to sink teeth in the food for which it had waited so long. But the man had waited long, and the lacerated hand closed on the jaw. Slowly, while the wolf struggled feebly and the hand clutched feebly, the other hand crept across to a grip. Five minutes later the whole weight of the man's body was on top of the wolf. The hands had not sufficient strength to choke the wolf, but the face of the man was pressed close to the throat of the wolf and the mouth of the man was full of hair. At the end of half an hour the man was aware of a warm trickle in his throat. It was not pleasant. It was like molten lead being forced into his stomach, and it was forced by his will alone. Later the man rolled over on his back and slept.

There were some members of a scientific expedition on the whale-ship BEDFORD. From the deck they remarked a strange object on the shore. It was moving down the beach toward the water. They were unable to classify it, and, being scientific men, they climbed into the whale-boat alongside and went ashore to see. And they saw something that was alive but which could hardly be called a man. It was blind, unconscious. It squirmed along the ground like some monstrous worm. Most of its efforts were ineffectual, but it was persistent, and it writhed and twisted and went ahead perhaps a score of feet an hour.

Three weeks afterward the man lay in a bunk on the whale-ship BEDFORD, and with tears streaming down his wasted cheeks told who he was and what he had undergone. He also babbled incoherently of his mother, of sunny Southern California, and a home among the orange groves and flowers.

The days were not many after that when he sat at table with the scientific men and ship's officers. He gloated over the spectacle of so much food, watching it anxiously as it went into the mouths of others. With the disappearance of each mouthful an expression of deep regret came into his eyes. He was quite sane, yet he hated those men at mealtime. He was haunted by a fear that the food would not last. He inquired of the cook, the cabin-boy, the captain, concerning the food stores. They reassured him countless times; but he could not believe them, and pried cunningly about the lazarette to see with his own eyes.

It was noticed that the man was getting fat. He grew stouter with each day. The scientific men shook their heads and theorized. They limited the man at his meals, but still his girth increased and he swelled prodigiously under his shirt.

The sailors grinned. They knew. And when the scientific men set a watch on the man, they knew too. They saw him slouch for'ard after breakfast, and, like a mendicant, with outstretched palm, accost a sailor. The sailor grinned and passed him a fragment of sea biscuit. He clutched it avariciously, looked at it as a miser looks at gold, and thrust it into his shirt bosom. Similar were the donations from other grinning sailors.

The scientific men were discreet. They let him alone. But they privily examined his bunk. It was lined with hardtack; the mattress was stuffed with hardtack; every nook and cranny was filled with hardtack. Yet he was sane. He was taking precautions against another possible famine – that was all. He would recover from it, the scientific men said; and he did, ere the BEDFORD'S anchor rumbled down in San Francisco Bay.

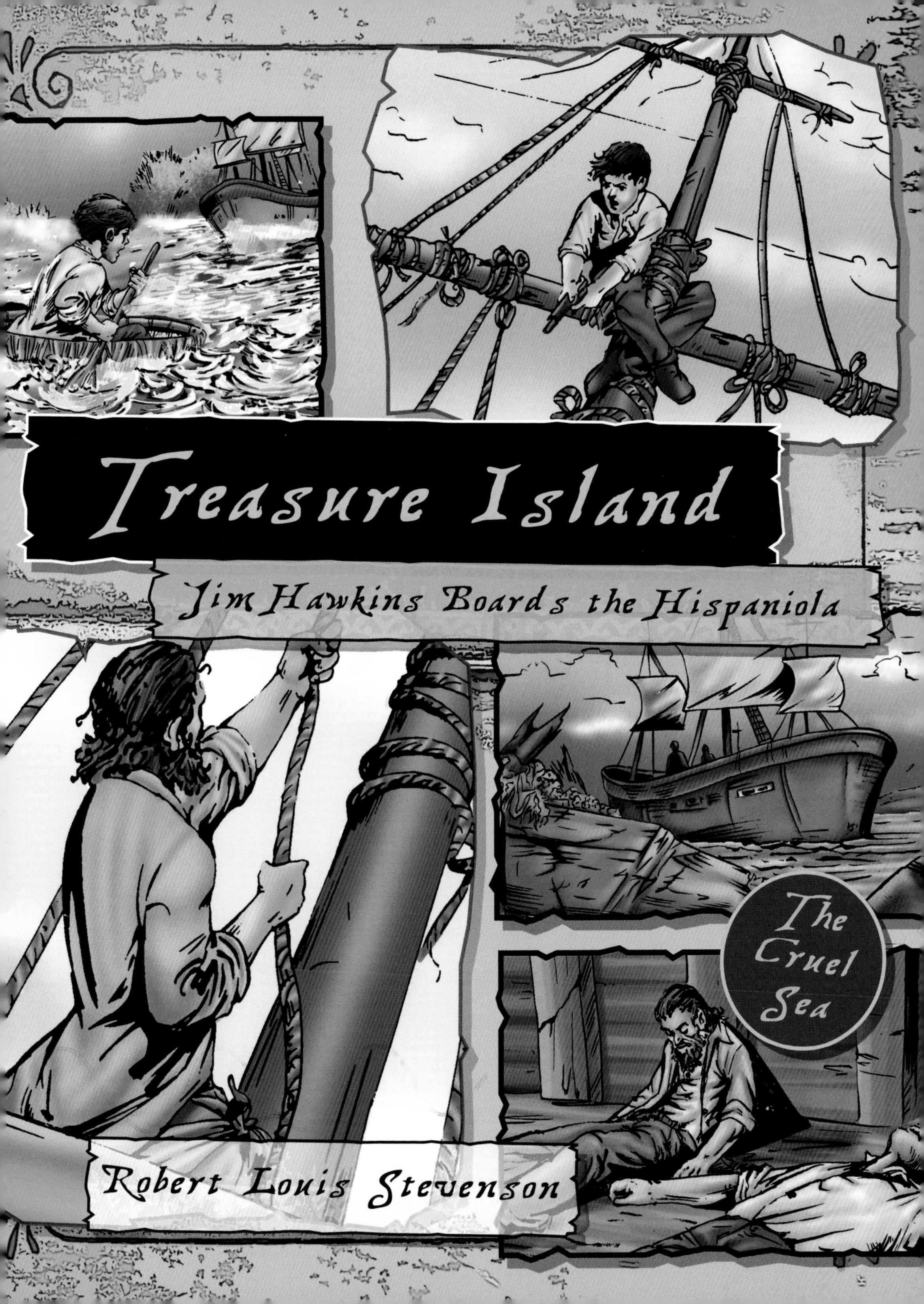
Treasure Island
Jim Hawkins Boards the Hispaniola
The Cruel Sea
Robert Louis Stevenson

The story so far

Jim Hawkins is a young boy who has had the luck to find a map left in the chest of an old pirate, giving the location of the treasure horde of Captain Flint, a notorious pirate. Hawkins travels with his companions, Squire Trelawney, Doctor Livesey and Captain Smollett, aboard the *Hispaniola* to a desert island to find the treasure, but unluckily the crew they hire turn out to be Flint's old crew, led by the one-legged cook Long John Silver. The crew mutiny when they reach the island, and take the ship. Jim and his companions have been defending their lives ashore, but Jim has been separated from the others and encounters an island castaway who has lent him a primitive boat, called a coracle, to help him make his way round the island.

Jim Hawkins Boards the Hispaniola from

Treasure Island

by

Robert Louis Stevenson

There was a great, smooth swell upon the sea. The wind blowing steady and gentle from the south, there was no contrariety between that and the current, and the billows rose and fell unbroken.

Had it been otherwise, I must long ago have perished; but as it was, it is surprising how easily and securely my little and light boat could ride. Often, as I still lay at the bottom and kept no more than an eye above the gunwale, I would see a big blue summit heaving close above me; yet the coracle would but bounce a little, dance as if on springs, and subside on the other side into the trough as lightly as a bird.

I began after a little to grow very bold and sat up to try my skill at paddling. But even a small change in the disposition of the weight will produce violent changes in the behaviour of a coracle. And I had hardly moved before the boat, giving up at once her gentle dancing movement, ran straight down a slope of water so steep that it made me giddy, and struck her nose, with a spout of spray, deep into the side of the next wave.

I was drenched and terrified, and fell instantly back into my old position, whereupon the coracle seemed to find her head again and led me as softly as before among the billows. It was plain she was not to be interfered with, and at that rate, since I could in no way influence her course, what hope had I left of reaching land?

I began to be horribly frightened, but I kept my head, for all that. First, moving with all care, I gradually baled out the coracle with my sea-cap; then, getting my eye once more above the gunwale, I set myself to study how it was she managed to slip so quietly through the rollers.

I found each wave, instead of the big, smooth glossy mountain it looks from shore or from a vessel's deck, was for all the world like any range of hills on dry land, full of peaks and smooth places and valleys. The coracle, left to herself, turning from side to side, threaded, so to speak, her way through these lower parts and avoided the steep slopes and higher, toppling summits of the wave.

'Well, now,' thought I to myself, 'it is plain I must lie where I am and not disturb the balance; but it is plain also that I can put the paddle over the side and from time to time, in smooth places, give her a shove or two towards land.' No sooner thought upon than done. There I lay on my elbows in the most trying attitude, and every now and again gave a weak stroke or two to turn her head to shore.

It was very tiring and slow work, yet I did visibly gain ground; and as we drew near the Cape of the Woods, though I saw I must infallibly miss that point, I had still made some hundred yards of easting. I was, indeed, close in. I could see the cool green tree-tops swaying together in the breeze, and I felt sure I should make the next promontory without fail.

It was high time, for I now began to be tortured with thirst. The glow of the sun from above, its thousandfold reflection from the waves, the sea-water that fell and dried upon me, caking my very lips with salt, combfiined to make my throat burn and my brain ache. The sight of the trees so near at hand had almost made me sick with longing, but the current had soon carried me past the point, and as the next reach of sea opened out, I beheld a sight that changed the nature of my thoughts.

Right in front of me, not half a mile away, I beheld the *Hispaniola* under sail. I made sure, of course, that I should be taken; but I was so distressed for want of water that I scarce knew whether to be glad or sorry at the thought, and long before I had come to a conclusion, surprise had taken entire possession of my mind and I could do nothing but stare and wonder.

The *Hispaniola* was under her main-sail and two jibs, and the beautiful white canvas shone in the sun like snow or silver. When I first sighted her, all her sails were drawing; she was lying a course about north-west, and I presumed the men on board were going round the island on their way back to the anchorage. Presently she began to fetch more and more to the westward, so that I thought they had sighted me and were going about in chase. At last, however, she fell right into the wind's eye, was taken dead aback, and stood there awhile helpless, with her sails shivering.

"Clumsy fellows," said I; "they must still be drunk as owls." And I thought how Captain Smollett would have set them skipping.

Meanwhile the schooner gradually fell off and filled again upon another tack, sailed swiftly for a minute or so, and brought up once more dead in the wind's eye. Again and again was this repeated. To and fro, up and down, north, south, east, and west, the *Hispaniola* sailed by swoops and dashes, and at each repetition ended as she had begun, with idly flapping canvas. It became plain to me that nobody was steering. And if so, where were the men? Either they were dead drunk or had deserted her, I thought, and perhaps if I could get on board I might return the vessel to her captain.

The current was bearing coracle and schooner southward at an equal rate. As for the latter's sailing, it was so wild and intermittent, and she hung each time so long in irons, that she certainly gained nothing, if she did not even lose. If only I dared to sit up and paddle, I made sure that I could overhaul her. The scheme had an air of adventure that inspired me, and the thought of the water breaker beside the fore companion doubled my growing courage.

Up I got, was welcomed almost instantly by another cloud of spray, but this time stuck to my purpose and set myself, with all my strength and caution, to paddle after the unsteered *Hispaniola*. Once I shipped a sea so heavy that I had to stop and bail, with my heart fluttering like a bird, but gradually I got into the way of the

thing and guided my coracle among the waves, with only now and then a blow upon her bows and a dash of foam in my face.

I was now gaining rapidly on the schooner; I could see the brass glisten on the tiller as it banged about, and still no soul appeared upon her decks. I could not choose but suppose she was deserted. If not, the men were lying drunk below, where I might batten them down, perhaps, and do what I chose with the ship.

For some time she had been doing the worse thing possible for me – standing still. She headed nearly due south, yawing, of course, all the time. Each time she fell off, her sails partly filled, and these brought her in a moment right to the wind again. I have said this was the worst thing possible for me, for helpless as she looked in this situation, with the canvas cracking like cannon and the blocks trundling and banging on the deck, she still continued to run away from me, not only with the speed of the current, but by the whole amount of her leeway, which was naturally great.

But now, at last, I had my chance. The breeze fell for some seconds, very low, and the current gradually turning her, the *Hispaniola* revolved slowly round her centre and at last presented me her stern, with the cabin window still gaping open and the lamp over the table still burning on into the day. The main-sail hung drooped like a banner. She was stock-still but for the current.

For the last little while I had even lost, but now redoubling my efforts, I began once more to overhaul the chase.

I was not a hundred yards from her when the wind came again

in a clap; she filled on the port tack and was off again, stooping and skimming like a swallow.

My first impulse was one of despair, but my second was towards joy. Round she came, till she was broadside on to me – round still till she had covered a half and then two thirds and then three quarters of the distance that separated us. I could see the waves boiling white under her forefoot. Immensely tall she looked to me from my low station in the coracle.

And then, of a sudden, I began to comprehend. I had scarce time to think – scarce time to act and save myself. I was on the summit of one swell when the schooner came stooping over the next. The bowsprit was over my head. I sprang to my feet and leaped, stamping the coracle under water. With one hand I caught the jib-boom, while my foot was lodged between the stay and the brace; and as I still clung there panting, a dull blow told me that the schooner had charged down upon and struck the coracle and that I was left without retreat on the *Hispaniola.*

I HAD scarce gained a position on the bowsprit when the flying jib flapped and filled upon the other tack, with a report like a gun. The schooner trembled to her keel under the reverse, but next moment, the other sails still drawing, the jib flapped back again and hung idle.

This had nearly tossed me off into the sea; and now I lost no time, crawled back along the bowsprit, and tumbled head foremost on the deck.

I was on the lee side of the forecastle, and the mainsail, which was still drawing, concealed from me a certain portion of the after-deck. Not a soul was to be seen. The planks, which had not been swabbed since the mutiny, bore the print of many feet, and an empty bottle, broken by the neck, tumbled to and fro like a live thing in the scuppers.

Suddenly the *Hispaniola* came right into the wind. The jibs behind me cracked aloud, the rudder slammed to, the whole ship gave a sickening heave and shudder, and at the same moment the main-boom swung inboard, the sheet groaning in the blocks, and showed me the lee after-deck.

There were the two watchmen, sure enough: red-cap on his back, as stiff as a handspike, with his arms stretched out like those of a crucifix and his teeth showing through his open lips; Israel Hands propped against the bulwarks, his chin on his chest, his hands lying open before him on the deck, his face as white, under its tan, as a tallow candle.

For a while the ship kept bucking and sidling like a vicious horse, the sails filling, now on one tack, now on another, and the boom swinging to and fro till the mast groaned aloud under the strain. Now and again too there would come a cloud of light sprays over the bulwark and a heavy blow of the ship's bows against the swell; so much heavier weather was made of it by this great rigged ship than by my home-made, lop-sided coracle, now gone to the bottom of the sea.

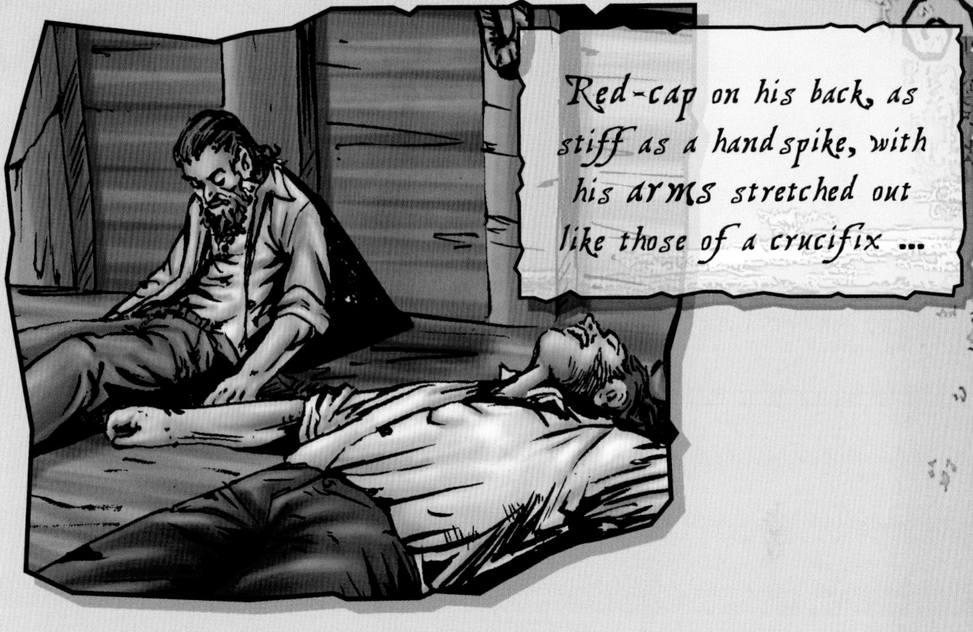

At every jump of the schooner, red-cap slipped to and fro, but – what was ghastly to behold – neither his attitude nor his fixed teeth-disclosing grin was anyway disturbed by this rough usage. At every jump too, Hands appeared still more to sink into himself and settle down upon the deck, his feet sliding ever the farther out, and the whole body canting towards the stern, so that his face became, little by little, hid from me; and at last I could see nothing beyond his ear and the frayed ringlet of one whisker.

At the same time, I observed, around both of them, splashes of dark blood upon the planks and began to feel sure that they had killed each other in their drunken wrath.

While I was thus looking and wondering, in a calm moment, when the ship was still, Israel Hands turned partly round and with a low moan writhed himself back to the position in which I had seen him first. The moan, which told of pain and deadly weakness, and the way in which his jaw hung open went right to my heart. But when I remembered the talk I had overheard from the apple barrel, all pity left me.

I walked aft until I reached the main-mast.

"Come aboard, Mr. Hands," I said ironically.

He rolled his eyes round heavily, but he was too far gone to express surprise. All he could do was to utter one word, "Brandy."

It occurred to me there was no time to lose, and dodging the boom as it once more lurched across the deck, I slipped aft and down the companion stairs into the cabin.

It was such a scene of confusion as you can hardly fancy. All the lockfast places had been broken open in quest of the chart. The floor was thick with mud where ruffians had sat down to drink or consult after wading in the marshes round their camp. The bulkheads, all painted in clear white and beaded round with gilt, bore a pattern of dirty hands. Dozens of empty bottles clinked together in corners to the rolling of the ship. One of the doctor's medical books lay open on the table, half of the leaves gutted out, I suppose, for pipelights. In the midst of all this the lamp still cast a smoky glow, obscure and brown as umber.

I went into the cellar; all the barrels were gone, and of the bottles a most surprising number had been drunk out and thrown away. Certainly, since the mutiny began, not a man of them could ever have been sober.

Foraging about, I found a bottle with some brandy left, for Hands; and for myself I routed out some biscuit, some pickled fruits, a great bunch of raisins, and a piece of cheese. With these I came on deck, put down my own stock behind the rudder head and well out of the coxswain's reach, went forward to the water-breaker, and had a good deep drink of water, and then, and not till then, gave Hands the brandy. He must have drunk a gill before he took the bottle from his mouth.

"Aye," said he, "by thunder, but I wanted some o' that!"

I had sat down already in my own corner and begun to eat.

"Much hurt?" I asked him.

He grunted, or rather, I might say, he barked.

"If that doctor was aboard," he said, "I'd be right enough in a couple of turns, but I don't have no manner of luck, you see, and that's what's the matter with me. As for that swab, he's good and dead, he is," he added, indicating the man with the red cap. "He warn't no seaman anyhow. And where mought you have come from?"

"Well," said I, "I've come aboard to take possession of this ship, Mr. Hands; and you'll please regard me as your captain until further notice."

He looked at me sourly enough but said nothing. Some of the colour had come back into his cheeks, though he still looked very sick and still continued to slip out and settle down as the ship banged about.

"By the by," I continued, "I can't have these colours, Mr. Hands; and by your leave, I'll strike 'em. Better none than these."

And again dodging the boom, I ran to the colour lines, handed down their cursed black flag, and chucked it overboard.

"God save the king!" said I, waving my cap. "And there's an end to Captain Silver!"

He watched me keenly and slyly, his chin all the while on his breast.

"I reckon," he said at last, "I reckon, Cap'n Hawkins, you'll kind of want to get ashore now. S'pose we talks."

"Why, yes," says I, "with all my heart, Mr. Hands. Say on." And I went back to my meal with a good appetite.

"This man," he began, nodding feebly at the corpse " – O'Brien were his name, a rank Irelander – this man and me got the canvas on her, meaning for to sail her back. Well, HE'S dead now, he is – as dead as bilge; and who's to sail this ship, I don't see. Without I gives you a hint, you ain't that man, as far's I can tell. Now, look here, you gives me food and drink and a old scarf or ankecher to tie my wound up, you do, and I'll tell you how to sail her, and that's about square all round, I take it."

"I'll tell you one thing," says I: "I'm not going back to Captain Kidd's anchorage. I mean to get into North Inlet and beach her quietly there."

"To be sure you did," he cried. "Why, I ain't sich an infernal lubber after all. I can see, can't I? I've tried my fling, I have, and

I've lost, and it's you has the wind of me. North Inlet? Why, I haven't no ch'ice, not I! I'd help you sail her up to Execution Dock, by thunder! So I would."

Well, as it seemed to me, there was some sense in this. We struck our bargain on the spot. In three minutes I had the *Hispaniola* sailing easily before the wind along the coast of Treasure Island, with good hopes of turning the northern point ere noon and beating down again as far as North Inlet before high water, when we might beach her safely and wait till the subsiding tide permitted us to land.

Then I lashed the tiller and went below to my own chest, where I got a soft silk handkerchief of my mother's. With this, and with my aid, Hands bound up the great bleeding stab he had received in the thigh, and after he had eaten a little and had a swallow or two more of the brandy, he began to pick up visibly, sat straighter up, spoke louder and clearer, and looked in every way another man.

The breeze served us admirably. We skimmed before it like a bird, the coast of the island flashing by and the view changing every minute. Soon we were past the high lands and bowling beside low, sandy country, sparsely dotted with dwarf pines, and soon we were beyond that again and had turned the corner of the rocky hill that ends the island on the north.

I was greatly elated with my new command, and pleased with the bright, sunshiny weather and these different prospects of the coast. I had now plenty of water and good things to eat, and my conscience, which had smitten me hard for my desertion, was quieted by the great conquest I had made. I should, I think, have had nothing left me to desire but for the eyes of the coxswain as they followed me derisively about the deck and the odd smile that appeared continually on his face. It was a smile that had in it something both of pain and weakness – a haggard old man's smile; but there was, besides that, a grain of derision, a shadow of treachery, in his expression as he craftily watched, and watched, and watched me at my work.

The wind, serving us to a desire, now hauled into the west. We could run so much the easier from the north-east corner of the island to the mouth of the North Inlet. Only, as we had no power to anchor and dared not beach her till the tide had flowed a good deal farther, time hung on our hands. The coxswain told me how to lay the ship to; after a good many trials I succeeded, and we both sat in silence over another meal.

"Cap'n," said he at length with that same uncomfortable smile, "here's my old shipmate, O'Brien; s'pose you was to heave him overboard. I ain't partic'lar as a rule, and I don't take no blame for settling his hash, but I don't reckon him ornamental now, do you?"

"I'm not strong enough, and I don't like the job; and there he lies, for me," said I.

"This here's an unlucky ship, this *Hispaniola*, Jim," he went on, blinking. "There's a power of men been killed in this *Hispaniola* – a sight o' poor seamen dead and gone since you and me took ship to Bristol. I never seen sich dirty luck, not I. There was this here O'Brien now – he's dead, ain't he? Well now, I'm no scholar, and you're a lad as can read and figure, and to put it straight, do you take it as a dead man is dead for good, or do he come alive again?"

"You can kill the body, Mr. Hands, but not the spirit; you must know that already," I replied. "O'Brien there is in another world, and may be watching us."

"Ah!" says he. "Well, that's unfort'nate – appears as if killing parties was a waste of time. Howsomever, sperrits don't reckon for much, by what I've seen. I'll chance it with the sperrits, Jim. And now, you've spoke up free, and I'll take it kind if you'd step down into that there cabin and get me a – well, a – shiver my timbers! I can't hit the name on 't; well, you get me a bottle of wine, Jim –

this here brandy's too strong for my head."

Now, the coxswain's hesitation seemed to be unnatural, and as for the notion of his preferring wine to brandy, I entirely disbelieved it. The whole story was a pretext. He wanted me to leave the deck – so much was plain; but with what purpose I could in no way imagine. His eyes never met mine; they kept wandering to and fro, up and down, now with a look to the sky, now with a flitting glance upon the dead O'Brien. All the time he kept smiling and putting his tongue out in the most guilty, embarrassed manner, so that a child could have told that he was bent on some deception. I was prompt with my answer, however, for I saw where my advantage lay and that with a fellow so densely stupid I could easily conceal my suspicions to the end.

"Some wine?" I said. "Far better. Will you have white or red?"

"Well, I reckon it's about the blessed same to me, shipmate," he replied; "so it's strong, and plenty of it, what's the odds?"

"All right," I answered. "I'll bring you port, Mr. Hands. But I'll have to dig for it."

With that I scuttled down the companion with all the noise I could, slipped off my shoes, ran quietly along the sparred gallery, mounted the forecastle ladder, and popped my head out of the fore companion. I knew he would not expect to see me there, yet I took every precaution possible, and certainly the worst of my suspicions proved too true.

He had risen from his position to his hands and knees, and

though his leg obviously hurt him pretty sharply when he moved – for I could hear him stifle a groan – yet it was at a good, rattling rate that he trailed himself across the deck. In half a minute he had reached the port scuppers and picked, out of a coil of rope, a long knife, or rather a short dirk, discoloured to the hilt with blood. He looked upon it for a moment, thrusting forth his under jaw, tried the point upon his hand, and then, hastily concealing it in the bosom of his jacket, trundled back again into his old place against the bulwark.

This was all that I required to know. Israel could move about, he was now armed, and if he had been at so much trouble to get rid of me, it was plain that I was meant to be the victim. What he would do afterwards – whether he would try to crawl right across the island from North Inlet to the camp among the swamps or whether he would fire Long Tom, trusting that his own comrades

In half a minute he had reached the port scuppers and picked a long knife discoloured to the hilt with blood.

might come first to help him – was, of course, more than I could say.

Yet I felt sure that I could trust him in one point, since in that our interests jumped together, and that was in the disposition of the schooner. We both desired to have her stranded safe enough, in a sheltered place, and so that, when the time came, she could be got off again with as little labour and danger as might be; and until that was done I considered that my life would certainly be spared.

While I was thus turning the business over in my mind, I had not been idle with my body. I had stolen back to the cabin, slipped once more into my shoes, and laid my hand at random on a bottle of wine, and now, with this for an excuse, I made my reappearance on the deck.

Hands lay as I had left him, all fallen together in a bundle and with his eyelids lowered as though he were too weak to bear the light. He looked up, however, at my coming, knocked the neck off the bottle like a man who had done the same thing often, and took a good swig, with his favourite toast of "Here's luck!" Then he lay quiet for a little, and then, pulling out a stick of tobacco, begged me to cut him a quid.

"Cut me a junk o' that," says he, "for I haven't no knife and hardly strength enough, so be as I had. Ah, Jim, Jim, I reckon I've missed stays! Cut me a quid, as'll likely be the last, lad, for I'm for my long home, and no mistake."

"Well," said I, "I'll cut you some tobacco, but if I was you and thought myself so badly, I would go to my prayers like a Christian man."

"Why?" said he. "Now, you tell me why."

"Why?" I cried. "You were asking me just now about the dead. You've broken your trust; you've lived in sin and lies and blood; there's a man you killed lying at your feet this moment, and you ask me why! For God's mercy, Mr. Hands, that's why."

I spoke with a little heat, thinking of the bloody dirk he had hidden in his pocket and designed, in his ill thoughts, to end me with. He, for his part, took a great draught of the wine and spoke with the most unusual solemnity.

"For thirty years," he said, "I've sailed the seas and seen good and bad, better and worse, fair weather and foul, provisions running out, knives going, and what not. Well, now I tell you, I never seen good come o' goodness yet. Him as strikes first is my fancy; dead men don't bite; them's my views – amen, so be it. And now, you look here," he added, suddenly changing his tone, "we've had about enough of this foolery. The tide's made good enough by now. You just take my orders, Cap'n Hawkins, and we'll sail slap in and be done with it."

All told, we had scarce two miles to run; but the navigation was delicate, the entrance to this northern anchorage was not only narrow and shoal, but lay east and west, so that the schooner must be nicely handled to be got in. I think I was a good, prompt subaltern, and I am very sure that Hands was an excellent pilot, for we went about and about and dodged in, shaving the banks, with a certainty and a neatness that were a pleasure to behold.

Scarcely had we passed the heads before the land closed around us. The shores of North Inlet were as thickly wooded as those of the southern anchorage, but the space was longer and narrower and more like, what in truth it was, the estuary of a river. Right before us, at the southern end, we saw the wreck of a ship in the last stages of dilapidation. It had been a great vessel of three masts but had lain so long exposed to the injuries of the weather that it was hung about with great webs of dripping seaweed, and on the deck of it shore bushes had taken root and now flourished thick with flowers. It was a sad sight, but it showed us that the anchorage was calm.

"Now," said Hands, "look there; there's a pet bit for to beach a ship in. Fine flat sand, never a cat's paw, trees all around of it, and flowers a-blowing like a garding on that old ship."

"And once beached," I inquired, "how shall we get her off again?"

"Why, so," he replied: "you take a line ashore there on the other side at low water, take a turn about one of them big pines; bring it back, take a turn around the capstan, and lie to for the tide. Come high water, all hands take a pull upon the line, and off she comes as sweet as natur'. And now, boy, you stand by. We're near the bit now, and she's too much way on her. Starboard a little – so – steady – starboard – larboard a little – steady – steady!"

So he issued his commands, which I breathlessly obeyed, till, all

of a sudden, he cried, "Now, my hearty, luff!" And I put the helm hard up, and the *Hispaniola* swung round rapidly and ran stem on for the low, wooded shore.

The excitement of these last manoeuvres had somewhat interfered with the watch I had kept hitherto, sharply enough, upon the coxswain. Even then I was still so much interested, waiting for the ship to touch, that I had quite forgot the peril that hung over my head and stood craning over the starboard bulwarks and watching the ripples spreading wide before the bows. I might have fallen without a struggle for my life had not a sudden disquietude seized upon me and made me turn my head. Perhaps I had heard a creak or seen his shadow moving with the tail of my eye; perhaps it was an instinct like a cat's; but, sure enough, when I looked round, there was Hands, already half-way towards me, with the dirk in his right hand.

We must both have cried out aloud when our eyes met, but while mine was the shrill cry of terror, his was a roar of fury like a charging bully's. At the same instant, he threw himself forward and I leapt sideways towards the bows. As I did so, I let go of the tiller, which sprang sharp to leeward, and I think this saved my life, for it struck Hands across the chest and stopped him, for the moment, dead.

Before he could recover, I was safe out of the corner where he had me trapped, with all the deck to dodge about. Just forward of the main-mast I stopped, drew a pistol from my pocket, took a cool aim, though he had already turned and was once more coming directly after me, and drew the trigger. The hammer fell, but there followed neither flash nor sound; the priming was useless with sea-water. I cursed myself for my neglect. Why had not I, long before, reprimed and reloaded my only weapons? Then I should not have been as now, a mere fleeing sheep before this butcher.

Wounded as he was, it was wonderful how fast he could move, his grizzled hair tumbling over his face, and his face itself as red as a red ensign with his haste and fury. I had no time to try my other pistol, nor indeed much inclination, for I was sure it would be useless. One thing I saw plainly: I must not simply retreat before him, or he would speedily hold me boxed into the bows, as a moment since he had so nearly boxed me in the stern. Once so caught, and nine or ten inches of the blood-stained dirk would be my last experience on this side of eternity. I placed my palms against the main-mast, which was of a goodish bigness, and waited, every nerve upon the stretch.

Seeing that I meant to dodge, he also paused; and a moment or two passed in feints on his part and corresponding movements upon mine. It was such a game as I had often played at home about the rocks of Black Hill Cove, but never before, you may be sure, with such a wildly beating heart as now. Still, as I say, it was a boy's game, and I thought I could hold my own at it against an elderly seaman with a wounded thigh. Indeed my courage had begun to rise so high that I allowed myself a few darting thoughts on what would be the end of the affair, and while I saw certainly that I could spin it out for long, I saw no hope of any ultimate escape.

Well, while things stood thus, suddenly the *Hispaniola* struck, staggered, ground for an instant in the sand, and then, swift as a blow, canted over to the port side till the deck stood at an angle of forty-five degrees and about a puncheon of water splashed into the scupper holes and lay, in a pool, between the deck and bulwark.

We were both of us capsized in a second, and both of us rolled, almost together, into the scuppers, the dead red-cap, with his arms still spread out, tumbling stiffly after us. So near were we, indeed, that my head came against the coxswain's foot with a crack that made my teeth rattle. Blow and all, I was the first afoot again, for Hands had got involved with the dead body. The sudden canting of the ship had made the deck no place for running on; I had to find some new way of escape, and that upon the instant, for my foe was almost touching me. Quick as thought, I sprang into the mizzen shrouds, rattled up hand over hand, and did not draw a breath till I was seated on the cross-trees.

I had been saved by being prompt; the dirk had struck not half a foot below me as I pursued my upward flight; and there stood Israel Hands with his mouth open and his face upturned to mine, a perfect statue of surprise and disappointment.

Now that I had a moment to myself, I lost no time in changing the priming of my pistol, and then, having one ready for service, and to make assurance doubly sure, I proceeded to draw the load of the other and recharge it afresh from the beginning.

My new employment struck Hands all of a heap; he began to see the dice going against him, and after an obvious hesitation, he also hauled himself heavily into the shrouds, and with the dirk in his teeth, began slowly and painfully to mount. It cost him no end of time and groans to haul his wounded leg behind him, and I had quietly finished my arrangements before he was much more than a third of the way up. Then, with a pistol in either hand, I addressed him.

"One more step, Mr. Hands," said I, "and I'll blow your brains out! Dead men don't bite, you know," I added with a chuckle.

He stopped instantly. I could see by the working of his face that he was trying to think, and the process was so slow and laborious

that, in my new-found security, I laughed aloud. At last, with a swallow or two, he spoke, his face still wearing the same expression of extreme perplexity. In order to speak he had to take the dagger from his mouth, but in all else he remained unmoved.

"Jim," says he, "I reckon we're fouled, you and me, and we'll have to sign articles. I'd have had you but for that there lurch, but I don't have no luck, not I; and I reckon I'll have to strike, which comes hard, you see, for a master mariner to a ship's younker like you, Jim."

I was drinking in his

words and smiling away, as conceited as a cock upon a wall, when, all in a breath, back went his right hand over his shoulder. Something sang like an arrow through the air; I felt a blow and then a sharp pang, and there I was pinned by the shoulder to the mast. In the horrid pain and surprise of the moment – I scarce can say it was by my own volition, and I am sure it was without a conscious aim – both my pistols went off, and both escaped out of my hands. They did not fall alone; with a choked cry, the coxswain loosed his grasp upon the shrouds and plunged head first into the water.

The Coral Island
Shipwreck!
R M Ballantyne
The Cruel Sea

The story so far

When three boys are marooned on a desert island after being shipwrecked, they think they are in paradise. Ralph Rover – the narrator of the story – and his companions Jack and Peterkin, find themselves on a beautiful coral island in Polynesia. With no provisions, and just a handful of useful items, they set about finding food and making a fire. Little do they know that the island is not paradise, and hard times lay ahead of them.

Shipwreck!

from

The Coral Island

by

R M Ballantyne

It was a bright, beautiful, warm day when our ship spread her canvas to the breeze and sailed for the regions of the south. Oh, how my heart bounded with delight as I listened to the merry chorus of the sailors while they hauled at the ropes and got in the anchor! The captain shouted; the men ran to obey; the noble ship bent over to the breeze, and the shore gradually faded from my view; while I stood looking on, with a kind of feeling that the whole was a delightful dream.

The first thing that struck me as being different from anything I had yet seen during my short career on the sea, was the hoisting of the anchor on deck and lashing it firmly down with ropes, as if we had now bid adieu to the land for ever and would require its services no more.

"There, lass!" cried a broad-shouldered jack-tar, giving the fluke of the anchor a hearty slap with his hand after the housing was completed – "there, lass, take a good nap now, for we sha'n't ask you to kiss the mud again for many a long day to come!"

And so it was. That anchor did not "kiss the mud" for many long days afterwards; and when at last it did, it was for the last time!

There were a number of boys in the ship, but two of them were my special favourites. Jack Martin was a tall, strapping, broad-shouldered youth of eighteen, with a handsome, good-humoured, firm face. He had had a good education, was clever and hearty and lion-like in his actions, but mild and quiet in disposition. Jack was a general favourite, and had a peculiar fondness for me. My other companion was Peterkin Gay. He was little, quick, funny, decidedly mischievous, and about fourteen years old. But Peterkin's mischief was almost always harmless, else he could not have been so much beloved as he was.

"Hallo, youngster!" cried Jack Martin, giving me a slap on the shoulder the day I joined the ship, "come below and I'll show you your berth. You and I are to be messmates; and I think we shall be good friends, for I like the look o' you."

Jack was right. He and I, and Peterkin afterwards, became the best and staunchest friends that ever tossed together on the stormy waves.

I shall say little about the first part of our voyage. We had the usual amount of rough weather and calm; also we saw many strange fish rolling in the sea, and I was greatly delighted one day by seeing a shoal of flying-fish dart out of the water and skim through the air about a foot above the surface. They were pursued by dolphins, which feed on them; and one flying-fish, in its terror, flew over the ship, struck on the rigging, and fell upon the deck. Its wings were just fins elongated; and we found that they could never fly far at a time, and never mounted into the air like birds, but skimmed along the surface of the sea. Jack and I had it for dinner, and found it remarkably good.

When we approached Cape Horn, at the southern extremity of America, the weather became very cold and stormy, and the sailors began to tell stories about the furious gales and the dangers of that terrible cape.

"Cape Horn," said one, "is the most horrible headland I ever

doubled. I've sailed round it twice already, and both times the ship was a'most blow'd out o' the water."

"I've been round it once," said another; "an' that time the sails were split, and the ropes frozen in the blocks so that they wouldn't work, and we wos all but lost."

"An' I've been round it five times," cried a third; "an' every time wos wuss than another, the gales wos so tree-mendous!"

"And I've been round it, no times at all," cried Peterkin with an impudent wink in his eye, "an' that time I wos blow'd inside out!"

Nevertheless we passed the dreaded cape without much rough weather, and in the course of a few weeks afterwards were sailing gently, before a warm tropical breeze, over the Pacific Ocean. Thus we proceeded on our voyage – sometimes bounding merrily before a fair breeze; at other times floating calmly on the glassy wave and fishing for the curious inhabitants of the deep, all of which, although the sailors thought little of them, were strange, and interesting, and very wonderful to me.

At last we came among the Coral Islands of the Pacific; and I shall never forget the delight with which I gazed – when we chanced to pass one – at the pure white, dazzling shores, and the verdant palm-trees, which looked bright and beautiful in the sunshine. And often did we three long to be landed on one, imagining that we should certainly find perfect happiness there! Our wish was granted sooner than we expected.

One night, soon after we entered the tropics, an awful storm burst upon our ship. The first squall of wind carried away two of our masts, and left only the foremast standing. Even this, however, was more than enough, for we did not dare to hoist a rag of sail on it. For five days the tempest raged in all its fury. Everything was swept off the decks, except one small boat. The steersman was lashed to the wheel lest he should be washed away, and we all gave ourselves up for lost. The captain said that he had no idea where we were, as we had been blown far out of our course; and we feared much that we might get among the dangerous coral reefs which are so numerous in the Pacific. At daybreak on the sixth morning of the gale we saw land ahead; it was an island encircled by a reef of coral, on which the waves broke in fury. There was calm water within this reef, but we could see only one narrow opening into it. For this opening we steered; but ere we reached it a tremendous wave broke on our stern, tore the rudder completely off, and left us at the mercy of the winds and waves.

"It's all over with us now, lads!" said the captain to the men. "Get the boat ready to launch; we shall be on the rocks in less than half-an-hour."

The men obeyed in gloomy silence, for they felt that there was little hope of so small a boat living in such a sea.

"Come, boys," said Jack Martin, in a grave tone, to me and Peterkin, as we stood on the quarter-deck awaiting our fate – "come, boys; we three shall stick together. You see it is impossible that the little boat can reach the shore, crowded with men. It will be sure to upset, so I mean rather to trust myself to a large oar. I see through the telescope that the ship will strike at the tail of the reef, where the waves break into the quiet water inside; so if we manage to cling to the oar till it is driven over the breakers, we may perhaps gain the shore. What say you? Will you join me?"

We gladly agreed to follow Jack, for he inspired us with confidence – although I could perceive, by the sad tone of his voice, that he had little hope; and indeed, when I looked at the white waves that lashed the reef and boiled against the rocks as if in fury, I felt that there was but a step between us and death. My heart sank within me; but at that moment my thoughts turned to my beloved mother, and I remembered those words, which were among the last that she said to me: "Ralph, my dearest child, always remember, in the hour of danger, to look to your Lord and Saviour Jesus Christ. He alone is both able and willing to save your body and your soul." So I felt much comforted when I thought thereon.

The ship was now very near the rocks. The men were ready with the boat, and the captain beside them giving orders, when a tremendous wave came towards us. We three ran towards the bow to lay hold of our oar, and had barely reached it when the wave fell on the deck with a crash like thunder. At the same moment the ship struck; the foremast broke off close to the deck and went over the side, carrying the boat and men along with it. Our oar got entangled with the wreck, and Jack seized an axe to cut it free; but owing to the motion of the ship, he missed the cordage and struck the axe deep into the oar. Another wave, however, washed it clear of the wreck. We all seized hold of it, and the next instant we were struggling in the wild sea. The last thing I saw was the boat whirling in the surf, and all the sailors tossed into the foaming waves. Then I became insensible.

On recovering from my swoon I found myself lying on a bank of soft grass, under shelter of an overhanging rock, with Peterkin on his knees by my side, tenderly bathing my temples with water, and endeavouring to stop the blood that flowed from a wound in my forehead.

There is a strange and peculiar sensation experienced in recovering from a state of insensibility which is almost indescribable: a sort of dreamy, confused consciousness; a half-waking, half-sleeping condition, accompanied with a feeling of weariness, which, however, is by no means disagreeable. As I slowly recovered, and heard the voice of Peterkin inquiring whether I felt better, I thought that I must have overslept myself, and should be sent to the masthead for being lazy; but before I could leap up in haste, the thought seemed to vanish suddenly away, and I fancied that I must have been ill. Then a balmy breeze fanned my cheek; and I thought of home, and the garden at the back of my father's cottage with its luxuriant flowers, and the sweet-scented honeysuckle that my dear mother trained so carefully upon the trellised porch. But the roaring of the surf put these delightful thoughts to flight, and I was back again at sea, watching the dolphins and the flying-fish, and reefing topsails off the wild and stormy Cape Horn. Gradually the roar of the surf became louder and more distinct. I thought of being wrecked far, far away from my native land, and slowly opened my eyes to meet those of my companion Jack, who, with a look of intense anxiety, was gazing into my face.

"Speak to us, my dear Ralph!" whispered Jack tenderly. "Are you better now?"

I smiled and looked up, saying, "Better! Why, what do you mean, Jack? I'm quite well."

"Then what are you shamming for, and frightening us in this

way?" said Peterkin, smiling through his tears; for the poor boy had been really under the impression that I was dying.

I now raised myself on my elbow, and putting my hand to my forehead, found that it had been cut pretty severely, and that I had lost a good deal of blood.

"Come, come, Ralph," said Jack, pressing me gently backward, "lie down, my boy; you're not right yet. Wet your lips with this water; it's cool and clear as crystal. I got it from a spring close at hand. There, now, don't say a word – hold your tongue," he said, seeing me about to speak. "I'll tell you all about it, but you must not utter a syllable till you have rested well."

"Oh, don't stop him from speaking, Jack!" said Peterkin, who, now that his fears for my safety were removed, busied himself in erecting a shelter of broken branches in order to protect me from the wind – which, however, was almost unnecessary, for the rock beside which I had been laid completely broke the force of the gale. "Let him speak, Jack; it's a comfort to hear that he's alive after lying there stiff and white and sulky for a whole hour, just like an Egyptian mummy. Never saw such a fellow as you are, Ralph – always up to mischief. You've almost knocked out all my teeth and more than half-choked me, and now you go shamming dead! It's very wicked of you, indeed it is."

While Peterkin ran on in this style my faculties became quite clear again, and I began to understand my position. "What do you mean by saying I half-choked you, Peterkin?" said I.

"What do I mean? Is English not your mother-tongue? or do you want me to repeat it in French by way of making it clearer? Don't you remember?"

"I remember nothing," said I, interrupting him, "after we were thrown into the sea."

"Hush, Peterkin!" said Jack; "you're exciting Ralph with your nonsense. I'll explain it to you. You recollect that, after the ship struck, we three sprang over the bow into the sea? Well, I noticed that the oar struck your head and gave you that cut on the brow which nearly stunned you, so that you grasped Peterkin round the neck without knowing apparently what you were about. In doing so, you pushed the telescope – which you clung to as if it had been your life – against Peterkin's mouth –"

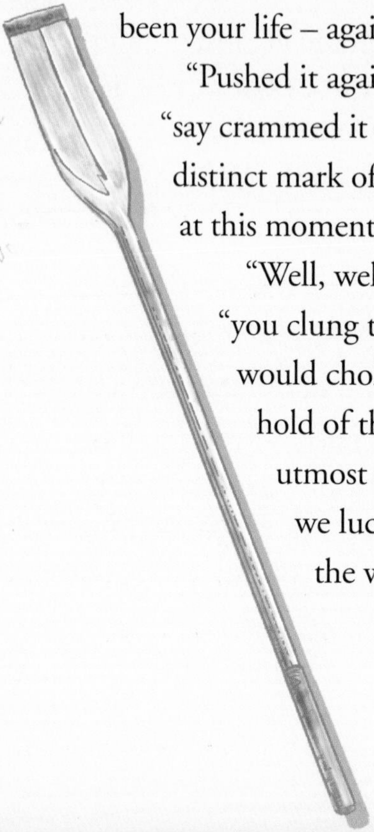

"Pushed it against his mouth!" interrupted Peterkin; "say crammed it down his throat! Why, there's a distinct mark of the brass rim on the back of my gullet at this moment!"

"Well, well, be that as it may," continued Jack, "you clung to him, Ralph, till I feared you really would choke him. But I saw that he had a good hold of the oar; so I exerted myself to the utmost to push you towards the shore, which we luckily reached without much trouble, for the water inside the reef is quite calm."

"But the captain and crew, what of

them?" I inquired anxiously.

Jack shook his head.

"Are they lost?"

"No, they are not lost, I hope; but, I fear, there is not much chance of their being saved. The ship struck at the very tail of the island on which we are cast. When the boat was tossed into the sea it fortunately did not upset, although it shipped a good deal of water, and all the men managed to scramble into it; but before they could get the oars out, the gale carried them past the point and away to leeward of the island. After we landed I saw them endeavouring to pull towards us; but as they had only one pair of oars out of the eight that belonged to the boat, and as the wind was blowing right in their teeth, they gradually lost ground. Then I saw them put about and hoist some sort of sail – a blanket, I fancy, for it was too small for the boat – and in half-an-hour they were out of sight."

"Poor fellows!" I murmured sorrowfully.

"But the more I think about it I've better hope of them," continued Jack in a more cheerful tone. "You see, Ralph, I've read a great deal about these South Sea Islands, and I know that in many places they are scattered about in thousands over the sea, so they're almost sure to fall in with one of them before long."

"I'm sure I hope so," said Peterkin earnestly. "But what has become of the wreck, Jack? I saw you clambering up the rocks there while I was watching Ralph. Did you say she had gone to pieces?"

"No, she has not gone to pieces; but she has gone to the bottom," replied Jack. "As I said before, she struck on the tail of the island and stove in her bow; but the next breaker swung her clear, and she floated away to leeward. The poor fellows in the boat made a hard struggle to reach her, but long before they came near her she filled and went down. It was after she had foundered that I saw them trying to pull to the island."

There was a long silence after Jack had ceased speaking, and I have no doubt that each was revolving in his mind our extraordinary position. For my part, I cannot say that my reflections were very agreeable. I knew that we were on an island, for Jack had said so; but whether it was inhabited or not, I did not know. If it should be inhabited, I felt certain, from all I had heard of South Sea Islanders, that we should be roasted alive and eaten. If it should turn out to be uninhabited, I fancied that we should be starved to death. "Oh," thought I, "if the ship had only struck on the rocks we might have done pretty well, for we could have obtained provisions from her, and tools to enable us to build a shelter; but now – alas! alas! we are lost!" These last words I uttered aloud in my distress.

"Lost, Ralph!" exclaimed Jack, while a smile overspread his hearty countenance. "Saved, you should have said. Your cogitations seem to have taken a wrong road, and led you to a wrong conclusion."

"Do you know what conclusion I have come to?" said Peterkin.

"I have made up my mind that it's capital – first-rate – the best thing that ever happened to us, and the most splendid prospect that ever lay before three jolly young tars. We've got an island all to ourselves. We'll take possession in the name of the king. We'll go and enter the service of its black inhabitants. Of course we'll rise, naturally, to the top of affairs: white men always do in savage countries. You shall be king, Jack; Ralph, prime minister; and I shall be—"

"The court-jester," interrupted Jack.

"No," retorted Peterkin; "I'll have no title at all. I shall merely accept a highly responsible situation under government; for you see, Jack, I'm fond of having an enormous salary and nothing to do."

"But suppose there are no natives?"

"Then we'll build a charming villa, and plant a lovely garden round it, stuck all full of the most splendiferous tropical flowers; and we'll farm the land, plant, sow, reap, eat, sleep, and be merry."

"But to be serious," said Jack, assuming a grave expression of countenance – which, I observed, always had the effect of checking Peterkin's disposition to make fun of everything – "we are really in rather an uncomfortable position. If this is a desert island, we shall have to live very much like the wild beasts; for we have not a tool of any kind – not even a knife."

"Yes, we have that," said Peterkin, fumbling in his trousers pocket, from which he drew forth a small penknife with only one blade, and that was broken.

"Well, that's better than nothing. – But come," said Jack, rising; "we are wasting our time in talking instead of doing. – You seem well enough to walk now, Ralph. – Let us see what we have got in our pockets; and then let us climb some hill and ascertain what sort of island we have been cast upon, for, whether good or bad, it seems likely to be our home for some time to come."

We now seated ourselves upon a rock, and began to examine into our personal property. When we reached the shore after being wrecked, my companions had taken off part of their clothes and spread them out in the sun to dry; for although the gale was raging fiercely, there was not a single cloud in the bright sky. They had also stripped off most part of my wet clothes and spread them also on the rocks. Having resumed our garments, we now searched all our pockets with the utmost care, and laid their contents out on a flat stone before us; and now that our minds were fully alive to our condition, it was with no little anxiety that we turned our several pockets inside out in order that nothing might escape us. When all was collected together, we found that our worldly goods consisted of the following articles:

First, a small penknife with a single blade, broken off about the middle and very rusty, besides having two or three notches on its edge. (Peterkin said of this, with his usual pleasantry, that it would do for a saw as well as a knife, which was a great advantage.)

Second, an old German-silver pencil-case without any lead in it. Third, a piece of whip-cord about six yards long. Fourth, a sailmaker's needle of a small size. Fifth, a ship's telescope, which I happened to have in my hand at the time the ship struck, and which I had clung to firmly all the time I was in the water; indeed, it was with difficulty that Jack got it out of my grasp when I was lying insensible on the shore. I cannot understand why I kept such a firm hold of this telescope. They say that a drowning man will clutch at a straw. Perhaps it may have been some such feeling in me, for I did not know that it was in my hand at the time we were wrecked. However, we felt some pleasure in having it with us now – although we did not see that it could be of much use to us, as the glass at the small end was broken to pieces. Our sixth article was a brass ring which Jack always wore on his little finger.

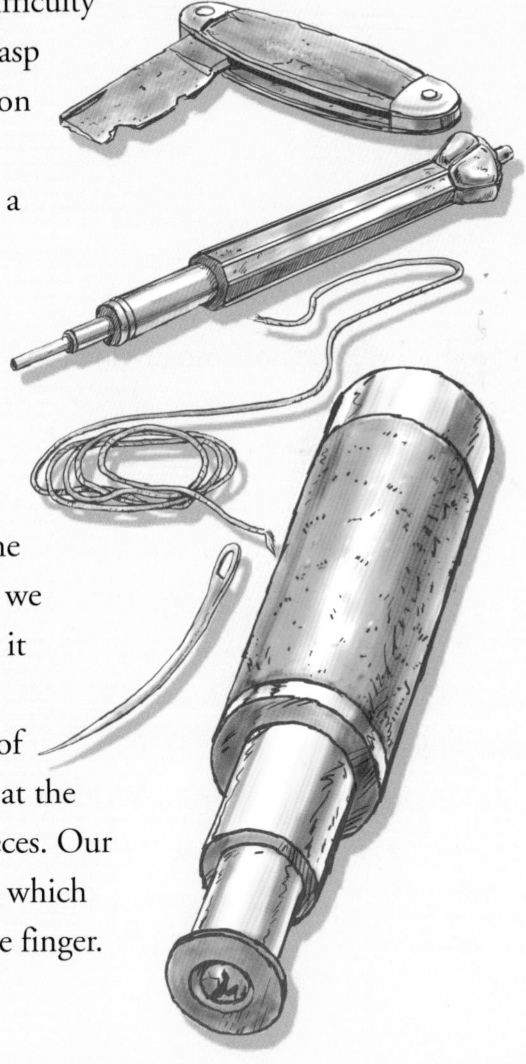

I never understood why he wore it; for Jack was not vain of his appearance, and did not seem to care for ornaments of any kind. Peterkin said, "it was in memory of the girl he left behind him!" But as he never spoke of this girl to either of us, I am inclined to think that Peterkin was either jesting or mistaken. In addition to these articles, we had a little bit of tinder and the clothes on our backs. These last were as follows:

Each of us had on a pair of stout canvas trousers and a pair of sailors' thick shoes. Jack wore a red flannel shirt, a blue jacket, and a red Kilmarnock bonnet or nightcap, besides a pair of worsted socks, and a cotton pocket-handkerchief with sixteen portraits of Lord Nelson printed on it and a union-jack in the middle. Peterkin had on a striped flannel shirt – which he wore outside his trousers and belted round his waist, after the manner of a tunic – and a round black straw hat. He had no jacket, having thrown it off just before we were cast into the sea; but this was not of much consequence, as the climate of the island proved to be extremely mild – so much so, indeed, that Jack and I often preferred to go about without our jackets. Peterkin had also a pair of white cotton socks and a blue handkerchief with white spots all over it. My own costume consisted of a blue flannel shirt, a blue jacket, a black cap, and a pair of

worsted socks, besides the shoes and canvas trousers already mentioned. This was all we had, and besides these things we had nothing else; but when we thought of the danger from which we had escaped, and how much worse off we might have been had the ship struck on the reef during the night, we felt very thankful that we were possessed of so much, although, I must confess, we sometimes wished that we had had a little more.

While we were examining these things and talking about them, Jack suddenly started and exclaimed:

"The oar! We have forgotten the oar!"

"What good will that do us?" said Peterkin. "There's wood enough on the island to make a thousand oars."

"Ay, lad," replied Jack; "but there's a bit of hoop-iron at the end of it, and that may be of much use to us."

"Very true," said I; "let us go fetch it." And with that we all three rose and hastened down to the beach. I still felt a little weak from loss of blood, so that my companions soon began to leave me behind; but Jack perceived this, and, with his usual considerate good-nature, turned back to help me. This was now the first time that I had looked well about me since landing, as the spot where I had been laid was covered with thick bushes, which almost hid the country from our view. As we now emerged from among these and walked down the sandy beach together, I cast my eyes about, and truly my heart glowed within me and my spirits rose at the beautiful prospect which I beheld on every side. The gale had suddenly died away, just as if it had blown furiously till it dashed our ship upon the rocks, and had nothing more to do after accomplishing that. The island on which we stood was hilly, and covered almost everywhere with the most beautiful and richly coloured trees, bushes, and shrubs, none of which I knew the names of at that time—except, indeed, the cocoa-nut palms, which I recognised at once from the many pictures that I had seen of them before I left home. A sandy beach of dazzling whiteness lined this bright-green shore, and upon it there fell a gentle ripple of the sea. This last astonished me much, for I recollected that at home the sea used to fall in huge billows on the shore long after a storm had subsided. But on casting my glance out to sea the cause became apparent. About a mile distant from the shore I saw the great billows of the ocean rolling like a green wall, and falling with a long, loud roar upon a low coral reef, where they were dashed into white foam and flung up in clouds of spray. This spray sometimes flew exceedingly high, and every here and there a beautiful rainbow was formed for a moment among the falling drops. We afterwards found that this coral reef extended quite round the island, and formed a natural breakwater to it. Beyond this, the sea rose and tossed violently from the effects of the storm; but between the reef and the shore it was as calm and as smooth as a pond.

My heart was filled with more delight than I can express at sight of so many glorious objects, and my thoughts turned suddenly to the contemplation of the Creator of them all. I mention this the more gladly, because at that time, I am ashamed to say, I very seldom thought of my Creator, although I was constantly surrounded by the most beautiful and wonderful of His works. I observed, from the expression of my companion's countenance, that he too derived much joy from the splendid scenery, which was all the more agreeable to us after our long voyage on the salt sea. There the breeze was fresh and cold; but here it was delightfully mild, and when a puff blew off the land it came laden with the most exquisite perfume that can be imagined. While we thus gazed we were startled by a loud "Huzza!" from Peterkin, and on looking towards the edge of the sea we saw him capering and jumping about like a monkey, and ever and anon tugging with all his might at something that lay upon the shore.

"What an odd fellow he is, to be sure!" said Jack, taking me by the arm and hurrying forward. "Come, let us hasten to see what it is."

"Here it is, boys – hurrah! Come along! Just what we want!" cried Peterkin as we drew near, still tugging with all his power. "First-rate; just the very ticket!"

I need scarcely say to my readers that my companion Peterkin was in the habit of using very remarkable and peculiar phrases. And I am free to confess that I did not well understand the meaning of some of them – such, for instance, as "the very ticket;" but I think it my duty to recount everything relating to my adventures with a strict regard to truthfulness in as far as my memory serves me, so I write, as nearly as possible, the exact words that my companions spoke. I often asked Peterkin to explain what he meant by "ticket," but he always answered me by going into fits of laughter. However, by observing the occasions on which he used it, I came to understand that it meant to show that something was remarkably good or fortunate.

On coming up we found that Peterkin was vainly endeavouring to pull the axe out of the oar into which, it will be remembered, Jack struck it while endeavouring to cut away the cordage among which it had become entangled at the bow of the ship. Fortunately for us, the axe had remained fast in the oar, and even now all Peterkin's strength could not draw it out of the cut.

"Ah, that is capital indeed!" cried Jack, at the same time giving the axe a wrench that plucked it out of the tough wood. "How fortunate this is! It will be of more value to us than a hundred knives, and the edge is quite new and sharp."

"I'll answer for the toughness of the handle, at any rate!" cried Peterkin; "my arms are nearly pulled out of the sockets. But see here, our luck is great. There is iron on the blade." He pointed to a piece of hoop-iron as he spoke, which had been nailed round the blade of the oar to prevent it from splitting.

This also was a fortunate discovery. Jack went down on his knees, and with the edge of the axe began carefully to force out the nails. But as they were firmly fixed in, and the operation blunted our axe, we carried the oar up with us to the place where we had

left the rest of our things, intending to burn the wood away from the iron at a more convenient time.

"Now, lads," said Jack after we had laid it on the stone which contained our little all, "I propose that we should go to the tail of the island, where the ship struck, which is only a quarter of a mile off; and see if anything else has been thrown ashore. I don't expect anything, but it is well to see. When we get back here it will be time to have our supper and prepare our beds."

"Agreed!" cried Peterkin and I together, as, indeed, we would have agreed to any proposal that Jack made; for, besides his being older and much stronger and taller than either of us, he was a very clever fellow, and, I think, would have induced people much older than himself to choose him for their leader, especially if they required to be led on a bold enterprise.

Now as we hastened along the white beach, which shone so brightly in the rays of the setting sun that our eyes were quite dazzled by its glare, it suddenly came into Peterkin's head that we had nothing to eat except the wild berries which grew in profusion at our feet.

"What shall we do, Jack?" said he with a rueful look. "Perhaps they may be poisonous!"

"No fear," replied Jack confidently. "I have observed that a few of them are not unlike some of the berries that grow wild on our own native hills. Besides, I saw one or two strange birds eating them just a few minutes ago, and what won't kill the birds won't kill us. But look up there, Peterkin," continued Jack, pointing to the branched head of a cocoa-nut palm. "There are nuts for us in all stages."

"So there are!" cried Peterkin, who, being of a very unobservant nature, had been too much taken up with other things to notice anything so high above his head as the fruit of a palm-tree. But whatever faults my young comrade had, he could not be blamed for want of activity or animal spirits. Indeed, the nuts had scarcely been pointed out to him when he bounded up the tall stem of the tree like a squirrel, and in a few minutes returned with three nuts, each as large as a man's fist.

"You had better keep them till we return," said Jack. "Let us finish our work before eating."

"So be it, captain; go ahead!" cried Peterkin, thrusting the nuts into his trousers pocket. "In fact, I don't want to eat just now; but I would give a good deal for a drink. Oh, that I could find a spring! but I don't see the smallest sign of one hereabouts. I say, Jack, how does it happen that you seem to be up to everything? You have told us the names of half-a-dozen trees already, and yet you say that you were never in the South Seas before."

"I'm not up to everything, Peterkin, as you'll find out ere long," replied Jack with a smile; "but I have been a great reader of books of travel and adventure all my life, and that has put me up to a good many things that you are, perhaps, not acquainted with."

"Oh, Jack, that's all humbug! If you begin to lay everything to the credit of books, I'll quite lose my opinion of you," cried Peterkin with a look of contempt. "I've seen a lot o' fellows that were always poring over books, and when they came to try to do anything, they were no better than baboons!"

"You are quite right," retorted Jack; "and I have seen a lot of fellows, who never looked into books at all, who knew nothing about anything except the things they had actually seen, and very little they knew even about these. Indeed, some were so ignorant that they did not know that cocoa-nuts grew on cocoa-nut trees!"

I could not refrain from laughing at this rebuke, for there was much truth in it as to Peterkin's ignorance.

"Humph! maybe you're right," answered Peterkin; "but I

would not give tuppence for a man of books if he had nothing else in him."

"Neither would I," said Jack; "but that's no reason why you should run books down, or think less of me for having read them. Suppose, now, Peterkin, that you wanted to build a ship, and I were to give you a long and particular account of the way to do it, would not that be very useful?"

"No doubt of it," said Peterkin, laughing.

"And suppose I were to write the account in a letter instead of telling you in words, would that be less useful?"

"Well – no, perhaps not."

"Well, suppose I were to print it and send it to you in the form of a book, would it not be as good and useful as ever?"

"Oh, bother! Jack, you're a philosopher, and that's worse than anything!" cried Peterkin with a look of pretended horror.

"Very well, Peterkin, we shall see," returned Jack, halting under the shade of a cocoa-nut tree. "You said you were thirsty just a minute ago. Now jump up that tree and bring down a nut – not a ripe one; bring a green, unripe one."

Peterkin looked surprised, but seeing that Jack was in earnest, he obeyed.

"Now cut a hole in it with your penknife and clap it to your mouth, old fellow," said Jack.

Peterkin did as he was directed, and we both burst into uncontrollable laughter at the changes that instantly passed over his expressive countenance. No sooner had he put the nut to his mouth, and thrown back his head in order to catch what came out of it, than his eyes opened to twice their ordinary size with astonishment, while his throat moved vigorously in the act of swallowing. Then a smile and a look of intense delight overspread his face, except, indeed, the mouth, which, being firmly fixed to the hole in the nut, could not take part in the expression; but he endeavoured to make up for this by winking at us excessively with his right eye. At length he stopped, and drawing a long breath, exclaimed:

"Nectar! Perfect nectar! I say, Jack, you're a Briton – the best fellow I ever met in my life – Only taste that!" said he, turning to me and holding the nut to my mouth. I immediately drank, and certainly I was much surprised at the delightful liquid that flowed copiously down my throat. It was extremely cool, and had a sweet taste, mingled with acid; in fact, it was the likest thing to lemonade I ever tasted, and was most grateful and refreshing. I handed the nut to Jack, who, after tasting it, said, "Now, Peterkin, you unbeliever! I never saw or tasted a cocoa-nut in my life before, except those sold in shops at home; but I once read that the green nuts contain that stuff; and you see it is true."

"And, pray," asked Peterkin, "what sort of 'stuff' does the ripe nut contain?"

"A hollow kernel," answered Jack, "with a liquid like milk in it; but it does not satisfy thirst so well as hunger. It is very wholesome food, I believe."

"Meat and drink on the same tree!" cried Peterkin; "washing in the sea, lodging on the ground – and all for nothing! My dear boys, we're set up for life! It must be the ancient Paradise – hurrah!" and Peterkin tossed his straw hat in the air and ran along the beach, hallooing like a madman with delight.

We afterwards found, however, that these lovely islands were very unlike Paradise in many things. But more of this in its proper place.

We had now come to the point of rocks on which the ship had struck, but did not find a single article, although we searched carefully among the coral rocks, which at this place jutted out so far as nearly to join the reef that encircled the island. Just as we were about to return, however, we saw something black floating in a little cove that had escaped our observation. Running forward, we drew it from the water, and found it to be a long, thick, leather boot, such as fishermen at home wear; and a few paces farther on, we picked up its fellow.

We at once recognised these as having belonged to our captain, for he had worn them during the whole of the storm in order to guard his legs from the waves and spray that constantly washed over our decks. My first thought on seeing them was that our dear captain had been drowned; but Jack soon put my mind more at rest on that point by saying that if the captain had been drowned with the boots on, he would certainly have been washed ashore along with them, and that he had no doubt whatever he had

kicked them off while in the sea that he might swim more easily.

Peterkin immediately put them on; but they were so large that, as Jack said, they would have done for boots, trousers, and vest too. I also tried them; but although I was long enough in the legs for them, they were much too large in the feet for me. So we handed them to Jack, who was anxious to make me keep them; but as they fitted his large limbs and feet as if they had been made for him, I would not hear of it, so he consented at last to use them. I may remark, however, that Jack did not use them often, as they were extremely heavy.

It was beginning to grow dark when we returned to our encampment; so we put off our visit to the top of a hill till next day, and employed the light that yet remained to us in cutting down a quantity of boughs and the broad leaves of a tree of which none of us knew the name. With these we erected a sort of rustic bower, in which we meant to pass the night. There was no absolute necessity for this, because the air of our island was so genial and balmy that we could have slept quite well without any shelter; but we were so little used to sleeping in the open air that we did not quite relish the idea of lying down without any covering over us. Besides, our bower would shelter us from the night-dews or rain, if any should happen to fall. Having strewed the floor with leaves and dry grass, we bethought ourselves of supper.

But it now occurred to us, for the first time, that we had no means of making a fire.

"Now, there's a fix! What shall we do?" said Peterkin, while we both turned our eyes to Jack, to whom we always looked in our difficulties. Jack seemed not a little perplexed.

"There are flints enough, no doubt, on the beach," said he; "but they are of no use at all without a steel. However, we must try." So saying, he went to the beach, and soon returned with two flints. On one of these he placed the tinder, and endeavoured to ignite it; but it was with great difficulty that a very small spark was struck out of the flints, and the tinder, being a bad, hard piece, would not catch. He then tried the bit of hoop-iron, which would not strike fire at all; and after that the back of the axe, with no better success. During all these trials Peterkin sat with his hands in his pockets, gazing with a most melancholy visage at our comrade, his face growing longer and more miserable at each successive failure.

"Oh dear!" he sighed; "I would not care a button for the cooking of our victuals – perhaps they don't need it – but it's so dismal to eat one's supper in the dark, and we have had such a capital day that it's a pity to finish off in this glum style. Oh, I have it!" he cried, starting up: "the spy-glass – the big glass at the end is a burning-glass!"

"You forget that we have no sun," said I.

Peterkin was silent. In his sudden recollection of the telescope he had quite overlooked the absence of the sun.

"Ah, boys, I've got it now!" exclaimed Jack, rising and cutting a branch from a neighbouring bush, which he stripped of its leaves. "I recollect seeing this done once at home. Hand me the bit of whip-cord." With the cord and branch Jack soon formed a bow. Then he cut a piece about three inches long off the end of a dead branch, which he pointed at the two ends. Round this he passed the cord of the bow, and placed one end against his chest, which was protected from its point by a chip of wood; the other point he placed against the bit of tinder, and then began to saw vigorously with the bow, just as a blacksmith does with his drill while boring a hole in a piece of iron. In a few seconds the tinder began to smoke; in less than a minute it caught fire; and in less than a quarter of an hour we were drinking our lemonade and eating cocoa-nuts round a fire that would have roasted an entire

sheep, while the smoke, flames, and sparks flew up among the broad leaves of the overhanging palm-trees, and cast a warm glow upon our leafy bower.

That night the starry sky looked down through the gently rustling trees upon our slumbers, and the distant roaring of the surf upon the coral reef was our lullaby.

Kidnapped
The Loss of the Brig
Robert Louis Stevenson
The Cruel Sea

The story so far

Set in Scotland, in 1751, *Kidnapped* tells the story of David Balfour, a young boy of seventeen. On his father's death, he seeks out his only other living relative, his Uncle Ebenezer, but the old man has persuaded a ship's captain, Hoseason, to kidnap David and sell him as a slave in the Americas. After they have set sail, they run down another boat, from which only one man is saved, the bold and dashing Alan Breck. However, during a terrible storm the ship is wrecked upon rocks. David manages to escape and is washed ashore on a small island. There he is stranded until some fishermen tell him that he can escape from the island at low tide.

The Loss of the Brig
from

Kidnapped

by

Robert Louis Stevenson

It was already late at night, and as dark as it ever would be at that season of the year (and that is to say, it was still pretty bright), when Hoseason clapped his head into the round-house door.

"Here," said he, "come out and see if ye can pilot."

"Is this one of your tricks?" asked Alan.

"Do I look like tricks?" cries the captain. "I have other things to think of – my brig's in danger!"

By the concerned look of his face, and, above all, by the sharp tones in which he spoke of his brig, it was plain to both of us he was in deadly earnest; and so Alan and I, with no great fear of treachery, stepped on deck.

The sky was clear; it blew hard, and was bitter cold; a great deal of daylight lingered; and the moon, which was nearly full, shone brightly. The brig was close hauled, so as to round the southwest corner of the Island of Mull, the hills of which (and Ben More above them all, with a wisp of mist upon the top of it) lay full upon the lar-board bow. Though it was no good point of sailing for the Covenant, she tore through the seas at a great rate, pitching and straining, and pursued by the westerly swell.

Altogether it was no such ill night to keep the seas in; and I had begun to wonder what it was that sat so heavily upon the captain, when the brig rising suddenly on the top of a high swell, he pointed and cried to us to look. Away on the lee bow, a thing like a fountain rose out of the moonlit sea, and immediately after we heard a low sound of roaring.

"What do ye call that?" asked the captain, gloomily.

"The sea breaking on a reef," said Alan. "And now ye ken where it is; and what better would ye have?"

"Ay," said Hoseason, "if it was the only one."

And sure enough, just as he spoke there came a second fountain farther to the south.

"There!" said Hoseason. "Ye see for yourself. If I had kent of these reefs, if I had had a chart, or if Shuan had been spared, it's not sixty guineas, no, nor six hundred, would have made me risk my brig in sic a stoneyard! But you, sir, that was to pilot us, have ye never a word?"

"I'm thinking," said Alan, "these'll be what they call the Torran Rocks."

"Are there many of them?" says the captain.

"Truly, sir, I am nae pilot," said Alan; "but it sticks in my mind there are ten miles of them."

Mr. Riach and the captain looked at each other.

"There's a way through them, I suppose?" said the captain.

"Doubtless," said Alan, "but where? But it somehow runs in my mind once more that it is clearer under the land."

"So?" said Hoseason. "We'll have to haul our wind then, Mr. Riach; we'll have to come as near in about the end of Mull as we can take her, sir; and even then we'll have the land to kep the wind off us, and that stoneyard on our lee. Well, we're in for it now, and may as well crack on."

With that he gave an order to the steersman, and sent Riach to the foretop. There were only five men on deck, counting the officers; these being all that were fit (or, at least, both fit and willing) for their work. So, as I say, it fell to Mr. Riach to go aloft, and he sat there looking out and hailing the deck with news of all he saw.

"The sea to the south is thick," he cried; and then, after a while, "it does seem clearer in by the land."

"Well, sir," said Hoseason to Alan, "we'll try your way of it. But

I think I might as well trust to a blind fiddler. Pray God you're right."

"Pray God I am!" says Alan to me. "But where did I hear it? Well, well, it will be as it must."

As we got nearer to the turn of the land the reefs began to be sown here and there on our very path; and Mr. Riach sometimes cried down to us to change the course. Sometimes, indeed, none too soon; for one reef was so close on the brig's weather board that when a sea burst upon it the lighter sprays fell upon her deck and wetted us like rain.

The brightness of the night showed us these perils as clearly as

by day, which was, perhaps, the more alarming. It showed me, too, the face of the captain as he stood by the steersman, now on one foot, now on the other, and sometimes blowing in his hands, but still listening and looking and as steady as steel. Neither he nor Mr. Riach had shown well in the fighting; but I saw they were brave in their own trade, and admired them all the more because I found Alan very white.

"Ochone, David," says he, "this is no the kind of death I fancy!"

"What, Alan!" I cried, "you're not afraid?"

"No," said he, wetting his lips, "but you'll allow, yourself, it's a cold ending."

By this time, now and then sheering to one side or the other to avoid a reef, but still hugging the wind and the land, we had got round Iona and begun to come alongside Mull. The tide at the tail of the land ran very strong, and threw the brig about. Two hands were put to the helm, and Hoseason himself would sometimes lend a help; and it was strange to see three strong men throw their weight upon the tiller, and it (like a living thing) struggle against and drive them back. This would have been the greater danger had not the sea been for some while free of obstacles. Mr. Riach, besides, announced from the top that he saw clear water ahead.

"Ye were right," said Hoseason to Alan. "Ye have saved the brig, sir. I'll mind that when we come to clear accounts." And I believe he not only meant what he said, but would have done it; so high a place did the Covenant hold in his affections.

But this is matter only for conjecture, things having gone otherwise than he forecast.

"Keep her away a point," sings out Mr. Riach. "Reef to windward!"

And just at the same time the tide caught the brig, and threw the wind out of her sails. She came round into the wind like a top, and the next moment struck the reef with such a dunch as threw us all flat upon the deck, and came near to shake Mr. Riach from his place upon the mast.

I was on my feet in a minute. The reef on which we had struck was close in under the southwest end of Mull, off a little isle they call Earraid, which lay low and black upon the larboard. Sometimes the swell broke clean over us; sometimes it only ground the poor brig upon the reef, so that we could hear her beat herself to pieces; and what with the great noise of the sails, and the singing of the wind, and the flying of the spray in the moonlight, and the sense of danger, I think my head must have been partly turned, for I could scarcely understand the things I saw.

Presently I observed Mr. Riach and the seamen busy round the skiff, and, still in the same blank, ran over to assist them; and as soon as I set my hand to work, my mind came clear again. It was no very easy task, for the skiff lay amidships and was full of hamper, and the breaking of the heavier seas continually forced us to give over and hold on; but we all wrought like horses while we could.

Meanwhile such of the wounded as could move came clambering out of the fore-scuttle and began to help; while the rest that lay helpless in their bunks harrowed me with screaming and begging to be saved.

The captain took no part. It seemed he was struck stupid. He stood holding by the shrouds, talking to himself and groaning out aloud whenever the ship hammered on the rock. His brig was like wife and child to him; he had looked on, day by day, at the mishandling of poor Ransome; but when it came to the brig, he seemed to suffer along with her.

All the time of our working at the boat, I remember only one other thing: that I asked Alan, looking across at the shore, what country it was; and he answered, it was the worst possible for him, for it was a land of the Campbells.

We had one of the wounded men told off to keep a watch upon the seas and cry us warning. Well, we had the boat about ready to be launched, when this man sang out pretty shrill: "For God's sake, hold on!" We knew by his tone that it was something more than ordinary; and sure enough, there followed a sea so huge that it lifted the brig right up and canted her over on her beam. Whether the cry came too late, or my hold was too weak, I know not; but at the sudden tilting of the ship I was cast clean over the bulwarks into the sea.

I went down, and drank my fill, and then came up, and got a blink of the moon, and then down again. They say a man sinks a

I went down, and drank my fill, and then came up, and got a blink of the moon, and then down again.

third time for good. I cannot be made like other folk, then; for I would not like to write how often I went down, or how often I came up again. All the while, I was being hurled along, and beaten upon and choked, and then swallowed whole; and the thing was so distracting to my wits, that I was neither sorry nor afraid.

Presently, I found I was holding to a spar, which helped me somewhat. And then all of a sudden I was in quiet water, and began to come to myself.

It was the spare yard I had got hold of, and I was amazed to see how far I had travelled from the brig. I hailed her, indeed; but it was plain she was already out of cry. She was still holding together; but whether or not they had yet launched the boat, I was too far off and too low down to see.

While I was hailing the brig, I spied a tract of water lying between us where no great waves came, but which yet boiled white all over and bristled in the moon with rings and bubbles. Sometimes the whole tract swung to one side, like the tail of a live serpent; sometimes, for a glimpse, it would all disappear and then boil up again. What it was I had no guess, which for the time increased my fear of it; but I now know it must have been the roost or tide race, which had carried me away so fast and tumbled me about so cruelly, and at last, as if tired of that play, had flung out me and the spare yard upon its landward margin.

I now lay quite becalmed, and began to feel that a man can die of cold as well as of drowning. The shores of Earraid were close in; I could see in the moonlight the dots of heather and the sparkling of the mica in the rocks.

"Well," thought I to myself, "if I cannot get as far as that, it's strange!"

I had no skill of swimming, Essen Water being small in our neighbourhood; but when I laid hold upon the yard with both arms, and kicked out with both feet, I soon begun to find that I was moving. Hard work it was, and mortally slow; but in about an hour of kicking and splashing, I had got well in between the points of a sandy bay surrounded by low hills.

The sea was here quite quiet; there was no sound of any surf; the moon shone clear; and I thought in my heart I had never seen a place so desert and desolate. But it was dry land; and when at last it grew so shallow that I could leave the yard and wade ashore upon my feet, I cannot tell if I was more tired or more grateful. Both, at least, I was: tired as I never was before that night; and grateful to God as I trust I have been often, though never with more cause.

With my stepping ashore I began the most unhappy part of my adventures. It was half-past twelve in the morning, and though the wind was broken by the land, it was a cold night. I dared not sit down (for I thought I should have frozen), but took off my shoes and walked to and fro upon the sand, bare-foot, and beating my breast with infinite weariness. There was no sound of man or cattle; not a cock crew, though it was about the hour of their first waking; only the surf broke outside in the distance, which put me in mind of my perils and those of my friend. To walk by the sea at that hour of the morning, and in a place so desert-like and lonesome, struck me with a kind of fear.

As soon as the day began to break I put on my shoes and climbed a hill – the ruggedest scramble I ever undertook – falling, the whole way, between big blocks of granite, or leaping from one to another. When I got to the top the dawn was come. There was no sign of the brig, which must have lifted from the reef and sunk. The boat, too, was nowhere to be seen. There was never a sail upon the ocean; and in what I could see of the land was neither house nor man.

I was afraid to think what had befallen my shipmates, and afraid to look longer at so empty a scene. What with my wet clothes and weariness, and my belly that now began to ache with hunger, I had enough to trouble me without that. So I set off eastward along the south coast, hoping to find a house where I might warm myself, and perhaps get news of those I had lost. And at the worst, I considered the sun would soon rise and dry my clothes.

After a little, my way was stopped by a creek or inlet of the sea, which seemed to run pretty deep into the land; and as I had no means to get across, I must needs change my direction to go about the end of it. It was still the roughest kind of walking; indeed the whole, not only of Earraid, but of the neighbouring part of Mull (which they call the Ross) is nothing but a jumble of granite rocks with heather in among. At first the creek kept narrowing as I had looked to see; but presently to my surprise it began to widen out again. At this I scratched my head, but had still no notion of the truth: until at last I came to a rising ground, and it burst upon me all in a moment that I was cast upon a little barren isle, and cut off on every side by the salt seas.

Instead of the sun rising to dry me, it came on to rain, with a thick mist; so that my case was lamentable.

I stood in the rain, and shivered, and wondered what to do, till it occurred to me that perhaps the creek was fordable. Back I went to the narrowest point and waded in. But not three yards from shore, I plumped in head over ears; and if ever I was heard of more, it was rather by God's grace than my own prudence. I was no wetter (for that could hardly be), but I was all the colder for this mishap; and having lost another hope was the more unhappy.

And now, all at once, the yard came in my head. What had carried me through the roost would surely serve me to cross this little quiet creek in safety. With that I set off, undaunted, across the top of the isle, to fetch and carry it back. It was a weary tramp in all ways, and if hope had not buoyed me up, I must have cast myself down and given up. Whether with the sea salt, or because I was growing fevered, I was distressed with thirst, and had to stop, as I went, and drink the peaty water out of the hags.

I came to the bay at last, more dead than alive; and at the first glance, I thought the yard was something farther out than when I left it. In I went, for the third time, into the sea. The sand was smooth and firm, and shelved gradually down, so that I could wade out till the water was almost to my neck and the little waves splashed into my face. But at that depth my feet began to leave me, and I durst venture in no farther. As for the yard, I saw it bobbing very quietly some twenty feet beyond.

I had borne up well until this last disappointment; but at that I came ashore, and flung myself down upon the sands and wept.

The time I spent upon the island is still so horrible a thought to me, that I must pass it lightly over. In all the books I have read of people cast away, they had either their pockets full of tools, or a chest of things would be thrown upon the beach along with them, as if on purpose. My case was very different. I had nothing in my pockets but money and Alan's silver button; and being inland bred, I was as much short of knowledge as of means.

I knew indeed that shell-fish were counted good to eat; and among the rocks of the isle I found a great plenty of limpets, which at first I could scarcely strike from their places, not knowing quickness to be needful. There were, besides, some of the little shells that we call buckies; I think periwinkle is the English name. Of these two I made my whole diet, devouring them cold and raw as I found them; and so hungry was I, that at first they seemed to me delicious.

I knew indeed that shell-fish were counted good to eat; and among the rocks of the isle I found a great plenty of limpets.

Perhaps they were out of season, or perhaps there was something wrong in the sea about my island. But at least I had no sooner eaten my first meal than I was seized with giddiness and retching, and lay for a long time no better than dead. A second trial of the same food (indeed I had no other) did better with me, and revived my strength. But as long as I was on the island, I never knew what to expect when I had eaten; sometimes all was well, and sometimes I was thrown into a miserable sickness; nor could I ever distinguish what particular fish it was that hurt me.

All day it streamed rain; the island ran like a sop, there was no dry spot to be found; and when I lay down that night, between two boulders that made a kind of roof, my feet were in a bog.

The second day I crossed the island to all sides. There was no one part of it better than another; it was all desolate and rocky; nothing living on it but game birds which I lacked the means to kill, and the gulls which haunted the outlying rocks in a prodigious number. But the creek, or strait, that cut off the isle from the main-land of the Ross, opened out on the north into a bay, and the bay again opened into the Sound of Iona; and it was the neighbourhood of this place that I chose to be my home; though if I had thought upon the very name of home in such a spot, I must have burst out weeping.

I had good reasons for my choice. There was in this part of the isle a little hut of a house like a pig's hut, where fishers used to sleep when they came there upon their business; but the turf roof of it had fallen entirely in; so that the hut was of no use to me, and gave me less shelter than my rocks. What was more important, the shell-fish on which I lived grew there in great plenty; when the tide was out I could gather a peck at a time: and this was doubtless a convenience. But the other reason went deeper. I had become in no way used to the horrid solitude of the isle, but still looked round me on all sides (like a man that was hunted), between fear and hope that I might see some human creature coming. Now, from a little up the hillside over the bay, I could catch a sight of the great, ancient church and the roofs of the people's houses in Iona. And on the other hand, over the low country of the Ross, I saw smoke go up, morning and evening, as if from a homestead in a hollow of the land.

I used to watch this smoke, when I was wet and cold, and had my head half turned with loneliness; and think of the fireside and the company, till my heart burned. It was the same with the roofs of Iona. Altogether, this sight I had of men's homes and comfortable lives, although it put a point on my own sufferings, yet it kept hope alive, and helped me to eat my raw shell-fish (which had soon grown to be a disgust), and saved me from the sense of horror I had whenever I was quite alone with dead rocks, and fowls, and the rain, and the cold sea.

I say it kept hope alive; and indeed it seemed impossible that I should be left to die on the shores of my own country, and within view of a church-tower and the smoke of men's houses. But the second day passed; and though as long as the light lasted I kept a bright look-out for boats on the Sound or men passing on the Ross, no help came near me. It still rained, and I turned in to sleep, as wet as ever, and with a cruel sore throat, but a little comforted, perhaps, by having said good-night to my next neighbours, the people of Iona.

Charles the Second declared a man could stay outdoors more days in the year in the climate of England than in any other. This was very like a king, with a palace at his back and changes of dry clothes. But he must have had better luck on his flight from Worcester than I had on that miserable isle. It was the height of the summer; yet it rained for more than twenty-four hours, and did not clear until the afternoon of the third day.

This was the day of incidents. In the morning I saw a red deer, a buck with a fine spread of antlers, standing in the rain on the top of the island; but he had scarce seen me rise from under my rock, before he trotted off upon the other side. I supposed he must have swum the strait; though what should bring any creature to Earraid, was more than I could fancy.

A little after, as I was jumping about after my limpets, I was startled by a guinea-piece, which fell upon a rock in front of me and glanced off into the sea. When the sailors gave me my money again, they kept back not only about a third of the whole sum, but my father's leather purse; so that from that day out, I carried my gold loose in a pocket with a button. I now saw there must be a hole, and clapped my hand to the place in a great hurry. But this was to lock the stable door after the steed was stolen. I had left the shore at Queensferry with near on fifty pounds; now I found no more than two guinea-pieces and a silver shilling.

It is true I picked up a third guinea a little after, where it lay shining on a piece of turf. That made a fortune of three pounds and four shillings, English money, for a lad, the rightful heir of an estate, and now starving on an isle at the extreme end of the wild Highlands.

This state of my affairs dashed me still further; and, indeed my plight on that third morning was truly pitiful. My clothes were beginning to rot; my stockings in particular were quite worn through, so that my shanks went naked; my hands had grown quite soft with the continual soaking; my throat was very sore, my strength had much abated, and my heart so turned against the horrid stuff I was condemned to eat, that the very sight of it came near to sicken me.

And yet the worst was not yet come.

There is a pretty high rock on the northwest of Earraid, which (because it had a flat top and overlooked the Sound) I was much in the habit of frequenting; not that ever I stayed in one place, save when asleep, my misery giving me no rest. Indeed, I wore myself down with continual and aimless goings and comings in the rain.

As soon, however, as the sun came out, I lay down on the top of that rock to dry myself. The comfort of the sunshine is a thing I cannot tell. It set me thinking hopefully of my deliverance, of which I had begun to despair; and I scanned the sea and the Ross with a fresh interest. On the south of my rock, a part of the island jutted out and hid the open ocean, so that a boat could thus come quite near me upon that side, and I be none the wiser.

Well, all of a sudden, a coble with a brown sail and a pair of fishers aboard of it, came flying round that corner of the isle, bound for Iona. I shouted out, and then fell on my knees on the rock and reached up my hands and prayed to them. They were near enough to hear – I could even see the colour of their hair; and there was no doubt but they observed me, for they cried out in the Gaelic tongue, and laughed. But the boat never turned aside, and flew on, right before my eyes, for Iona.

I could not believe such wickedness, and ran along the shore from rock to rock, crying on them piteously even after they were out of reach of my voice, I still cried and waved to them; and when they were quite gone, I thought my heart would have burst. All the time of my troubles I wept only twice. Once, when I could not reach the yard, and now, the second time, when these fishers turned a deaf ear to my cries. But this time I wept and roared like a wicked child, tearing up the turf with my nails, and grinding my face in the earth. If a wish would kill men, those two fishers would never have seen morning, and I should likely have died upon my island.

When I was a little over my anger, I must eat again, but with such loathing of the mess as I could now scarce control. Sure enough, I should have done as well to fast, for my fishes poisoned me again. I had all my first pains; my throat was so sore I could scarce swallow; I had a fit of strong shuddering, which clucked my teeth together; and there came on me that dreadful sense of illness, which we have no name for either in Scotch or English. I thought I should have died, and made my peace with God, forgiving all men, even my uncle and the fishers; and as soon as I had thus made up my mind to the worst, clearness came upon me; I observed the night was falling dry; my clothes were dried a good deal; truly, I was in a better case than ever before, since I had landed on the isle; and so I got to sleep at last, with a thought of gratitude.

The next day (which was the fourth of this horrible life of mine) I found my bodily strength run very low. But the sun shone, the air was sweet, and what I managed to eat of the shell-fish agreed well with me and revived my courage.

I was scarce back on my rock (where I went always the first thing after I had eaten) before I observed a boat coming down the Sound, and with her head, as I thought, in my direction.

I began at once to hope and fear exceedingly; for I thought these men might have thought better of their cruelty and be coming back to my assistance. But another disappointment, such as yesterday's, was more than I could bear. I turned my back, accordingly, upon the sea, and did not look again till I had counted many hundreds. The boat was still heading for the island. The next time I counted the full thousand, as slowly as I could, my heart beating so as to hurt me. And then it was out of all question. She was coming straight to Earraid!

I could no longer hold myself back, but ran to the seaside and out, from one rock to another, as far as I could go. It is a marvel I

was not drowned; for when I was brought to a stand at last, my legs shook under me, and my mouth was so dry, I must wet it with the sea-water before I was able to shout.

All this time the boat was coming on; and now I was able to perceive it was the same boat and the same two men as yesterday. This I knew by their hair, which the one had of a bright yellow and the other black. But now there was a third man along with them, who looked to be of a better class.

As soon as they were come within easy speech, they let down

their sail and lay quiet. In spite of my supplications, they drew no nearer in, and what frightened me most of all, the new man tee-hee'd with laughter as he talked and looked at me.

Then he stood up in the boat and addressed me a long while, speaking fast and with many wavings of his hand. I told him I had no Gaelic; and at this he became very angry, and I began to suspect he thought he was talking English. Listening very close, I caught the word "whateffer" several times; but all the rest was Gaelic and might have been Greek and Hebrew for me.

"Whatever," said I, to show him I had caught a word.

"Yes, yes – yes, yes," says he, and then he looked at the other men, as much as to say, "I told you I spoke English," and began again as hard as ever in the Gaelic.

This time I picked out another word, "tide." Then I had a flash of hope. I remembered he was always waving his hand towards the mainland of the Ross.

"Do you mean when the tide is out – ?" I cried, and could not finish.

"Yes, yes," said he. "Tide."

At that I turned tail upon their boat (where my adviser had once more begun to tee-hee with laughter), leaped back the way I had come, from one stone to another, and set off running across the isle as I had never run before. In about half an hour I came out upon the shores of the creek; and, sure enough, it was shrunk into a little trickle of water, through which I dashed, not above my knees, and landed with a shout on the main island.

A sea-bred boy would not have stayed a day on Earraid; which is only what they call a tidal islet, and except in the bottom of the neaps, can be entered and left twice in every twenty-four hours, either dry-shod, or at the most by wading. Even I, who had the tide going out and in before me in the bay, and even watched for the ebbs, the better to get my shellfish – even I (I say) if I had sat down to think, instead of raging at my fate, must have soon guessed the secret, and got free. It was no wonder the fishers had not understood me. The wonder was rather that they had ever guessed my pitiful illusion, and taken the trouble to come back. I had starved with cold and hunger on that island for close upon one hundred hours. But for the fishers, I might have left my bones there, in pure folly. And even as it was, I had paid for it pretty dear, not only in past sufferings, but in my present case; being clothed like a beggar-man, scarce able to walk, and in great pain of my sore throat.

I have seen wicked men and fools, a great many of both; and I believe they both get paid in the end; but the fools first.

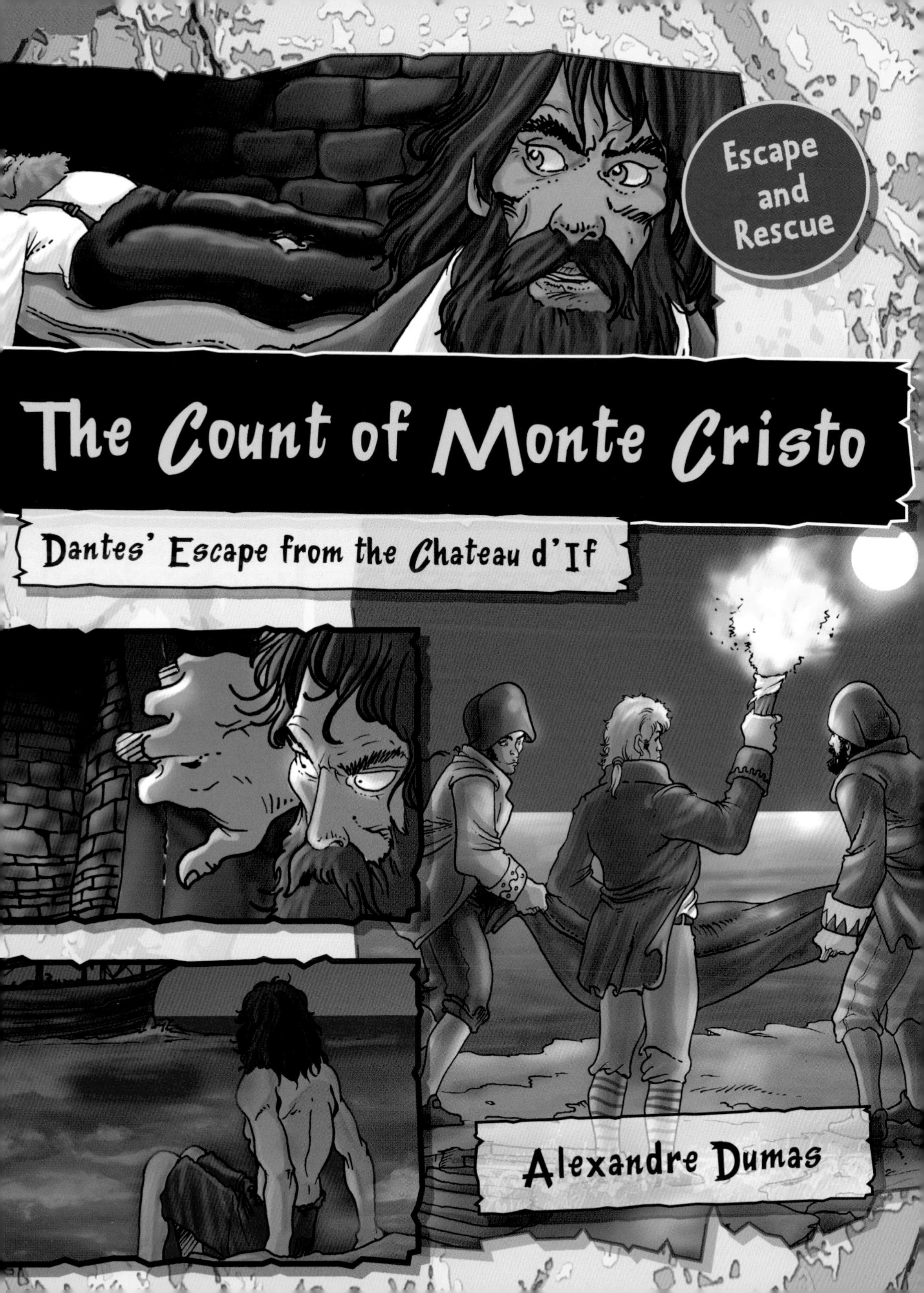
Escape and Rescue
The Count of Monte Cristo
Dantes' Escape from the Chateau d'If
Alexandre Dumas

The story so far

Edmond Dantes, a sailor in Napoleonic France, has been imprisoned in the notorious Chateau d'If, a prison on a Mediterranean island. His crime was to be found carrying a treacherous letter. After years of solitary confinement, he has met up with the prisoner in the next cell through an underground tunnel. The other prisoner is an older man, a priest called Faria, who has taught Dantes many things, and tells him the location of a great treasure he has hidden. Faria suffers from an illness that may kill him at any time. Dantes has saved his life once before by giving him his medicine at the right moment, but Faria knows he hasn't long left to live.

Dantes' Escape from the Chateau d'If
from

The Count of Monte Cristo

by

Alexandre Dumas

One night Edmond awoke suddenly, believing that he heard someone calling him. He opened his eyes upon utter darkness. His name, or rather a plaintive voice which essayed to pronounce his name, reached him. He sat up in bed and a cold sweat broke out upon his brow. Undoubtedly the call came from Faria's dungeon. "Alas," murmured Edmond; "can it be?"

He moved his bed, drew up the stone, rushed into the passage, and reached the opposite extremity; the secret entrance was open. By the light of the wretched and wavering lamp, of which we have spoken, Dantes saw the old man, pale, but yet erect, clinging to the bedstead. His features were writhing with those horrible symptoms which he already knew, and which had so seriously alarmed him when he saw them for the first time.

"Alas, my dear friend," said Faria in a resigned tone, "you understand, do you not, and I need not attempt to explain to you?"

Edmond uttered a cry of agony, and, quite out of his senses, rushed towards the door, exclaiming, "Help, help!" Faria had just sufficient strength to restrain him.

"Silence," he said, "or you are lost. We must now only think of you, my dear friend, and so act as to render your captivity supportable or your flight possible. It would require years to do again what I have done here, and the results would be instantly destroyed if our jailers knew we had communicated with each other. Besides, be assured, my dear Edmond, the dungeon I am about to leave will not long remain empty; some other unfortunate being will soon take my place, and to him you will appear like an angel of salvation. Perhaps he will be young, strong, and enduring, like yourself, and will aid you in your escape, while I have been but a hindrance. You will no longer have half a dead body tied to you as a drag to all your movements. At length providence has done something for you; he restores to you more than he takes away, and it was time I should die."

Edmond could only clasp his hands and exclaim, "Oh, my friend, my friend, speak not thus!" and then resuming all his presence of mind, which had for a moment staggered under this blow, and his strength, which had failed at the words of the old man, he said, "Oh, I have saved you once, and I will save you a second time!" And raising the foot of the bed, he drew out the phial, still a third filled with the red liquor.

"See," he exclaimed, "there remains still some of the magic draught. Quick, quick! tell me what I must do this time; are there any fresh instructions? Speak, my friend; I listen."

"There is not a hope," replied Faria, shaking his head, "but no matter; God wills it that man whom he has created, and in whose heart he has so profoundly rooted the love of life, should do all in his power to preserve that existence, which, however painful it may be, is yet always so dear."

"Oh, yes, yes!" exclaimed Dantes; "and I tell you that I will save you yet."

"Well, then, try. The cold gains upon me. I feel the blood flowing towards my brain. These horrible chills, which make my teeth chatter and seem to dislocate my bones, begin to pervade my whole frame; in five minutes the malady will reach its height, and in a quarter of an hour there will be nothing left of me but a corpse."

"Oh!" exclaimed Dantes, his heart wrung with anguish.

"Do as you did before, only do not wait so long, all the springs of life are now exhausted in me, and death," he continued, looking at his paralyzed arm and leg, "has but half its work to do. If, after having made me swallow twelve drops instead of ten, you see that I do not recover, then pour the rest down my throat. Now lift me on my bed, for I can no longer support myself."

Edmond took the old man in his arms, and laid him on the bed.

"And now, my dear friend," said Faria, "sole consolation of my wretched existence, – you whom heaven gave me somewhat late, but still gave me, a priceless gift, and for which I am most grateful, – at the moment of separating from you forever, I wish you all the happiness and all the prosperity you so well deserve. My son, I bless thee!" The young man cast himself on his knees, leaning his head against the old man's bed.

"Listen, now, to what I say in this my dying moment. The treasure of the Spadas exists. God grants me the boon of vision unrestricted by time or space. I see it in the depths of the inner cavern. My eyes pierce the inmost recesses of the earth, and are dazzled at the sight of so much riches. If you do escape, remember that the poor abbe, whom all the world called mad, was not so. Hasten to Monte Cristo – avail yourself of the fortune – for you have indeed suffered long enough." A violent convulsion attacked the old man. Dantes raised his head and saw Faria's eyes injected with blood. It seemed as if a flow of blood had ascended from the chest to the head.

"Adieu, adieu!" murmured the old man, clasping Edmond's hand convulsively – "adieu!"

"Oh, no, – no, not yet," he cried; "do not forsake me! Oh, succor him! Help – help – help!"

"Hush – hush!" murmured the dying man, "that they may not separate us if you save me!"

"You are right. Oh, yes, yes; be assured I shall save you! Besides, although you suffer much, you do not seem to be in such agony as you were before."

"Do not mistake. I suffer less because there is in me less strength to endure. At your age we have faith in life; it is the privilege of youth to believe and hope, but old men see death more clearly. Oh, 'tis here – 'tis here – 'tis over – my sight is gone – my senses fail! Your hand, Dantes! Adieu – adieu!" And raising himself by a final effort, in which he summoned all his faculties, he said, – "Monte Cristo, forget not Monte Cristo!" And he fell back on the bed. The crisis was terrible, and a rigid form with twisted limbs, swollen eyelids, and lips flecked with bloody foam, lay on the bed of torture, in place of the intellectual being who so lately rested there.

Dantes took the lamp, placed it on a projecting stone above the bed, whence its tremulous light fell with strange and fantastic ray on the distorted countenance and motionless, stiffened body. With steady gaze he awaited confidently the moment for administering the restorative.

When he believed that the right moment had arrived, he took the knife, pried open the teeth, which offered less resistance than before, counted one after the other twelve drops, and watched; the phial contained, perhaps, twice as much more. He waited ten minutes, a quarter of an hour, half an hour, – no change took place. Trembling, his hair erect, his brow bathed with perspiration, he counted the seconds by the beating of his heart. Then he thought it was time to make the last trial, and he put the phial to the purple lips of Faria, and without having occasion to force open his jaws, which had remained extended, he poured the whole of the liquid down his throat.

The draught produced a galvanic effect, a violent trembling pervaded the old man's limbs, his eyes opened until it was fearful to gaze upon them, he heaved a sigh which resembled a shriek, and then his convulsed body returned gradually to its former immobility, the eyes remaining open.

Half an hour, an hour, an hour and a half elapsed, and during this period of anguish, Edmond leaned over his friend, his hand applied to his heart, and felt the body gradually grow cold, and the heart's pulsation become more and more deep and dull, until at length it stopped; the last movement of the heart ceased, the face became livid, the eyes remained open, but the eyeballs were glazed. It was six o'clock in the morning, the dawn was just breaking, and its feeble ray came into the dungeon, and paled the ineffectual light of the lamp. Strange shadows passed over the countenance of the dead man, and at times gave it the appearance of life. While the struggle between day and night lasted, Dantes still doubted; but as soon as the daylight gained the pre-eminence, he saw that he was alone with a corpse. Then an invincible and extreme terror seized upon him, and he dared not again press the hand that hung out of bed, he dared no longer to gaze on those fixed and vacant eyes, which he tried many times to close, but in vain – they opened again as soon as shut. He extinguished the lamp, carefully concealed it, and then went away, closing as well as

As soon as the daylight gained the pre-eminence, he saw that he was alone with a corpse.

he could the entrance to the secret passage by the large stone as he descended.

It was time, for the jailer was coming. On this occasion he began his rounds at Dantes' cell, and on leaving him he went on to Faria's dungeon, taking thither breakfast and some linen. Nothing betokened that the man know anything of what had occurred. He went on his way.

Dantes was then seized with an indescribable desire to know what was going on in the dungeon of his unfortunate friend. He therefore returned by the subterraneous gallery, and arrived in time to hear the exclamations of the turnkey, who called out for help. Other turnkeys came, and then was heard the regular tramp of soldiers. Last of all came the governor.

Edmond heard the creaking of the bed as they moved the corpse, heard the voice of the governor, who asked them to throw water on the dead man's face; and seeing that, in spite of this application, the prisoner did not recover, they sent for the doctor. The governor then went out, and words of pity fell on Dantes' listening ears, mingled with brutal laughter.

"Well, well," said one, "the madman has gone to look after his treasure. Good journey to him!"

"With all his millions, he will not have enough to pay for his shroud!" said another.

"Oh," added a third voice, "the shrouds of the Chateau d'If are not dear!"

"Perhaps," said one of the previous speakers, "as he was a churchman, they may go to some expense in his behalf."

"They may give him the honours of the sack."

Edmond did not lose a word, but comprehended very little of what was said. The voices soon ceased, and it seemed to him as if every one had left the cell. Still he dared not to enter, as they might have left some turnkey to watch the dead. He remained, therefore, mute and motionless, hardly venturing to breathe. At the end of an hour, he heard a faint noise, which increased. It was the governor who returned, followed by the doctor and other attendants. There was a moment's silence, – it was evident that the doctor was examining the dead body. The inquiries soon commenced.

The doctor analyzed the symptoms of the malady to which the prisoner had succumbed, and declared that he was dead. Questions and answers followed in a nonchalant manner that made Dantes indignant, for he felt that all the world should have for the poor abbe a love and respect equal to his own.

"I am very sorry for what you tell me," said the governor, replying to the assurance of the doctor, "that the old man is really dead; for he was a quiet, inoffensive prisoner, happy in his folly, and required no watching."

"Ah," added the turnkey, "there was no occasion for watching him: he would have stayed here fifty years, I'll answer for it, without any attempt to escape."

"Still," said the governor, "I believe it will be requisite, notwithstanding your certainty, and not that I doubt your science, but in discharge of my official duty, that we should be perfectly assured that the prisoner is dead." There was a moment of complete silence, during which Dantes, still listening, knew that the doctor was examining the corpse a second time.

"You may make your mind easy," said the doctor; "he is dead. I will answer for that."

"You know, sir," said the governor, persisting, "that we are not content in such cases as this with such a simple examination. In spite of all appearances, be so kind, therefore, as to finish your duty by fulfilling the formalities described by law."

"Let the irons be heated," said the doctor; "but really it is a useless precaution." This order to heat the irons made Dantes shudder. He heard hasty steps, the creaking of a door, people going and coming, and some minutes afterwards a turnkey entered, saying, —

"Here is the brazier, lighted." There was a moment's silence, and then was heard the crackling of burning flesh, of which the peculiar and nauseous smell penetrated even behind the wall where Dantes was listening in horror. The perspiration poured forth upon the young man's brow, and he felt as if he should faint.

"You see, sir, he is really dead," said the doctor; "this burn in the heel is decisive. The poor fool is cured of his folly, and delivered from his captivity."

"Wasn't his name Faria?" inquired one of the officers who

accompanied the governor.

"Yes, sir; and, as he said, it was an ancient name. He was, too, very learned, and rational enough on all points which did not relate to his treasure; but on that, indeed, he was intractable."

"It is the sort of malady which we call monomania," said the doctor.

"You had never anything to complain of?" said the governor to the jailer who had charge of the abbe.

"Never, sir," replied the jailer, "never; on the contrary, he sometimes amused me very much by telling me stories. One day, too, when my wife was ill, he gave me a prescription which cured her."

"Ah, ah!" said the doctor, "I did not know that I had a rival; but I hope, governor, that you will show him all proper respect."

"Yes, yes, make your mind easy, he shall be decently interred in the newest sack we can find. Will that satisfy you?"

"Must this last formality take place in your presence, sir?" inquired a turnkey.

"Certainly. But make haste – I cannot stay here all day." Other footsteps, going and coming, were now heard, and a moment afterwards the noise of rustling canvas reached Dantes' ears, the bed creaked, and the heavy footfall of a man who lifts a weight sounded on the floor; then the bed again creaked under the weight deposited upon it.

"This evening," said the governor.

"Will there be any mass?" asked one of the attendants.

"That is impossible," replied the governor. "The chaplain of the chateau came to me yesterday to beg for leave of absence, in order to take a trip to Hyeres for a week. I told him I would attend to the prisoners in his absence. If the poor abbe had not been in such a hurry, he might have had his requiem."

"Pooh, pooh;" said the doctor, with the impiety usual in persons of his profession; "he is a churchman. God will respect his profession, and not give the devil the wicked delight of sending him a priest." A shout of laughter followed this brutal jest. Meanwhile the operation of putting the body in the sack was going on.

"This evening," said the governor, when the task was ended.

"At what hour?" inquired a turnkey.

"Why, about ten or eleven o'clock."

"Shall we watch by the corpse?"

"Of what use would it be? Shut the dungeon as if he were alive – that is all." Then the steps retreated, and the voices died away in the distance; the noise of the door, with its creaking hinges and bolts ceased, and a silence more sombre than that of solitude ensued, – the silence of death, which was all-pervasive, and struck its icy chill to the very soul of Dantes. Then he raised the flag-stone cautiously with his head, and looked carefully around the chamber. It was empty, and Dantes emerged from the tunnel.

On the bed, at full length, and faintly illuminated by the pale

light that came from the window, lay a sack of canvas, and under its rude folds was stretched a long and stiffened form; it was Faria's last winding-sheet, – a winding-sheet which, as the turnkey said, cost so little. Everything was in readiness. A barrier had been placed between Dantes and his old friend. No longer could Edmond look into those wide-open eyes which had seemed to be penetrating the mysteries of death; no longer could he clasp the hand which had done so much to make his existence blessed. Faria, the beneficent and cheerful companion, with whom he was accustomed to live so intimately, no longer breathed. He seated himself on the edge of that terrible bed, and fell into melancholy and gloomy revery.

Alone – he was alone again – again condemned to silence – again face to face with nothingness! Alone! – never again to see the face, never again to hear the voice of the only human being who united him to earth! Was not Faria's fate the better, after all – to solve the problem of life at its source, even at the risk of horrible suffering? The idea of suicide, which his friend had driven away and kept away by his cheerful presence, now hovered like a phantom over the abbe's dead body.

"If I could die," he said, "I should go where he goes, and should assuredly find him again. But how to die? It is very easy," he went on with a smile; "I will remain here, rush on the first person that opens the door, strangle him, and then they will guillotine me." But excessive grief is like a storm at sea, where the frail bark is tossed from the depths to the top of the wave. Dantes recoiled from the idea of so infamous a death, and passed suddenly from despair to an ardent desire for life and liberty.

"Die? oh, no," he exclaimed – "not die now, after having lived and suffered so long and so much! Die? yes, had I died years ago; but now to die would be, indeed, to give way to the sarcasm of destiny. No, I want to live; I shall struggle to the very last; I will yet win back the happiness of which I have been deprived. Before I die I must not forget that I have my executioners to punish, and perhaps, too, who knows, some friends to reward. Yet they will forget me here, and I shall die in my dungeon like Faria." As he said this, he became silent and gazed straight before him like one overwhelmed with a strange and amazing thought. Suddenly he arose, lifted his hand to his brow as if his brain wore giddy, paced twice or thrice round the dungeon, and then paused abruptly by the bed.

"Just God!" he muttered, "whence comes this thought? Is it from thee? Since none but the dead pass freely from this dungeon, let me take the place of the dead!" Without giving himself time to reconsider his decision, and, indeed, that he might not allow his thoughts to be distracted from his desperate resolution, he bent over the appalling shroud, opened it with the knife which Faria had made, drew the corpse from the sack, and bore it along the tunnel to his own chamber, laid it on his couch, tied around its head the rag he wore at night around his own, covered it with his counterpane, once again kissed the ice-cold brow, and tried vainly to close the resisting eyes, which glared horribly, turned the head towards the wall, so that the jailer might, when he brought the evening meal, believe that he was asleep, as was his frequent custom; entered the tunnel again, drew the bed against the wall, returned to the other cell, took from the hiding-place the needle and thread, flung off his rags, that they might feel only naked flesh beneath the coarse canvas, and getting inside the sack, placed himself in the posture in which the dead body had been laid, and sewed up the mouth of the sack from the inside.

He would have been discovered by the beating of his heart, if by any mischance the jailers had entered at that moment. Dantes might have waited until the evening visit was over, but he was afraid that the governor would change his mind, and order the dead body to be removed earlier. In that case his last hope would have been destroyed. Now his plans were fully made, and this is what he intended to do. If while he was being carried out the grave-diggers should discover that they were bearing a live instead of a dead body, Dantes did not intend to give them time to recognize him, but with a sudden cut of the knife, he meant to open the sack from top to bottom, and, profiting by their alarm, escape; if they tried to catch him, he would use his knife to better purpose.

If they took him to the cemetery and laid him in a grave, he would allow himself to be covered with earth, and then, as it was night, the grave-diggers could scarcely have turned their backs before he would have worked his way through the yielding soil and escaped. He hoped that the weight of earth would not be so great that he could not overcome it. If he was detected in this and the earth proved too heavy, he would be stifled, and then – so much the better, all would be over. Dantes had not eaten since the preceding evening, but he had not thought of hunger, nor did he think of it now. His situation was too precarious to allow him even time to reflect on any thought but one.

The first risk that Dantes ran was, that the jailer, when he brought him his supper at seven o'clock, might perceive the change that had been made; fortunately, twenty times at least, from misanthropy or fatigue, Dantes had received his jailer in bed, and then the man placed his bread and soup on the table, and went away without saying a word. This time the jailer might not be as silent as usual, but speak to Dantes, and seeing that he received no reply, go to the bed, and thus discover all.

When seven o'clock came, Dantes' agony really began. His hand placed upon his heart was unable to redress its throbbings, while, with the other he wiped the perspiration from his temples. From time to time chills ran through his whole body, and clutched his heart in a grasp of ice. Then he thought he was going to die. Yet the hours passed on without any unusual disturbance, and Dantes knew that he had escaped the first peril. It was a good augury. At length, about the hour the governor had appointed, footsteps were heard on the stairs. Edmond felt that the moment had arrived, summoned up all his courage, held his breath, and would have been happy if at the same time he could have repressed the throbbing of his veins. The footsteps – they were double – paused at the door – and Dantes guessed that the two grave-diggers had come to seek him – this idea was soon converted into certainty, when he heard the noise they made in putting down the hand-bier. The door opened, and a dim light reached Dantes' eyes through the coarse sack that covered him; he saw two shadows approach his bed, a third remaining at the door with a torch in its hand. The two men, approaching the ends of the bed, took the sack by its extremities.

"He's heavy though for an old and thin man," said one, as he raised the head.

"They say every year adds half a pound to the weight of the bones," said another, lifting the feet.

"Have you tied the knot?" inquired the first speaker.

"What would be the use of carrying so much more

weight?" was the reply, "I can do that when we get there."

"Yes, you're right," replied the companion.

'What's the knot for?' thought Dantes.

They deposited the supposed corpse on the bier. Edmond stiffened himself in order to play the part of a dead man, and then the party, lighted by the man with the torch, who went first, ascended the stairs. Suddenly he felt the fresh and sharp night air, and Dantes knew that the mistral was blowing. It was a sensation in which pleasure and pain were strangely mingled. The bearers went on for twenty paces, then stopped, putting the bier down on the ground. One of them went away, and Dantes heard his shoes striking on the pavement.

"Where am I?" he asked himself.

"Really, he is by no means a light load!" said the other bearer, sitting on the edge of the hand-barrow. Dantes' first impulse was to escape, but fortunately he did not attempt it.

"Give us a light," said the other bearer, "or I shall never find what I am looking for." The man with the torch complied, although not asked in the most polite terms.

"What can he be looking for?" thought Edmond. "The spade, perhaps." An exclamation of satisfaction indicated that the grave-digger had found the object of his search. "Here it is at last," he said, "not without some trouble though."

"Yes," was the answer, "but it has lost nothing by waiting."

As he said this, the man came towards Edmond, who heard a

heavy metallic substance laid down beside him, and at the same moment a cord was fastened round his feet with sudden and painful violence.

"Well, have you tied the knot?" inquired the grave-digger, who was looking on.

"Yes, and pretty tight too, I can tell you," was the answer.

"Move on, then." And the bier was lifted once more, and they proceeded.

They advanced fifty paces farther, and then stopped to open a door, then went forward again. The noise of the waves dashing against the rocks on which the chateau is built, reached Dantes' ear distinctly as they went forward.

"Bad weather!" observed one of the bearers; "not a pleasant night for a dip in the sea."

"Why, yes, the abbe runs a chance of being wet," said the other; and then there was a burst of brutal laughter. Dantes did not comprehend the jest, but his hair stood erect on his head.

"Well, here we are at last," said one of them. "A little farther – a little farther," said the other. "You know very well that the last was stopped on his way, dashed on the rocks, and the governor told us next day that we were careless fellows."

They ascended five or six more steps, and then Dantes felt that they took him, one by the head and the other by the heels, and swung him to and fro. "One!" said the grave-diggers, "two! three!" And at the same instant Dantes felt himself flung into the air like a wounded bird, falling, falling, with a rapidity that made his blood curdle. Although drawn downwards by the heavy weight which hastened his rapid descent, it seemed to him as if the fall lasted for a century.

At last, with a horrible splash, he darted like an arrow into the ice-cold water, and as he did so he uttered a shrill cry, stifled in a moment by his immersion beneath the waves.

Dantes had been flung into the sea, and was dragged into its depths by a thirty-six pound shot tied to his feet. The sea is the cemetery of the Chateau d'If.

Dantes, although stunned and almost suffocated, had sufficient presence of mind to hold his breath, and as his right hand (prepared as he was for every chance) held his knife open, he rapidly ripped up the sack, extricated his arm, and then his body; but in spite of all his efforts to free himself from the shot, he felt it dragging him down still lower. He then bent his body, and by a desperate effort severed the cord that bound his legs, at the moment when it seemed as if he were actually strangled. With a mighty leap he rose to the surface of the sea, while the shot dragged down to the depths the sack that had so nearly become his shroud.

Dantes waited only to get breath, and then dived, in order to avoid being seen. When he arose a second time, he was fifty paces from where he had first sunk. He saw overhead a black and tempestuous sky, across which the wind was driving clouds that occasionally suffered a twinkling star to appear; before him was the

One!
Two!
Three!

vast expanse of waters, sombre and terrible, whose waves foamed and roared as if before the approach of a storm. Behind him, blacker than the sea, blacker than the sky, rose phantom-like the vast stone structure, whose projecting crags seemed like arms extended to seize their prey, and on the highest rock was a torch lighting two figures. He fancied that these two forms were looking at the sea; doubtless these strange grave-diggers had heard his cry. Dantes dived again, and remained a long time beneath the water. This was an easy feat to him, for he usually attracted a crowd of spectators in the bay before the lighthouse at Marseilles when he swam there, and was unanimously declared to be the best swimmer in the port. When he came up again the light had disappeared.

He must now get his bearings. Ratonneau and Pomegue are the nearest islands of all those that surround the Chateau d'If, but Ratonneau and Pomegue are inhabited, as is also the islet of Daume. Tiboulen and Lemaire were therefore the safest for Dantes' venture. The islands of Tiboulen and Lemaire are a league from the Chateau d'If; Dantes, nevertheless, determined to make for them. But how could he find his way in the darkness of the night? At this moment he saw the light of Planier, gleaming in front of him like a star. By leaving this light on the right, he kept the Island of Tiboulen a little on the left; by turning to the left, therefore, he would find it. But, as we have said, it was at least a league from the Chateau d'If to this island. Often in prison Faria had said to him, when he saw him idle and inactive, "Dantes, you must not give way to this listlessness; you will be drowned if you seek to escape, and your strength has not been properly exercised and prepared for exertion." These words rang in Dantes' ears, even beneath the waves; he hastened to cleave his way through them to see if he had not lost his strength. He found with pleasure that his captivity had taken away nothing of his power, and that he was still master of that element on whose bosom he had so often sported as a boy.

Fear, that relentless pursuer, clogged Dantes' efforts. He listened for any sound that might be audible, and every time that he rose to the top of a wave he scanned the horizon, and strove to penetrate the darkness. He fancied that every wave behind him was a pursuing boat, and he redoubled his exertions, increasing rapidly his distance from the chateau, but exhausting his strength. He swam on still, and already the terrible chateau had disappeared in the darkness. He could not see it, but he felt its presence. An hour passed, during which Dantes, excited by the feeling of freedom, continued to cleave the waves. "Let us see," said he, "I have swum above an hour, but as the wind is against me, that has retarded my speed; however, if I am not mistaken, I must be close to Tiboulen. But what if I were mistaken?" A shudder passed over him. He sought to tread water, in order to rest himself; but the sea was too violent, and he felt that he could not make use of this means of recuperation.

"Well," said he, "I will swim on until I am worn out, or the cramp seizes me, and then I shall sink;" and he struck out with the energy of despair.

Suddenly the sky seemed to him to become still darker and more dense, and heavy clouds seemed to sweep down towards him; at the same time he felt a sharp pain in his knee. He fancied for a moment that he had been shot, and listened for the report; but he heard nothing. Then he put out his hand, and encountered an obstacle and with another stroke knew that he had gained the shore.

Before him rose a grotesque mass of rocks, that resembled nothing so much as a vast fire petrified at the moment of its most fervent combustion. It was the Island of Tiboulen. Dantes rose, advanced a few steps, and, with a fervent prayer of gratitude, stretched himself on the granite, which seemed to him softer than down. Then, in spite of the wind and rain, he fell into the deep, sweet sleep of utter exhaustion. At the expiration of an hour Edmond was awakened by the roar of thunder. The tempest was let loose and beating the atmosphere with its mighty wings; from time to time a flash of lightning stretched across the heavens like a fiery serpent, lighting up the clouds that rolled on in vast chaotic waves.

Dantes had not been deceived – he had reached the first of the two islands, which was, in fact, Tiboulen. He knew that it was barren and without shelter; but when the sea became more calm, he resolved to plunge into its waves again, and swim to Lemaire, equally arid, but larger, and consequently better adapted for concealment.

An overhanging rock offered him a temporary shelter, and

scarcely had he availed himself of it when the tempest burst forth in all its fury. Edmond felt the trembling of the rock beneath which he lay; the waves, dashing themselves against it, wetted him with their spray. He was safely sheltered, and yet he felt dizzy in the midst of the warring of the elements and the dazzling brightness of the lightning. It seemed to him that the island trembled to its base, and that it would, like a vessel at anchor, break moorings, and bear him off into the centre of the storm. He then recollected that he had not eaten or drunk for four-and-twenty hours. He extended his hands, and drank greedily of the rainwater that had lodged in a hollow of the rock.

As he rose, a flash of lightning, that seemed to rive the remotest heights of heaven, illumined the darkness. By its light, between the Island of Lemaire and Cape Croiselle, a quarter of a league distant, Dantes saw a fishing-boat driven rapidly like a spectre before the power of winds and waves. A second after, he saw it again, approaching with frightful rapidity. Dantes cried at the top of his voice to warn them of their danger, but they saw it themselves. Another flash showed him four men clinging to the shattered mast and the rigging, while a fifth clung to the broken rudder.

The men he beheld saw him undoubtedly, for their cries were carried to his ears by the wind. Above the splintered mast a sail rent to tatters was waving; suddenly the ropes that still held it gave way, and it disappeared in the darkness of the night like a vast sea-bird. At the same moment a violent crash was heard, and cries of

distress. Dantes from his rocky perch saw the shattered vessel, and among the fragments the floating forms of the hapless sailors. Then all was dark again.

Dantes ran down the rocks at the risk of being himself dashed to pieces; he listened, he groped about, but he heard and saw nothing – the cries had ceased, and the tempest continued to rage. By degrees the wind abated, vast gray clouds rolled towards the west, and the blue firmament appeared studded with bright stars. Soon a red streak became visible in the horizon, the waves whitened, a light played over them, and gilded their foaming crests with gold. It was day.

Dantes stood mute and motionless before this majestic spectacle, as if he now beheld it for the first time; and indeed since his captivity in the Chateau d'If he had forgotten that such scenes were ever to be witnessed. He turned towards the fortress, and looked at both sea and land. The gloomy building rose from the bosom of the ocean with imposing majesty and seemed to dominate the scene. It was about five o'clock. The sea continued to get calmer.

"In two or three hours," thought Dantes, "the turnkey will enter my chamber, find the body of my poor friend, recognize it, seek for me in vain, and give the alarm. Then the tunnel will be discovered; the men who cast me into the sea and who must have heard the cry I uttered, will be questioned. Then boats filled with armed soldiers will pursue the wretched fugitive. The cannon will warn everyone to refuse shelter to a man wandering about naked and famished. The police of Marseilles will be on the alert by land, whilst the governor pursues me by sea. I am cold, I am hungry. I have lost even the knife that saved me. O my God, I have suffered enough surely! Have pity on me, and do for me what I am unable to do for myself."

As Dantes (his eyes turned in the direction of the Chateau d'If) uttered this prayer, he saw off the farther point of the Island of Pomegue a small vessel with lateen sail skimming the sea like a gull in search of prey; and with his sailor's eye he knew it to be a Genoese tartan. She was coming out of Marseilles harbour, and was standing out to sea rapidly, her sharp prow cleaving through the waves. "Oh," cried Edmond, "to think that in half an hour I could join her, did I not fear being questioned, detected, and conveyed back to Marseilles! What can I do? What story can I invent? under pretext of trading along the coast, these men, who are in reality smugglers, will prefer selling me to doing a good action. I must wait. But I cannot – I am starving. In a few hours my strength will be utterly exhausted; besides, perhaps I have not been missed at the fortress. I can pass as one of the sailors wrecked last night. My story will be accepted, for there is no one left to contradict me."

As he spoke, Dantes looked toward the spot where the fishing-vessel had been wrecked, and started. The red cap of one of the sailors hung to a point of the rock and some timbers that had formed part of the vessel's keel, floated at the foot of the crag. In an instant Dantes' plan was formed. He swam to the cap, placed it on his head, seized one of the timbers, and struck out so as to cut across the course the vessel was taking.

"I am saved!" murmured he. And this conviction restored his strength.

He soon saw that the vessel, with the wind dead ahead, was tacking between the Chateau d'If and the tower of Planier. For an instant he feared lest, instead of keeping in shore, she should stand out to sea; but he soon saw that she would pass, like most vessels bound for Italy, between the islands of Jaros and Calaseraigne.

However, the vessel and the swimmer insensibly neared one another, and in one of its tacks the tartan bore down within a quarter of a mile of him. He rose on the waves, making signs of distress; but no one on board saw him, and the vessel stood on another tack. Dantes would have shouted, but he knew that the wind would drown his voice.

It was then he rejoiced at his precaution in taking the timber, for without it he would have been unable, perhaps, to reach the vessel – certainly to return to shore, should he be unsuccessful in attracting attention.

Dantes, though almost sure as to what course the vessel would take, had yet watched it anxiously until it tacked and stood towards him. Then he advanced; but before they could meet, the vessel again changed her course. By a violent effort he rose half out of the water, waving his cap, and uttering a loud shout peculiar to sailers. This time he was both seen and heard, and the tartan instantly steered towards him. At the same time, he saw they were about to lower the boat.

An instant after, the boat, rowed by two men, advanced rapidly towards him. Dantes let go of the timber, which he now thought to be useless, and swam vigorously to meet them. But he had reckoned too much upon his strength, and then he realized how serviceable the timber had been to him. His arms became stiff, his legs lost their flexibility, and he was almost breathless.

He shouted again. The two sailors redoubled their efforts, and one of them cried in Italian, "Courage!"

The word reached his ear as a wave which he no longer had the strength to surmount passed over his head. He rose again to the surface, struggled with the last desperate effort of a drowning man, uttered a third cry, and felt himself sinking, as if the fatal cannon shot were again tied to his feet. The water passed over his head, and the sky turned gray. A convulsive movement again brought him to the surface. He felt himself seized by the hair, then he saw and heard nothing. He had fainted.

When he opened his eyes Dantes found himself on the deck of the tartan. His first care was to see what course they were taking. They were rapidly leaving the Chateau d'If behind. Dantes was so exhausted that the exclamation of joy he uttered was mistaken for a sigh.

As we have said, he was lying on the deck. A sailor was rubbing his limbs with a woollen cloth; another, whom he recognized as the one who had cried out "Courage!" held a gourd full of rum to his mouth; while the third, an old sailer, at once the pilot and captain, looked on with that egotistical pity men feel for a misfortune that they have escaped yesterday, and which may overtake them tomorrow.

A few drops of the rum restored suspended animation, while the friction of his limbs restored their elasticity.

"Who are you?" said the pilot in bad French.

"I am," replied Dantes, in bad Italian, "a Maltese sailor. We were coming from Syracuse laden with grain. The storm of last night overtook us at Cape Morgion, and we were wrecked on these rocks."

"Where do you come from?"

"From these rocks that I had the good luck to cling to while our captain and the rest of the crew were all lost. I saw your vessel, and fearful of being left to perish on the desolate island, I swam off on a piece of wreckage to try and intercept your course. You have saved my life, and I thank you," continued Dantes. "I was lost when one of your sailors caught hold of my hair."

"It was I," said a sailor of a frank and manly appearance; "and it was time, for you were sinking."

"Yes," returned Dantes, holding out his hand, "I thank you again."

"I almost hesitated, though," replied the sailor; "you looked more like a brigand than an honest man, with your beard six inches, and your hair a foot long." Dantes recollected that his hair and beard had not been cut all the time he was at the Chateau d'If.

"Yes," said he, "I made a vow, to our Lady of the Grotto not to cut my hair or beard for ten years if I were saved in a moment of danger; but to-day the vow expires."

"Now what are we to do with you?" said the captain.

"Alas, anything you please. My captain is dead; I have barely escaped; but I am a good sailor. Leave me at the first port you make; I shall be sure to find employment."

"Do you know the Mediterranean?"

"I have sailed over it since my childhood."

"You know the best harbours?"

"There are few ports that I could not enter or leave with a bandage over my eyes."

"I say, captain," said the sailor who had cried "Courage!" to Dantes, "if what he says is true, what hinders his staying with us?"

"If he says true," said the captain doubtingly. "But in his present condition he will promise anything, and take his chance of keeping it afterwards."

"I will do more than I promise," said Dantes.

"We shall see," returned the other, smiling.

"Where are you going?" asked Dantes.

"To Leghorn."

"Then why, instead of tacking so frequently, do you not sail nearer the wind?"

"Because we should run straight on to the Island of Rion."

"You shall pass it by twenty fathoms."

"Take the helm, and let us see what you know." The young man took the helm, felt to see if the vessel answered the rudder promptly and seeing that, without being a first-rate sailer, she yet was tolerably obedient.

"To the sheets," said he. The four seamen, who composed the crew, obeyed, while the pilot looked on. "Haul taut." – They obeyed.

"Belay." This order was also executed; and the vessel passed, as Dantes had predicted, twenty fathoms to windward.

"Bravo!" said the captain.

"Bravo!" repeated the sailors. And they all looked with astonishment at this man whose eye now disclosed an intelligence and his body a vigour they had not thought him capable of showing.

"You see," said Dantes, quitting the helm, "I shall be of some use to you, at least during the voyage. If you do not want me at Leghorn, you can leave me there, and I will pay you out of the first wages I get, for my food and the clothes you lend me."

"Ah," said the captain, "we can agree very well, if you are reasonable."

"Give me what you give the others, and it will be all right," returned Dantes.

"That's not fair," said the seaman who had saved Dantes; "for you know more than we do."

"What is that to you, Jacopo?" returned the Captain. "Every one is free to ask what he pleases."

"That's true," replied Jacopo; "I only make a remark."

"Well, you would do much better to find him a jacket and a pair of trousers, if you have them."

"No," said Jacopo; "but I have a shirt and a pair of trousers."

"That is all I want," interrupted Dantes. Jacopo dived into the hold and soon returned with what Edmond wanted.

"Now, then, do you wish for anything else?" said the patron.

"A piece of bread and another glass of the capital rum I tasted, for I have not eaten or drunk for a long time." He had not tasted food for forty hours. A piece of bread was brought, and Jacopo offered him the gourd.

"Larboard your helm," cried the captain to the steersman. Dantes glanced that way as he lifted the gourd to his mouth; then paused with hand in mid-air.

"Hollo! what's the matter at the Chateau d'If?" said the captain.

A small white cloud, which had attracted Dantes' attention,

crowned the summit of the bastion of the Chateau d'If. At the same moment the faint report of a gun was heard. The sailors looked at one another.

"What is this?" asked the captain.

"A prisoner has escaped from the Chateau d'If, and they are firing the alarm gun," replied Dantes. The captain glanced at him, but he had lifted the rum to his lips and was drinking it with so much composure, that suspicions, if the captain had any, died away.

"At any rate," murmured he, "if it be, so much the better, for I have made a rare acquisition." Under pretence of being fatigued, Dantes asked to take the helm; the steersman, glad to be relieved, looked at the captain, and the latter by a sign indicated that he might abandon it to his new comrade. Dantes could thus keep his eyes on Marseilles.

"What is the day of the month?" asked he of Jacopo, who sat down beside him.

"The 28th of February."

"In what year?"

"In what year – you ask me in what year?"

"Yes," replied the young man, "I ask you in what year!"

"You have forgotten then?"

"I got such a fright last night," replied Dantes, smiling, "that I have almost lost my memory. I ask you what year is it?"

"The year 1829," returned Jacopo. It was fourteen years day for day since Dantes' arrest. He was nineteen when he entered the Chateau d'If; he was thirty-three when he escaped. A sorrowful smile passed over his face; he asked himself what had become of Mercedes, who must believe him dead. Then his eyes lighted up with hatred as he thought of the three men who had caused him so long and wretched a captivity. He renewed against Danglars, Fernand, and Villefort the oath of implacable vengeance he had made in his dungeon. This oath was no longer a vain menace; for the fastest sailer in the Mediterranean would have been unable to overtake the little tartan, that with every stitch of canvas set was flying before the wind to Leghorn.

Escape and Rescue
The Prisoner of Zenda
A New Use for a Tea-table
Anthony Hope

The story so far

Rudolf Rassendyll is impersonating the King of Ruritania, whom he closely resembles. The impersonation was meant to be for one night only, but the real King was kidnapped and Rassendyll has been forced to continue the deception. He is falling deeply in love with the king's cousin, Princess Flavia, and has to avoid the attacks of Black Michael, a duke who is holding the real King, and plotting to take the throne. The duke's supporters, usually called The Six, are with him. Rassendyll has also encountered the Duke's cast-off mistress, Antoinette de Mauban.

A New Use for a Tea-table
from

The Prisoner of Zenda

by

Anthony Hope

If I were to detail the ordinary events of my daily life at this time, they might prove instructive to people who are not familiar with the inside of palaces; if I revealed some of the secrets I learnt, they might prove of interest to the statesmen of Europe. I intend to do neither of these things. I should be between the Scylla of dullness and the Charybdis of indiscretion, and I feel that I had far better confine myself strictly to the underground drama which was being played beneath the surface of Ruritanian politics. I need only say that the secret of my imposture defied detection. I made mistakes. I had bad minutes: it needed all the tact and graciousness whereof I was master to smooth over some apparent lapses of memory and unmindfulness of old acquaintances of which I was guilty. But I escaped, and I attribute my escape, as I have said before, most of all, to the very audacity of the enterprise. It is my belief that, given the necessary physical likeness, it was far easier to pretend to be King of Ruritania than it would have been to personate my next-door neighbour. One day Sapt came into my room. He threw me a letter, saying:

"That's for you – a woman's hand, I think. But I've some news for you first."

"What's that?"

"The King's at the Castle of Zenda," said he.

"How do you know?"

"Because the other half of Michael's Six are there. I had enquiries made, and they're all there – Lauengram, Krafstein, and young Rupert Hentzau: three rogues, too, on my honour, as fine as live in Ruritania."

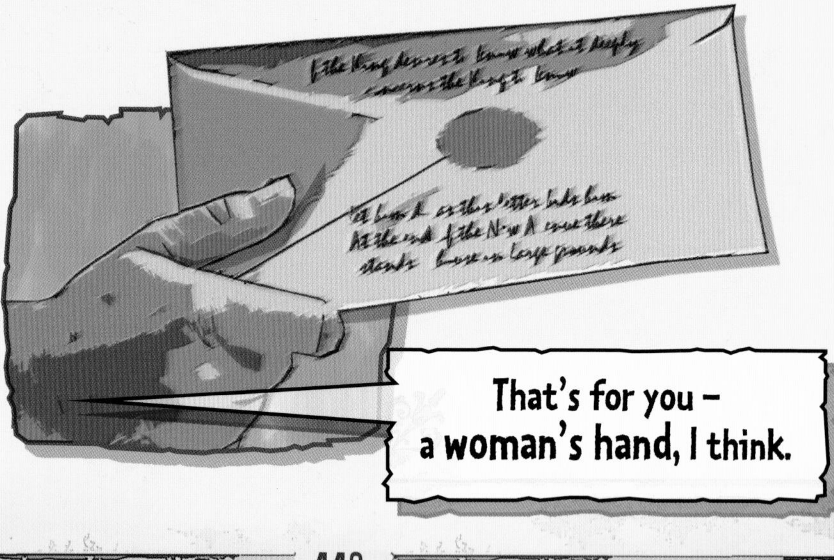

"Well?"

"Well, Fritz wants you to march to the Castle with horse, foot, and artillery."

"And drag the moat?" I asked.

"That would be about it," grinned Sapt, "and we shouldn't find the King's body then."

"You think it's certain he's there?"

"Very probable. Besides the fact of those three being there, the drawbridge is kept up, and no one goes in without an order from young Hentzau or Black Michael himself. We must tie Fritz up."

"I'll go to Zenda," said I.

"You're mad."

"Some day."

"Oh, perhaps. You'll very likely stay there though, if you do."

"That may be, my friend," said I carelessly.

"His Majesty looks sulky," observed Sapt. "How's the love affair?"

"Damn you, hold your tongue!" I said.

He looked at me for a moment, then he lit his pipe. It was quite true that I was in a bad temper, and I went on perversely:

"Wherever I go, I'm dodged by half a dozen fellows."

"I know you are; I send 'em," he replied composedly.

"What for?"

"Well," said Sapt, puffing away, "it wouldn't be exactly inconvenient for Black Michael if you disappeared. With you gone, the old game that we stopped would be played – or he'd have a shot at it."

"I can take care of myself."

"De Gautet, Bersonin, and Detchard are in Strelsau; and any one of them, lad, would cut your throat as readily – as readily as I would Black Michael's, and a deal more treacherously. What's the letter?"

I opened it and read it aloud:

"If the King desires to know what it deeply concerns the King to know, let him do as this letter bids him. At the end of the New Avenue there stands a house in large grounds. The house has a portico, with a statue of a nymph on it. A wall encloses the garden; there is a gate in the wall at the back. At twelve o'clock tonight, if the King enters alone by that gate, turns to the right, and walks twenty yards, he will find a summerhouse, approached by a flight of six steps. If he mounts and enters, he will find someone who will tell him what touches most dearly his life and his throne. This is written by a faithful friend. He must be alone. If he neglects the invitation his life will be in danger. Let him show this to no one, or he will ruin a woman who loves him: Black Michael does not pardon."

"No," observed Sapt, as I ended, "but he can dictate a very pretty letter."

I had arrived at the same conclusion, and was about to throw the letter away, when I saw there was more writing on the other side.

"Hallo! there's some more."

"If you hesitate," the writer continued, "consult Colonel Sapt –"

"Eh," exclaimed that gentleman, genuinely astonished. "Does she take me for a greater fool than you?"

I waved to him to be silent.

"Ask him what woman would do most to prevent the duke from marrying his cousin, and therefore most to prevent him becoming king? And ask if her name begins with – A?"

I sprang to my feet. Sapt laid down his pipe.

"Antoinette de Mauban, by heaven!" I cried.

"How do you know?" asked Sapt.

I told him what I knew of the lady, and how I knew it. He nodded.

"It's so far true that she's had a great row with Michael," said he, thoughtfully.

"If she would, she could be useful," I said.

"I believe, though, that Michael wrote that letter."

"So do I, but I mean to know for certain. I shall go, Sapt."

"No, I shall go," said he.

"You may go as far as the gate."

"I shall go to the summer-house."

"I'm hanged if you shall!"

I rose and leant my back against the mantelpiece.

"Sapt, I believe in that woman, and I shall go."

"I don't believe in any woman," said Sapt, "and you shan't go."

"I either go to the summer-house or back to England," said I.

Sapt began to know exactly how far he could lead or drive, and when he must follow.

"We're playing against time," I added. "Every day we leave the King where he is there is fresh risk. Every day I masquerade like this, there is fresh risk. Sapt, we must play high; we must force the game."

"So be it," he said, with a sigh.

To cut the story short, at half-past eleven that night Sapt and I mounted our horses. Fritz was again left on guard, our destination not being revealed to him. It was a very dark night. I wore no sword, but I carried a revolver, a long knife, and a bull's-eye lantern. We arrived outside the gate. I dismounted. Sapt held out his hand.

"I shall wait here," he said. "If I hear a shot, I'll –"

"Stay where you are; it's the King's only chance. You mustn't come to grief too."

"You're right, lad. Good luck!"

I pressed the little gate. It yielded, and I found myself in a wild sort of shrubbery. There was a grass-grown path and, turning to the right as I had been bidden, I followed it cautiously. My lantern was closed, the revolver was in my hand. I heard not a sound. Presently a large dark object loomed out of the gloom ahead of me. It was the summer-house. Reaching the steps, I mounted them and found myself confronted by a weak, rickety wooden door, which hung upon the latch. I pushed it open and walked in. A woman flew to me and seized my hand.

"Shut the door," she whispered.

I obeyed and turned the light of my lantern on her. She was in evening dress, arrayed very sumptuously, and her dark striking beauty was marvellously displayed in the glare of the bull's-eye. The summer-house was a bare little room, furnished only with a couple of chairs and a small iron table, such as one sees in a tea garden or an open-air cafe.

"Don't talk," she said. "We've no time. Listen! I know you, Mr. Rassendyll. I wrote that letter at the duke's orders."

"So I thought," said I.

"In twenty minutes three men will be here to kill you."

"Three – the three?"

"Yes. You must be gone by then. If not, tonight you'll be killed –"

"Or they will."

"Listen, listen! When you're killed, your body will be taken to a low quarter of the town. It will be found there. Michael will at once arrest all your friends – Colonel Sapt and Captain von Tarlenheim first – proclaim a state of siege in Strelsau, and send a messenger to Zenda. The other three will murder the King in the Castle, and the duke will proclaim either himself or the princess – himself, if he is strong enough. Anyhow, he'll marry her, and become king in fact, and soon in name. Do you see?"

"It's a pretty plot. But why, madame, do you –?"

"Say I'm a Christian – or say I'm jealous. My God! shall I see him marry her? Now go; but remember – this is what I have to tell you – that never, by night or by day, are you safe. Three men follow you as a guard. Is it not so? Well, three follow them; Michael's three are never two hundred yards from you. Your life is not worth a moment if ever they find you alone. Now go. Stay, the gate will be guarded by now. Go down softly, go past the summer-house, on for a hundred yards, and you'll find a ladder against the wall. Get over it, and fly for your life."

"And you?" I asked.

"I have my game to play too. If he finds out what I have done, we shall not meet again. If not, I may yet – But never mind. Go at once."

"But what will you tell him?"

"That you never came – that you saw through the trick."

I took her hand and kissed it.

"Madame," said I, "you have served the King well tonight. Where is he in the Castle?"

She sank her voice to a fearful whisper. I listened eagerly.

"Across the drawbridge you come to a heavy door; behind that lies – Hark! What's that?"

There were steps outside.

"They're coming! They're too soon! Heavens! they're too soon!" and she turned pale as death.

"They seem to me," said I, "to be in the nick of time."

"Close your lantern. See, there's a chink in the door. Can you see them?"

I put my eye to the chink. On the lowest step I saw three dim figures. I cocked my revolver. Antoinette hastily laid her hand on mine.

"You may kill one," said she. "But what then?"

A voice came from outside – a voice that spoke perfect English.

"Mr. Rassendyll," it said.

I made no answer.

"We want to talk to you. Will you promise not to shoot till we've done?"

"Have I the pleasure of addressing Mr. Detchard?" I said.

"Never mind names."

"Then let mine alone."

"All right, sire. I've an offer for you."

I still had my eye to the chink. The three had mounted two steps more; three revolvers pointed full at the door.

"Will you let us in? We pledge our honour to observe the truce."

"Don't trust them," whispered Antoinette.

"We can speak through the door," said I.

"But you might open it and fire," objected Detchard; "and though we should finish you, you might finish one of us. Will you give your honour not to fire while we talk?"

"Don't trust them," whispered Antoinette again.

A sudden idea struck me. I considered it for a moment. It seemed feasible.

"I give my honour not to fire before you do," said I; "but I won't let you in. Stand outside and talk."

"That's sensible," he said.

The three mounted the last step, and stood just outside the door. I laid my ear to the chink. I could hear no words, but Detchard's head was close to that of the taller of his companions (De Gautet, I guessed).

"H'm! Private communications," thought I. Then I said aloud: "Well, gentlemen, what's the offer?"

"A safe-conduct to the frontier, and fifty thousand pounds English."

"No, no," whispered Antoinette in the lowest of whispers. "They are treacherous."

"That seems handsome," said I, reconnoitring through the chink. They were all close together, just outside the door now.

I had probed the hearts of the ruffians, and I did not need Antoinette's warning. They meant to "rush" me as soon as I was engaged in talk.

"Give me a minute to consider," said I; and I thought I heard a laugh outside.

I turned to Antoinette.

"Stand up close to the wall, out of the line of fire from the door," I whispered.

"What are you going to do?" she asked in fright.

"You'll see," said I.

I took up the little iron table. It was not very heavy for a man of my strength, and I held it by the legs. The top, protruding in front of me, made a complete screen for my head and body. I fastened my closed lantern to my belt and put my revolver in a handy pocket. Suddenly I saw the door move ever so slightly – perhaps it was the wind, perhaps it was a hand trying it outside.

I drew back as far as I could from the door, holding the table in the position that I have described. Then I called out:

"Gentlemen, I accept your offer, relying on your honour. If you will open the door—"

"Open it yourself," said Detchard.

"It opens outwards," said I. "Stand back a little, gentlemen, or I shall hit you when I open it."

I went and fumbled with the latch. Then I stole back to my place on tiptoe.

"I can't open it!" I cried. "The latch has caught."

"Tut! I'll open it!" cried Detchard. "Nonsense, Bersonin, why not? Are you afraid of one man?"

I smiled to myself. An instant later the door was flung back. The gleam of a lantern showed me the three close together outside, their revolvers levelled. With a shout, I charged at my utmost pace across the summer-house and through the doorway. Three shots rang out and battered into my shield. Another moment, and I leapt out and the table caught them full and square, and in a tumbling, swearing, struggling mass, they and I and that brave table, rolled down the steps of the summerhouse to the ground below. Antoinette de Mauban shrieked, but I rose to my feet, laughing aloud.

De Gautet and Bersonin lay like men stunned. Detchard was under the table, but, as I rose, he pushed it from him and fired again. I raised my revolver and took a snap shot; I heard him curse, and then I ran like a hare, laughing as I went, past the summer-house and along by the wall. I heard steps behind me, and turning round I fired again for luck. The steps ceased.

"Please God," said I, "she told me the truth about the ladder!" for the wall was high and topped with iron spikes.

Yes, there it was. I was up and over in a minute. Doubling

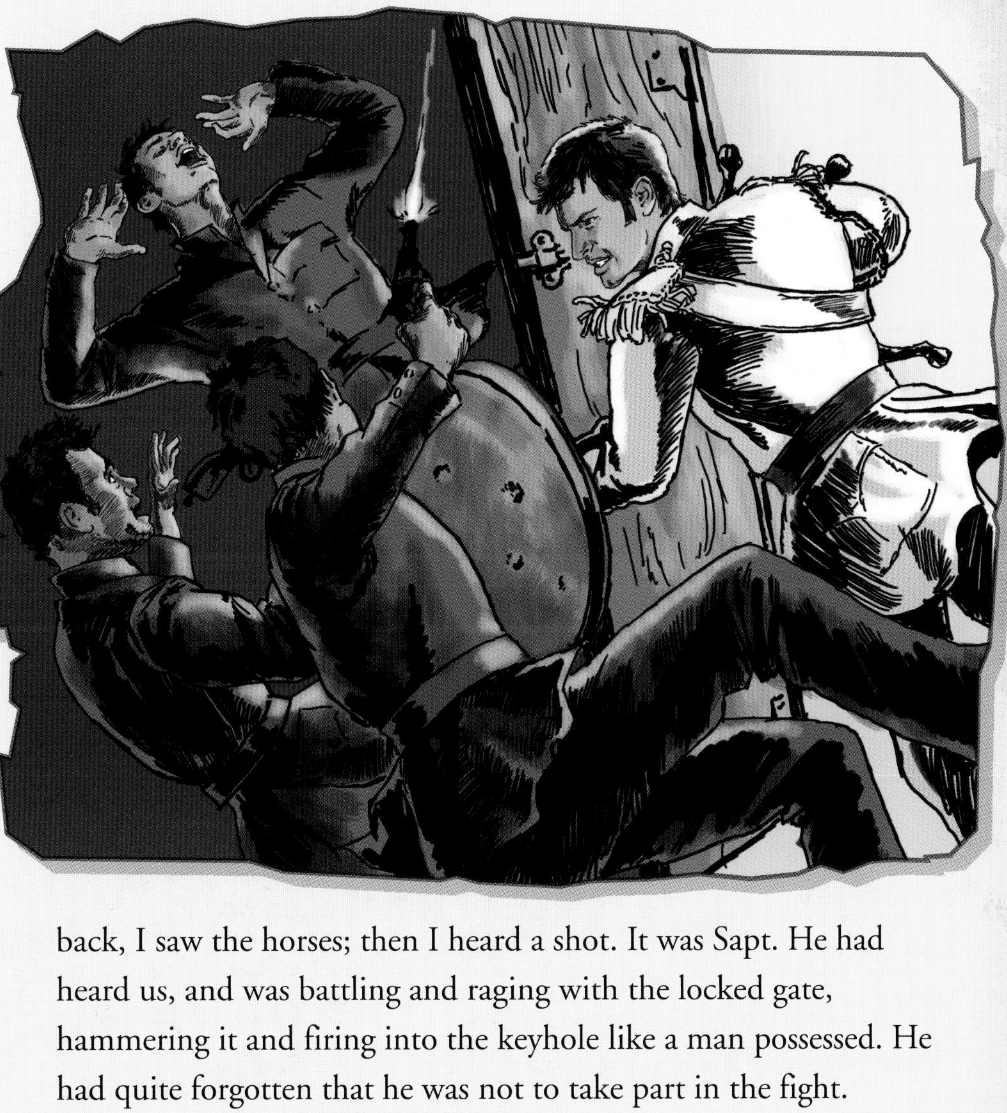

back, I saw the horses; then I heard a shot. It was Sapt. He had heard us, and was battling and raging with the locked gate, hammering it and firing into the keyhole like a man possessed. He had quite forgotten that he was not to take part in the fight. Whereat I laughed again, and said, as I clapped him on the shoulder:

"Come home to bed, old chap. I've got the finest tea-table story that ever you heard!"

He started and cried: "You're safe!" and wrung my hand. But a moment later he added:

"And what the devil are you laughing at?"

"Four gentlemen round a tea-table," said I, laughing still, for it had been uncommonly ludicrous to see the formidable three altogether routed and scattered with no more deadly weapon than an ordinary tea-table.

Moreover, you will observe that I had honourably kept my word, and not fired till they did.

Robinson Crusoe
Fighting the Cannibals
Daniel Defoe
scape
and
Rescue

The story so far

Robinson Crusoe, a native of England, has been shipwrecked for many years on a desert island. He has good stores, including guns, which he rescued from the shipwreck. Crusoe has known for some time that cannibals occasionally visit his island to feast on their prisoners, and on one of their previous trips, he befriended a man who escaped them, whom he has made his servant and named Friday.

Fighting the Cannibals

from

Robinson Crusoe

by

Daniel Defoe

I was busy one morning when I called to Friday, and bid him to go to the sea-shore and see if he could find a turtle or a tortoise, a thing which we generally got once a week, for the sake of the eggs as well as the flesh. Friday had not been long gone when he came running back, and flew over my outer wall or fence, like one that felt not the ground or the steps he set his foot on; and before I had time to speak to him he cries out to me, "O master! O master! O sorrow! O bad!"

"What's the matter, Friday?" says I.

"O yonder there," says he, "one, two, three canoes; one, two, three!" By this way of speaking I concluded there were six; but on inquiry I found there were but three. "Well, Friday," says I, "do not be frightened." So I heartened him up as well as I could. However, I saw the poor fellow was most terribly scared, for nothing ran in his head but that they were come to look for him, and would cut him in pieces and eat him; and the poor fellow trembled so that I scarcely knew what to do with him. I comforted him as well as I could, and told him I was in as much danger as he, and that they would eat me as well as him. "But," says I, "Friday, we must resolve to fight them. Can you fight, Friday?"

"Me shoot," says he, "but there come many great number."

"No matter for that," said I again; "our guns will fright them that we do not kill." So I asked him whether, if I resolved to defend him, he would defend me, and stand by me, and do just as I bid him. He said, "Me die when you bid die, master." So I went and fetched a good dram of rum and gave him; for I had been so good a husband of my rum that I had a great deal left. When we had drunk it, I made him take the two fowling- pieces, which we always carried, and loaded them with large swan-shot, as big as small pistol-bullets. Then I took four muskets, and loaded them with two slugs and five small bullets each; and my two pistols I loaded with a brace of bullets each. I hung my great sword, as usual, naked by my side, and gave Friday his hatchet. When I had thus prepared myself, I took my perspective glass, and went up to the side of the hill, to see what I could discover; and I found

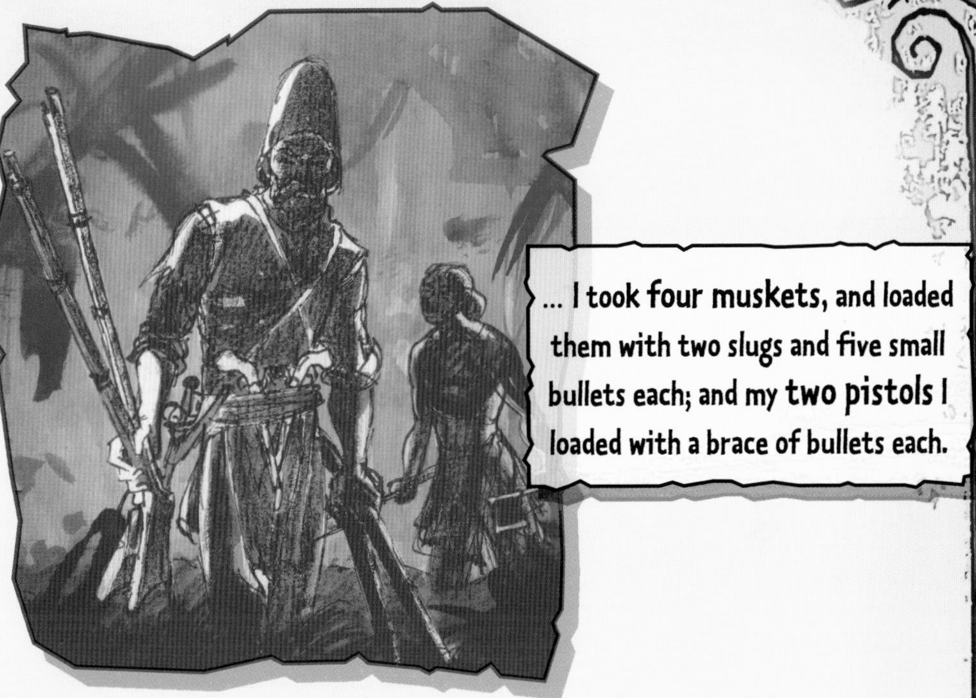

quickly by my glass that there were one-and-twenty savages, three prisoners, and three canoes; and that their whole business seemed to be the triumphant banquet upon these three human bodies: a barbarous feast, indeed! but nothing more than, as I had observed, was usual with them. I observed also that they had landed, not where they had done when Friday made his escape, but nearer to my creek, where the shore was low, and where a thick wood came almost close down to the sea. This, with the abhorrence of the inhuman errand these wretches came about, filled me with such indignation that I came down again to Friday, and told him I was resolved to go down to them and kill them all; and asked him if he would stand by me. He had now got over his fright, and his spirits being a little raised with the dram I had given him, he was very cheerful, and told me, as before, he would die when I bid die.

In this fit of fury I divided the arms which I had charged, as before, between us; I gave Friday one pistol to stick in his girdle, and three guns upon his shoulder, and I took one pistol and the other three guns myself; and in this posture we marched out. I took a small bottle of rum in my pocket, and gave Friday a large bag with more powder and bullets; and as to orders, I charged him to keep close behind me, and not to stir, or shoot, or do anything till I bid him, and in the meantime not to speak a word. In this posture I fetched a compass to my right hand of near a mile, as well to get over the creek as to get into the wood, so that I could come within shot of them before I should be discovered, which I had seen by my glass it was easy to do.

While I was making this march, my former thoughts returning, I began to abate my resolution: I do not mean that I entertained any fear of their number, for as they were naked, unarmed wretches, it is certain I was superior to them – nay, though I had been alone. But it occurred to my thoughts, what call, what occasion, much less what necessity I was in to go and dip my hands in blood, to attack people who had neither done or intended me any wrong? who, as to me, were innocent, and whose barbarous customs were their own disaster, being in them a token, indeed, of God's having left them, with the other nations of that part of the world, to such stupidity, and to such inhuman courses, but did not call me to take upon me to be a judge of their actions, much less an executioner of His justice – that whenever He thought fit He would take the cause into His own hands, and by national vengeance punish them as a people for national crimes, but that, in the meantime, it was none of my business – that it was true Friday might justify it, because he was a declared enemy and in a state of war with those very particular people, and it was lawful for him to attack them – but I could not say the same with regard to myself. These things were so warmly pressed upon my thoughts all the way as I went, that I resolved I would only go and place myself near them that I might observe their barbarous feast, and that I would act then as God should direct; but that unless something offered that was more a call to me than yet I knew of, I would not meddle with them.

With this resolution I entered the wood, and, with all possible wariness and silence, Friday following close at my heels, I marched till I came to the skirts of the wood on the side which was next to them, only that one corner of the wood lay between me and them. Here I called softly to Friday, and showing him a great tree which was just at the corner of the wood, I bade him go to the tree, and bring me word if he could see there plainly what they were doing. He did so, and came immediately back to me, and told me they might be plainly viewed there – that they were all about their fire, eating the flesh of one of their prisoners, and that another lay bound upon the sand a little from them, whom he said they would kill next; and this fired the very soul within me. He told me it was not one of their nation, but one of the bearded men he had told me of, that came to their country in the boat. I was filled with horror at the very naming of the white bearded man; and going to the tree, I saw plainly by my glass a white man, who lay upon the beach of the sea with his hands and his feet tied with flags, or things like rushes, and that he was an European, and had clothes on.

There was another tree and a little thicket beyond it, about fifty yards nearer to them than the place where I was, which, by going a little way about, I saw I might come at undiscovered, and that then I should be within half a shot of them; so I withheld my passion, though I was indeed enraged to the highest degree; and going back about twenty paces, I got behind some bushes, which held all the way till I came to the other tree, and then came to a little rising ground, which gave me a full view of them at the distance of about eighty yards.

I had now not a moment to lose, for nineteen of the dreadful wretches sat upon the ground, all close huddled together, and had just sent the other two to butcher the poor Christian, and bring him perhaps limb by limb to their fire, and they were stooping down to untie the bands at his feet. I turned to Friday. "Now, Friday," said I, "do as I bid thee." Friday said he would. "Then, Friday," says I, "do exactly as you see me do; fail in nothing." So I set down one of the muskets and the fowling-piece upon the ground, and Friday did the like by his, and with the other musket I took my aim at the savages, bidding him to do the like; then asking

him if he was ready, he said, "Yes."

"Then fire at them," said I; and at the same moment I fired also.

Friday took his aim so much better than I, that on the side that he shot he killed two of them, and wounded three more; and on my side I killed one, and wounded two. They were, you may be sure, in a dreadful consternation: and all of them that were not hurt jumped upon their feet, but did not immediately know which way to run, or which way to look, for they knew not from whence their destruction came. Friday kept his eyes close upon me, that, as I had bid him, he might observe what I did; so, as soon as the first shot was made, I threw down the piece, and took up the fowling-piece, and Friday did the like; he saw me cock and present; he did the same again. "Are you ready, Friday?" said I.

"Yes," says he.

"Let fly, then," says I, "in the name of God!" and with that I fired again among the amazed wretches, and so did Friday; and as our pieces were now loaded with what I call swan-shot, or small pistol-bullets, we found only two drop; but so many were wounded that they ran about yelling and screaming like mad creatures, all bloody, and most of them miserably wounded; whereof three more fell quickly after, though not quite dead.

"Now, Friday," says I, laying down the discharged pieces, and taking up the musket which was yet loaded, "follow me," which he did with a great deal of courage; upon which I rushed out of the wood and showed myself, and Friday close at my foot. As soon as I perceived they saw me, I shouted as loud as I could, and bade Friday do so too, and running as fast as I could, which, by the way, was not very fast, being loaded with arms as I was, I made directly towards the poor victim, who was, as I said, lying upon the beach or shore, between the place where they sat and the sea. The two butchers who were just going to work with him had left him at the surprise of our first fire, and fled in a terrible fright to the seaside, and had jumped into a canoe, and three more of the rest made the same way. I turned to Friday, and bade him step forwards and fire at them; he understood me immediately, and running about forty

... running as fast as I could ... I made directly towards the poor victim ...

yards, to be nearer them, he shot at them; and I thought he had killed them all, for I saw them all fall of a heap into the boat, though I saw two of them up again quickly; however, he killed two of them, and wounded the third, so that he lay down in the bottom of the boat as if he had been dead.

While my man Friday fired at them, I pulled out my knife and cut the flags that bound the poor victim; and loosing his hands and feet, I lifted him up, and asked him in the Portuguese tongue what he was. He answered in Latin, Christianus; but was so weak and faint that he could scarce stand or speak. I took my bottle out of my pocket and gave it him, making signs that he should drink, which he did; and I gave him a piece of bread, which he ate. Then

I asked him what countryman he was: and he said, Espagniole; and being a little recovered, let me know, by all the signs he could possibly make, how much he was in my debt for his deliverance. "Seignior," said I, with as much Spanish as I could make up, "we will talk afterwards, but we must fight now: if you have any strength left, take this pistol and sword, and lay about you." He took them very thankfully; and no sooner had he the arms in his hands, but, as if they had put new vigour into him, he flew upon his murderers like a fury, and had cut two of them in pieces in an instant; for the truth is, as the whole was a surprise to them, so the poor creatures were so much frightened with the noise of our pieces that they fell down for mere amazement and fear, and had no more power to attempt their own escape than their flesh had to resist our shot; and that was the case of those five that Friday shot at in the boat; for as three of them fell with the hurt they received, so the other two fell with the fright.

I kept my piece in my hand still without firing, being willing to keep my charge ready, because I had given the Spaniard my pistol and sword: so I called to Friday, and bade him run up to the tree from whence we first fired, and fetch the arms which lay there that had been discharged, which he did with great swiftness; and then giving him my musket, I sat down myself to load all the rest again, and bade them come to me when they wanted. While I was loading these pieces, there happened a fierce engagement between the Spaniard and one of the savages, who made at him with one of their great wooden swords, the weapon that was to have killed him before, if I had not prevented it. The Spaniard, who was as bold and brave as could be imagined, though weak, had fought the Indian a good while, and had cut two great wounds on his head; but the savage being a stout, lusty fellow, closing in with him, had thrown him down, being faint, and was wringing my sword out of his hand; when the Spaniard, though undermost, wisely quitting the sword, drew the pistol from his girdle, shot the savage through the body, and killed him upon the spot, before I, who was running to help him, could come near him.

Friday, being now left to his liberty, pursued the flying wretches, with no weapon in his hand but his hatchet: and with that he despatched those three who as I said before, were wounded at first, and fallen, and all the rest he could come up with: and the Spaniard coming to me for a gun, I gave him one of the fowling-pieces, with which he pursued two of the savages, and wounded them both; but as he was not able to run, they both got from him into the wood, where Friday pursued them, and killed one of them, but the other was too nimble for him; and though he was wounded, yet had plunged himself into the sea, and swam with all his might off to those two who were left in the canoe; which three in the canoe, with one wounded, that we knew not whether he died or no, were all that escaped our hands of one-and-twenty. The account of the whole is as follows: Three killed at our first shot from the tree; two killed at the next shot; two killed by Friday in the boat; two killed by Friday of those at first wounded; one killed by Friday in the wood; three killed by the Spaniard; four killed, being found dropped here and there, of the wounds, or killed by Friday in his chase of them; four escaped in the boat, whereof one wounded, if not dead – twenty-one in all.

Those that were in the canoe worked hard to get out of gun-shot, and though Friday made two or three shots at them, I did not find that he hit any of them. Friday would fain have had me take one of their canoes, and pursue them; and indeed I was very anxious about their escape, lest, carrying the news home to their people, they should come back perhaps with two or three hundred of the canoes and devour us by mere multitude; so I consented to pursue them by sea, and running to one of their canoes, I jumped in and bade Friday follow me: but when I was in the canoe I was surprised to find another poor creature lie there, bound hand and foot, as the Spaniard was, for the slaughter, and almost dead with fear, not knowing what was the matter; for he had not been able to look up over the side of the boat, he was tied so hard neck and heels, and had been tied so long that he had really but little life in him.

I immediately cut the twisted flags or rushes which they had bound him with, and would have helped him up; but he could not stand or speak, but groaned most piteously, believing, it seems, still, that he was only unbound in order to be killed. When Friday came to him I bade him speak to him, and tell him of his deliverance; and pulling out my bottle, made him give the poor wretch a dram, which, with the news of his being delivered, revived him, and he sat up in the boat. But when Friday came to hear him speak, and look in his face, it would have moved any one to tears to have seen how Friday kissed him, embraced him, hugged him, cried, laughed, hallooed, jumped about, danced, sang; then cried again, wrung his hands, beat his own face and head; and then sang and jumped about again like a distracted creature. It was a good while before I could make him speak to me or tell me what was the matter; but when he came a little to himself he told me that it was his father.

It is not easy for me to express how it moved me to see what ecstasy and filial affection had worked in this poor savage at the sight of his father, and of his being delivered from death; nor indeed can I describe half the extravagances of his affection after this: for he went into the boat and out of the boat a great many times: when he went in to him he would sit down by him, open his breast, and hold his father's head close to his bosom for many minutes together, to nourish it; then he took his arms and ankles, which were numbed and stiff with the binding, and chafed and rubbed them with his hands; and I, perceiving what the case was, gave him some rum out of my bottle to rub them with, which did them a great deal of good.

This affair put an end to our pursuit of the canoe with the other savages, who were now almost out of sight; and it was happy for us that we did not, for it blew so hard within two hours after, and before they could be got a quarter of their way, and continued blowing so hard all night, and that from the north-west, which was against them, that I could not suppose their boat could live, or that they ever reached their own coast.

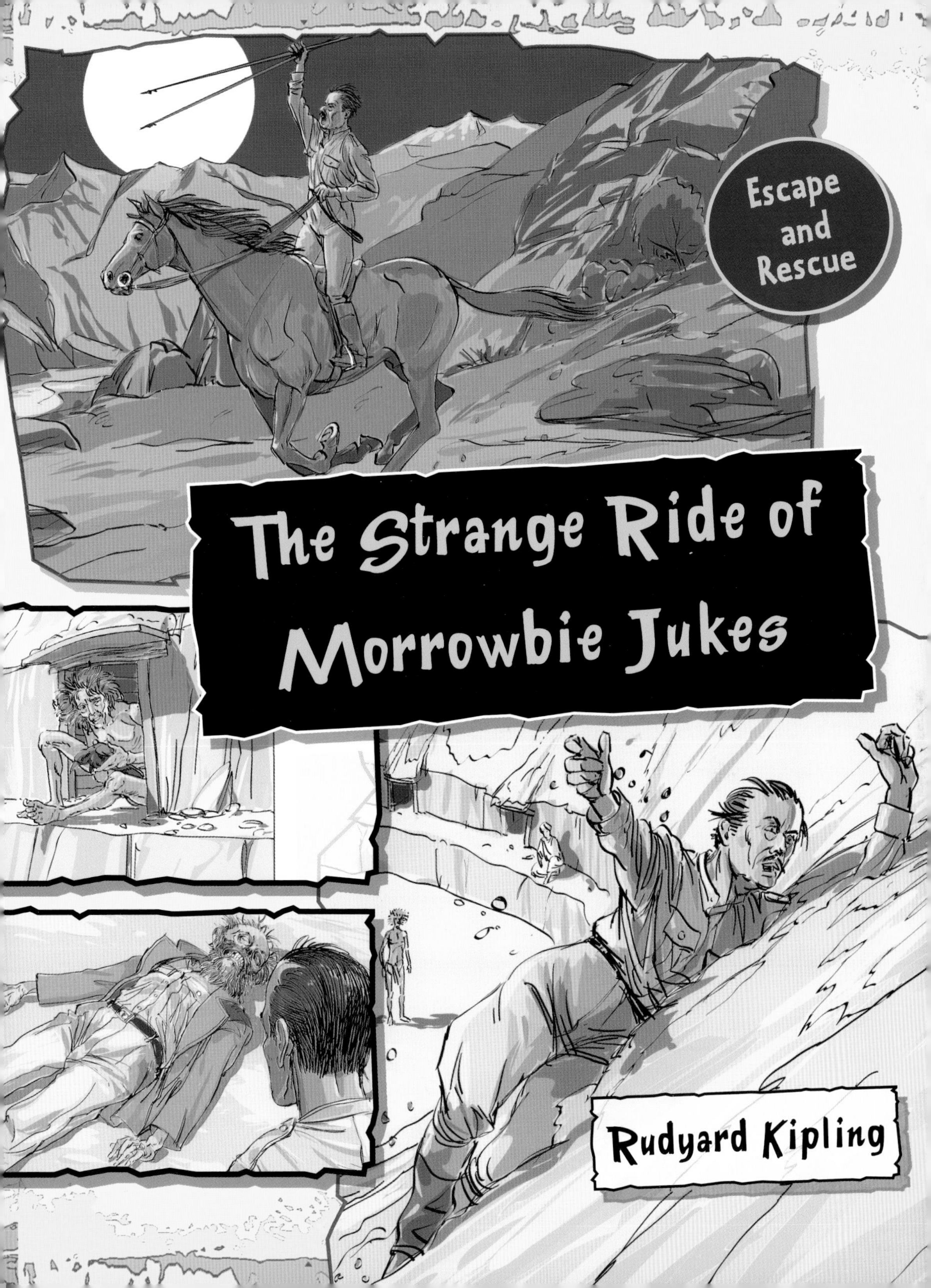
Escape and Rescue
The Strange Ride of Morrowbie Jukes
Rudyard Kipling

The Strange Ride of Morrowbie Jukes

by

Rudyard Kipling

Alive or dead – there is no other way.
Native Proverb.

There is, as the conjurers say, no deception about this tale. Jukes by accident stumbled upon a village that is well known to exist, though he is the only Englishman who has been there. A somewhat similar institution used to flourish on the outskirts of Calcutta, and there is a story that if you go into the heart of Bikanir, which is in the heart of the Great Indian Desert, you shall come across not a village but a town where the Dead who did not die but may not live have established their headquarters. And, since it is perfectly true that in the same Desert is a wonderful city where all the rich moneylenders retreat after they have made their fortunes (fortunes so vast that the owners cannot trust even the strong hand of the Government to protect them, but take refuge in the waterless sands), and drive sumptuous C-spring barouches, and buy beautiful girls and decorate their palaces with gold and ivory and Minton tiles and mother-o'-pearl, I do not see why Jukes's tale should not be true. He is a Civil Engineer, with a head for plans and distances and things of that kind, and he certainly would not take the trouble to invent imaginary traps. He could earn more by doing his legitimate work. He never varies the tale in the telling, and grows very hot and indignant when he thinks of the disrespectful treatment he received. He wrote this quite straightforwardly at first, but he has since touched it up in places and introduced Moral Reflections, thus:

In the beginning it all arose from a slight attack of fever. My work necessitated my being in camp for some months between Pakpattan and Mubarakpur – a desolate sandy stretch of country as every one who has had the misfortune to go there may know. My coolies were neither more nor less exasperating than other gangs, and my work demanded sufficient attention to keep me from moping, had I been inclined to so unmanly a weakness.

On the 23 December, 1884, I felt a little feverish. There was a full moon at the time, and, in consequence, every dog near my tent was baying it. The brutes assembled in twos and threes and drove me frantic. A few days previously I had shot one loud-mouthed singer and suspended his carcass in terrorem about fifty yards from my tent-door. But his friends fell upon, fought for, and ultimately devoured the body: and, as it seemed to me, sang their hymns of thanksgiving afterward with renewed energy.

The light-headedness which accompanies fever acts differently on different men. My irritation gave way, after a short time, to a fixed determination to slaughter one huge black and white beast who had been foremost in song and first in flight throughout the evening. Thanks to a shaking hand and a giddy head I had already missed him twice with both barrels of my shotgun, when it struck me that my best plan would be to ride him down in the open and finish him off with a hog-spear. This, of course, was merely the semi-delirious notion of a fever patient; but I remember that it struck me at the time as being eminently practical and feasible.

I therefore ordered my groom to saddle Pornic and bring him round quietly to the rear of my tent. When the pony was ready, I stood at his head prepared to mount and dash out as soon as the dog should again lift up his voice. Pornic, by the way, had not been out of his pickets for a couple of days; the night air was crisp and chilly; and I was armed with a specially long and sharp pair of persuaders with which I had been rousing a sluggish cob that afternoon. You will easily believe, then, that when he was let go he went quickly. In one moment, for the brute bolted as straight as a die, the tent was left far behind, and we were flying over the smooth sandy soil at racing speed. In another we had passed the wretched dog, and I had almost forgotten why it was that I had taken horse and hog-spear.

The delirium of fever and the excitement of rapid motion through the air must have taken away the remnant of my senses. I have a faint recollection of standing upright in my stirrups, and of brandishing my hog-spear at the great white Moon that looked down so calmly on my mad gallop; and of shouting challenges to the camel-thorn bushes as they whizzed past. Once or twice, I believe, I swayed forward on Pornic's neck, and literally hung on by my spurs – as the marks next morning showed.

The wretched beast went forward like a thing possessed, over what seemed to be a limitless expanse of moonlit sand. Next, I remember, the ground rose suddenly in front of us, and as we

topped the ascent I saw the waters of the Sutlej shining like a silver bar below. Then Pornic blundered heavily on his nose, and we rolled together down some unseen slope.

I must have lost consciousness, for when I recovered I was lying on my stomach in a heap of soft white sand, and the dawn was beginning to break dimly over the edge of the slope down which I had fallen. As the light grew stronger I saw that I was at the bottom of a horseshoe-shaped crater of sand, opening on one side directly on to the shoals of the Sutlej. My fever had altogether left me, and, with the exception of a slight dizziness in the head, I felt no bad effects from the fall over night.

Pornic, who was standing a few yards away, was naturally a good deal exhausted, but had not hurt himself in the least. His saddle, a favorite polo one, was much knocked about, and had been twisted under his belly. It took me some time to put him to rights, and in the meantime I had ample opportunities of observing the spot into which I had so foolishly dropped.

At the risk of being considered tedious, I must describe it at length; inasmuch as an accurate mental picture of its peculiarities will be of material assistance in enabling the reader to understand what follows.

Imagine then, as I have said before, a horseshoe-shaped crater of sand with steeply graded sand walls about thirty-five feet high. (The slope, I fancy, must have been about 65.) This crater enclosed a level piece of ground about fifty yards long by thirty at its broadest part, with a rude well in the centre. Round the bottom of the crater, about three feet from the level of the ground proper, ran a series of eighty-three semi-circular, ovoid, square, and multilateral holes, all about three feet at the mouth. Each hole on inspection showed that it was carefully shored internally with driftwood and bamboos, and over the mouth a wooden drip-board projected, like the peak of a jockey's cap, for two feet. No sign of life was visible in these tunnels, but a most sickening stench pervaded the entire amphitheatre – a stench fouler than any which my wanderings in Indian villages have introduced me to.

Having remounted Pornic, who was as anxious as I to get back to camp, I rode round the base of the horseshoe to find some place whence an exit would be practicable. The inhabitants, whoever they might be, had not thought fit to put in an appearance, so I was left to my own devices. My first attempt to 'rush' Pornic up the steep sand-banks showed me that I had fallen into a trap exactly on the same model as that which the ant-lion sets for its prey. At each step the shifting sand poured down from above in tons, and rattled on the drip-boards of the holes like small shot. A couple of ineffectual charges sent us both rolling down to the bottom, half choked with the torrents of sand; and I was constrained to turn my attention to the river-bank.

Here everything seemed easy enough. The sand hills ran down to the river edge, it is true, but there were plenty of shoals and shallows across which I could gallop Pornic, and find my way back to terra firma by turning sharply to the right or the left. As I led Pornic over the sands I was startled by the faint pop of a rifle across the river; and at the same moment a bullet dropped with a sharp 'whit' close to Pornic's head.

There was no mistaking the nature of the missile – a regulation Martini-Henry 'picket'. About five hundred yards away a country-boat was anchored in midstream; and a jet of smoke drifting away from its bows in the still morning air showed me whence the delicate attention had come. Was ever a respectable gentleman in such an impasse? The treacherous sand slope allowed no escape from a spot which I had visited most involuntarily, and a promenade on the river frontage was the signal for a bombardment from some insane native in a boat. I'm afraid that I lost my temper very much indeed.

Another bullet reminded me that I had better save my breath to cool my porridge; and I retreated hastily up the sands and back to the horseshoe, where I saw that the noise of the rifle had drawn sixty-five human beings from the badger-holes which I had up till that point supposed to be untenanted. I found myself in the midst of a crowd of spectators – about forty men, twenty women, and one child who could not have been more than five years old. They were all scantily clothed in that salmon-colored cloth which one associates with Hindu mendicants, and, at first sight, gave me the impression of a band of loathsome fakirs. The filth and repulsiveness of the assembly were beyond all description, and I shuddered to think what their life in the badger-holes must be.

Even in these days, when local self-government has destroyed the greater part of a native's respect for a Sahib, I have been accustomed to a certain amount of civility from my inferiors, and on approaching the crowd naturally expected that there would be some recognition of my presence. As a matter of fact there was; but it was by no means what I had looked for.

The ragged crew actually laughed at me – such laughter I hope I may never hear again. They cackled, yelled, whistled and howled as I walked into their midst: some of them literally throwing themselves down on the ground in convulsions of unholy mirth. In a moment I had let go Pornic's head, and, irritated beyond expression at the morning's adventure, commenced cuffing those nearest to me with all the force I could. The wretches dropped under my blows like nine-pins, and the laughter gave place to wails for mercy; while those yet untouched clasped me round the knees, imploring me in all sorts of uncouth tongues to spare them.

In the tumult, and just when I was feeling very much ashamed of myself for having thus easily given way to my temper, a thin, high voice murmured in English from behind my shoulder: "Sahib! Sahib! Do you not know me? Sahib, it is Gunga Dass, the telegraph-master."

I spun round quickly and faced the speaker.

Gunga Dass (I have, of course, no hesitation in mentioning the man's real name) I had known four years before as a Deccanee

Brahmin loaned by the Punjab Government to one of the Khalsia States. He was in charge of a branch telegraph-office there, and when I had last met him was a jovial, full-stomached, portly Government servant with a marvellous capacity for making bad puns in English – a peculiarity which made me remember him long after I had forgotten his services to me in his official capacity. It is seldom that a Hindu makes English puns.

Now, however, the man was changed beyond all recognition. Caste-mark, stomach, slate-colored continuations, and unctuous speech were all gone. I looked at a withered skeleton, turbanless and almost naked, with long matted hair and deep-set codfish-eyes. But for a crescent-shaped scar on the left cheek – the result of an accident for which I was responsible – I should never have known him. But it was indubitably Gunga Dass, and – for this I was thankful – an English-speaking native who might at least tell me the meaning of all that I had gone through that day.

The crowd retreated to some distance as I turned toward the miserable figure, and ordered him to show me some method of escaping from the crater. He held a freshly plucked crow in his hand, and in reply to my question climbed slowly on a platform of sand which ran in front of the holes, and commenced lighting a fire there in silence. Dried bents, sand-poppies, and driftwood burn quickly; and I derived much consolation from the fact that he lit them with an ordinary sulphur-match. When they were in a bright glow, and the crow was neatly spitted in front thereof,

Gunga Dass began without a word of preamble:

"There are only two kinds of men, Sar. The alive and the dead. When you are dead, you are dead, but when you are alive you live." (Here the crow demanded his attention for an instant as it twirled before the fire in danger of being burned to a cinder.) "If you die at home and do not die when you come to the ghât to be burned you come here."

The nature of the reeking village was made plain now, and all that I had known or read of the grotesque and the horrible paled before the fact just communicated by the ex-Brahmin. Sixteen years ago, when I first landed in Bombay, I had been told by a wandering Armenian of the existence, somewhere in India, of a place to which such Hindus as had the misfortune to recover from trance or catalepsy were conveyed and kept, and I recollect laughing heartily at what I was then pleased to consider a traveller's tale. Sitting at the bottom of the sand-trap, the memory of Watson's Hotel, with its swinging punkahs, white-robed attendants, and the sallow-faced Armenian, rose up in my mind as vividly as a photograph, and I burst into a loud fit of laughter. The contrast was too absurd!

Gunga Dass, as he bent over the unclean bird, watched me curiously. Hindus seldom laugh, and his surroundings were not such as to move Gunga Dass to any undue excess of hilarity. He removed the crow solemnly from the wooden spit and as solemnly devoured it. Then he continued his story, which I give in his own words:

"In epidemics of the cholera you are carried to be burned almost before you are dead. When you come to the riverside the cold air, perhaps, makes you alive, and then, if you are only little alive, mud is put on your nose and mouth and you die conclusively. If you are rather more alive, more mud is put; but if you are too lively they let you go and take you away. I was too lively, and made protestation with anger against the indignities that they endeavoured to press upon me. In those days I was Brahmin and proud man. Now I am dead man and eat" – here he eyed the well-gnawed breast bone with the first sign of emotion that I had seen in him since we met – "crows, and other things. They took me from my sheets when they saw that I was too lively and gave me medicines for one week, and I survived successfully. Then they sent me by rail from my place to Okara Station, with a man to take care of me; and at Okara Station we met two other men, and they conducted we three on camels, in the night, from Okara Station to this place, and they propelled me from the top to the bottom, and the other two succeeded, and I have been here ever since two and a half years. Once I was Brahmin and proud man, and now I eat crows."

"There is no way of getting out?"

"None of what kind at all. When I first came I made experiments frequently and all the others also, but we have always succumbed to the sand which is precipitated upon our heads."

"But surely," I broke in at this point, "the river-front is open, and it is worth while dodging the bullets; while at night" –

I had already matured a rough plan of escape which a natural instinct of selfishness forbade me sharing with Gunga Dass. He, however, divined my unspoken thought almost as soon as it was formed; and, to my intense astonishment, gave vent to a long low chuckle of derision – the laughter, be it understood, of a superior or at least of an equal.

"You will not" – he had dropped the Sir completely after his opening sentence – "make any escape that way. But you can try. I have tried. Once only."

The sensation of nameless terror and abject fear which I had in vain attempted to strive against overmastered me completely. My long fast – it was now close upon ten o'clock, and I had eaten nothing since tiffin on the previous day – combined with the violent and unnatural agitation of the ride had exhausted me, and I verily believe that, for a few minutes, I acted as one mad. I hurled myself against the pitiless sand-slope. I ran round the base of the crater, blaspheming and praying by turns. I crawled out among the sedges of the river-front, only to be driven back each time in an agony of nervous dread by the rifle-bullets which cut up the sand round me – for I dared not face the death of a mad dog among that hideous crowd – and finally fell, spent and raving, at the curb of the well. No one had taken the slightest notice of an exhibition which makes me blush hotly even when I think of it now.

Two or three men trod on my panting body as they drew water, but they were evidently used to this sort of thing, and had no time to waste upon me. The situation was humiliating, Gunga Dass, indeed, when he had banked the embers of his fire with sand, was at some pains to throw half a cupful of fetid water over my head, an attention for which I could have fallen on my knees and thanked him, but he was laughing all the while in the same mirthless, wheezy key that greeted me on my first attempt to force the shoals. And so, in a semi-comatose condition, I lay till noon. Then, being only a man after all, I felt hungry, and intimated as much to Gunga Dass, whom I had begun to regard as my natural

protector. Following the impulse of the outer world when dealing with natives, I put my hand into my pocket and drew out four annas. The absurdity of the gift struck me at once, and I was about to replace the money.

Gunga Dass, however, was of a different opinion, "Give me the money," said he; "all you have, or I will get help, and we will kill you!" All this as if it were the most natural thing in the world!

A Briton's first impulse, I believe, is to guard the contents of his pockets; but a moment's reflection convinced me of the futility of differing with the one man who had it in his power to make me comfortable; and with whose help it was possible that I might eventually escape from the crater. I gave him all the money in my possession, Rs. 9-8-5 – nine rupees eight annas and five pie – for I always keep small change as bakshish when I am in camp. Gunga Dass clutched the coins, and hid them at once in his ragged loin-cloth, his expression changing to something diabolical as he looked round to assure himself that no one had observed us.

"Now I will give you something to eat," said he.

What pleasure the possession of my money could have afforded him I am unable to say; but inasmuch as it did give him evident delight I was not sorry that I had parted with it so readily, for I had no doubt that he would have had me killed if I had refused. One does not protest against the vagaries of a den of wild beasts; and my companions were lower than any beasts. While I devoured what Gunga Dass had provided, a coarse chapatti and a cupful of the foul well-water, the people showed not the faintest sign of curiosity – that curiosity which is so rampant, as a rule, in an Indian village.

I could even fancy that they despised me. At all events they treated me with the most chilling indifference, and Gunga Dass was nearly as bad. I plied him with questions about the terrible village, and received extremely unsatisfactory answers. So far as I could gather, it had been in existence from time immemorial – whence I concluded that it was at least a century old – and during that time no one had ever been known to escape from it. (I had to control myself here with both hands, lest the blind terror should lay hold of me a second time and drive me raving round the crater.) Gunga Dass took a malicious pleasure in emphasizing this point and in watching me wince. Nothing that I could do would induce him to tell me who the mysterious 'They' were.

"It is so ordered," he would reply, "and I do not yet know anyone who has disobeyed the orders."

"Only wait till my servants find that I am missing," I retorted, "and I promise you that this place shall be cleared off the face of the earth, and I'll give you a lesson in civility, too, my friend."

"Your servants would be torn in pieces before they came near this place; and, besides, you are dead, my dear friend. It is not your fault, of course, but none the less you are dead and buried."

At irregular intervals supplies of food, I was told, were dropped down from the land side into the amphitheatre, and the inhabitants fought for them like wild beasts. When a man felt his death coming on he retreated to his lair and died there. The body was sometimes dragged out of the hole and thrown onto the sand, or allowed to rot where it lay.

The phrase "thrown on to the sand" caught my attention, and I asked Gunga Dass whether this sort of thing was not likely to breed a pestilence.

"That," said he, with another of his wheezy chuckles, "you may see for yourself subsequently. You will have much time to make observations."

Whereat, to his great delight, I winced once more and hastily continued the conversation: "And how do you live here from day to day? What do you do?" The question elicited exactly the same answer as before – coupled with the information that "this place is like your European heaven; there is neither marrying nor giving in marriage."

Gunga Dass has been educated at a Mission School, and, as he himself admitted, had he only changed his religion "like a wise man," might have avoided the living grave which was now his portion. But as long as I was with him I fancy he was happy.

Here was a Sahib, a representative of the dominant race, helpless as a child and completely at the mercy of his native neighbours. In a deliberate lazy way he set himself to torture me as a schoolboy would devote a rapturous half-hour to watching the agonies of an impaled beetle, or as a ferret in a blind burrow might glue himself comfortably to the neck of a rabbit. The burden of his conversation was that there was no escape "of no kind whatever," and that I should stay here till I died and was "thrown on to the sand." If it were possible to forejudge the conversation of the Damned on the advent of a new soul in their abode, I should say that they would speak as Gunga Dass did to me throughout that long afternoon. I was powerless to protest or answer; all my energies being devoted to a struggle against the inexplicable terror that threatened to overwhelm me again and again. I can compare the feeling to nothing except the struggles of a man against the overpowering nausea of the Channel passage – only my agony was of the spirit and infinitely more terrible.

As the day wore on, the inhabitants began to appear in full strength to catch the rays or the afternoon sun, which were now sloping in at the mouth of the crater. They assembled in little knots, and talked among themselves without even throwing a glance in my direction. About four o'clock, as far as I could judge, Gunga Dass rose and dived into his lair for a moment, emerging with a live crow in his hands. The wretched bird was in a most draggled and deplorable condition, but seemed to be in no way afraid of its master. Advancing cautiously to the river front, Gunga Dass stepped from tussock to tussock until he had reached a smooth patch of sand directly in the line of the boat's fire. The occupants of the boat took no notice. Here he stopped, and, with a couple of dexterous turns of the wrist, pegged the bird on its back with outstretched wings. As was only natural, the crow began to shriek at once and beat the air with its claws. In a few seconds the clamour had attracted the attention of a bevy of wild crows on a shoal a few hundred yards away, where they were discussing something that looked like a corpse. Half a dozen

crows flew over at once to see what was going on, and also, as it proved, to attack the pinioned bird. Gunga Dass, who had lain down on a tussock, motioned to me to be quiet, though I fancy this was a needless precaution. In a moment, and before I could see how it happened, a wild crow, who had grappled with the shrieking and helpless bird, was entangled in the latter's claws, swiftly disengaged by Gunga Dass, and pegged down beside its companion in adversity. Curiosity, it seemed, overpowered the rest of the flock, and almost before Gunga Dass and I had time to withdraw to the tussock, two more captives were struggling in the upturned claws of the decoys. So the chase – if I can give it so dignified a name – continued until Gunga Dass had captured seven crows. Five of them he throttled at once, reserving two for further operations another day. I was a good deal impressed by this, to me, novel method of securing food, and complimented Gunga Dass on his skill.

"It is nothing to do," said he. "Tomorrow you must do it for me. You are stronger than I am."

This calm assumption of superiority upset me not a little, and I answered peremptorily; – "Indeed, you old ruffian! What do you think I have given you money for?"

"Very well," was the unmoved reply. "Perhaps not tomorrow, nor the day after, nor subsequently; but in the end, and for many years, you will catch crows and eat crows, and you will thank your European God that you have crows to catch and eat."

I could have cheerfully strangled him for this; but judged it best under the circumstances to smother my resentment. An hour later I was eating one of the crows; and, as Gunga Dass had said, thanking my God that I had a crow to eat. Never as long as I live shall I forget that evening meal. The whole population were squatting on the hard sand platform opposite their dens, huddled over tiny fires of refuse and dried rushes. Death, having once laid his hand upon these men and forborne to strike, seemed to stand aloof from them now; for most of our company were old men, bent and worn and twisted with years, and women aged to all appearance as the Fates themselves. They sat together in knots and talked – God only knows what they found to discuss – in low equable tones, curiously in contrast to the strident babble with which natives are accustomed to make day hideous. Now and then an access of that sudden fury which had possessed me in the morning would lay hold on a man or woman; and with yells and imprecations the sufferer would attack the steep slope until, baffled and bleeding, he fell back on the platform incapable of moving a limb. The others would never even raise their eyes when this happened, as men too well aware of the futility of their fellows' attempts and wearied with their useless repetition. I saw four such outbursts in the course of that evening.

Gunga Dass took an eminently business-like view of my situation, and while we were dining – I can afford to laugh at the recollection now, but it was painful enough at the time – propounded the terms on which he would consent to "do" for me. My nine rupees eight annas, he argued, at the rate of three annas a day, would provide me with food for fifty-one days, or about seven weeks; that is to say, he would be willing to cater for me for that length of time. At the end of it I was to look after myself. For a further consideration – videlicet my boots – he would be willing to allow me to occupy the den next to his own, and would supply me with as much dried grass for bedding as he could spare.

"Very well, Gunga Dass," I replied; "to the first terms I cheerfully agree, but, as there is nothing on earth to prevent my killing you as you sit here and taking everything that you have" (I thought of the two invaluable crows at the time), "I flatly refuse to give you my boots and shall take whichever den I please."

The stroke was a bold one, and I was glad when I saw that it had succeeded, Gunga Dass changed his tone immediately, and disavowed all intention of asking for my boots. At the time it did not strike me as at all strange that I, a Civil Engineer, a man of thirteen years' standing in the Service, and, I trust, an average Englishman, should thus calmly threaten murder and violence against the man who had, for a consideration it is true, taken me under his wing. I had left the world, it seemed, for centuries. I was as certain then as I am now of my own existence, that in the accursed settlement there was no law save that of the strongest; that the living dead men had thrown behind them every canon of the world which had cast them out; and that I had to depend for my own life on my strength and vigilance alone. The crew of the ill-fated Mignonette are the only men who would understand my frame of mind. "At present," I argued to myself, "I am strong and a match for six of these wretches. It is imperatively necessary that I should, for my own sake, keep both health and strength until the hour of my release comes – if it ever does."

Fortified with these resolutions, I ate and drank as much as I could, and made Gunga Dass understand that I intended to be his master, and that the least sign of insubordination on his part would be visited with the only punishment I had it in my power to inflict – sudden and violent death. Shortly after this I went to bed. That is to say, Gunga Dass gave me a double armful of dried bents which I thrust down the mouth of the lair to the right of his, and followed myself, feet foremost; the hole running about nine feet into the sand with a slight downward inclination, and being neatly shored with timbers. From my den, which faced the river-front, I was able to watch the waters of the Sutlej flowing past under the light of a young moon and compose myself to sleep as best I might.

The horrors of that night I shall never forget. My den was nearly as narrow as a coffin, and the sides had been worn smooth and greasy by the contact of innumerable naked bodies, added to which it smelled abominably. Sleep was altogether out of question to one in my excited frame of mind. As the night wore on, it seemed that the entire amphitheatre was filled with legions of unclean devils that, trooping up from the shoals below, mocked the unfortunates in their lairs.

Personally I am not of an imaginative temperament, – very few Engineers are, – but on that occasion I was as completely prostrated with nervous terror as any woman. After half an hour or so, however, I was able once more to calmly review my chances of escape. Any exit by the steep sand walls was, of course, impracticable. I had been thoroughly convinced of this some time before. It was possible, just possible, that I might, in the uncertain moonlight, safely run the gauntlet of the rifle shots. The place was so full of terror for me that I was prepared to undergo any risk in leaving it. Imagine my delight, then, when after creeping stealthily to the river-front I found that the infernal boat was not there. My freedom lay before me in the next few steps!

By walking out to the first shallow pool that lay at the foot of the projecting left horn of the horseshoe, I could wade across, turn the flank of the crater, and make my way inland. Without a moment's hesitation I marched briskly past the tussocks where Gunga Dass had snared the crows, and out in the direction of the smooth white sand beyond. My first step from the tufts of dried grass showed me how utterly futile was any hope of escape; for, as I put my foot down, I felt an indescribable drawing, sucking motion of the sand below. Another moment and my leg was swallowed up nearly to the knee. In the moonlight the whole surface of the sand seemed to be shaken with devilish delight at my disappointment. I struggled clear, sweating with terror and exertion, back to the tussocks behind me and fell on my face.

My only means of escape from the semicircle was protected with a quicksand!

How long I lay I have not the faintest idea; but I was roused at last by the malevolent chuckle of Gunga Dass at my ear. "I would advise you, Protector of the Poor" (the ruffian was speaking English) "to return to your house. It is unhealthy to lie down here. Moreover, when the boat returns, you will most certainly be rifled at." He stood over me in the dim light, of the dawn, chuckling and laughing to himself.

Suppressing my first impulse to catch the man by the neck and

throw him on to the quicksand, I rose sullenly and followed him to the platform below the burrows.

Suddenly, and futilely as I thought while I spoke, I asked: – "Gunga Dass, what is the good of the boat if I can't get out anyhow?" I recollect that even in my deepest trouble I had been speculating vaguely on the waste of ammunition in guarding an already well protected foreshore.

Gunga Dass laughed again and made answer: "They have the boat only in daytime. It is for the reason that there is a way. I hope we shall have the pleasure of your company for much longer time. It is a pleasant spot when you have been here some years and eaten roast crow long enough."

I staggered, numbed and helpless, toward the fetid burrow allotted to me, and fell asleep. An hour or so later I was awakened by a piercing scream – the shrill, high-pitched scream of a horse in pain. Those who have once heard that will never forget the sound. I found some little difficulty in scrambling out of the burrow. When I was in the open, I saw Pornic, my poor old Pornic, lying dead on the sandy soil. How they had killed him I cannot guess. Gunga Dass explained that horse was better than crow, and "greatest good of greatest number is political maxim. We are now Republic, Mister Jukes, and you are entitled to a fair share of the beast. If you like, we will pass a vote of thanks. Shall I propose?"

Yes, we were a Republic indeed! A Republic of wild beasts penned at the bottom of a pit, to eat and fight and sleep till we died. I attempted no protest of any kind, but sat down and stared at the hideous sight in front of me. In less time almost than it takes me to write this, Pornic's body was divided, in some unclean way or other; the men and women had dragged the fragments on to the platform and were preparing their morning meal. Gunga Dass cooked mine. The almost irresistible impulse to fly at the sand walls until I was wearied laid hold of me afresh, and I had to struggle against it with all my might. Gunga Dass was offensively jocular till I told him that if he addressed another remark of any kind whatever to me I should strangle him where he sat. This silenced him till silence became insupportable, and I bade him say something.

"You will live here till you die like the other Feringhi," he said, coolly, watching me over the fragment of gristle that he was gnawing.

"What other Sahib, you swine? Speak at once, and don't stop to tell me a lie."

"He is over there," answered Gunga Dass, pointing to a burrow-mouth about four doors to the left of my own. "You can see for yourself. He died in the burrow as you will die, and I will die, and as all these men and women and the one child will also die."

"For pity's sake tell me all you know about him. Who was he? When did he come, and when did he die?"

This appeal was a weak step on my part. Gunga Dass only leered and replied: "I will not – unless you give me something first."

Then I recollected where I was, and struck the man between the eyes, partially stunning him. He stepped down from the platform at once, and, cringing and fawning and weeping and attempting to embrace my feet, led me round to the burrow which he had indicated.

"I know nothing whatever about the gentleman, Your God be my witness that I do not. He was as anxious to escape as you were, and he was shot from the boat, though we all did all things to prevent him from attempting. He was shot here." Gunga Dass laid his hand on his lean stomach and bowed, to the earth.

"Well, and what then? Go on!"

"And then – and then, Your Honour, we carried him into his house and gave him water, and put wet cloths on the wound, and he laid down in his house and gave up the ghost."

"In how long? In how long?"

"About half an hour, after he received his wound. I call Vishnu to witness," yelled the wretched man, "that I did everything for him. Everything which was possible, that I did!"

He threw himself down on the ground and clasped my ankles. But I had my doubts about Gunga Dass's benevolence, and kicked him off as he lay protesting.

"I believe you robbed him of everything he had. But I can find out in a minute or two. How long was the Sahib here?"

"Nearly a year and a half. I think he must have gone mad. But hear me swear, Protector of the Poor! Won't Your Honour hear me swear that I never touched an article that belonged to him? What is Your Worship going to do?"

I had taken Gunga Dass by the waist and had hauled him on to the platform opposite the deserted burrow. As I did so I thought of my wretched fellow-prisoner's unspeakable misery among all these horrors for eighteen months, and the final agony of dying like a rat in a hole, with a bullet-wound in the stomach. Gunga Dass fancied I was going to kill him and howled pitifully. The rest of the population, in the plethora that follows a full flesh meal, watched us without stirring.

"Go inside, Gunga Dass," said I, "and fetch it out."

I was feeling sick and faint with horror now. Gunga Dass nearly rolled off the platform and howled aloud.

"But I am Brahmin, Sahib – a high-caste Brahmin. By your soul, by your father's soul, do not make me do this thing!"

"Brahmin or no Brahmin, by my soul and my father's soul, in you go!" I said, and, seizing him by the shoulders, I crammed his head into the mouth of the burrow, kicked the rest of him in, and, sitting down, covered my face with my hands.

At the end of a few minutes I heard a rustle and a creak; then Gunga Dass in a sobbing, choking whisper speaking to himself; then a soft thud – and I uncovered my eyes.

The dry sand had turned the corpse entrusted to its keeping into a yellow-brown mummy. I told Gunga Dass to stand off while I examined it. The body – clad in an olive-green hunting-suit much stained and worn, with leather pads on the shoulders – was that of a man between thirty and forty, above middle height, with light, sandy hair, long moustache, and a rough unkempt beard. The left canine of the upper jaw was missing, and a portion of the lobe of the right ear was gone. On the second finger of the left hand was a ring – a shield-shaped bloodstone set in gold, with a monogram that might have been either 'B.K.' or 'B.L'. On the third finger of the right hand was a silver ring in the shape of a coiled cobra, much worn and tarnished. Gunga Dass deposited a handful of trifles he had picked out of the burrow at my feet, and, covering the face of the body with my handkerchief, I turned to examine these. I give the full list in the hope that it may lead to the identification of the unfortunate man:

1. Bowl of a briarwood pipe, serrated at the edge; much worn and blackened; bound with string at the screw.
2. Two patent-lever keys; wards of both broken.
3. Tortoise-shell-handled penknife, silver or nickel, name-plate, marked with monogram 'B.K'.
4. Envelope, postmark undecipherable, bearing a Victorian stamp, addressed to 'Miss Mon' – (rest illegible) – 'ham' – 'nt'.

The dry **sand** had turned the **corpse** entrusted to its keeping into a **yellow-brown mummy.**

5. Imitation crocodile-skin notebook with pencil. First forty-five pages blank; four and a half illegible; fifteen others filled with private memoranda relating chiefly to three persons – a Mrs. L. Singleton, abbreviated several times to 'Lot Single', 'Mrs. S. May' and 'Garmison', referred to in places as 'Jerry' or 'Jack'.
6. Handle of small-sized hunting-knife. Blade snapped short. Buck's horn, diamond cut, with swivel and ring on the butt; fragment of cotton cord attached.

It must not be supposed that I inventoried all these things on the spot as fully as I have here written them down. The notebook first attracted my attention, and I put it in my pocket with a view to studying it later on. The rest of the articles I conveyed to my burrow for safety's sake, and there, being a methodical man, I inventoried them. I then returned to the corpse and ordered Gunga Dass to help me to carry it out to the river-front. While we were engaged in this, the exploded shell of an old brown cartridge dropped out of one of the pockets and rolled at my feet. Gunga Dass had not seen it; and I fell to thinking that a man does not carry exploded cartridge-cases, especially 'browns', which will not bear loading twice, about with him when shooting. In other words, that cartridge-case has been fired inside the crater. Consequently there must be a gun somewhere. I was on the verge of asking Gunga Dass, but checked myself, knowing that he would lie. We laid the body down on the edge of the quicksand by the tussocks. It was my intention to push it out and let it be swallowed up – the only possible mode of burial that I could think of. I ordered Gunga Dass to go away.

Then I gingerly put the corpse out on the quicksand. In doing so, it was lying face downward, I tore the frail and rotten khaki shooting-coat open, disclosing a hideous cavity in the back. I have already told you that the dry sand had, as it were, mummified the body. A moment's glance showed that the gaping hole had been caused by a gun-shot wound; the gun must have been fired with the muzzle almost touching the back. The shooting-coat, being intact, had been drawn over the body after death, which must have been instantaneous. The secret of the poor wretch's death was plain to me in a flash. Someone of the crater, presumably Gunga Dass, must have shot him with his own gun – the gun that fitted the brown cartridges. He had never attempted to escape in the face of the rifle-fire from the boat.

I pushed the corpse out hastily, and saw it sink from sight literally in a few seconds. I shuddered as I watched. In a dazed, half-conscious way I turned to peruse the notebook. A stained and discoloured slip of paper had been inserted between the binding and the back, and dropped out as I opened the pages. This is what it contained: "Four out from crow-clump: three left; nine out; two right; three back; two left; fourteen out; two left; seven out; one left; nine back; two right; six back; four right; seven back." The paper had been burned and charred at the edges. What it meant I could not understand. I sat down on the dried bents turning it over and over between my fingers, until I was aware of Gunga Dass standing immediately behind me with glowing eyes and outstretched hands.

"Have you got it?" he panted. "Will you not let me look at it also? I swear that I will return it."

"Got what? Return what?" I asked.

"That which you have in your hands. It will help us both." He stretched out his long, bird-like talons, trembling with eagerness,

"I could never find it," he continued. "He had secreted it about his person. Therefore I shot him, but nevertheless I was unable to obtain it."

Gunga Dass had quite forgotten his little fiction about the rifle-bullet. I received the information perfectly calmly. Morality is blunted by consorting with the Dead who are alive.

"What on earth are you raving about? What is it you want me to give you?"

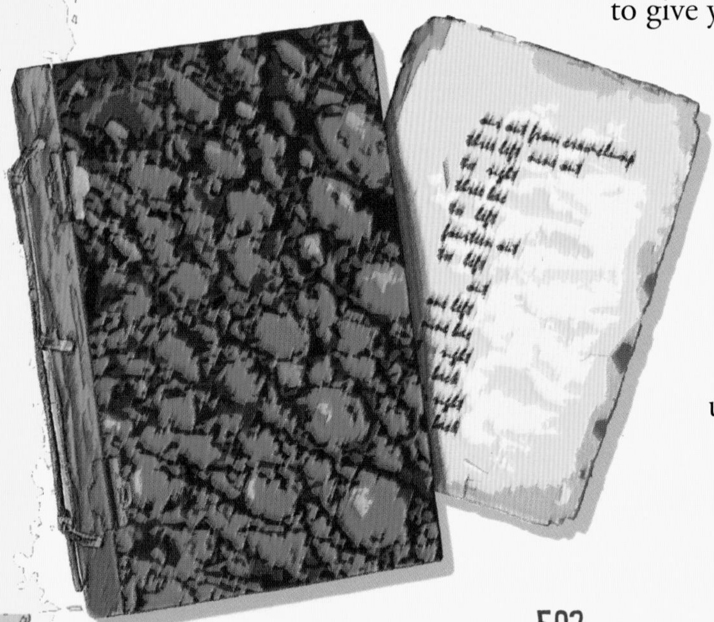

"The piece of paper in the notebook. It will help us both. Oh, you fool! You fool! Can you not see what it will do for us? We shall escape!" His voice rose

almost to a scream, and he danced with excitement before me. I own I was moved at the chance of getting away.

"Don't skip! Explain yourself. Do you mean to say that this slip of paper will help us? What does it mean?"

"Read it aloud! Read it aloud! I beg and I pray you to read it aloud."

I did so. Gunga Dass listened delightedly, and drew an irregular line in the sand with his fingers.

"See now! It was the length of his gun-barrels without the stock. I have those barrels. Four gun-barrels out from the place where I caught crows. Straight out; do you follow me? Then three left – Ah! how well I remember when that man worked it out night after night. Then nine out, and so on. Out is always straight before you across the quicksand. He told me so before I killed him."

"But if you knew all this why didn't you get out before?"

"I did not know it. He told me that he was working it out a year and a half ago, and how he was working it out night after night when the boat had gone away, and he could get out near the quicksand safely. Then he said that we would get away together. But I was afraid that he would leave me behind one night when he had worked it all out, and so I shot him. Besides, it is not advisable that the men who once get in here should escape. Only I, and I am a Brahmin."

The prospect of escape had brought Gunga Dass's caste back to him. He stood up, walked about and gesticulated violently.

Eventually I managed to make him talk soberly, and he told me how this Englishman had spent six months night after night in exploring, inch by inch, the passage across the quicksand; how he had declared it to be simplicity itself up to within about twenty yards of the river bank after turning the flank of the left horn of the horseshoe. This much he had evidently not completed when Gunga Dass shot him with his own gun.

In my frenzy of delight at the possibilities of escape I recollect shaking hands effusively with Gunga Dass, after we had decided that we were to make an attempt to get away that very night. It was weary work waiting throughout the afternoon.

About ten o'clock, as far as I could judge, when the Moon had just risen above the lip of the crater, Gunga Dass made a move for his burrow to bring out the gun-barrels whereby to measure our path. All the other wretched inhabitants had retired to their lairs long ago. The guardian boat drifted down-stream some hours before, and we were utterly alone by the crow-clump. Gunga Dass, while carrying the gun-barrels, let slip the piece of paper which was to be our guide. I stooped down hastily to recover it, and, as I did so, I was aware that the diabolical Brahmin was aiming a violent blow at the back of my head with the gun-barrels. It was too late to turn round. I must have received the blow somewhere on the nape of my neck. A hundred thousand fiery stars danced before my eyes, and I fell forward senseless at the edge of the quicksand.

When I recovered consciousness, the Moon was going down, and I was sensible of intolerable pain in the back of my head. Gunga Dass had disappeared and my mouth was full of blood. I lay down again and prayed that I might die without more ado. Then the unreasoning fury which I have before mentioned laid hold upon me, and I staggered inland toward the walls of the crater. It seemed that some one was calling to me in a whisper – "Sahib! Sahib! Sahib!" exactly as my bearer used to call me in the mornings. I fancied that I was delirious until a handful of sand fell at my feet, Then I looked up and saw a head peering down into the amphitheatre – the head of Dunnoo, my dog-boy, who attended to my collies. As soon as he had attracted my attention, he held up his hand and showed a rope. I motioned, staggering to and fro the while, that he should throw it down. It was a couple of leather punkah-ropes knotted together, with a loop at one end. I slipped the loop over my head and under my arms; heard Dunnoo urge something forward; was conscious that I was being dragged, face downward, up the steep sand slope, and the next instant found myself choked and half fainting on the sand hills overlooking the crater. Dunnoo, with his face ashy grey in the moonlight, implored me not to stay but to get back to my tent at once.

It seems that he had tracked Pornic's footprints fourteen miles across the sands to the crater; had returned and told my servants, who flatly refused to meddle with any one, white or black, once

fallen into the hideous Village of the Dead; whereupon Dunnoo had taken one of my ponies and a couple of punkah-ropes, returned to the crater, and hauled me out as I have described.

To cut a long story short, Dunnoo is now my personal servant on a gold mohur a month – a sum which I still think far too little for the services he has rendered. Nothing on earth will induce me to go near that devilish spot again, or to reveal its whereabouts more clearly than I have done. Of Gunga Dass I have never found a trace, nor do I wish to do. My sole motive in giving this to be published is the hope that some one may possibly identify, from the details and the inventory which I have given above, the corpse of the man in the olive-green hunting-suit.

Author Biographies

R M Ballantyne 1825–1894

The Coral Island (p343)

Robert Ballantyne was one of Victorian England's best-loved writers of high-action adventure books. As a boy of sixteen, he worked as a fur trader in the wilds of Canada, and his first book was based on his adventures there. His subsequent stories took place in all corners of the globe.

R D Blackmore 1825–1900

Lorna Doone (p65)

Although a popular writer in his time, Blackmore is mainly remembered for his novel *Lorna Doone*, a tale set in Exmoor, which popularized the Devon countryside for Victorian England. A friend described Blackmore as 'proud, shy, reticent, strong-willed, sweet-tempered, and self-centred.'

Sir Arthur Conan Doyle 1859–1930

The Adventure of the Speckled Band (p11); *The Lost World* (p157)

Arthur Doyle trained as a doctor and used one of his old professors as inspiration for his best-known creation, Sherlock Holmes. Doyle wanted to be known for his more serious works, and killed off Holmes in a story. However, public outcry forced him to bring the character back for further adventures.

Guy de Maupassant 1850–1893

The Hand (p53)

Frenchman Guy de Maupassant is one of the great masters of the short story. He died insane at the age of forty-two, and his epitaph, which he wrote himself, reads: 'I have coveted everything, and taken pleasure in nothing.'

Daniel Defoe 1660–1731

Robinson Crusoe (p453)

Journalist, poet, novelist, prisoner and spy, Defoe led a life of uncertainty and adventure. Before the age of seven, he had lived through the Great Fire of London, the plague (although not personally) and an attack by the French fleet. *Robinson Crusoe* is his best-known novel.

Charles Dickens 1812–1870

Oliver Twist (p79)

When Dickens was ten, his father was imprisoned for debt and the young boy was put to work in a factory, blackening boots. This early experience helped to make him a passionate social reformer, using his hugely popular novels to expose hypocrisy among the rich and the terrible conditions of the poor at the time.

Alexandre Dumas 1802–1870

The Count of Monte Cristo (p399)

The grandson of a French general and an Afro-Caribbean slave, Dumas was shunned by the establishment in his lifetime. However, his novels – especially *The Three Musketeers, The Count of Monte Cristo* and the *Man in the Iron Mask* – were immensely popular and brought him a great deal of wealth.

Anthony Hope 1863–1933

The Prisoner of Zenda (p113; p437)

Hope was a cousin of Kenneth Grahame who wrote *The Wind in the Willows.* The plot for *The Prisoner of Zenda,* Hope's best-known work, came to him whilst walking in a London street and he completed the first draft in four weeks.

Rudyard Kipling 1865–1936

The Strange Ride of Morrowbie Jukes (p469)

Kipling was the author of classic works such as the poem 'If', the *Just So Stories* and *The Jungle Book*. He was born in India, and at the age of seven was sent to live in England with his sister Trix, to protect him from the harsh climate. It was a miserable experience that he never forgot.

Jack London 1876–1916

Love of Life (p281)

Born in California into a poor family, London lived a hard, rough life as a sailor (he claimed he was also a pirate), a gold prospector and a tramp. He served time in prison, but always longed to write, and achieved success with his first book, *The Call of the Wild*.

E Nesbit 1858–1924

The Railway Children (p99)

Edith Nesbit wrote over forty books of fiction for children, and has been called the first modern children's writer. She created the idea of combining realistic characters and settings with magical elements, and her books include *The Railway Children*, *The Five Children and It* and *The Treasure Seekers*.

H Rider Haggard 1856–1925

King Solomon's Mines (p231)

According to one story, Rider Haggard didn't think much of Robert Louis Stevenson's *Treasure Island* when it first appeared in 1883, and made a bet with his brother that he could write a better book. The result was *King Solomon's Mines*, written in six weeks, based on the African landscapes and hunters he had known as a young man.

Robert Louis Stevenson 1850–1894

Treasure Island (p315); *Kidnapped* (p375)

Stevenson wrote in a wide range of genres, including poetry, children's books, travel, modern and historical novels, essays and thrillers. He died, aged just forty-four, on the South Pacific island of Samoa, having created several classics, including *Treasure Island, Dr Jekyll and Mr Hyde*, and *A Child's Garden of Verses.*

Jules Verne 1828–1905

Journey to the Centre of the Earth (p181)

Sometimes called the father of science fiction, Jules Verne's novels predicted future scientific developments including space travel, television, aircraft, the Internet and submarines. He is one of the most translated authors of all time.